One Of

This edition first published 2016 by Fahrenheit Press

www.Fahrenheit-Press.com

Copyright © Paul Charles 2016

The right of Paul Charles to be identified as the author of this work has been asserted by him in accordance with the Copyright, Designs and Patents Act 1988.

All rights reserved. No part of this publication may be reproduced, stored in a retrieval system, or transmitted in any form, or by any means, electronic, mechanical, photocopying, recording or otherwise, without permission in writing from the publisher.

F 4 E

One Of Our Jeans Is Missing

By

Paul Charles

Fahrenheit Press

PART ONE

BEFORE

Chapter One.

When you're talking, I mean when I'm talking, I hear this voice in my head saying these exact same words. But I often wonder do other people hear my voice the same way. Like now, for instance: Do you hear me talking in the same quiet tones I can hear from myself? And if you can, do you wonder how I can tell you what I'm about to tell you with such a calm voice?

I mean it's just another story of ordinary people and I certainly couldn't claim that any of us, any of us involved, is special or anything like that. I guess what I'm trying to say is, things happen. It's not that you start out wanting to be involved in a drama. No really, I'm serious! The majority of us grow up in good families. We are brought up, I believe, knowing that in order to have an easier life there has to be order. When you get down to it, it really is as simple as that.

The laws of the land are there simply to protect us. The rules of our forefathers tend to keep the wheels of society running smoothly for most of us. Fundamentally there is no real advantage to breaking the law. Is there? I mean, really? When you think about it, it is much better to know that when you hear the screech of the tyres and the wail of the siren, the police car won't be pulling up outside your house.

But you meet people, don't you? You interact with them, they (and others) interact with you and before you know it something is happening and you don't know what it is, do you Mr Jones? When I first moved down to London I remember thinking that living life was a bit like being in a car that was out of control. You might not crash into something, but on the other hand, you just might. I guess what I'm trying to suggest here is that it's totally beyond your control. I think it is the ability to close your eyes at the appropriate moment and push the accelerator to the floor that gets you through this thing they call life.

Now that I've started to talk I'm no longer preoccupied with how my voice sounds and so I feel a bit better about telling you all of this. I find it takes a while to get started up, to get to that point where I tune out of the sound of the voice and the effect of the words, and the story takes over. And I have to tell you that this is a story that took over my life completely.

It is the story of how five people woke up one morning to find themselves involved in a mystery. Well, the real problem was that we didn't know if a certain member of our five had woken up at all. But, as they frequently say in the movies, 'Let's start at the beginning'.

Chapter Two.

My name is David Buchanan. I moved from Northern Ireland to Wimbledon on September 27, 1967. I didn't leave the wee North because of the Troubles – that happened somewhat later and has absolutely nothing whatsoever to do with this tale. I grew up in a small village in County Derry called Castlemartin. I loved my parents – I still do, and they love me. I had a happy childhood and enjoyed my time in Castlemartin. Okay, no problems so far.

I moved to London, not because I wanted to get away from anywhere, but because I wanted to go somewhere. I suppose if there had to be a single deciding factor in why I chose London, it would be music. I've always been into music in a big way, especially the music of Bob Dylan – a fact you no doubt noted in the earlier silent quote. I find that slightly strange, you know, the fact that I would still claim to be a fan of Bob Dylan. I've been listening to him now since the mid-sixties, but as I enter my fiftieth year, still claiming to be a fan, I find myself wondering what the One Direction fans will be claiming in thirty-five years' time. That's a bit cruel I know, but you see, that's one of the things about music isn't it? It's not enough that you like certain types of music. No, don't you see, it's much more than that; people are equally passionate about the music they don't like.

But we don't need to get into that now, for although music has always been a big part of my life, it is just a part of this story, not the main part of this story. Well, at least not directly.

London, legend had it, was the world's music capital and so I caught the Belfast to Heysham Ferry and connecting train down into Euston on September 27, 1967. It was a wee bit more complex than that, the bit about going to London for an interview and getting a job and fixing up accommodation and all that, but it's really of no importance here. Aside from anything else, I can't talk about my work. Don't fret; you're not really missing much. Work to me has always been nothing more, nor less, than a way to finance my lifestyle. I started out my life this way. At the stage I might have started to feel ambitious I was, as you'll see, preoccupied (perhaps even obsessed) with something (someone) else. So my job has always been a means to an end and I have to say I'm happy about that. I do what I do as well as I need to, but I never take my work home with me, neither mentally nor physically.

Anyway, as autumn fell, along with the smog, I was in London and visiting the Marquee Club as often as my salary would permit. Homesickness – an illness as great as any I've experienced – lessened somewhat at Christmas when, during my first trip home, I found myself looking forward to returning to London. It might have been something to do with a wee girl from County Clare, whose passing comments on my desert boots I took as encouragement. I was staying in a youth hostel, located at 14 Inner Park Road, which was quite close to Wimbledon Common but the easy to remember number of its heavily used in-house phone box – Putney 1978 – testified to the fact that it was midway between Wimbledon and Putney. The girl from Clare had moved into the hostel just before Christmas. Anyway, following the holidays I invited her out, well actually, invited her in would be more accurate, if the truth be told. We sat in the hostel's resident's lounge on our first – and only – date, drinking tea and discussing my desert boots. It's the truth. There was nothing else we found to talk about. Yes, true but sad, very sad.

The Clare lass went off (immediately) with one of the other residents – a Bristol lad, independently wealthy but with no desert boots – and I was left consoling myself to Dylan's 'It's All Over Now Baby Blue'. But it was a step forward. I'd been using 'Love Minus Zero/No Limits' (another Dylan classic) to get over my long-haired ex from back home in Castlemartin. Although maybe ex is a bit grand a word for Colette. We'd been stepping out together for several months, as in going out for long walks and discussing everything under the sun, and occasionally enjoying an innocent kiss or two along the way. Innocent kisses and half-hearted fumbling were the sum total of my experience at that stage. They were half-hearted in that neither of us wanted it to develop into anything physical, as in completely physical. Actually I have a feeling now, and I've thought about this a lot, that perhaps Colette was up for something more than half-hearted fumbling in those days. She didn't find a willing partner in me though; I wasn't ready for any of that.

Then I got stuck into London life. I met the fools that a young fool meets. I'd meet people who came into the hostel, they'd become mates and then… they'd move out. You'd lose contact and start the process over again. It didn't bother me; with a few exceptions, people come in and out of my life, and when they go it's no big deal. I don't consider, or care, whether it's a flaw in my character. It doesn't matter. You see, I'm not exactly what you would call a loner but I seem to be quite content in my own company, always have been for as long as I can remember.

So, I started to find my way around the city. It was easy. I worked out the route from Wimbledon to the Marquee Club in Wardour Street, W1. The nearest tube was Piccadilly Circus and I figured out everything else relative to that particular route.

I've always devoured books and am a devoted fan of both movies and music, so my world revolved around hours spent sitting in the cinema, browsing through bookshops and record stores – mostly Goodness Records on

Wimbledon Bridge and, for imports, Musicland, Piccadilly Circus – and listening to people like Taste, Joe Cocker, Spooky Tooth, Cheese, Free, Traffic and Clark Hutchinson in the Marquee Club. When I couldn't afford to 'Go up the West End,' I'd visit the Toby Jug in Tolworth.

Without thinking about it too much, I found the hair on my head growing and a growth appearing on my top lip – a growth that has remained to this day. My choice in clothes, while never outlandish, grew ever more liberal. I favoured granddad shirts in various colours (included even a few tie dye specials) and darker shades of loon pants. Okay, I'll own up: I went through a period of fifteen months when I quite liked a pair of black and white checked hipsters. I also seem to remember getting a lot of wear out of a pair of corduroy shoes and, of course, the aforementioned desert boots. My uniform was completed by an old, black pinstripe waistcoat, which I bought in a jumble sale for three (old) pence and wore until the arms nearly dropped back on! Penny for penny the best buy of my life. During working hours I was dressed as soberly, but not as expensively, as a judge.

In a heartbeat, it seemed, one and a half years had passed. I've found it happens that way in my life. Time just waves you goodbye, passes, and later when I try to reflect on what happened during the period under consideration, I can't think of one significant milestone or incident. Perhaps it's for the best, eh?

But the thing I can remember, and remember vividly, is the day I first met the two Jeans.

Chapter Three.

I was sitting in the residents' lounge of the hostel. It was a Saturday, the best time to relax in the lounge as the majority of the residents of the self-same establishment took off at the weekends. I was reading the New Musical Express, probably for the tenth time since buying it the previous morning on my way to work, and was planning the weekend's entertainment when, from out of the blue, I heard:

'Aye up, what goes on in 'ere then?'

I looked up to see two heads peeking out from behind the half opened door. It had been the bottom head that had spoken. She was blonde and her friend was a silky brunette.

'Hello, I'm Jean and this is my best friend, Jean. Who are you?' the blonde one offered, in her strong Northern English accent, before smiling and stepping into the lounge. Her friend stumbled in behind her and was now shyly stealing looks at me over the first Jean's shoulder.

'Sorry, I thought you said you were called Jean,' I began, confused and putting the NME to one side.

'Yes, I'm Jean Kerr,' the blonde girl said.

'And I'm Jean Simpson,' the brunette one added immediately.

'But who are you?' the blonde one asked again.

'You'll be glad to know I'm not a Gene, as in Autry,' I said. I don't really know why I said that.

Well, I suppose I do. I consciously forced myself to say it. I said it rather than say my actual name and maybe hello, and goodbye, before returning to my NME. That would have been my usual response. But maybe by that point I'd spent just a few too many weekends by myself in the residents' lounge to ignore the interruption. Here were two girls – stunning, both of them – and they were my captive audience. They were either here looking for someone (highly unlikely on the weekend) or they'd just moved into the hostel and were doing the rounds. Maybe I could be their guide.

As I said, it was a Saturday afternoon and the majority of the residents wouldn't be back at the hostel until after work on Monday evening, which gave me at least a thirty-six hour head start over the rest of the gang.

'Oh we know that,' the blonde Jean replied, in her thick northern accent.

'You'd never be a Gene, as in Simmons, wearing desert boots like those,' the other half of the double act segued perfectly.

Okay, I was outnumbered. Surely it was a good time for me to retire gracefully.

'My name is David Buchanan,' I replied, rising from my sofa by the window and walking across with hand extended.

'Oh, he's Irish! That's lovely, and so well-mannered to boot,' Miss Kerr said, taking my hand.

She had quite a limp wrist (I find myself continually being tempted to add 'to be honest' to everything. Like just there, I was about to say, 'She had quite a limp wrist, to be honest'. But there wouldn't be much point in telling you that if I wasn't going to tell you the truth now would there? Anyway, forgive me if I occasionally slip it in; it's just a foible of mine and doesn't mean the rest of this isn't truthful). So, she had a limp wrist, as I say, which was surprising because she was quite solid. Not fat, just solid. She wore black, calf-length leather boots, a black and white, knee-length skirt and a black three-quarter length leather coat over a white blouse.

I'm a starer; did I tell you that already? Well I am, I'm a starer, one who stares. I still held the blonde, Jean Kerr's, limp hand and my eyes were glued to her full breasts. Frightfully rude I know, but there you go. Even though it was March she had a tan, an all-year-round tan, and I'll tell you what her all-year-round tan did – it made it easier to see through her blouse to the white bra underneath. You find yourself staring and then you find yourself caught staring, and then you pretend you weren't staring at all.

Not that Jean Kerr seemed to care. In fact, she seemed the kind of girl who doesn't really care if they do or don't. She seemed that way on the first day and she turned out to be exactly that. She wore her sexuality as carelessly as she wore her leather jacket. It was an accessory, sometimes maybe even a necessity. But, just like the leather coat, sometimes she'd be just as happy to take it off and leave it at home. Maybe I should have said leather boots there rather than leather coat. The point being that it's much more of a relief to take off boots than it is to remove a jacket, don't you think? Yes, I do too, and I think that's probably how it was for Jean Kerr.

Jean Simpson on my other hand – sorry, sorry, I meant on the other hand – stepped out from behind her friend for the first time and took my hand. She was the slighter of the two but had a much firmer handshake and there was... well... just that something altogether different from her blonde friend. She was more... more charged, more... mysterious, yes mysterious, that's it. Jean Simpson was more mysterious than Jean Kerr. She had short (ish) dark hair to her friend's long, flowing, blonde mane. She hardly wore any make-up at all to her friend's heavily made-up face. Maybe the make-up was just subtler – I don't remember. But I do remember that she wore a blue miniskirt, which displayed absolutely brilliant legs. I don't think I've ever seen a better pair of legs in my life.

Now this might be a suitable place to pause for a few seconds. Legs! Can anyone tell me why they provide such endless attraction? We can broaden the subject a little if you'd like to include the 'two Bs': breasts and bums. All of them are important to me, so it's probably best we discuss them early on. As I've already admitted, I really do love legs. I loved Jean Simpson's legs the same way I love Barbara Parkins' legs, and the same way I love Linda Cristal's legs. The male opinion on the perfect pair of legs seems to differ somewhat from the female opinion. Men seem to prefer solid and muscular around the thighs and a bit (just a bit mind you) chunky around the calf, while women seem to prefer them thinner, spindly even. Actually getting back to Barbara Parkins and Linda Cristal for a quick final moment before we pass them by totally, I should also admit that I am also rather partial to a beautiful pair of lips. Barbara Parkins – in particular, she really has beautiful lips. And Jean Simpson's lips were just as beautiful!

But that's not what I wanted to talk about. I wanted to talk about why it is that I think those particular people are beautiful. They say that beauty is in the eye of the beholder and that the real beauty comes from within. But I can't see within Barbara Parkins, I couldn't tell you what Linda Cristal's thoughts are on global warming and, to be quite honest, I don't give a feck what she thinks about economic climate in Outer Closetobankruptia. I'm happier not knowing whether she has bad breath or if she leaves nail clippings or dirty laundry everywhere. Or wondering if she would shoo you off with 'I'm not in the mood'. No, I'm totally content for her to warm my heart whenever she does, and maybe she's attractive to me because I don't know all these things about her. But m y big question is: why am I attracted to her in the first place? Basically we're talking about meat packaged in skin, aren't we? A bit basic, I know, but that's the truth. I think I've worked out the reason why men need to find women attractive – why? Well the procreation of man- and womankind – of course! But I've never been able to work out the reason behind why we're so attracted to them.

Let's take the bum, for instance. Men positively drool over the exterior posterior. Men will hold back while climbing the stairs on a double-decker bus, just in the hope of catching a glimpse. I've watched men stare at the reflection of passing women in shop windows. That probably says a lot about me; the fact that these men are staring at these wondrous things of beauty and I'm more fascinated with the male activity.

While we're at it, here's another thing: the feature in question that beguiles us all so, may, in fact, be nothing more than an illusion. What's turning us on, is not perhaps the bum itself, but more the way that bum fits into a pair of jeans (sorry, no pun intended). Don't you see? It's the same with breasts. The Wonderbra is a marvellous invention but the basis of its success is deception. Even lips, I'm told, can greatly benefit from discreet injections.

Perhaps both men and women have to appear to be beautiful because our privates are perhaps not our best feature? Could that be it? I don't know. I just know that the female species is magnetic to me. This would all dovetail perfectly were I to say, 'And that day in the residents' lounge of the hostel, I was to fall passionately in love with Jean Simpson.' Not true. Call me shallow if you must, but on that first day I was much more intrigued with the glitzier Jean Kerr.

I also think she was the most anxious to make a connection.

Maybe there was a bit of a competitive thing going on between the two of them. Maybe Jean Kerr wanted to be the first of the two Jeans to have a London friend or, in my case, perhaps more appropriately, a friend in London.

'Goodness,' I can hear you all saying, 'he's a quick worker.'

Not so. At first, we became friends. Not real friends, of course, we just knew of each other and acknowledged each other whenever we met. We had a few drinks, went to see a few movies together and occasionally tried, in vain, to find the Windmill of Wimbledon Common. Our relationship was kinda like 'Yeah, and so what?' I got to know Jean Simpson even less, mainly due to the fact that I was one of her friend's friends.

Another nine months passed, quick as a flash, and it was time for me to move out of the hostel. I wasn't happy to see the back of it, nor was I sad to go. It was time to move, and so I rented a flat in 14 Rostrevor Road, which was off Alexandra Road, which ran parallel to the railway tracks down in Wimbledon. As well as having a place of my own (actually shared with another chap from the hostel, but that's a mere technicality) I could also sleep for an extra fifteen minutes each morning, as I now didn't have to catch a bus (the number 93) to catch a train to get to work.

I figured that would be the end of Jean – Jean Kerr, I mean – but no. In fact, the opposite was true and our relationship moved to another gear. I used to envy the hostel residents who were off out of a night, to spend the evening round a friend's flat in town. It always sounded so sophisticated – quite the thing, don't you see. Now that I was seeing it from the outside, I realised very quickly it wasn't all it was cracked up to be. Instead of staying put in the hostel, waiting for tomorrow to come, you'd stay put in a bedsit or a shared flat, waiting for the very same tomorrow.

And that's exactly what Jean Kerr and I would do. She would come down to the flat, I'd make her a cup of tea or coffee and we'd eat a couple of Jacob's Kimberley biscuits and then she'd eat a few more, and we'd talk about stuff, and then I'd walk her to the bus and she'd scoot off back to the hostel to tell Jean Simpson all about the splendid evening she'd just enjoyed.

In fact, Jean Kerr took to telling everyone who'd listen that I scrubbed up well. I suppose by default we were becoming boyfriend and girlfriend. Mind you, at this stage we hadn't even kissed. But I do believe our new status had something to do with the fact that the other Jean had taken to dropping into their conversations some details about a chap she had met. Yes, a Scottish lad by the name of John Harrison appeared to be making the same transition from 'friend' to 'boyfriend' with Jean Simpson as Jean Kerr's Irishman was making with her.

However, there was one big difference between the two couples; Jean and John's relationship was slightly more complicated in that John was still involved, to a degree, with his previous girlfriend, Mary, who was, I'm led to believe, aggressively resisting becoming his ex.

Anyway, Jean would pass on to me little titbits of information about John Harrison. You know, things like he was a great cartoonist – a hobby not a career; things like he'd a great job in the Civil Serpents with excellent prospects; things like he was very serious about Jean and as soon as he could get out of the relationship with Mary Skeffington (for that was her name, Mary Skeffington) he wanted to become engaged to Jean Simpson.

I couldn't imagine how anyone would want to disentangle themselves from one with such a sophisticated name as Mary Skeffington. It's a name to positively sing out loud! I could imagine her, with her rosy cheeks and Home Counties outfit and her two kids with similar classic looks, wandering through the extensive grounds of their Cotswolds' home, receiving lessons on nature from their doting mother.

'So is John engaged to Mary Skeffington?' I asked the blonde Jean, one evening after we'd watched Ready Steady Go on a crappy black and white television I'd bought for fifteen pounds.

'For heaven's sake, Dave,' Jean guffawed, 'you never listen to me, do you? No, no and no, they are most certainly not engaged!'

I try hard never to listen to anyone who calls me Dave. I hate being called Dave. My name is David, not Dave

– nor Davy, nor Davey, nor even DB, as someone at work insists on calling me.

'Well then, if he's not engaged, I don't really see what the problem is about him marrying Jean,' I started.

'They're not getting married, for heaven's sake,' she gasped, gulping for air from beneath half a mouthful of tea. The tea, which missed me, splattered all over my threadbare red carpet. The stain it created would probably ensure that I lost my deposit to the landlord, but Jean wouldn't even let me go and fetch a cloth. 'Who told you they're getting married? She wouldn't get married without telling me first – I'm her best friend! She's not going to get married before me.'

All of a sudden she eyed me as though I'd moved ten places up her list of prospects.

'No, sorry – of course I meant engaged,' I explained, falling back down the list again. 'I meant, if he's not betrothed to Mary, then I don't really see what the problem is with him getting engaged to Jean. Perhaps they'll marry later.'

'Well,' Jean replied, breaking into a whisper (the northern accent is beautiful and all, but it doesn't really have the same charm when whispered, does it?) 'Well,' she whispered again, 'apparently Mary's a bit possessive; she's totally in love with John and thought they were going to be together forever and ever.'

'I can see how that could be a bit of a problem down the line, particularly at the wedding,' I offered.

'It's no joke, David,' Jean replied, her eyes full of resolve. She sat down beside me on my bed.

No, no – not like that! I should explain. You see, during the day and early part of the evening my bed doubles as a sofa. So sitting on the bed beside me wasn't normally a big thing, except this time it was. For she took my ears in her hands, pulled my face closer to hers, stuck her lips on mine and inserted her tongue into my mouth. She had her eyes closed by this point. I only know this because mine were open. Well, I'd been told that this stuff was also a fine spectator sport and so I wanted to spectate, if you know what I mean. There she was, tickling my tonsils for a few minutes, her tongue tasting of coffee and her lipstick tasting sticky, almost unpleasant. Then, as quick as it had started it had stopped. She put me down again, went back to her chair, picked up a magazine and started to flick through it again as though nothing had happened.

Colour me shocked. What was that all about? Up to that point neither of us had showed even the slightest bit of interest in sexual over- (or under-) tones.

'What was that all about?' I'd thought it, so I felt I should say it, and so I did.

'I'm having a hard time at work at the minute,' she said. Honest to goodness, that's what she said.

And at that moment I decided I'd better carry around a spare bottle of aftershave with me, just in case she ever got fired. Actually, I'm not even sure I would – the kiss hadn't really been up to much; so lifeless, so sexless, so nothing. In fact, she did nothing for me in that department and I'm equally sure I did nothing for her.

'Then,' I hear you say, 'how come you ended up in bed together three nights later?'

Chapter Four.

I blame Mary Skeffington.
No, seriously, it was her fault. Mary Skeffington was to blame.
Jean (Kerr) felt that Jean (Simpson) was worried that Mary (Skeffington) was making a last ditch attempt to keep John (Harrison). So Jean (Simpson) agreed to become engaged to John and the other Jean, perhaps motivated by not wanting to face the same fate as Mary, took me (David Buchanan) to my sofa and transformed it into a bed.
So how exactly did she do it? Well Jean, ever the seductress, started it all off.
'I'm not a virgin, you know.'
'Oh really,' I replied. I didn't really know whether to add 'that's nice' or 'that's sad'.
But I didn't get a chance to add anything, because she then tried to glue her lips to mine and in a quick break for air she added, 'And I'm on the pill, so you needn't worry.'
Okay. Right!
It was like I was a spectator at my own inauguration. And then, after the initial act, it was like she was a spectator of me spectating at my own inauguration; she just lay there, looking like she'd really rather prefer to be reading the copy of Edna O'Brien's Factory Girls I knew she had in her bag. She was fully clothed, except for having removed that one vital, flimsy garment from beneath her skirt, and continuing to hold them in her right hand throughout the proceedings. There was a bit of 'Could you move over that way a bit, I

can't breathe', and then some huffing and puffing – no moaning nor groaning, mind you – and a 'There, that's better'. And then she merely settled down to allow me to get my task out of the way.

It was all quite businesslike, rather too businesslike if you ask me. Lacking in passion, I'd have to say. Did I say lacking in passion? Make that devoid of passion. It was more functional than romantic; functional as in when you go to the toilet. And more a number one than a number two at that. Ah, that's probably too much information, not to mention unnecessary, sorry about that. Anyway, what I mean to say is that it was nowhere near as satisfying as my numerous practice runs had been.

Five minutes later and it was all over, as pleasant as catching a train to work. She dusted herself down, smoothed her clothes, and went off to make a cup of tea and reinstate her precious Marks and Spencer undies, and not necessarily in that order either.

But that was it, we'd done it; I'd done the thing that had preoccupied my every waking thought for probably the previous four years and, if I'd still been living in Castlemartin, would have preoccupied my every waking thought for at least the following four. When the moment had finally arrived I hadn't been scared like I'd been told I was going to be. But then again it wasn't exactly the wild thing.

However, by doing it, we had become something.

In the moments after, it appeared that Jean definitely felt we'd passed some point together – like we'd bonded or become soulmates, or something equally momentous. She even took to calling me 'Pet'. I, on the other hand, to be perfectly honest (there I go again – I really must learn to stop saying that) was more bemused by the whole affair. A few minutes later she returned with two cups of tea and a meagre portion of beans on toast, and started rabbiting on about how she was having trouble at work and how she felt her supervisor didn't like her, and because he didn't like her she wasn't going to be able to get on, and how depressed she was about it all. She rambled on and on about how much of a pranny she felt he was. From what she was saying, his biggest sin seemed to be that he used the word 'super' too often; everyone and everything was either 'super' or 'not super'. Jean Simpson's boss, she moaned, was just brill and was really helpful and supportive. Up until that point I hadn't realised that they weren't working in the same office, not even the same building in fact. I'd always assumed they were working together.

Then Jean Kerr started to fill me in on the latest episode in Jean and John's relationship. There was good news and bad news (for Jean Kerr, that was). The bad news was that Jean and John were engaged now. As in, they were definitely going to get married. But the good news was that they couldn't afford to get married for at least the next couple of years.

'How are you getting on at work, David?' Jean Kerr then said, no obvious seam in the conversation.

'Yeah,' I replied casually. 'Okay I suppose; it pays the rent with enough left over for my records, books, movies and gigs. So I've no complaints. They just let me get on with it.'

'You're good at what you do,' she said, not really knowing what I did.

I'd signed a little bit of paper known as the Official Secrets Act, which forbade me to tell anyone exactly what it was I did.

'You should apply yourself more. You're a bright boy; you'd get a promotion, more money and benefits, and all of that.'

'But I'm okay. I don't need more money.'

She looked at me like I'd just told her I had a socially transmitted disease.

'Don't be stupid lad! Aye, of course we need more money,' she said, breaking into her full northern accent, which she'd taken to avoiding recently.

Originally I'd believed the two Jeans to be from Yorkshire, but then I came to discover that they were in fact from Derbyshire. Not that this was the main thing troubling my mind at that moment. Did you notice that she used the royal 'we'? I certainly did, and I couldn't believe it. But there was more to come.

'Haven't you got enough records and books, David?' she continued, her eyes scaling my generously packed shelves. 'You should start saving your money. You never know what we might need it for.'

Ten minutes later I was alone in my room, the unpleasant taste of her lipstick still fresh on my lips. It was impossible to remove. I'd tried, oh how I'd tried.

And that, my friends, is how I lost my virginity – to Jean Kerr and not to Peyton Place's Barbara Parkins, as I so often dreamed. I couldn't help but feel that it had all been planned – not exactly a trap, but it was like I'd missed out on a few chapters of the book: hang on, how did they get from nothing, to a single kiss, to full-on sex? What happened to the romance and the wining and the dining? And the intrigue, and the not knowing, and the not being able to walk home some nights from being doubled up in pain? What happened to love? Exactly! What had happened to love?

Search me; all I can remember was enjoying the beans on toast and the cold cup of tea that followed more than the actual deed.

The thing here, I feel I should say, was that all of the above was from my perspective; you know, how things had happened from my point of view. If you asked Jean Kerr about that night she'd surely see it differently. Perhaps she'd enjoyed the whole thing tremendously, maybe thought I was a gentleman for not pushing things. Felt that she needed to take charge. Maybe she thought we needed to take the leap into the romantic bliss we'd been avoiding. That is how she could have told the same story. But the point I'm trying to make is: how we all can experience the exact same set of facts and come to a totally different conclusion. It's incredible really, isn't it? But you try to tell me which of us had interpreted the facts correctly? I was there and I am one of the parties involved, and I couldn't tell you which of the above views is the more accurate. The only conclusion I can come to is that we each have our own sense of reality.

Mind you, my guessing what she thought was not all fantasy. I remember her telling me about a conversation she'd had with Jean Simpson. Jean Simpson had always claimed that she was going to remain a virgin until the day she got married. But Jean Kerr had warned Jean Simpson that she would have to have sex with her man in order to keep him. So there!

But that wasn't any problem of mine. No, my problem was that the relationship that I wasn't supposed to be having with Jean Kerr was running out of control. The clues to her master plan were all glaring at me, staring me in the face, smirking at every mention of promotion, saving, 'wasting money on records and books' and, the big one, having sex with her boy (me) in order to keep him.

Jean Kerr was also not a virgin. Did that mean that she'd been down this road before? Having sex while away in London was one thing but sleeping with someone in a tiny, tight-knit community like those found in Derby or Castlemartin was another thing altogether.

I needed to find out a little about Jean's past. I mean, not in an uncaring or inconsiderate way. She always looked as though she was trying to put a brave face on things, like she was always smiling but the more you got to know her the more you realised that the smile only ran as deep as her make-up. And whatever her problems were – with work, with past relationships, with life in general – if I wasn't part of the solution, I was most definitely going to become part of the problem. I wanted to be neither. I'd kinda just drifted into this, and unless I was prepared to do something about it, someone was bound to get hurt. So I needed to check out the old boyfriend situation, you know, on the Q.T.

The only person in possession of that knowledge was Jean Simpson.

Chapter Five.

The task of discovering this info from the same Miss Simpson was easier said than done. Yes, I knew Jean Kerr's best friend and she knew me. But we rarely saw each other when Jean Kerr wasn't around, and when we did, it was like a quick nod to each other on the street. It wasn't like she went to the Marquee Club and I'd bump into her a couple of times a week or anything like that. So even if I met her accidentally, in passing, I'd still be a long way from finding the link to inviting her for a cup of tea or coffee and then steering the conversation to Jean Kerr's past.

But guess what? Guess who laid the much-needed rendezvous out on a plate for me? Yes, the very same Jean Kerr.

One weekend in November, she'd arranged to go up North to visit with her parents. It was a couple of weeks after we'd shared an intimate moment for the first time – that would have been November 1969 for the historians. I wasn't keen on there being another repeat performance for there had already been two further performances, and neither had been any more spiritually rewarding than the first. Extremely ungallant, I know, but things happen, what can I tell you.

Anyway, the opening came quite out of the blue.

'Our Jean's down,' Jean Kerr started.

'Oh,' I replied.

'Yes. Mary Skeffington is causing problems again. She's been on to John parents and guess what?'

'What?'

'She told them that she and John had been sleeping together, for heaven's sake, and that she might be pregnant and she's devastated because John's dating someone else.'

'Oh!' I replied. You might think I'm a man (perhaps boy) of little words but it's really hard to talk and read the NME at the same time.

'So now John has to go to his parents this weekend as well, and he's very worried as poor Jean is going to be in London all by herself because I'm not going to be here with her. So, I want you to be a pet, Pet, and take her to the cinema on Saturday and then out for a nice meal somewhere, cheer her up like, yes?'

'Well,' I replied, folding up my NME and dumping it on the floor, 'I had planned to go to the Marquee to see Taste but I could maybe scrap that. Have you mentioned your idea to Jean?'

'Yes, and she said you wouldn't want to take her out, and I told her you definitely would want to see her. I know it'll be terribly boring for you, Pet, but she's my best friend and I'd like you to do it for me.'

'Okay.'

'Okay?' she said as she got up from the sofa, for it was a sofa on that particular night. She picked up my discarded NME and folded it in two before placing it neatly with numerous other publications under the dead television set. 'I thought you'd take some persuading and I hadn't even got going yet.'

That's exactly what I'd been worried about, and I was fast developing a preference to practising by myself.

'Well,' I began, rising from the sofa and making my escape, 'she's probably gutted about John, the marriage and all of that, so don't worry, I'll be happy to take her out for the night.'

'Not too happy I hope,' she shouted at me over her shoulder, as she took a couple of dirty cups out to the sink.

She shot me a look, which would curl milk even before it had a chance to leave the udder.

Saturday night came sooner than expected, with Jean Simpson arriving at my flat two hours early.
'What's this I hear about you ditching the Marquee Club to take me to the ABC cinema?' she said, before I could even get a 'hello' in. Then she smiled, showing off the finest set of white teeth I'd ever seen. Jean Kerr had obviously relished informing her of my plans for the evening – no doubt with a little of the 'Look how I've got this boy to put himself out for you!' kind of vibe.
'If it isn't too late, I'd love to see that group over an evening at the flicks.'
Well, this was going far better than expected.
'Your wish is my command,' I replied, as I invited her inside.
She seemed slightly hesitant, possibly something to do with the potential dangers of being alone with an unknown boy, in an unknown flat. The danger seemed to pass when she heard my flatmate rattling about from deep within. Now, if you were to ask me I would have to say that it was potentially more dangerous for a girl to be alone in a flat with two boys. But I needn't have worried about that – when he eventually appeared, my flatmate, being my flatmate, gave me one of those 'you dirty old dog!' looks, made his excuses and left. I thought this would have made Jean nervous, due to her previous doorstep performance, but no. Not at all in fact, because by now she was perfectly relaxed and comfortable browsing her way through my record collection, her wine-coloured duffle coat (the one that Jean Kerr hoped her friend would give up to a jumble sale) thrown across the bed (sorry, make that sofa). Beneath the duffle coat, she was wearing a black miniskirt over black stockings, and a black cardigan over a black blouse. She appeared to have just washed her hair; it was smooth and

looked silky, very silky. All in all, she gave the impression that she was far from perturbed about the recently reported ongoing problems between her and John Harrison.

'Goodness, Jean told me you'd a lot of records but I never imagined it was this many!' she began and a few seconds later continued with, 'Traffic – Mr. Fantasy! Augh, I just love this record; would you put it on for me please? Stevie Winwood – he's got such a sexy voice. I adored his singing with the Spencer Davis Group; 'I'm A Man', ah, that just gets me every time. I can't believe that someone can sing that good and then play such great Hammond Organ, and then on top of that make his guitar sing so sweetly. I love his guitar work on 'Dear Mr. Fantasy'.'

Now, why couldn't Jean Kerr have ever said something like that? That was my first thought – do you know what my second thought was? I'll tell you. I bet myself that anyone as passionate about music as Jean Simpson clearly would never lie on my sofa (bed) like a sack of potatoes. Yes, I know that probably sounds a bit cruel, not to mention ungallant, but that was my second thought and I did tell you I would reveal it.

Two hours and three albums later (the aforementioned Traffic, Joe Cocker and Abbey Road) and we were hastily making our departure into the chilly night. The journey to the Marquee Club – a walk down to Wimbledon tube station, tube to Piccadilly Circus, changing at Earls Court, and another walk through Soho to Wardour Street – had never passed so quickly, so engrossed were we in our conversation about music and movies. We didn't exactly agree about everything, mind; whereas she was into Tamla Motown, I was more into the Atlantic Records type of soul. And whereas I was into the Beatles, she was more of a Rolling Stones fan. But she knew her (green) onions. So much so that I started to wonder how she'd ever become a friend of Jean Kerr's. Not that this was a subject I wanted to raise – I didn't want to endure any 'Well at least I've never slept with her' retorts.

Weirdly enough, I remember a lot about that night. I particularly remember that Taste were absolutely amazing. I remember that Jean Simpson was totally mesmerised by the three musicians on stage: John Wilson – the one-man orchestra – on drums; the lanky Charlie McCracken on bass guitar; and Rory Gallagher on guitar and vocals. Rory was always such an exciting musician on stage, at times looking like he was connected directly into the mains himself. Jean – not to mention the rest of the audience – was blown away by Rory's guitar playing. You see the band were just hitting their peak and were about to come over-ground, if you know what I mean. They were packing out clubs up and down the country and this group of people – fans, by another name – had all tuned into them via word of mouth. Pretty soon Taste would get a proper record deal and the rest of their meteoric rise would be history, but on that particular night in the Marquee Club it was simply a case of a band at their musical best, turning on a packed house.

I hope that doesn't sound too elitist because it's definitely not meant to. But everyone in the Marquee Club that night – with the sweat dripping down the black walls, like indoor rain, and the floor so caked in beer you had to continuously move your feet for fear of sticking to a spot for eternity – yes, every single one of the six hundred and fifty people packed into that room (which was meant to hold four hundred at most) felt they were witnessing something very special.

When we left the club at about eleven o'clock, Jean Simpson was literally on cloud nine.

'I don't want to go back to Wimbledon just yet,' she began breathlessly, as we automatically headed in the direction of the tube station.

'That's fine, I'm in no hurry,' I replied, knowing that when we did return to Wimbledon she'd go her way and I'd go mine, and that would be the end of my little plan to find out more about the mysterious past of her best friend Jean Kerr.

'Is this what it's like every night?' she asked, linking her arm with mine. I knew it wasn't a sign of anything remotely intimate – it was more for security.

'Pretty much, although that was a wee bit special,' I replied, slowing down our pace a little.

'Goodness David, and we thought you were a bit weird, always heading up the West End to these clubs. Jean and I used to joke about it.'

'You did?'

'Yeah. We wondered what you were really up to. We thought maybe strip clubs, sex clubs and suchlike.' She paused to laugh for a few seconds. 'Mind you, what you were in fact up to is, in its own way, quite exotic, isn't it?'

'Absolutely,' I confirmed emphatically.

'But how did you find out about this secret world?'

'Well, if I was to trace it back I suppose, for me, it would've started with a neighbour of mine back in Magherafelt. His name was Martin McClelland but his stage name was Martin Dean…'

'Stage name?' she quizzed me in amusement.

'He was in a wee local group, The Blues by Five and he wrote a few songs and anyway he got picked up by a showband–'

'A showband?'

'You know, like an eight-piece group that acted like a human juke box in the Irish ballrooms,' I continued, speeding up my reply in the hope there would be no more interruptions; I was struggling to find a way to describe the legendary Irish showbands. 'So Martin McClelland joined this local outfit called The Playboys and changed his name to Martin Dean–'

'After Dean Martin?' she interrupted enthusiastically, seeming very happy to finally recognise one of the names.

'After his favourite singer Dean Martin,' I smiled, 'and Martin was always playing his record player, and I'd pick up bits and pieces, not really that fussed about it at the time, to be honest. But I did register how keen he was on his music. Then I heard The Beatles on Radio Luxembourg. That was the first time in my life I can remember music stopping me in my tracks. I can still hear it vividly: I was in our house. My mum was ironing with the radio on in the background. I was busy, very busy, doing nothing and 'Love Me Do' came on, and it was so raw it grabbed me by the throat. The thing I couldn't really come to terms with was that although it was this raw sound, it was also extremely pleasing to the ear. God, I'm beginning to sound like the NME.'

'Sorry, whose enemy?'

'No, no sorry! A music paper called the New Musical Express, NME for short,' I explained, feeling a little self-conscious. I'd heard my own voice just then and it had thrown me.

'Goodness no, not at all! I'm totally intrigued by whatever it is that has made you so single-minded. Tell me more,' she said, rubbing her hands gleefully and pulling me even closer to her in the process.

'Okay,' I said, 'well, up to then I'd always listened to what my mother and Martin Dean were listening to. My mum's favourites were anything, and I do mean anything, by Frank Sinatra or 'What Do You Want To Make Those Eyes at Me For?'

'Emile Ford?'

'That's the one. But whatever it was, whether it was my mum's or Martin's music, it was always in the background for me while I was doing something else. But the Beatles compelled me to stop and listen to them, they demanded my attention.'

'And they certainly got it,' Jean added, breaking into another of her awkward smiles.

'So they did. As you can imagine in the wilds of Ulster, there wasn't much of an outlet for this kind of music and after that moment in the kitchen, 'Love Me Do' and my first taste of The Beatles, I was hungry for it. I started listening to Radio Luxembourg and I remember they had this introduction offer on the NME.'

'The New Musical... don't tell me, don't tell me! I want to get to know all this stuff... The New Musical... Express, yes, that's it! The New Musical Express,' she concluded proudly, using our interlinked arms to pull us tighter again.

'That's it. So the NME took me into the weird and wonderful world of all these new bands, and for as long as I can remember I've been reading about all the exciting comings and goings at the Marquee Club. So when I came over here I nearly tripped over myself in my haste to get to the club, and ever since it's been an amazing voyage of discovery,' I said, no longer hearing my voice. I was about to stop at that point but suddenly a flash came into my mind. 'But Stevie Winwood and Traffic and Mr. Fantasy and The Spencer Davis Group – you knew all about them. How come?'

'Well, I know this'll sound rather shallow,' she started, pulling us so close I could no longer see her face, 'but Stevie is just so cute looking, and so I joined the Spencer Davis Group Fan Club and that's kept me in touch a bit about him. But the rest of this, I mean, I've never heard about Taste before in my life, yet that was one of the most exciting night's entertainment I've ever experienced!'

I couldn't help but think 'What about your time with John Harrison?' but I didn't say it. We were walking in the direction of the only thing I knew would be open at that time, The Golden Spoon in Leicester Square.

'We'll go Dutch,' she announced, as we walked across the square towards it. 'Okay?'

'Sounds fine to me,' I said, and meant it; I was happy she felt that way and happy she had insisted on buying her own ticket to the Marquee Club. That's not me being sexist or anything. I was – in fact, we both were – Jean Kerr's friends, and no matter how much I was beginning to like Jean Simpson, I'd no time for doing to someone else what I wouldn't like done to me. It was as simple as that. Not that I'm suggesting that if I had bought her a ticket to the concert and then a bite of supper we'd have... 'Wishful thinking,' I hear you say, before you start shouting at me to 'Shut up and get on with it.' Okay, that sounds fine to me, but if I'm to shut up, how am I to get on with it?

'Have you ever brought Jean to one of these concerts?' Jean asked.

'Gigs, they're called gigs, and no I haven't. I think she thinks they're a waste of money–'

'And that you'll grow out of them.'

'Really?'

'Oh goodness, I've been frightfully disloyal – please don't tell her I told you that!'

How many times in civilisation have those exact words 'Please don't tell her (or him) I told you that' signalled the end of a relationship? Or, perhaps more importantly, the beginning of another?

The Golden Spoon turned out to be a convenient place to take a break in the conversation because it allowed me to pick my next question carefully. 'Opportunist,' I hear you say. Hey, so what? They also say that there's a war of the sexes going on out there.

'Did Jean tell you any of her other plans for me?' We were now reading the menus and I could have gone for a bigger question, but I wanted to start small, work my way in. Jean Simpson probably felt she should answer because of her earlier indiscretion, but at the same time if I'd gone for the kill too soon – say, for instance 'Does she tell you everything about us?' – well, she could very easily have laughed that one off with a 'Wouldn't you like to know'.

As it happened, Jean was blushing, and I couldn't quite figure out whether that was because my plan had worked and she knew she had to tell me something of substance or whether she was stalling for time in order to come up with a bit of fancy footwork.

'Well now, this could get interesting,' she began with a sigh. 'You must have an inkling that our Jean has got most of her life mapped out? And I think it would be safe to say that you're a part of it.'

'Sorry?'

'Oh come on,' Jean teased, as she repeatedly hit the menu against her chin.

I kept getting myself into these situations where I thought I was missing a few chapters in what was going on around me. A wee bit like Dylan's, 'meanwhile, life goes on all around without you'. A lot like it, in fact.

Yes okay, so I wasn't so naive that I was completely shocked that Jean Kerr's plans involved me. But the words 'most of her life mapped out' and 'you're part of it' clawed desperately in my throat on the way down, making them impossible to swallow.

'We never really discuss much of anything, it's not really that kind of a relationship,' I admitted, not really appreciating exactly what I was saying.

But Jean did.

'I know, I know, I've heard that you don't really have much time for the small stuff.'

I looked her straight in her baby-blue eyes. She started to blush again – she had a habit of blushing, did our Jean Simpson.

'So you do discuss everything,' I said, rather pleased that my little trap had worked.

'Goodness, she's doing it again!' Jean said, choosing to ignore my last question.

'She's doing what again?' I asked innocently.

'Jean... she has this habit of going ahead and making plans, making these great plans for her life, and then when they don't fall into place for her, she goes off the rails. Since we met – we were both around five at the time, she moved into the house next to ours – she's always been "making plans",' she said, doing a fairly passable imitation of Jean's strong accent which was in fact quite close to her own but slightly more sterilised. 'You know, in our very first chat – and I'll remind you she was five years old! – she told me everything she wanted to do with her life. Be beautiful; have a very successful career – I had to ask her what a career was; get married and have two beautiful children – both girls; have a house and two cars; and all of it before she was twenty-seven.'

'Why twenty-seven for heaven's sake?' I asked, innocent of the real issue.

What was the real issue? Well, it seemed to be that I was the man who fitted into Jean's master plan. I was to marry, father two girls and have a career so successful that a) I could keep up with my wife's equally successful career and b) we could jointly afford to buy a house and two cars. I didn't even like cars. I had no intention of ever learning to drive. Particularly now that it just might be the one great way to disqualify myself from Jean's dream.

'Oh apparently it's got something to do with one of the Brontë Sisters.'

'Right. That figures. Tell me... ahm... you kind of implied that this had already happened with someone else... who?'

'Ah, now that's really very sad as well,' Jean said, just as the waitress came over to the table.

Again something was left hanging in the air.

Thankfully I had the menu to use as a pretend distraction. You see, the thing I found about The Golden Spoon was that the food was pretty average, but they were always open late and, most importantly, their milkshakes and pancakes were brilliant. I'd known before I sat down exactly what I wanted; I was going to have my regular order of a pineapple milkshake and a round of pancakes with butterscotch sauce. Oh so delicious – just the thought of it made me forget, albeit temporarily, about Jean Kerr.

'What about some nourishment?!' Jean Simpson said in disbelief after the waitress had taken our order and left.

She had opted for a more staid omelette but without the listed chips.

'Oh it's okay, I get enough of that from Dylan and The Beatles. Anyway, you were about to tell me about Jean's last plan.'

'Goodness, look – please never mention any of this to her, or anyone else. I would've thought she'd have told you some of it by now, after what you two have been up to,' she said, playing with the salt and pepper cellars in front of her.

I was sure I was blushing slightly. Not from embarrassment of what Jean Kerr and I had done (just about), or from the fact that Jean Simpson knew about that; no, I was blushing from the fact that I was imagining what it would be like to do the same with someone as passionate as Jean Simpson. I was convinced it wouldn't be a spectator sport like it was with Jean Kerr. I thought it would be much more of an equal participant sport. But sadly I'd never know, would I? We were both friends with Jean Kerr, and that ruled out any involvement other than verbal between Jean Simpson and me.

'Don't worry, I'd never tell,' I said remorsefully.

'Well, it's one of those childhood sweetheart type of tales,' she sighed, taking a large breath while still retaining the smile in her eyes, 'basically, she met a mutual neighbour, Brian, when we were eleven, and from then on they were inseparable. They were always scurrying off somewhere, making plans or talking about her plans. The thing is, though, to him Jean was a friend – just a friend. By the time he reached seventeen he started to take an interest in boys.'

'You meant… girls there didn't you?' I said, cutting across her, thinking the obvious wasn't possible.

'No,' she said, leaning in over the table and dropping her voice to a whisper. She needn't have worried really, the majority of The Golden Spoon's clientele were couples preoccupied with each other, plus a couple of drunks who wouldn't have woken up even if the Vanilla

Fudge (the American heavy rock band, not another milkshake) had been playing full blast at the next table.

'No David, I meant boys. Brian liked boys. Jean genuinely thought he was suffering with an illness, and she kept thinking and telling everyone that he would get better. She continued making her plans figuring that Brian's predicament was nothing more than a minor setback.'

'And what happened?' I said, after a natural break, which was filled by our food being delivered to the table.

'He disappeared.'

'What he left the village?'

'No, he just disappeared. Fell right off the face of the Earth. It was like he'd never existed. Neither the police nor his parents ever heard from him again.'

'So nobody knows what happened to him?'

'No. After Jean got over it, and that took some time, she said that she thought he'd run away with another boy, but because he was so ashamed of his illness he never bothered to contact anyone again.'

'And that was it?' I asked, between sips of my milkshake.

'That was it. Jean stayed in her house for ages. She put on a bit of weight and started to have to try harder to keep her glamorous looks. And when she started to come out again, I kept trying to tell her to let things happen by themselves, to try to be a bit more natural, go with the flow.'

'Sounds like good advice to me,' I said, hiking my shoulders.

'I thought so, but it was wasted on Jean. It's just like… She's the local girl that everyone, including herself, feels is the girl most likely to succeed and she is so desperate to make the prediction come true that she'll stop at nothing in her endeavours to make it so,' she announced and then looked over her shoulders before continuing, 'I mean, look at you two. You'd hardly even been out together or anything and next minute you're riding her. Now John and I, we're going to get married. We've been going out twice a week and once he sorts out all this rubbish with bloody Mary Skeffington, then we'll start to save seriously and plan the wedding. But we've barely kissed.'

I laughed, partly from the fact that I found it hard to believe that someone as passionate as Jean Simpson was even capable of barely kissing. I would have thought that when those lips made contact, sparks would fly! Hey, but what do I know, this was all new to me. I was also laughing about the fact that she used the word riding to describe the sexual act. I hadn't heard that since I'd left home. No, I don't mean 'home' as in my house, you know my parents walking around my house talking about riding, for they definitely did not! No, I meant 'home' as in my village, Castlemartin, in Northern Ireland. I quite like the word 'riding'; it seems to be quite an apt word to describe the act. There is nothing gross about the word, nor about the act for that matter, and that's why I like the word. I was just surprised to hear Jean Simpson use it.

'You mean you're going to tell me that you're not…' I started and then found myself swimming into troubled waters. I mean, Jean wasn't scared about saying what she thought but I still found it difficult to discuss this particular topic with girls.

'No, David, John and I are not going to have sex until we are married,' she offered, jumping in to save me.

'But, I mean it's none of my business and all of that, but don't you feel that you'll be a… you know… a bit…'

'Horny?'

'No I wasn't actually going to say that exact word, I was going to say a bit frustrated?' I replied, loving her straight-talking the more the night progressed. I'd never enjoyed such an explicit conversation with a girl before in my life.

'Well, David, if we are "a bit frustrated" then perhaps we'll have to… you know… ourselves… solo?' She was mid-bite of her omelette and for the first time that evening struggling to find a word, but still through it all she was upbeat and appeared to be enjoying the conversation as much as I was.

'Yes, yes. I know,' I said, and we laughed and blushed simultaneously.

'Mary Skeffington,' I started, cleaning the last of the delicious butterscotch sauce from my plate, 'what's her problem?'

'Well, basically I'd say it's that she's still in love with John.'

'Even though she knows he's left her for another woman.'

'But don't you see, David, even if he has left her, she still clearly feels the same way about him. It just means that she was genuinely in love with him. I can't abide those who say "Well, I don't love him any more because he doesn't love me!" You love someone or you don't love someone, it's as simple as that. Now, they may not return your love, but I don't think real love is subject to conditions. It's not that feeble. It's like a bolt of lightning that knocks your socks off. And you can't do anything about it. You have to live with it.'

'Yeah, I think I get all of that,' I said, starting off as unconfident as a new foal trying to find it's legs, 'it's just that surely when this bolt of lightning strikes it would be impossible to control it and curtail it and put it on hold for a couple of years of engagement.'

Yeah, a shaky start but I felt I was watching the little foal now run confidently across the paddock. Not so.

'You're just slightly confused. You're talking about lust. I'm talking about love. We all know how you mix the two up, David Buchanan.'

Chapter Six.

The next time I saw Jean Simpson I had to rescue her. 'Agh,' I hear you say. One more time, this time altogether: 'Agh!'

All in all, the night in question turned out to be quite the eventful evening. Not only did I get to rescue Jean Simpson, but I also got to meet both John Harrison and Mary Skeffington, and I got to escort Jean Kerr. Yes, it was definitely action-packed all right.

We were off to a party, you see – an Irish friend of John's was hosting it. That's all I could find out about him, the fact that he was Irish.

'Yeah,' Jean said, as she busied herself applying her make-up. Remind me to tell you more about that later. 'He's called Tiger and he's from somewhere called Lisburn, do you know him?'

You know, I was genuinely beginning to think that most of London believed that if you were Irish, you knew every other Irish person in London.

'Well, funny you should say that, but just at the point that you're about to leave Ireland,' I began, my tongue tickling the skin in my mouth, 'the IPB–'

'The IPB?' she said, if only to prove she was listening to me.

'The IPB – the Irish Patriotic Board. So, as I was saying, the IPB meet you and give you a directory with the names of all the Irish people living in London. I've been through it once and I can remember plenty of Patricks and Seamus's and Liams and Seans and Kathleens and

Catherines and Roisins, and I've just about memorised all their faces, but I can't for the life of me remember a Tiger.'

'Oh super, what a great idea to give you a directory before you leave your homeland! Perhaps you could check it again, see if you can't find this "Tiger" in there? It would be truly excellent if we knew all about him before we get to the party; our Jean would be soooooo impressed.'

'Ah, that could be a problem, you see,' I replied, struggling with where to go with it; wind-ups are only fun if the other person is at least suspicious that you might be attempting one. Jean hadn't a clue, so I was probably bordering on being rude. But I decided to go on with it anyway.

'Really? Why?' she said, between brushing up a rosy hue on her cheeks with one of her numerous make-up brushes.

'Well, they don't put people in the directory if they're members of an illegal operation.'

'For heaven's sake,' she shouted, mid-flick of her brush, never once taking her eyes from her reflection in the mirror, 'you don't mean Tiger's a member of the—'

'We don't need to go into that,' I said. The fun had completely gone from the game. It was a bit like fish jumping out of the river and right into your fishing net.

While I remember it, let's just backtrack a little here. Jean Kerr had taken to applying her make-up in my flat these days. I assumed it was a sign of her being comfortable with me. Perhaps it was some sort of ritualistic intimacy. But whatever it was, she wasn't a pleasant sight before applying her make-up.

I don't think I'm being rude here, do you? I mean, do you think I'm being rude? Okay, let's think about it. Why do girls wear make-up? To look good, feel better, be more attractive to the opposite sex? A combination of all of the above? Jean Simpson hardly wears any make-up. Okay? Is this because she's better looking than her friend? Maybe she has less confidence than her friend? Or could it be that her friend, Jean Kerr, is so desperate for love that she wants to be attractive to all men? Maybe Jean Simpson wants to hide from men and she feels that by wearing little or no make-up she can disappear into the crowd more easily. This is going off on perhaps too much of a tangent, but I have to admit that it is always something that has intrigued me. And it's not that I have an aversion to girls wearing make-up – my ex in Ireland positively plastered it on and she was stunning. Barbara Parkins, the object of many of my daydreams, wears a lot of make-up and to me she's the bee's knees. I won't go into the fact that bee's knees are probably not the most attractive things on Earth because I think, and hope, you know what I mean.

Now, here's another interesting thing: when I originally met the two Jeans, neither of them had a boyfriend. So had I approached Jean Simpson first, would I be her boyfriend now instead of John Harrison? I mean why not? I like her a lot – she's attractive, unlike Jean Kerr; she doesn't mind really smiling a bit, unlike Jean Kerr; she loves music and going to gigs, unlike Jean Kerr; and made-up or not, she is very sensual, unlike Jean Kerr. So my point would have to be: did I end up with Jean Kerr just because she was the blonde one who trowelled on the make-up? But then again, I wasn't really attracted to Jean Kerr in the first place, she just must have caught my attention because she was more glitzy than her friend and as a result of her initially catching my attention we kind of drifted together and you know what, on reflection the drifting together was achieved only because she was steering said driftwood in that direction. So there, that's my theory totally shot down in flames.

'Get back to the party!' I hear you shout. Well, as it happens, I was just about to do that.

The party was in a spacious, second floor, two bedroom flat in Deacon Road, Kingston-upon-Thames. The flat was so packed that the partygoers spilled into the lounge, kitchen, bathroom and one of the bedrooms (Tiger had private use of the other), and down into the hallway and stairwell. Tiger must have had tolerant neighbours because the noise could be heard from the end of the street.

The walls of the flat were adorned with posters of Tiger's hero, Jimi Hendrix. There was a large (ish) 'Keep Off The Grass' sign, stolen (I believe) from nearby Richmond Park, which took pride of place on the mantelpiece above the redundant gas fire. Red bulbs were in every reachable socket and the two roadside flashing orange warning lights, he'd also nicked, added to the ambience.

Tiger was in his bedroom for the first forty or so minutes of our visit. I only know this because when the two Jeans inquired as to the whereabouts of Sue, their friend from Jean's office, I heard them being told through fits of giggles that she was in the bedroom with a certain Tiger in her tank! Jean Kerr had been shocked and rushed off to find us drinks while Jean Simpson had laughed so much she had to visit the toilet. I could tell she was preoccupied with John Harrison. He had always been due to arrive late, but now it was even later than that. When she returned, we got to small talking about how much she'd enjoyed our trip to the Marquee Club. She also said that she'd found it refreshing that she could be out with a boy and that he was decent enough not to try anything on. In fact, I think she said that it was quite refreshing. I wondered did she mean boring.

'For heaven's sake, of course he's not going to try to get off with me best mate!' Jean Kerr cut in, as, laden with drinks, she made her way through the crowd.

I always hated that saying 'get off with'. Jean Kerr used it a lot. Jean Simpson didn't.

'And besides, our Jean, you're nearly married!' she added as she doled out the drinks.

'Shush,' Jean Simpson hissed, 'someone will hear you – Mary Skeffington might have friends here tonight. God, I hope she doesn't come.'

As the two Jeans departed together to see another friend from work – Jean Kerr's office this time – I overheard

Miss Kerr saying proudly, 'Can you believe that about Sue and Tiger?' before Jean Simpson broke into a loud fit of the giggles again.

'Poor Tiger,' I said to no one in particular, 'that'll be the talk of everyone's office on Monday morning.'

'Sorry?' this posh voice from behind me offered in genuine interest.

'Sorry?' I replied a little taken aback.

'I thought you just said something to me.'

'No, well, I was saying something but it was to myself,' I replied, hiking my shoulders in a goofy pose.

'First sign of it you know.'

'What?' I replied, sipping my wine.

'Madness. You know, talking to one's self.'

'Or perhaps I was talking to the funniest person here,' I replied, deadpan.

'Oh jolly good; I could do with a laugh. Will you talk to me instead of yourself?'

'Well, as long as we don't ignore the me I was talking to, he's rather sensitive.'

'Maybe you are funny, or maybe you're just mad,' the woman said, before laughing. When she did, she showed off a perfect set of teeth, more perfect than Jean Simpson's in fact, which was quite an achievement. She leaned against the wall beside me and slid down until she was on her hunkers.

'It's quieter down here – why don't you join me?' she smiled from below.

Being a creature of comfort I found a couple of small beanbags and dragged them to our corner. She'd watched me complete the task while holding both our drinks.

'I say, a gentleman as well! Now, if only I could understand exactly what you were saying through that accent of yours we could have some splendid fun, I'm sure,' she said, flopping into her beanbag.

She was blonde like Jean Kerr, but unlike Jean my new friend's hair was natural. Hers was cut in a style similar to Cathy McGowan's and, like Cathy McGowan, she was continuously brushing it out of her eyes. She was wearing a pair of deep blue satin trousers with a tie-dye t-shirt and a red, large-stitch woollen waistcoat. She had black eyebrows, I kid you not. And not a spec of make-up. And although she wasn't beautiful in an actress or model sort of way, she was naturally quite stunning.

'What's your wine like?' she asked, smudging around to find a comfortable spot in the beanbag. Such spots of comfort are very hard to find but when you do manage to locate one, they are extremely rewarding. I was about to mention this but then I thought it might be taken as innuendo.

'I can think of no words other than red, cheap and wet,' I replied, just as I found my own comfortable spot.

'Ah,' she replied, 'I was thinking of changing – I think I've had enough G&Ts at this stage.'

Just then, as the speakers blasted with Hendrix's 'Purple Haze', a girl floated by with two glasses of wine in her hands.

'Excuse me, where did you get it?' my new friend asked, gesturing towards the glasses.

The girl, dressed all in black and with long, black hair, tried several times to get her instructions across. She was clearly already out of her brains, and in the end all she could muster was 'Ah blast, here! It's easier if I give you this and go back and get another round.' Judging by the way she swayed as she wandered off, she wasn't wrong.

As the sound of Hendrix increased a few decibels, my beanbag companion said, 'Ah, Tiger's reappeared.' She took a sip of her wine and continued, 'It's not as bad as you say it is. But then again they tell me the secret at parties is to tell everyone your favourite drink is crap so that there'll be more of it left for yourself.' She then looked at my drink, next at me and she broke into a smile as her green-eyed stare returned to my drink again.

I raised it to her.

'Right then, at least we all know where we stand.'

'Or sit.'

'Or sit,' she said, before laughing and raising her own glass.

'Listen, I'm David Buchanan.'

'Oh I say, you're not going to try to pick me up now are you?'

'No, not at all! And besides, it's a devil on the old back lifting someone out of a beanbag.'

'Ha. Ha. Ha,' she mocked.

'No, I wasn't trying to pick you up. I wouldn't, I've come with someone else.'

'So you really are a gentleman,' she said, going for another sip.

'Well,' I replied, I could actually hear the surprise in my voice, 'no, not really. It's just not something I would do, gentleman or not.'

'By any chance is this someone else you've come with, your girlfriend?'

'Well, not exactly, no,' I offered, surprised at the honesty of my own answer. I was trying to figure out if this was because I didn't consider Jean to be my girlfriend or, because, I liked this new girl enough to be subconsciously sending out a 'perhaps later' signal? And anyway, how do you send out a 'perhaps later' signal? Is that what I'd been doing my whole life? I mention this here because there just might be a degree of truth in it.

'Either she is your girlfriend or she isn't, David,' she replied, seeming to be enjoying the conversation.

I loved the way she said my name. She said it gently and, to my ears at least, she imbued it with great importance. People of breeding (and money) can do that. But you need the breeding and the money together.

'Well, what about if she was my friend?' I asked.

'If she was your friend, commonly referred to as just a good friend, then you could go find her now and tell her you'd met someone and you were chatting to them and something might happen and would she, your just good friend, be okay to find their own way home.'

'That would be a bit rude though, wouldn't it?' I replied, barely resisting the temptation to inquire whether something might happen.

'Well okay, so how would you deal with that situation, were that to be the situation?' She said, emphasising her italics – she sure liked her italics did this girl.

'Well, I'd tell the girl I just met that I'd arrived with someone, a friend, and that a friend is always a friend and never just a friend. I'd tell her I'd like to see her again and try to exchange numbers for another time and I'd see my original friend home.'

She eyed me up and down as she took in all this information, apparently assessing what I'd just said. I think it was during this moment that I fell for her, fell for her hook, line and sinker. In those precious few moments she replaced Barbara Parkins as the most attractive person I'd ever seen.

It's amazing, all the things that float round your head when you first meet a woman. We all seem to be doing the same thing, even if only subconsciously: 'Is there a potential relationship here?' you ask yourself. Your brain replies 'No!' but then you go, 'Well why on Earth not?' And the why on Earth not bit can be down to a million different things, ranging from the fact that they're married to they're too big, too small, too short, too tall, too forward, too shy. And each and every one of these factors has numerous subsections. Then if you miraculously manage to come across someone who finds his or her way through that series of assessments, then what happens? Well, then you'll discover that they are currently running their own series of equally stringent assessment tests on yourself. How much of this assessment is simply for a quick bonk and how much of it is to find the perfect life partner? Or is that all part of the same assessment? 'Yes, he's fine for a quick fling but not for a husband.' I'd be ever so lucky if that was what Mary Skeffington was thinking.

'What is your problem then, David?' she asked, adopting a serious tone, 'you're good looking, you dress well, you've got excellent manners, you don't swear all over the place and you don't seem to chase everything that's in a skirt, so there must be something wrong with you? I'm just intrigued to know what it is.'

To be perfectly honest my vanity hadn't let me get much further than 'you're good looking' – in fact, I was stuck in that statement for a few revolutions. Oh yeah, and then there was the bit about dressing well. What this? This little old waistcoat? Did you know it cost me thruppence at a jumble sale? These corduroy shoes (by that point I'd given up on the desert boots)? They're very comfortable. This clean, self-ironed, white shirt? It always seemed to look its best under the waistcoat and with simple black trousers. Before I'd a chance to bask too much in this glory she hit me again.

'So, are you going to tell your friend you've met someone?'

I hesitated for literally just one heartbeat too long while considering whether or not to ask, 'Have I met someone?' And whether or not I should tell Jean Kerr. But that moment's hesitation gave me away and she was down on me like a ton of bricks.

'My case rests, Your Honour,' she crowed. 'Guilty as charged. Take the man in the green corduroy shoes back to the cells. I'll charge him later when I find out the mitigating circumstances.'

'Ah, woe is me. It would be just my luck to get the hanging judge,' I groaned. The music was so loud that I now ventured to lean in close, in order that we could hear each other. But I wasn't expecting anything quite so exotic as the mixture of aromas that filled my nostrils as I moved in. I was scared I was going to start sniffing her in public – maybe that would also be another charge to add to my conviction list. But it nearly would have been worth it. Firstly she smelled clean, incredibly clean. I don't really know any other way to describe it; perhaps there was a lingering scent of the soap she'd used. Then there was a drop or two of her heather-tinted perfume and then just the ever so slight hint of perspiration. Yes, a totally intoxicating concoction.

'Okay, I'll save the black cap, but just for the moment. What facts do you want to be taken into consideration?'

'Well look, no disrespect to her or anything like that, but it's just that we seem to have drifted into some kind of relationship,' I reluctantly started off by way of explanation, and then I found that I was quite happy to be voicing these things. Since my conversation with Jean Simpson about Jean Kerr's plans for me, I had to admit to myself that I was genuinely concerned.

'Oh that old chestnut,' my new acquaintance said, chuckling before she helped herself to the remainder of her wine.

And you'll never guess what happened, at that precise moment the drunk lady in black was making her way very unsteadily towards us. This time she was balancing four glasses of wine in her hands and she mumbled and muttered something along the lines of 'I knew you'd be ready for another by the time I came back and this just seemed easier,' before she offered us the front two from the precarious cluster.

'I hope that generous gesture will encourage you to be lenient,' I said to my new friend. 'Look, I'm with a girl, but it's like we've jumped several of the stages in… all this.'

I swung my free hand out over the masses of partygoers all chatting to each other before continuing.

'And it's not that's she's even head over heels in love with me, but I do appear to fit the bill as far as she's concerned. I'm house trained and I don't go around getting into trouble or insulting people, or at least that's what she says. To be perfectly frank, I think she'd been in love once already and it didn't work out, so, you know, it's a bit like anything or anyone will do – I think she just wants to get on with it and get to the next part of the game. I think she's hoping that this is going to be a more enjoyable round for her. But she hasn't particularly enjoyed it so far. She's been getting herself down about it recently and I just keep thinking that it's not fair to pull the rug out from under her.'

'Have you ever told her that you love her?'

'No!'

'Never?'

'No.'

'Never even when it meant you might get lucky?'

'I haven't, honest,' I replied, and before I thought about what I was saying, I continued, 'I haven't needed to.'

I felt like I was betraying Jean Kerr in a way. Sure, this girl didn't know her but whatever Jean's faults were I shouldn't really be talking about her behind her back with a stranger. On the other hand I had never been able to discuss it with Jean herself, either. She would run a million miles rather than discuss something that didn't fit into her master plan.

'I apologise for being so indiscreet. I wasn't meaning to be disrespectful, it's just–'

'I can see your problem,' the judge began, 'and when I return from the toilet I'll give you my judgement.' With that she placed her glass of wine in my free hand, rolled out of her beanbag onto the floor, stood up, placed her hands in her back pockets, Betty Davis style, and headed off in the direction of the bathroom.

I sat amusing myself by watching people grow progressively drunker. I like a wee drink, as I have said, but I'm continuously intrigued by a human's capacity for alcohol. I think if you were from another planet and you visited Earth for a few days, say, for the purposes of this particular point I'm trying to make, on a Friday and Saturday, and you observed mankind, well, you literally wouldn't believe it. I mean, we spend most of our hard-earned cash pouring this vile liquid down our throats in vast quantities and then we either fall down, get aggressive with our fellow men or amorous with our fellow women (or sometimes even our fellow lamp posts, on both counts). Then we'll be sick and vomit the drink and very probably the day's intake of food all over our bathroom floor, which would need to be cleaned up the next morning, possibly even bringing up round two, which... well, hopefully you get the picture. Yes, I think our alien friends are going to report back to their masters that they don't need to worry about us strange Earth Beings; just give us several pints of lager and we'll be a pushover, literally. Don't be alarmed about this though; by the time they manage to make the return trip to invade Earth you, and your children, and your children's children, will be long gone.

I'd reached this point of intergalactic comfort just at the moment that Jean Simpson came wandering past.

'Any sign of John yet?' I asked, from my lowly position.

'No, David, no John!' she hissed in uncharacteristic bad humour. She also sounded a little drunk (due to the cider in her hand no doubt) and a lot preoccupied (due to the missing Mr Harrison). She wandered off without either looking at me or saying a further word.

Otis Redding's classic album Otis Blue was now being played at full blast. I was lost in 'Down in the Valley' when a thud to my left brought me to my senses. The hanging judge had returned and she had plonked herself back down in the beanbag beside me.

'Tell me David,' she said, clearing her throat for what sounded like her final statement before the sentence was passed, 'have you ever told any girl that you loved them?'

'No.'

'You say that with such conviction, not a moment's hesitation.'

'But I haven't! Believe me; I would know if I'd told someone I loved them. It would be the biggest moment of my life so far.'

She seemed to grow lost in her thoughts. I thought I was losing her so I said, as you do, 'Have you ever told anyone you loved them?'

'I have,' she replied, solemnly.

'And has anyone ever said those words to you?'

'They have.'

'And,' I said, continuing in my best Perry Mason voice, 'is there any chance that the person you've told you love is the same one who has told you they love you?'

'Yes.'

'Congratulations,' I declared, finding myself feeling slightly disappointed.

'That was then,' she muttered, glumly.

'And now?' I asked. They say in court you should never ask a question unless you are completely sure you want to hear the answer. I wasn't completely sure that I wanted to hear the answer. I wasn't sure I even cared. I just wanted to shift the burning hot spotlight away from myself.

'Now he's fallen for someone else.'

'No?'

'Yes!'

'Gagh,' I whistled. 'Ah well, you'll find someone else.'

I realised how crass I sounded as the words left my lips. But luckily the wine seemed to be taking effect on her, as she didn't register that little misstep.

'Yeah, I suppose so,' she said, not even trying to hide the fact that she was now indulging me, 'and you'll find someone else as well?'

'Well, that's not exactly true,' I offered, hoping I wasn't sounding like Leslie Philips (ask your parents if you need to).

'But you said…' she began, fluttering those eyelashes at me.

'Well, I suppose, you know, my friend is also with two other friends and maybe…' The ideas flowed and I was racing ahead of myself.

Honestly, before I'd a chance to say 'No, it wouldn't be right, another time perhaps', the judge had pounced on me with, 'There! Caught you! You're not quite the gentleman you appeared to be after all. You leave me no option but to sentence you to listen to Tiger talk about Jimi Hendrix for an hour! I hope you learn from your mistakes.'

I'd been well and truly wound up and it had worked, worked a treat, for her that is. Now I knew what it felt like to have the shoe on the other foot.

'So all of that stuff you told me about your romantic life wasn't true?'

'Sadly, it's all true,' she said, before sighing.

She put a hand on my shoulder to steady herself as she leaned in closer to my ear and once again her scents were hypnotising. I wondered if my breath smelled okay.

'In my case, my boyfriend and I had been friends since we were about eleven. Goodness, it sounds like that Cher song, 'Bang Bang': "We rode on a horse made of sticks. Bang! Bang! He shot me down. Bang! Bang! I hit the ground." Isn't that how the lyrics go?'

'Never been a fan, to be honest. I was already sickened by the number of times I had to endure 'I Got You Babe' on the radio.'

'Oh I loved it! Or at least I used to love it. I could see my boyfriend and myself in the words of that song.' The mention of her boyfriend appeared to realign her train of thought. 'Anyway, we went from friends to falling in love hook, line and sinker. I resisted it in the beginning – I knew what was happening and I resisted it. I just thought it was too easy. Neither of us had experience of the real world and we'd never known anyone other than each other really. I was convinced, in spite of my feelings, that we were just going through some pre-ordained motions. And I felt I wanted to have some say in the matter, you know. Yes, society does want to continue and for it to continue man needs to lie with woman and create more of the species, who do more of the same ad infinitum.'

'That's incredible,' I said, if only so that I could turn my mouth towards her ear and smell her instead of her smelling me. The scent was so intoxicating it made me forget what I was about to say. 'That's incredible,' I repeated, stumbling somewhat but then finding a thread. 'I think the same thing sometimes. I keep wondering what the whole attraction game is about. I mean, why are boys attracted to girls? You know, it's got to be more than hair, and smell and lips and eyes and—'

'Breasts and rears,' she added, filling in the awkward bits for me.

'Yes. Quite. Now you come to mention it, it's got to be more than that really, hasn't it? There's got to be something else that connects.'

'Yes there is, David – I was just getting to that point. There's the soul. That's when it all clicked for me. When I realised that he and I were meant to be together because our souls had connected. That was the point I stopped fighting it. Yes, there were other things as well. Like I didn't want the first time I made love to be with a stranger, a strange body. I knew him and he knew me. We'd grown up together. We'd seen each other's bodies maturing. I wasn't scared of him physically or sexually. I felt that was important. I felt that it was important that I didn't get to know a man through sleeping with him. I didn't want to start a relationship off with sex and mix up all the signals from there on in. That's why it was easy for us to do what we did; we were making a spiritual connection. Of course I wanted to do it with him; it wasn't a step I feared.'

'And I thought it was perfect, but it obviously wasn't. You see, I keep getting back to this: society and its rules, and the rules it uses to protect itself. If we hadn't slept together at the point we did, would we still be together? You know, okay, so you're not allowed or supposed to know this big secret until you vow to stay with each other forever and ever, Amen. It's a great secret and it's so important that you need to make a legally and spiritually binding agreement before you can partake. That way society ensures, to a degree, a monogamous relationship which is conducive to producing children, whereas if one thinks that one can keep changing partners, you know, trying to taste all the forbidden fruits out there, well you are less likely to want to bring children into the world to slow you down now, aren't you?'

'Good point,' I said, completely spellbound by her story. It was certainly better than any of the fantasy stories in the Mayfair magazine. I couldn't believe my ears really. Here was this beautiful young woman lounging beside me, telling me about sleeping with her boyfriend and the thought process she went through while deciding to sleep with him. Then this guy leaves her for someone else. I needed to hear more.

'So you broke up?' I asked, hoping to prompt her back into her tale.

'Well yes, but I don't think I should just let it go like that. I mean, I know he's making a big mistake and I feel that eventually he's going to realise this, and I just don't want to have fallen out of love with him by the time he wakes up. That would be so sad.'

Just then the two Jeans came through the doorway opposite us, arm in arm, with a man in the middle of them.

'David!' Jean Kerr gushed, 'this is Jean's boyfriend John, John this is…'

And that's as far as she got with her introduction.

John Harrison was staring at the judge sitting beside me. She was staring at him. She rose slowly to her feet, as dignified as she could from a beanbag, leaving her glass of wine with me. When she was steady (ish), she took back her glass of wine, turned and threw it all over John Harrison.

Then all hell broke loose.

Chapter Seven.

John shouted, 'Mary!'
Jean Simpson screamed, 'Mary Skeffington?'
Jean Kerr screeched, 'Fockin' bitch Mary fockin' Skeffington!' and threw her half pint of lager over Mary.

Mary ignored both of our Jeans and the lager, which was adding yet another shade to her shirt, and plunged straight at John Harrison. It wasn't a well-planned attack on her part, for when she landed on him she didn't know what to do next, other than shove him. The momentum she had built up in her few steps was enough to unbalance John and he fell over, with Mary on top of him. John clasped his hands around his head in order to protect himself from what he thought was going to be a barrage of punches. Jean Simpson had now dropped to her knees, flashing a bit of stocking top, and was trying to pull Mary off her man. Jean Kerr kept screeching: 'Fockin' this' and 'fockin' that' and 'fockin' her' and 'fockin' him' and fockin' every single thing. She was totally out of control. I tried to calm her down but she pushed me to one side with such force and pent up anger that I went flying across the room and straight back into the beanbag.

Embarrassing to admit this, but I was having great difficulty getting back out – I rolled this way and I rolled that way, but I couldn't find a way out of that blasted bag.

A crowd had started to gather now, and Jean Kerr seemed to be struggling with the zip on one of her boots. 'Fockin' useless expensive boots!' she screamed.

Jean Simpson was on top of Mary, who was still on top of John and still not sure what to do with him. Kent Walton would have been proud of the fight. Especially with all the stocking-top Jean Simpson was exposing as she tried to pin Mary to the floor. Unfortunately John was between Mary and the floor, and he was suffering the whole force of both of the girls.

Jean Kerr, in contrast to her friend, was exposing some stocking bottoms, as in stocking feet. She was throwing such a fit I expected she'd soon need another wee trip back up North to recover. She had been relatively quiet for a few moments. Boot off, however, she was back on her feet again, and I suddenly realised why she had been so defiantly trying to remove her boot as she swung it high above her head before using it to lay into poor Mary! But it was Jean Simpson who took the first blow. Nothing serious, it brushed her shoulder.

With all the screaming and shouting and jostling going on you'd have imagined there'd be blood flowing freely and the sound of bones cracking everywhere. But that's the thing about fights, isn't it? I mean real fights, they're so uncoordinated, so ungraceful, aren't they? Now fights in movies, they're a different thing altogether – they look almost like a form of ballet. Everything is perfectly orchestrated; the timing has to be perfect. The fight is lengthy and the balance of power shifts first in favour of the hero, then away from him, then back to him and away from him again until you are convinced he is about to lose the fight, and then miraculously the hero recovers and overpowers his opponent as the fight concludes. In the middle of all this, the hero's head had taken a serious battering.

Now, I don't know if you've ever accidentally bumped your head into a door, or post, or anything hard by accident, but you'd start to see stars, sparks and suchlike, wouldn't you? Your stomach would start to churn. Wouldn't it? You'd want to be sick, wouldn't you? Maybe you'd have concussion, perhaps a broken nose, perhaps a bloody eye. Maybe you'd like to lie down and cry. Now think of repeating this process several times in quick succession. You'd have to think that it would render you pretty immobile, wouldn't you? You wouldn't feel like just getting up, dusting yourself off, finding your hat (it would always be a white hat), dusting that off, straightening the brim and then strolling up to the beautiful heroine, before linking arms with her and heading off into the sunset now, would you? And all of the above only for you to appear in the next scene without a single blemish on your face, well apart from a knowing smirk that is.

Whereas in real fights you have screaming girls, like Jean Kerr, hitting their friends with a weapon no deadlier than a leather boot.

'Fockin' sorry!' Jean Kerr screamed, as James Brown's 'It's A Man's, Man's, Man's World' filled the speakers to distortion in the background. 'Let me at her, give me a clear fockin' shot, our Jean, I'll send her into the middle of next fockin' week, fockin' bitch!'

Jean Simpson all but ignored her best friend, so focused was she on the task at hand as Mary turned to defend herself against the onslaught. She was starting to overpower Jean Simpson, with John still cowering beneath her, and I was finally able to take stock of the situation.

First off, Jean Simpson's legs looked amazing, scene-stopping, just stunning. Perfect male-fantasy, super-heroine shape – muscular thighs with sublimely curved calves and petite ankles. So much so that Jean Simpson's wonderful legs were now the sole attraction in the packed room, and that's really saying something when you consider Jean Kerr's antics. I know, I know, I was meant to be ignoring the exposed legs, but I was there and you'll just have to take me words for it: Jean Simpson's legs were completely impossible to ignore. But, putting that aside, three against one just wasn't fair, especially when one of the three was intent on doing some serious damage.

Second off, if I pulled Jean Simpson away from Mary, there was a good chance that: a) Mary was going to make another of her effective charges, this time at the person she thought was her competitor for the affections of John Harrison; or b) Jean Kerr was going to take someone's head off. So I felt it was all relatively simple. I had to disentangle Mary, restrain her and then remove her from the scene altogether.

Disentanglement was easier said than done. Actually, I'm not 100 per cent sure that's a fact. But, however I did it, Jean Kerr was going to take it as some form of betrayal. Then again, I figured, I didn't really know this new Jean Kerr – this wild, blonde-maned pirate, one boot still on, the other raised and swooshing and swinging high in the air, desperate to connect with Mary's head. So, as Mary began to gain an edge over Jean Simpson, I quickly pulled Miss Simpson off of her altogether. I kept my arm firmly around her waist. She kept kicking out like she was riding an imaginary bicycle, so that when I turned to face Jean Kerr, I was using Jean Simpson as a shield. I was guilty of assuming that one friend wouldn't hit the other.

Not so.

Jean was by this point so enraged she had to hit someone, anyone, and Jean Simpson would have to do for now.

'Let me fockin' at her!' she kept screaming, referring, I thought, to Mary. John, now benefiting from a lighter load, was now pushing Mary off of him and stumbling to his feet. Right, here was my opportunity. 'Hi John, good to meet you! I'm David Buchanan. Hold this one, will you, while I get Mary out of here before some serious damage is done,' I said, thrusting Jean Simpson into his arms.

He smiled feebly and grabbed hold of the girl, placing her behind him with himself now between the two Jeans. That was when Jean Kerr made her first real successful connection of the encounter: her boot and John's head. John slumped to the floor in a heap and both Jeans immediately dropped to their knees and started to fuss over him.

Here was my perfect opportunity: I grabbed Mary by the hand and got her the hell out of there.

She didn't offer too much resistance.

Chapter Eight.

'So you're Mary Skeffington?' I said. I hadn't let go of her hand and she hadn't tried to break free. We were walking away from the party and we could still hear the music, with John Lennon's subtle confession of an affair in 'Norwegian Wood' filling the night air. You had to say one thing about our host Tiger, he certainly had very accommodating neighbours in Deacon Road.

'And here I was trying to retain a little mystery by not telling you my name,' Mary replied breathlessly. 'I can't believe it; my heart's still beating like a drum.'

She innocently took my hand and placed it near to where her heart was. Coincidently this position was quite close to another part of her anatomy and I had to convince myself I was feeling for a heartbeat and nothing else.

I continued to experience the pounding of her heart but all too soon she'd realised exactly what she'd done by her gesture and she smiled a gentle smile and whispered, 'Okay, we'll count that as your payment for saving me. But don't get any ideas.'

On that we turned and walked in the general direction of Kingston Overground Station, still hand in hand.

'So John Harrison is the boy you were talking about?'

'So the mad Jean Kerr is the girl you were talking about?' she replied.

I shrugged in response. I was glad in a way that she was aware of everything now, no skeletons hiding in the cupboard, or wardrobe, or wherever skeletons stay (I do have to confess that I've never ever come across a skeleton in either a cupboard or a wardrobe). We walked on, hand in hand, lost in our own thoughts.

'So, Jean Kerr is not going to be a happy bunny the next time you see her?' she eventually said.

I was impressed with that. I mean, you could have forgiven her for being preoccupied about her own situation with John and the repercussions of recent events. But no, she'd been thinking about Jean Kerr and me.

'You poor boy,' she continued, breaking into a throaty laugh, 'she's probably going to lay into you with the other one of her boots.'

'It's lucky she doesn't play football!' I said only half joking. 'I couldn't believe that – she was just... totally bizarre.'

'Actually, it would be funny if it wasn't so scary,' she added before sighing. 'Well, now you know both sides of the story, do you think there is any chance John will get back with me?'

That's what I like, I thought, nice, wee, easy questions.

'What can I tell you? I mean on one side you have the fact that John and Jean Simpson haven't really known each other all that long and they only see each other twice a week and–'

'And...' she said, 'you were going to say that they haven't slept together yet.'

'In this instance, it could be important.'

'No, sadly in this case I think it will only serve to make her more attractive. On top of which John is very single-minded. Once he sets his sights on something, he just keeps his head down and works to achieve it at all costs. So if they've made their plans, he'll be happy to only see her twice a week. He'll be buzzing away like a busy little bee, hatching all their long-term plans. I bet he'll have worked out a savings plan for both of them. In a way it'll be like she doesn't exist.'

Sounded like someone else I knew.

'You know, all these sacrifices will be for their own good but in reality, he really likes the hermit life, saving away all the time. You can imagine that when he gets married it won't stop there; he'll start saving for his retirement.'

'Then what is it about him that he'd have two beautiful women fighting over him?' I asked dejectedly.

'I'm in love with him. I don't really know why, but I am. That's the way it works isn't it? You really have no choice over who you fall for, do you? I imagine she loves him as well. You really think she's beautiful?'

You see, there's another intriguing thing: I had said, 'Then what is it about him that would have two beautiful women fighting over him?' Notice the two beautiful women section. That is to say, I was also paying Mary Skeffington a compliment. I mean, I didn't ask the question just so I could pay her a compliment. I suppose, if I'm perfectly honest, the subtext, if there was one, was, 'What's he got that I haven't?' But we don't ever admit to such thoughts, do we? So, whatever way you shake it and bake it, it was a compliment for both of them. However, Mary Skeffington only took note of the point that I thought Jean Simpson was beautiful.

'Yeah,' I replied. I was being as honest as I knew how.

'Well then, why didn't you pick up with her instead of the mad one and then all of this wouldn't have happened, would it?'

'My case entirely, Your Honour,' I replied. 'But it's not the way it works, is it? Like you said, we have absolutely no control in any of this. We like to pretend we have, but the reality is that we don't. Take me, for instance: I've drifted into a situation I don't really want to be in. Yet supposedly I'm meant to be in control of all of my emotional moves. Yes, I might fool myself into thinking that I'm only doing it because she's liberal with her favours, but then I've always felt the favours of those given liberally are not as rewarding as those given sparingly. Not quite as precious, if you know what I mean.'

I hope she knew what I meant because I didn't want to give the more vivid description, as in she lies there like a sack of potatoes. No, long term I didn't think I'd be doing myself any favours by being that honest. But then Mary Skeffington nodded and I took that as a sign that she did know what I meant, so I continued.

'Now, I'm always telling myself that I can get out of this, this relationship with Jean Kerr, whenever I want to and, you know, every time I think of ending it I come up with an excuse as to why I shouldn't. You know, she's about to go home for a time because she's ill, and it's not fair to break it off before she goes. But even thinking that is wrong, because in my mind there is really nothing to break off. But in her mind there clearly is. In another situation, you could see months, perhaps even years passing, and then talk of marriage and then thinking well I won't say no just now, for fear of upsetting her, and before you know it you wake up in a loveless marriage ten years later. But the point I'm trying to make here is that we really have no control over whom we fall for. So because of that it's rarely going to be tidy.'

'I do hear what you're saying, David, but it still would have been more convenient for everyone if you'd picked up with the other Jean. I saw the way you were ogling her bare legs during the scuffle – I kept looking over at you to see what to do, to see if you were going to do anything to help me and each time I couldn't help but notice that your eyes were nearly popping out of their sockets at her stocking tops. I started to think I hadn't dressed properly for the wrestling match. Yes, you'd have done all of us a favour if you'd picked her instead of jungle woman.'

'Well, all things considered, even if I had picked up with the other Jean, what's to say that John still wouldn't have gone off with someone else entirely? There must have been something lacking… I mean…' I faltered, realising where I was taking this.

'I know exactly what you mean,' she said confidently. 'There must have been something lacking in our relationship for him to be receptive to the charms of Jean Simpson. Or maybe he just… maybe he just fell in love with her.'

'But he couldn't have done that if he'd really been in love with you?' I offered, scratching my chin in the hope she would realise that this was just a thought and not a statement.

'You therefore honestly think that if someone falls in love, that's it for life?'

'If they are really in love, yes, of course.'

'You poor, naive boy you; don't you realise that people change, they grow apart, they have different interests, different goals? That's what happens in life.'

'No,' I said defiantly, 'that's just a bunch of excuses for something which wasn't real love in the first place.'

'You really believe that?'

'With all of my heart.'

'You're such a romantic.'

'Is that a crime, Your Honour?' I asked.

'Unusual in one so young,' she replied.

'But then again, look at yourself: you're fighting desperately for a love you don't want to lose. You told me yourself that by the time John realises what's happened, the love would have died.'

'I do love him, David, and I'm scared that it's already over and all this fighting of mine to save it is nothing more than damage limitation on my part, as in a delaying tactic to accepting the fact that it really is over. How long do you think it takes for love to die David?'

Now there's a question to chill the heart even further on a cold and windy November night.

Chapter Nine.

Just in case you were thinking that I took advantage of the vulnerable Mary Skeffington that evening, I have to report to you that this is not my style and, even if it was, I'm very sure Mary would have been well able to look after herself. In fact, I left her to her flat in Gladstone Road, Wimbledon, a long straight road close to Wimbledon Theatre that was so long and steep it looked like it might go all the way to Heaven. I walked back up Broadway, over Wimbledon Bridge past the train (and tube) station, where Wimbledon Hill Road started, then a quick first right into Alexandra Road, took the fourth on the left into Rostrevor Road, which was only about a fifteen-minute walk from her flat but took me thirty that night. Just long enough to go through things in my head and make a few plans.

The big decision, and an easy one to make, was that I had to break up with Jean Kerr. It had to be done, and quickly. Apart from which, I certainly didn't want to see a repeat performance of her freaking out.

I'd like to say that I acted properly and I went round to see her, to tell her that it had to stop, that what we were doing was unfair, particularly to her. Tell her that I was sorry if I hurt her. All very honourable I'm sure you'll agree. But that's not the way it happened.

No, that's not the way it happened at all, because she dumped me!

And not only that, she sent Jean Simpson to tell me it was all over. That she'd caught me trying to chat up Mary

Skeffington and that I'd saved Mary from getting a good hiding. A hiding she'd deserved.

And she didn't wait long, either – Jean Simpson was round the following afternoon. Sundays for me are a day for lazing around, and when Jean called on me at about three o'clock I was listening to a couple of new albums I'd bought the previous morning.

I find it a bit frustrating with new albums. I mean, I can't really listen to them properly until I know them, and I can't get to know them until I've listened to them a few times. So there I was, trying to get to know Bob Dylan's Nashville Skyline and Esther & Abi Ofarim's Ofarim Concert – Live 1969.

Nashville Skyline was particularly intriguing. Dylan had come off his motorbike in Woodstock, Upstate New York, and had supposedly broken his neck. In the space of the several months' recuperation, he'd gone from lean, mean and punky, to filled out, bearded and appearing to age into the father of the younger version of himself.

The Ofarim album shows just how shallow I can be at times. I bought it not because I was particularly a fan of the duo but because I was a fan of Esther's great legs. Jean Kerr kept telling me that it wasn't exactly a case of Mrs Ofarim having great legs, no, it was just more a case that she wasn't scared of showing a lot, if not all, of them in her micro skirts! On reflection, Miss Kerr may not have been wrong.

Anyway, there I was, slumming it on a lazy Sunday afternoon, listening over and over to a song called 'Lay Lady Lay' and enjoying Zimmerman-inspired thoughts when Jean Simpson turned up. 'I'll let you be in my dreams if I can be in yours' – Dylan said that. 'The devil always sends the prettiest messengers' – Dylan never said that, I did, because the devil had a habit of doing just that. For Jean was wearing a plaited Black Watch Tartan miniskirt, dense white stockings, ankle-length black boots, a white polo neck jumper and her trusted duffle coat, which she flamboyantly threw across my sofa. As she did so she gave a little twirl which umbrella'd her skirt, exposing the thigh that had been on show to great effect the previous night. Was this a bit of a performance for my sole benefit, or merely an accident? I couldn't figure out which.

'Listen,' she started, immediately taking a seat on the sofa beside her duffle coat and smoothing out her skirt in the direction of her knees, 'you're in big trouble, David Buchanan.'

'What, all because I saved a wee girl from sure massacre at the hand, or should that be foot, of Jean's boot?'

She looked at me with a kind of quizzical look that implied, 'Are you alright in the head?'

Instead she said, 'Well that, plus the fact that we all saw you trying to chat her up.'

'I was only talking to the wee girl!' I gasped in desperation.

'Well,' Jean continued, breaking into a semi-smile for the first time since she'd arrived, 'you'll still get hung for stealing no matter if it's a sheep or a lamb, so for goodness sake, why don't you take Mary Skeffington and give her a good ride and get her off my, and John's, back?'

'Thank you very much. So, it's a case of, as I'm already in the dog house, why don't I do you a favour while I'm there and keep you out of trouble?' I snapped, only half in jest. 'And what's in it for me?'

'Oh,' she replied coyly, and swept some hair from her face and put it behind her ear, 'if you're very good I might give you another little twirl.'

So her little display earlier hadn't been an accident after all.

'With that particular enticement I'd love to take you up on your offer, but I'm afraid we might find that Mary Skeffington doesn't want to participate in our little scheme. She's got her own little scheme.'

'She can't possibly believe that she's going to get back with John?' Jean said, faking a huff.

'Look, I hate to take sides here – and I'm not – but have you ever considered it from her point of view? Eh?'

Jean rose from the sofa and inadvertently gave me a little twirl, and thrill, as she went over to my record player to turn down Bob Dylan.

'God, I can't abide his voice, David!' she said. I realised that she would never have been that rude, bordering on insulting one of my particular musical preferences, if I hadn't – in her eyes – taken Mary Skeffington's side in the fight at Tiger's Saturday night party. Though I tried not to betray the hurt I was experiencing.

'How do you bear to listen to him whining away all the time?' she continued, amplifying her revenge.

She didn't wait for a reply; music lowered, she returned to her sofa once more, affording me a quick flash again. It was a bittersweet signal, perhaps to reveal that she wasn't totally annoyed at me. If this was what she did by accident, I was beginning to wonder how she'd repay a real debt. My little mystery was quickly solved when she continued talking, following some staged clearing of the throat.

'I hope you enjoyed your little show, David, but that's all for now. Look, of course I've thought of how she must feel, but do you really think I should let that get in the way of how I feel?'

'Well, I guess I'm a little biased here but if he can fall out of love once, don't you think it could happen again, only next time you'd be on the receiving end?'

'But this time it's different!' she protested.

'How's it different, Jean? If you were sitting there telling me that you couldn't keep your hands off each other, that you were consumed with love for each other, I might look at it differently, you know. But you're going to see each other twice a week for the next two years until you've saved enough money to marry? I mean, come on Jean! Please don't forget John has already slept with Mary; he has experienced the magic. Are you sure he can wait two years? What if he starts to look elsewhere?'

'Well, you've been to the magical well too, and I don't see you bursting down any doors for more. Besides…' she replied coyly.

'Besides what?' I pushed.

'Well, girls learn to, you know…'

'I don't know, tell me,' I persisted.

'Well,' she said staring me right in the eyes, 'they… I mean … we, we learn to look after ourselves.'

'Oh,' I replied, feeling that I'd been firmly put in my place.

'Oh indeed, David Buchanan, and what's more, young man, I'm here to tell you that you won't be getting up to any more of your naughtiness with Jean Kerr. In fact, she sent me here to tell you that it's over between you two. And she says that you're not to come around to our new flat, trying to change her mind because she won't be home. She's going to her parents' for a few days to recharge her batteries.'

They'd recently moved into a flat together, still on the SW19 manor, not too far away from me, around in Alexandra Road. No. 18 Alexandra Road in fact. Jean Kerr had picked the location because of the security value of: a) having a lamp post just outside their front door; and b) being at near the start of Alexandra Road where there were houses on both side of the road. A little further up the road the houses stopped, affording the residents a perfect view of the railway tracks.

'I'm not surprised,' I offered, 'after last night I would've thought she needed a whole new set of batteries altogether.'

'So that's all you have to say?'

'Let's just say that I'm not unhappy with the situation.'

'Very polite David, very polite indeed, I'm sure,' she smirked, half mocking me. On reflection, perhaps you should make that a full mock.

'It makes it a lot easier this way, doesn't it? It resolves it all without anyone's feelings getting hurt.'

'And what about me?' she gushed, 'what about my feelings?'

'Sorry?' I thought I'd heard her wrong. I thought she'd said 'What about me and my feelings?'

'Well, if you and our Jean split up then what am I going to do?'

'Marry John and live happily ever after.'

'Yeah, yeah, I know all of that, but I thought you and I were going to become good friends. I mean, I really enjoyed going to the Marquee Club – that was so exciting to me. I'd never been to a proper club before. It's like being part of a secret society – there's a whole new language, a new world full of wonderful things, things like: the NME; gig; set; admission; the PA being crap; sticky floor; smelly toilets; support band; main band; interval; guitar solos; boring drum solos; amplifiers; microphones; encores, and club membership. I mean, I find it incredible that six hundred people all congregate in the one tiny place on the same night, at the same time, to hear brilliant music being made by someone I've never heard of before in my life. I mean, Taste have never been on the television, I've never heard them on the radio, I've never read about them in the papers but yet the place was packed to overflowing with people who knew all of their songs. Every time I go up the West End from now on, I'll keep wondering if there are other magical clubs hiding behind other closed doors and whether they're all packed with people listening to class music. Until our night at the Marquee Club I used to think that underground music was music performed by buskers in the tube stations.'

Jean paused for a moment; she looked like she was collecting her thoughts. So I kept quiet. After a few seconds she spoke again.

'And the other thing, the other important thing is that we can talk about things I'd never talk to John about.'

'Me too,' I admitted, 'I enjoy our frank discussions.'

It was true. I found it remarkable how easy it was to talk to this girl. I mean, I'd hardly spent any time with her but the time we did spend together we seemed to have a rapport that, personally speaking, I shared with no one else. There was no pretence in our relationship. I mean, there couldn't be, could there? Jean Simpson had made it perfectly clear to me that she intended to marry John Harrison. That was a fact, the fact. But there was something happening to her physically and... well, I don't really know, but there was certainly something going on I couldn't quite put my finger on. However any kind of relationship we would enjoy would have to be based around that fact she was going to get married in a few years. Yet, at the same time... Hey, I wasn't complaining. Bottom line was that she was great company, a bit of a hoot and she loved her music and, call me a cad if you want to, but I would also admit to enjoying the titillation involved in our candid conversations. I'd never made a connection before like the one I'd made with Jean Simpson, male or female. If I'm being perfectly honest I haven't made such a candid connection since either. So, again from a purely selfish standpoint, I didn't want to lose it.

'But look,' I continued, mustering up as much enthusiasm as possible, 'I don't see any reason why we should stop being friends, you know, why should we stop our chats. Or why we shouldn't go and see groups together. In fact, Bob Dylan's in town next week and I could probably get us a couple of tickets.'

'Very funny, I don't think.'

'No, but seriously – surely it's okay for us to be mates, I mean why on Earth shouldn't we?'

'Great!' she said springing up on to her feet, her sulk apparently over, 'that's what I was hoping you'd say. Yes, let's be friends, I'd like that. We'll have to keep it a secret from our Jean for a while. But leave that to me to look after.'

'Sure,' I replied. I couldn't think of what else to say; I was still replaying some of the conversation over in my head. The more I got to know this Jean the more she surprised me. I was finding it hard to believe this was the same apparently timid girl who had appeared from behind Jean's Kerr's coat-tails at the hostel not so long before.

She didn't give me the final twirl I'd been half expecting, but her words from earlier repeated over and over in my mind as I closed the door behind her. 'That's all for now,' were the words she had used as she'd flashed me a brief glimpse of her perfect legs.

Chapter Ten.

After a few months had passed, Jean Kerr was back in London, apparently recovered from whatever she needed to recover from. She'd taken to wearing loose-fitting clothes and looked strained about the eyes. I saw her occasionally, as in when passing her on the streets of Wimbledon; as I said, the two Jeans had moved into a flat in Alexandra Road. She was polite, as she'd be polite to someone she didn't know, which was somewhat appropriate since she kind of pretended that she didn't know me. I mean she'd blink her eyes twice and nod her head ever so slightly as a small sign of acknowledgement, but that was that.

Hey, I'm certainly not complaining. Jean Simpson would make a point of speaking to me whenever we met and she'd stop and ask me how I was doing and, when Jean Kerr would drift away from us, pretending to be window shopping, Jean Simpson would always whisper under her breath something like, 'We should go out together sometime soon. You're just going to have to give me a bit more time with our Jean,' or words to that effect.

I could see what she was trying to do; she was obviously letting time pass, but at the same time she was insisting on being seen by Jean Kerr to be making a connection with me so that when she announced (I hoped) that we were going to see a group together, it would seem natural. Seemed to me like a good plan.

In the meantime, I was settling down now to see what the next chapter in my exciting adventure would reveal. I mean, let's pause to consider it please: I'd been in London less than a year; I'd met and had been seduced by a glamorous blonde; I was having intimate conversations with both Mary Skeffington and Jean Simpson; I was in the city where all the great music was being created and performed. Every time I went into the Marquee Club to see one of these groups you could actually feel the beginning of something special starting to happen. (I hesitated from using the word 'big' there, mainly because at the time we didn't realise just how big underground music was going to become. And then by virtue of the definition, the minute it became popular and broke the surface of commercial success it ceased to be underground. But all that was in the future.)

For the time being, we would all distract ourselves with our favourite pastime: coming up with Top Five lists of this and that and every other thing.

Take for instance my Top Five underground groups, purely from my perspective, of course:

1. The Taste
2. Peter Green's Fleetwood Mac
3. Chicken Shack
4. Bakerloo Blues Band
5. Spirit of John Morgan

If I were still in Ireland I probably would have included The Interns; they'd possibly even be at the top of the list. I saw them a few times, and I'd rarely witnessed a band so powerful. Speaking of which, I saw The Moody Blues at Eel Pie Island; they were termed 'a progressive group' because they played 'progressive music'. That's what the NME and the Melody Maker said, so it must have been true. And so we move on to my Top Five progressive bands, which were:

1. Spooky Tooth
2. Traffic
3. The Moody Blues
4. Skid Row

5. Grannies Intentions

I feel it's worth noting here that the Skid Row I'm referring to above is the Irish trio of Brush Shiels, Gary Moore and Nollaig Bridgeman and not the American bunch of... pretenders who nicked the name a few decades later.

Hey, and while we're at it, and it will become clear in a moment why I'd lots of time to consider both lists and my navel, my Top Five albums of the time were:

1. Dylan Highway 61 Revisited
2. Dylan Another Side of Bob Dylan
3. Dylan Bringing it All Back Home
4. Beatles Rubber Soul
5. Dylan The Freewheelin' Bob Dylan

Van Morrison's Blowin' Your Mind! nearly made the Top Five – there's some amazing music on that album – but there can only be five in the Top Five, can't there? The other interesting thing, to me at least that is, is that the only entry apart from Dylan is the Beatles and that particular album (Rubber Soul) is the most overtly Dylan-influenced album the Fabs ever made.

So, as you can see from all these lists, my homesickness really was a very big issue with me in those days and distracting myself with music – in stereo, of course – and writing out lists was the best cure for it. In fact, I'd a list for everything. I eventually stopped making lists when I started to compile a list of my Top Five favourite lists – is that sad or what?

One of the final Top Fives I came up with was a list of my favourite women, and they were:

1. Barbara Parkins
2. Jean Simpson
3. Ann Burgess
4. Linda Cristal

5. Mary Skeffington

Barbara Parkins could be nowhere else but number one, and I scoured the papers for news of her and what she'd been doing since she'd left Peyton Place. Jean Simpson you know and I suppose, because she was committed to marry another, it really was a waste of a spot having her in the list at all. But then if one was intent on being that cruel, they could also say 'Well, it's also a waste having Barbara Parkins and Linda Cristal there.' Barbara was somewhere in America, probably fighting off Ryan O'Neal, while Linda Cristal was most likely way out west working on another movie with John Wayne or Jimmy Stewart. Who's Ann Burgess? Well that's another story, if not an entire book.

At number six – if I'd allowed myself a number six, which I didn't, as we were all very strict with our Top Five lists – would have been Judy Geeson, who'd not long since crashed onto the scene as the main female interest in the hit movie Here We Go Round the Mulberry Bush, but she was hardly going to walk into my local and start to chat me up either.

But that was part of the problem for me anyway. I hated the whole 'chatting-up girls' thing. To me it was so false, so unnatural, and after you'd successfully chatted someone up it took ages to undo the falseness of the original encounter so that you could really get to know the person. The problem was, once you did get to know the real person, there was a good chance that either she or you wouldn't really want to proceed any further!

You see, that's why I much prefer the way my friendships with both Mary Skeffington and Jean Simpson had developed. We all kind of drifted into each other's company, as it were, but they were natural relationships. Does that make sense? Of course, if I own up here and be completely honest there was as much a chance of a man landing on the Moon as there was of me having a proper relationship with Jean Simpson or Mary Skeffington. Jean

Simpson was about to get married and her best friend hated me. Mary Skeffington, on the other hand, was still chasing her ex, Jean Simpson's future husband, the totally implausible ladies' man John Harrison. Obviously it was going to take a lot of time for Mary to accept that it was finally over between her and John and then, when she eventually reached, and accepted, that conclusion it was going to take an even greater amount of time before she would get over him. Yeah, you're absolutely right; I'd no chance at all. But both the relationships were natural – I'll happily concede they weren't much, but at least they were that.

Well, now that I really think about it, the reality was that I'd only seen Mary on one occasion, and that had been a few months previous. And I've already told you about my brief encounters with Jean Simpson.

Then you know what happened?

Well, bugger me if Neil Armstrong didn't go and have a wee walk on the Moon! That was on July 21, 1969 – I remember the date clearly because first thing in the morning I received a postcard from Mary Skeffington (it had actually arrived the day before and I'd walked over it a few times in the hallway before realising it was for me). And then, just after lunchtime on the very same day, I received a phone call from Jean Simpson.

Mary's card was belated thanks, a very belated thanks, for looking after her on the fateful evening of the party. In an effort to show her appreciation, she had invited me out for dinner or a drink (my choice). It didn't take long for me to make a decision: I rang her immediately, as you do, and arranged to see her the following Saturday.

Jean's Simpson's contact was slightly more complicated than that. As I froze my whatsits off in the draughty hallway on the communal phone, she explained that she'd now got Jean to the point where she didn't mind her going out with me to see, in Jean Kerr's words, 'some smelly groups'. The next part of the plan was for Jean

Simpson to persuade her boyfriend to feel okay about it as well. The secret was he wasn't to know that he was being persuaded.

We were to meet in the Alexandra pub on the Wimbledon Hill Road, Wimbledon, on Wednesday evening, just so that John could see what a nice, unthreatening kind of chap I was. I assume she meant unthreatening in a sexual way and I'm not sure I could stomach that as a compliment.

Her passing shot was, 'It would be good if you just drifted in by accident, around eight thirty. Oh and by the way, our Jean's going to be there; she's part of the plan. Byeeeeeeeeeee.'

I was left talking to the electronic static of the phone – known as Wim 7440 – in the freezing cold before I realised she'd already disconnected.

Later that evening, as I've already said, someone took a step forward; the major difference was that his step was a giant leap for mankind.

Chapter Eleven.

I am trying to deal with this chronologically and the meeting with Jean Simpson was the first of the two, coming as it did the following Wednesday, as planned. In an effort to make the plan appear even more natural I arranged to go to the movies. I was going to watch Seventeen for the third time, but I thought it might not be the appropriate thing to do before our little charade, so instead I went to see Alfie, with Michael Caine strutting his stuff like he'd never done before, nor since for that matter. Alfie finished at 8.10 p.m., which meant that at a leisurely stroll I could be in the Alex pub around 8.30 p.m.

At 8.29 p.m. exactly, I ambled across St Mark's Place, leaving the stunning red bricked 1880s library building behind me, and straight into the pub and there sat the gang, to my extreme right, around a table in the corner window where Jean Kerr was noisily holding court. They didn't notice me enter – that was to my advantage, I felt, because I could then wander directly over to the bar while avoiding eye contact with them.

And my plan worked. After a few minutes I felt a tap on my shoulder – they'd strange plumbers in the Alex – no, seriously, I felt a tap on my shoulder and I turned around, doing my best impression of being surprised. Well, I did a fairly good impression because I was genuinely surprised, as I turned around to find neither of the Jeans, but one John Harrison.

'Hey man, how are you doing?'

I shook my head a few times in shock. He obviously took this as a sign that I didn't recognise him.

'It's John, John Harrison – Jean Simpson's betrothed. I met you at Tiger's party?' he said, spelling it out for me.

'Oh yeah! Oh hello,' I said, as I struggled to believe that he'd just told me he was someone's betrothed. Even my grandmother was hipper than that.

'I just wanted to thank you for stepping in and saving the day. Someone could've gotten hurt if you hadn't defused the situation.'

So that's what I'd done: I'd defused a situation.

'Nagh it's okay, really,' I said, as I examined this man.

He wasn't tall, he wasn't small, he wasn't fat, he wasn't thin, he wasn't dark, he wasn't light; he was an absolute middleman. He'd short, curly, brown hair and dark, bushy eyebrows, which almost met in the middle. Either it was just me, or John Harrison seemed to have trouble looking a person straight in the eye. Every time I looked straight at him, he'd look over one of my shoulders or even over my head. His ears looked just like the handles of the FA Cup and he'd a few moles on his face. He was dressed very Civil Serpenty, white shirt (top button undone), a yellow patterned tie, Fair Isle sleeveless sweater, grey flannels with lots of creases around the knees and upper legs, and black leather unpolished shoes. He looked like his mother had dressed him straight out of the Great Universal Stores (GUS to those in the know) catalogue. He smelled like a smoker to me. He was… cuddly. Yes, that's what he was, he was cuddly. How come one so cuddly could have two of the girls in my all-time Top Five fighting over him?

'Listen,' he said, 'why don't you go on over and join the girls and I'll get you a drink in? It's the least I can do. They're over there, in the corner.'

As I turned to look at the girls he added quickly in very conspiratorial tones, 'Oh and by the way, we're not allowed to discuss the fight in front of our Jean, Jean Kerr that is. That's on my Jean's instructions, okay?'

'Sure,' I said over my shoulder, as I made my way over to them thinking this should be interesting.

As I arrived, I could hear Jean Simpson conspiring with Jean Kerr to take advantage of her boyfriend, John Harrison. And the very same conspirator was also conspiring with her boyfriend behind her supposed best friend's back. A poor boy from Castlemartin didn't stand a chance in the middle of all of that conspiring now, did he?

While Jean Kerr was frosty, Jean Simpson was friendly, but not overly so. We small-chatted until John brought my drink across and then we small-chatted some more. Jean Kerr talked enthusiastically to only Jean and John, never once addressing me. In fact, she barely even looked at me the whole time. By her flawless performance, however, she was proving to at least two people at the table just how good a friend to Jean she really was.

John Harrison, as it turned out, was extremely sociable. That has to be said. He was very relaxed and brilliant at keeping the conversation going. He seemed interested in everything – everything that is apart from going to a sweaty club to see a group, a topic that Jean Simpson wasted no time in introducing. A topic that I felt she'd introduced just a wee bit too quickly. Apart from anything else, I was interested in John's main pastime, drawing. He doodled the whole time we were there, producing caricatures of all of us. I particularly loved the one he did of Jean Simpson; he seemed to be as fascinated with her miniskirt and her perfect legs as I was. Mind you, the main difference was he'd every right to be – he was going to be her husband. Nonetheless, I still found myself stealing a glance at her caricature every chance I could.

'I just wouldn't be interested, Jean,' he hissed, rolling his eyes and pausing to light up a Player.

'But it was such great fun the night I went there with David,' Jean protested.

'Yeah, I forgot to thank you for taking our Jean to the Marquee,' he said, addressing me as he eyed me up and down, working on another drawing. 'Whereabouts in Soho is this tent?'

'Oh for heaven's sake, John, it's not a tent, it's a club! It's only called the Marquee Club!' Jean Kerr said.

'He knows that, our Jean, he's only having us on,' Jean Simpson added.

John Harrison clearly enjoyed a wee private laugh to himself, as he continued studying me and drawing away. It kind of made me feel funny, you know, being aware that he was observing me so intently and intensely.

'No, it was fine, I always enjoy going,' I replied, trying to be as casual as possible, 'and it was good to have company, the company of someone who loves music so much.'

'Yeah,' he said, appearing to be studying the parting in my hair, 'but I also heard you behaved like a perfect gentleman. Not many of my friends would have done that. They'd all have tried to ravish her, and who'd blame them, eh?' John stopped his drawing, swapped the pencil from his left to his right – holding it between the same fingers as his ciggy – tickled Jean Simpson with his left, giggled for a few seconds and then put the pencil back in his left hand, put his ciggy back in between his lips, and continued to draw on both his ciggy and his page as his giggles subsided.

'Quite,' was the only word I could find to say as I felt my forehead and neck start to perspire.

'Let's just try it once, John Boy,' Jean pleaded.

'I'm sorry; I'd rather go to a football match.'

'But you don't even like football!' his future wife replied, puzzled.

'Exactly!' John crowed and rolled his eyes again, 'I would really rather go and stand with a bunch of loud-mouths watching twenty-two men with hairy knees and shorts, kick a pig's bladder around a field. We need to save our money, not waste it. Take our Jean with you.'

'But our Jean doesn't want to go either,' Jean Simpson said in exasperation.

'You've got to be kidding, our Jean; I'd have to bathe for a week afterwards,' Jean Kerr replied, dusting off some imaginary hair from her powder-blue, baggy dress and using her other hand to fan John's exhaled smoke away from her eyes.

Just when I thought Jean Simpson was about to retire defeated she winked at me before taking a sip of her red wine.

'I've just had a super idea,' Jean Kerr announced, looking like she'd just discovered the secret of Dylan's genius. She looked first to Jean Simpson and then to me before continuing, 'As you two love going to the Marquee Club so much, why don't you go together?'

Jean Simpson froze, waiting for a reaction from someone else. But John Harrison kept staring at me, then working on his sketch. It looked like it was being left to me to react first.

'That would be perfectly fine with me,' I offered, nonchalantly.

'She wouldn't cramp your style or anything like that?'

'Oh please John!' his Jean said, breaking her silence at last, 'David doesn't go out to these clubs to pull dolly birds; he goes to listen to his music. Don't you David?'

How do you answer a question like that? I decided in this case, as always, honestly was the best policy.

'Well now,' I started shakily enough, 'of course I go to listen to the music. However, were I to meet someone there, well, I don't think I'd say "Leave me alone, I'm listening to the music".' I shrugged my shoulders, hoping to imply 'I'm a man, after all, aren't I?' It was a difficult gesture because I was also trying to put into the gesture a bit of 'Of course, I'd never go with someone else's girlfriend!'

'Men!' Jean Kerr said and tutted, as Jean Simpson and John Harrison giggled at my attempt at bravado.

Jean Kerr was implying she'd expected no better. I think she was quite enjoying her role as the wronged woman – in fact, I bet if I hadn't been there she'd have had quite a bit extra to say.

'You've got a good point, David,' John said, pausing in his sketching for a few seconds in order to rub something out. He stubbed out the meagre remains of his ciggy butt in the crowded ashtray before he brushed the rubber waste from his book. Then he tilted his head to the left and looked proudly at his work. 'I mean, having someone like our Jean with you means you're never going to come across as a threatening solo male, so maybe you might even find it works to your advantage.'

He saw the frown appear on Jean Kerr's face about the same time I did.

'No offence, Jean, of course,' he continued after the pregnant pause, 'I mean, I thought you and David… oh gosh, help me here Jean,' and he looked at Miss Simpson, who seemed to be enjoying the exchange and happy to let him get on with cooking his own goose.

Poor John stuttered. 'I mean, if I thought that for one minute you and David… well, of course, I'd never suggest.'

Jean Kerr cast me a quick look, her head tilted back so that she could view me down the full length of her nose. 'Oh,' she smirked, 'they're welcome to him; just as long as he doesn't forget all about our Jean and doesn't let her fall into trouble.'

Now it was the turn of Jean Simpson to shoot Jean Kerr a killing look.

Goodness, this was great fun, and I would have enjoyed it a lot more if I hadn't been one of the participants.

Jean Simpson now saw the opportunity to fire off a few rounds of her own.

'Oh, you never know though, if John doesn't manage to shake off Mary Skeffington I might need to make a few connections of my own. I'm sure David wouldn't mind introducing me to a few of his long-haired friends at the Marquee Club.'

'Agh now Jean, I thought we'd put all that behind us! I told you I spoke to her mum and I put her mind at rest.'

'Really?' Jean Kerr chipped in, 'I didn't realise you'd discussed all this with Mary's mother! Isn't that just a wee bit over-familiar?'

'God, if it's not one of our Jeans on my case it's the other,' John said, before sighing and pushing hair that didn't exist out of his eyes. 'I mean, she'd been bad-mouthing me, saying I'd got her pregnant, which now, surprise, surprise, turns out to have been a false alarm. But in doing so she'd made her point that we'd been sleeping together–'

'John!' Jean Simpson hissed, 'I'm not sure it's absolutely necessary to be going over all of this now!'

'You started it,' he replied, just about returning the ball over the net.

Me? Well I was sitting there thinking here is a couple who were never going to make it long term. If you'd pushed me on the subject I'd have said that Jean Kerr and John Harrison were more the perfect couple. They both seemed to want to be in relationships where you didn't have to bother entirely about your partners. You know, you just got on with your own life and they – your betrothed, as John had referred to Jean Simpson – fell into step.

Then, Jean Kerr, the one who I'd assumed had been dropping hints about not mentioning the war before I arrived, was the one who actually brought the war into the conversation.

'If it hadn't been for him,' she said, looking directly at me, with such obvious utter contempt, 'I'd have given her a good hiding at Tiger's party and we'd have never heard from her again.'

'Yes, our Jean,' Jean Simpson lectured, 'and we'd have all ended up in jail. I get so depressed over how much of our lives are wasted discussing Mary Skeffington. Is there nothing else we can talk about?'

Jean Kerr seemed disappointed as John said, 'So tell me, David, which band are you going to take our Jean to see?'

'To hear John,' Jean corrected her boyfriend, 'we go to listen to bands not to look at them.'

'Right,' John replied, as he did a bit more correcting on his sketch, 'and which band would it be that you're going to go and listen to?'

'Well, I wouldn't mind hearing Jethro Tull. Personally speaking their music's a wee bit too much amplified-English-folk-music for me but they're an exciting live band, a bit wild and I hear that their guitarist, Mick Abrahams, is about to leave to form his own band, so I'd quite like to see them one more time before he does.'

'Jethro Tull, right, well, great I suppose. And when does all this take place?' John inquired, politely rolling his eyes again as he smiled. That was obviously one of his favourite gestures – he did it quite a lot.

'They're playing the Toby Jug in Tolworth, Wednesday night,' I said, as Jean Simpson looked on like a penguin waiting for the trainer to toss her a fish.

'Good, that's settled,' John announced happily, 'at least it doesn't interfere with our nights, Jean. We see each other every Tuesday and Thursday, you know.'

Jean Kerr now rolled her eyes the whole way to the heavens.

'So how much will all of this cost?' John asked, as he searched his back pocket for what I assumed would be a wallet.

'No, it's fine dear,' Jean said, looking rather pleased with herself that it had all turned out as she'd so carefully planned, 'we'll go Dutch, won't we David?'

'Of course,' I replied dutifully.

'What? You mean you'll each bring tulips?' John wisecracked, breaking into an uncontrollable fit of laughter, but at the same time appearing very relieved that he wasn't going to be asked to break into his wallet.

'Yes quite... dear,' Jean Simpson said, taking her turn to roll her eyes. 'Now, I'm sure David has other things to do.'

She stared me directly in the eyes with a, 'You have other things to do, don't you?' kind of stare.

'I'll get your telephone number from our Jean and give you a ring to fix up the details,' she continued as she dismissed me.

Now the more astute of you will remember that she had already rung me on the day that man first landed on the Moon. Yes exactly, that's what I'd been thinking as well. And at that moment she reminded me of the lady in Dylan's 'She Belongs to Me': 'She can take the dark out of the night-time and paint the daytime black.'

As I rose to leave, John Harrison handed me the sketch he'd been working on. It was of the two Jeans and me, and each of them was pulling one of my arms in the opposite direction.

Jean Kerr tut-tutted.

Jean Simpson had a puzzled look on her face.

John Harrison looked proud.

While each of them were preoccupied with their own thoughts, I quickly picked up and rolled the other three caricatures and quipped 'You don't mind if I take these as well?'

Before John had a chance to reply I'd carefully placed the drawings in my large inside pocket. As you might have already guessed, the reality was that I didn't give a fig for any of the drawings excepting the one where Jean Simpson was wearing her miniskirt and showing off those prized legs. Yes, with the drawing in my pocked I felt I benefited from an inner glow on that cold, cold night. I reached the flat in record time and couldn't wait to release the sketches from my inside pocket, and I positively drooled over Jean Simpson's fine pins for the next hour or so.

Chapter Twelve.

The thing about Mary Skeffington was that for someone so heartbroken she was so intent on having a great time, a hoot. If she had married, she'd now be a merry widow. I wonder what the term is for someone who was engaged but then was dumped? Yes, I know they've just been jilted, but you couldn't really say the merry jiltedee now, could you?

Yes, she was still passionately in love with John Harrison; yes, she was desperately scheming her way back into his affections, but she was not about to wrap herself in sackcloth and mark her face with ashes. Then again you'd also have to say that she was intelligent and the question had to be: How could such an intelligent woman not see and accept what the rest of the world knew; that it was over between her and John Harrison? John Harrison was betrothed to another. It was that simple.

Or was it?

Would John start to reconsider Mary Skeffington simply because, despite all he'd done to her by dumping her and humiliating her in public, she was still protesting her love for him? Would that make her more attractive in his eyes? She certainly couldn't have looked more attractive in my eyes than she did on that Wednesday night.

Unlike the night of the party, Mary was wearing make-up on this cold, cold Saturday night. Cosmetically speaking, she fell right between the two Jeans. She didn't shovel it on with a trowel like Jean Kerr, nor did she shyly add a hint here and there like Jean Simpson. She used some around her eyes, a bit on her cheeks to put a little colour into her natural whiteness and a strong, red lipstick. The thing that struck me though was how brilliantly clear her skin was – very white with not a blemish in sight.

Like the night of the party she kept brushing the hair from her eyes in a Cathy McGowan kind of way. It was funny seeing her dark, sharp eyebrows through her blonde fringe. She wasn't scared of looking you in the eyes, or catching your stare and holding it, and she seemed to continuously search my face for telltale looks that may have contradicted the words I was speaking. I couldn't work out if that was a by-product of her fall out with John or one of her natural qualities. Conversely, she wore her heart on her sleeve with her own facial expressions.

She was wearing a tight-fitting pair of Jackie Kennedy-type slacks which were tucked into a pair of brown, high-heeled, suede boots. Her top was a subtle red, sleeveless, high-necked jumper, which was perfectly set off with a well-worn and battle-scarred three-quarter length brown suede jacket. She refused to let the waiter take her jacket, insisting instead on letting it fall loosely over the back of her chair.

She spoke well, or proper as we used to say in Castlemartin. I know at the night of the party I'd said she'd a posh accent but on closer examination I found myself thinking she didn't really have an accent at all, it was just that she knew how to pronounce all her words properly. I admired that; you'll never know exactly how much I admired that. It seemed to me at that time in my life that everyone I spoke to seemed to start off every other sentence with, 'Pardon?'

I could see from Mary's eyes and the cute way she had of bobbing her nose around that she didn't exactly have to send my lines to Bletchley Park for decryption, but my accent was causing a few problems for her in the translation department. Key troubling words like: films; ate; eight; ask; Wimbledon; chimney; architect and suchlike seemed to raise eyebrows and questions marks when delivered in my Ulster accent. I'd recently found myself subconsciously earmarking words to avoid and seeking out acceptable substitutes.

'So David Buchanan,' she began, before I'd a chance to deploy another of my tricks, i.e. asking lots of questions, 'you know all about me and my love life, or lack of it, what about your romantic adventures? I think I got the gist about the mad Jean but what about others?'

We were sitting in Little Italy, which was just across the road from Wimbledon Theatre. It was cosy and as Val Doonican was currently entertaining the crowds across the road, we were sat at one of only three tables presently in use. (I'd already told her that I'd thought that the same Mr Doonican had released an album with one of the coolest, if somewhat inappropriate, titles, Val Doonican Rocks... But Gently.) The menu was very Italian and reasonably priced, and Mary made me promise that it would be her treat. She owed me a favour, she said, and she could afford it, she said.

'My life, what can I tell you? It's boring,' I replied.

'Now please, you know my comings and goings chapter and verse. In fact, everyone at that party seems to know the intimate details of my sex life. So cough up, David Buchanan, spill the beans.'

I wanted to say how much more interesting I felt it would be talking about her sex life instead, but I thought that might be better saved for later. Like five years later at this speed. So with the thought that the sooner I get on with it the sooner we can get round to her, I took a large breath and jumped right in.

'I, agh, I'd a very friendly, easy, fun-packed childhood. I was happy. I didn't really know what I wanted to do with my life and it didn't seem important to me to make a decision. I do remember when I was about eight or nine harbouring this passionate ambition about wanting to be a member of the RCMP.'

'Sorry, give me that again?' she asked politely.

I loved the sound of her voice; I just wished I could get her to talk more.

'The Royal Canadian Mounted Police.'

'The Mounties?' she gasped in disbelief. 'You wanted to be a member of the Mounties?'

'Yes, I was nine at the time and I loved their uniform, what with the hat and the red tunic, the white gloves with the wide-flared cuffs, and the riding britches with a wire clothes hanger down each leg. And I thought the fact that their motto was 'The Mounties always get their man' was far out.'

She took to a fit of the giggles. 'Unbelievable, David Buchanan! So what happened to change that?'

'The Beatles.'

'What, The Beatles as in you wanted to join The Beatles? I can see the similarity, as in dressing up in uniforms, plus they always get what they want, which seems to be an endless stream of number one hits.'

'No, not exactly, I mean I didn't want to join them. The fact that I don't have an ounce of musical talent in my body takes care of any ambitions in that direction! No, not at all in fact. But what they did was turn me on to music. Before that, music was always just a backdrop. The Beatles moved it into the main frame for me. Then I read that John Lennon and George Harrison were big fans of this American guy called Bob Dylan, so I bought one of his albums. I couldn't believe how directly he connected with me and I went out and bought all of his albums and here I am.'

'Sorry... you're in London because you bought all the Bob Dylan albums? I think we might be missing something there, David,' she said, before sipping on her wine while we waited for the meal to arrive.

She'd obviously done this so many times before that it was second nature to her. I was still, comparatively speaking, a novice. You see, back home in Castlemartin, people eat only in their houses. The only exception to that is a couple of fish and chip bars which had started to open in the few years just before I'd left. But basically food was a functional exercise back home, whereas in London it seemed to be more of a social adventure. So, what I'm saying is I was still at the follow-your-leader stage of dining, and in this case Mary Skeffington was my leader and I would gladly follow her wherever she wished to take me. Sadly, at this stage, she seemed intent on wanting to take me step-by-step and detail-by-detail through my past.

'Well as I said I didn't really have any ambitions…'

'Apart from The Mounties,' she said laughing.

'Yeah, apart from the Mounties,' I replied, too self-conscious to laugh at myself. 'I didn't really know what I wanted to do, but, I did know what I didn't want to do. Which was to end up tied down to a job and living the rest of my life serving it. I thought a much better idea would be to find something I could do and hopefully that something would pay me enough money that I could live my life freely. I knew it would be pretty hard to do that in Castlemartin and, because of the lure of music and thanks to the NME, I realised London would probably be the best starting point for me.'

'You found it easy to leave your family behind?' she asked, as the food arrived. I had ordered the exact same as her, tagliatelle, whatever that was, it was served in a cream sauce, and I now mirrored her choice of cutlery.

'I find it gets easier as time passes. It wasn't very easy at the beginning though. I mean, it was fine with my sister – she's about twelve years older than me and she's been married since I was nine, so we were never really very close. I am very close to my parents though,' I said, hearing my voice crack a little with emotion. I hoped it wasn't noticeable.

'Did your parents not mind you leaving?'

'They were…' I hesitated for a few beats, 'they were pretty grown up about it.'

She laughed. I was happy at that; I didn't want her to think I was making a cheap joke at my parent's expense.

'I mean, I think they both would've been happier if I'd stayed at home, but I think they felt that I'd make more of myself over here. It's probably harder for them you know, I've left a large gap in their lives, and while now I'm lucky enough to be filling up my gap with a new group of people in London, at the beginning it was very difficult. I just hadn't accounted for how hard the homesickness would hit me.'

'Yeah, I suppose because I've been lucky enough to be able to nip home for a weekend when I was missing my mother I've never really suffered from homesickness,' she offered quietly. 'What about girlfriends; did you leave any tearful Colleens at the airport?'

'At the docks, more like,' I replied, remembering my first fatiguing journey to London, endurable only because I felt I was at the start of a great adventure. 'I was seeing someone just before I left. Her name was Colette. Her name still is Colette, I'm sure.'

'Had you been seeing her long?'

'Probably a bit over a year,' I replied. The tagliatelle, which turned out to be plain old flattened spaghetti, was delicious and I wasn't making a dog's dinner out of eating it, so my confidence was rising.

'Goodness. That's a long time to date someone when you're a teenager. No plans for her to come over here?'

'No. It was never a possibility. Perhaps if I'd stayed in Ireland we would have… you know…'

'Settled down, got married, had kids?'

'Possibly, something like that I suppose, but I doubt it. Although, that seems to happen a lot in small villages; pretty soon you know everyone and you have to make your choice from them.'

'But isn't that a bit unfair on Colette? You know, if you'd stayed in Ireland she was the best of who was available and you'd have gotten it together?'

'No. No, it's nothing like that at all. We'd already agreed that we weren't really the ones for each other. She'd different goals. She was very happy to stay in Ireland. She'd no ambitions about travelling. She's part of a very tightly knit, large family and she's doing fine. Besides, she drops me a line now and then – she's met someone, and she likes him a lot and thinks he likes her. It's early days yet but she thinks it might work.'

'Does that hurt you?' Mary Skeffington asked. She seemed happy to have been distracted from her own disastrous love life for a time.

'Not really, I mean, I was a bit sad when I received her letter, you know – we'd kissed and cuddled a little, but not a lot. We were more mates, truth be told. It was more of a coincidence that we were of the opposite sex.'

'And that's been the love of your life apart from Mad Jean?' she continued, pausing only to use her napkin to dap the corners of her mouth. It was such a genteel gesture that I was convinced it showed her breeding. But she could've just as easily spotted someone doing it on the Forsythe Saga.

'Well, let's just say of the two I have fonder memories of Colette.'

'There's that gentleman slipping through again,' Mary said, with a warm smile. She really did have such beautiful teeth.

Girls, why are they made so absolutely beautiful if we're not meant to stare at them? I mean, I'm being pretty cool here telling you about this but… I couldn't believe I was out on the town with one so beautiful. And that so far she'd managed to get me to do most of the talking. I was thinking it was a shame that due to the fact she was still so hung up on John, I was never going to be able to feast my eyes on the rest of her body.

'I'm not sure about that,' I said, giving voice to some of my thoughts. 'But anyway, that's pretty much me – what about you, why are you in London?'

Before dessert had arrived she'd told me that she'd moved to London because John Harrison had moved to

London. In fact, pretty much everything she had ever done involved John Harrison. I hope that doesn't make her sound like some feeble girl who did everything for her man. That, quite simply, wasn't the case. She was very strong and ambitious; it just so happens that all her ambitions, until quite recently, were entwined with those of John Harrison. I think that was the thing that had shocked her the most. You know, the fact that as far as she was concerned they were a team. In a team you don't make sacrifices for each other, you just get on with whatever is best for the team. Only now in hindsight was she realising that some of the things she'd done could most definitely be described as 'sacrifices'. And when she really got down to it, she was slowly coming to the conclusion that every time one of them discussed giving way to the other, it was always she who stood back so that he could step forward.

'I hadn't seen it coming,' she claimed. 'In fact, I had absolutely no inkling. We met the two Jeans at another of Tiger's parties. Neither of us paid much attention to them, apart from the fact that they appeared to be sisters, and maybe stronger than sisters at that because they were sisters in name and not in blood.'

'At the night of the first party it was Jean Kerr who did all the talking, while the other Jean seemed a bit sheepish. I will say one thing though; since she's started dating John, she's come right out of her shell. No more riding on the other Jean's very large coat-tails.'

I had to agree with Mary on that one.

'It's funny that,' she said as desserts arrived, 'how when you're part of a couple for the first time, you seem to grow into it. You adopt the status of no longer being alone. I've been finding that now I'm alone, I'm feared. Maybe it's just because I'm a single girl or they think I'm desperate for a boy now that John has gone. I'm beginning to sense a little bit of closing of the ranks when I'm around.'

She stopped and dug her spoon into her Lancaster Lemon Tart (I found it strange that such a dish should be on the sweets menu in an Italian restaurant; perhaps these particular Italians were northern ones – northern Italy that is, not northern English), and she poked around in her dessert as if she was searching for gold or something. Maybe she was searching for words.

'David, I'm not the one who has done wrong,' she said, as a large tear started rolling down her left cheek. 'I'd never have looked at another man and here's John off chasing the first Jean who bats her eyelashes, rolls her 'a's at him and he's off. Dumped me and just because he's now in a couple and I'm not, I'm the one who's treated like a leper. As all his friends were our friends, now I've no friends.'

Her single teardrop was joined by another two and the trio were making their way slowly down her cheek.

'Well I'm your friend.'

That seemed to be the signal for the rest of her tears to pour out from her reservoir. How many tears do we have? We've all heard about the girl in the song who cried me a river. I hope that girl's boyfriend had a pair of wellies, but could you really ever reach a point when you've used up all your tears? Poor Mary Skeffington looked like she'd used up her entire reserve at this point. She wasn't a cry-baby or anything like that; she was actually quite spunky in her own way. It's just that, as near as I could figure, she'd given her all to someone, to something that she thought would last. Now that it hadn't lasted, she obviously felt that she'd lost a part of herself. I felt she was grieving more over that loss than over the loss of John Harrison, and that was probably why she was hurting so much. And... all of the above was most likely the reason why she'd never, ever give herself completely to anyone again. She'd always hold something back. Even if it was just a wee bit, it was going to be enough to stop her from ever having a deep relationship again. I told her all of this.

'Do you really think so?' she asked as we walked along the shop-packed Broadway over Wimbledon Bridge – the location of Goodness Records, now securely locked up –

and into Wimbledon Hill Road in the general direction of Wimbledon Common. We'd left the restaurant shortly after the final flow of tears. The waiter had been hovering with one of his 'Is everything okay, Madame?' lines. But it's true: men, boys, whatever, we all hate to see a woman cry. There's something instinctually protective in all of us and we always react to it. We'd paid the bill and left; sorry, make that she'd paid the bill and we left without saying much more. She said she'd like the evening to continue and that she'd like to walk around for a while, which I believe to be shorthand for she wouldn't be inviting me in for a coffee.

As we were turning into Worple Road, which even though it was close to the main high street (better known as Wimbledon Hill Road, very busy and buzzy in working hours), was pretty suburban, I shared my profound knowledge with her.

'Well, you'd have to admit it would account for how bad you feel.'

'You know,' she said, stopping mid-footpath and turning to face me, 'I think you might be right. I mean, I know I'm over John Harrison. I'm probably better off without him, but maybe I am allowing myself to dwell on our good times a little too much for my own good. You know what, I think you're absolutely right, David. That's so heartening, you know, to know why I feel so bad inside, why my insides are still being torn to pieces.'

'Do you think you wouldn't be feeling so bad if you and he hadn't made love?' I asked. Perhaps it was a bit of an insolent question but I wanted to know: Did making love with a girl create an additional bond or was it all just physical?

'No,' she replied succinctly, 'we weren't in love because we made love. We made love because we were in love in the first place and it seemed the most natural thing for us to do. So I guess what I'm saying is that whatever it was that we had, which I felt was special, was already there before we made love.'

We walked on into the still of the night while we both thought about what she'd just said.

'David,' she began a hundred yards or so later, 'I thought it was very beautiful what you said in the restaurant, about being my friend. That's what finally did me in. That's what made me cry so uncontrollably.'

During this part of the walk she'd taken my hand.

'It's not that I need a friend, although, as I said, I certainly don't seem to have too many of them floating around London. It's just that I do like you, and you've already showed your support in spite of your friends. So just for you to want to be my friend… well, that's beautiful.'

Mary seemed to be struggling with her words now. I kept quiet, willing her to continue.

'I guess what I'm trying to say here is that I think from the little I know of you, that when you say you'd like to be friends you don't mean it as the first step to you know–'

I made a grunt of some sort to interrupt her because I felt I knew where this conversation was going. I didn't know if I wanted her not to say it, just because if she even just thought those words, well, that would be enough to draw the line in the sand above which the relationship could only work. I'd have preferred us to avoid discussing the fact that we were only going to be friends, and not in the romantic sense of the word. True, it was understood that nothing would ever happen, but if the words were never actually stated as a fact, well, who knows what might happen in the future? But people – girls mostly – like to address this issue immediately, to state the obvious. Perhaps it's just so you know never to ever overstep the mark. But she'd started, and she certainly wasn't going to stop.

'No, no!' she protested. 'Let me get this out now or I'll never get it out! I know the whole speech about being "just good friends" – my mother had me well versed in that one.'

'Look it's fine, honest,' I said squeezing her hand, hoping I still wasn't too late to avoid those dreaded words.

Because of what I felt she was about to say, that may not have been the most appropriate thing to do.

'David, let me get this out,' she protested again, this time gently squeezing my hand in return. 'What I'm trying to say is that I'm still very confused over the John Harrison thing but I'd love for us to be good friends.'

Great, we'd got there. I was convinced this was more embarrassing for her than it was for me and I was happy now that she was off the hook; it's horrible witnessing people wrestling so tirelessly to free themselves.

'But the important piece is,' she continued, when I thought she should have finished saying her bit, now the damage was done. It's one thing putting a boy in his place, but then proceeding to rub his face in it? Well, that was just a little bit unnecessary now, wasn't it? Don't you think? 'I'm not entirely sure that I want us to be just good friends.'

Okay, I thought in italics, but didn't dare speak.

I walked her back to her flat in Gladstone Road. And that was it that night, apart from her saying she still had to figure a lot of things out, and her giving me her home and work phone numbers. And her giving me a goodnight kiss on the cheek. She said she liked being with me because I made her laugh. I loved her laughing; she had one of the most beautiful mouths you'd ever seen and, for one so sad, the most heart-warming laugh I'd ever witnessed.

She had this other thing I noticed that night for the first time; when she was feeling sad, her lips were closed, but when she was happy (and I'm not sure she was even aware she was doing this) the middle third of her beautiful lips was permanently parted, just slightly mind you. This made her appear to have a hint of a gentle smile on her face at all times. In fact, it was incredible, not to mention endearing, just how much her features were transformed by the slight opening and closing of her mid-lips.

Chapter Thirteen.

I have to admit, and I know it's not a very nice thing to say, but I was initially still a bit preoccupied with Mary Skeffington when I went to pick up Jean Simpson the following Wednesday evening for the Jethro Tull gig. Once inside the Jeans' first floor flat on Alexandra Road, my mind started to wander.

First off, Jean Kerr wasn't there, thank goodness; she'd taken another of her turns and had gone home to recover. Apparently work wasn't going as well as she'd hoped. Second off, Jean Simpson went out of her way to show me another of John Harrison's caricatures. This particular one was a bit 'ooh, la la.' Actually, it was a lot 'ooh, la la!'

John, from his vantage point, had obviously spotted Jean bending over to pick something up. As I've already mentioned, Jean liked to wear nothing but miniskirts. Sorry, let me just pause there a wee while: I mean of course she wears other clothes (tops, shoes, socks, even underwear…). What I mean to say is that she's always wearing those clothes with a miniskirt. Now, when you bend over in a miniskirt, well, there's not much left to the imagination, is there? I suppose I should have actually said when a beautiful girl in a miniskirt bends over, there's not much left to the imagination; if it was Frank Carson, Hilda Ogden or Harry Secombe wearing said miniskirt, well, I'm not so sure the overall effect would be quite so pleasing. I think you know what I'm on about.

John Harrison had just the eye for catching Jean Simpson's beautiful legs on paper. Of course, he'd used a bit of artistic licence, as though Jean had turned her head around to the artist/voyeur, and she'd an expression on her face that was a combination of being caught unawares and enjoying it. Maybe that's how they got their rocks off with each other, by imagining various saucy scenarios. With the vision before John, I wasn't sure he'd be able to last the two years or so to marriage. I certainly wouldn't have been able to.

But to me, the surprising fact in all of this was that it wasn't John who was showing me the drawing, but Jean herself! It's a bit like someone taking saucy photographs of their wife and then the wife going off to show it to another (frustrated) boy. Now I don't generally get frustrated, I just get on with life, but I have to tell you that this sketch did send my imagination running wild.

Even more so, why was she showing this drawing to me? And while we're on the subject, why had she put on that performance when she'd come round to my flat to tell me that Jean Kerr was ditching me? I mean, I wasn't complaining, no way. I suppose I'd just started to think that if there was a link between the two incidents, well perhaps… you know? On the other hand, maybe it was just a case of putting two and two together and coming up with five.

However, all that being said, she neglected to give me another of her twirls this time. Although she was wearing the same tartan mini and so, being thankful for small mercies, I thought no more of the subject. Lie! I thought about little else but her beautiful legs on the journey over to Tolworth. I even started to imagine that she'd made herself up better than she did when she went out with her future husband. What was that all about?

We talked a lot on the journey. Well, she talked mostly; I listened and thought about the sketch and the twirl. She told me all about John: how he was an only child; he'd just turned twenty; he hadn't had a big birthday party; and he was saving for his twenty-first! She wished he'd stopped smoking. She wished she could flatten his ears. She wished he could do something with his hair – it was so thick and curly that when he tried to grow it, it looked quite pathetic. I remember this bit the most, because she said that she liked my hair, she liked my eyebrows and she loved my eyelashes.

While that was all incredibly flattering, it seemed to me that for someone who was going to get married, she appeared to be paying quite a lot of attention to someone other than her fiancé. Who, I hear you ask? Oh that's very flattering, thank you very much; why me of course. But then again, maybe that wasn't actually the case if you had to ask the question.

Anyway, I've already said that John was an only child. His father had died when he was twelve – a hit-and-run victim, and the police had never traced the driver. John's mother had never remarried, choosing instead to enlist the invaluable help of her two sisters in raising Jean Simpson's chosen one.

He drove her mad with his meticulous planning and saving. Apparently he'd been saving all his life and at one stage had actually suggested to Jean that she give him all of her salary for safekeeping and he'd give it back in the form of an allowance! Though he was sussed enough not to persist when she refused.

But he dressed terribly. He didn't even think about it; wouldn't think about it, according to Jean. As long as he was warm in winter and cool in summer, he was happy. If last year's clothes still fit, he was happy to continue wearing them. If they didn't quite fit, his mother was an absolute demon on the old sewing machine.

According to Jean, she wished that John would dress a bit more like me! She particularly liked my waistcoat. She even went as far as to ask if I could give John a few pointers! I kind of laughed it off, as you do. Flattery and all of that, it's hard to know how to deal with it. Not that I'd much practice. But I can tell you, Jean Simpson was doing wonders for my self-confidence.

Mind you, I started to think – and I imagined you are probably thinking the same thing as I talk – if she liked me so much and she barely seemed to like John Harrison all that much, how come she wasn't with David Buchanan?

Well exactly, my sentiments entirely!

What else did she tell you about John, David? Well now, let me think. Yes that's it – she thought he was good enough with his drawings, cartoons and caricatures to do it professionally, to make a living from it. She thought he would make more of his life and, by association, their lives and, by indirect additional association, her life, were he to try to seek his fifteen minutes of glory with his drawings.

'There's no future in the Civil Service, you know – I'm forever telling Davi… sorry, so sorry, I mean John, of course I meant John. I'm always telling John that there's no future in the Civil Service and he should get out of there before it's too late.'

'And what does he say?' I felt compelled to ask.

'He always sings his wee Civil Service song:

A Civil Servant's weapon be
A cup of boiling scalding tea
One at ten and one at three
A Civil Servant's life for me.

I tried to laugh but I couldn't. It was just too painfully true.

We were in a quiet corner of the Toby Jug bar, having this wee chat before Jethro Tull went on. You could tell the band had quite a strong following of blues fans by the number of duffle coats on display in the gathering audience. The duffle coat brigade probably started this circuit in the first place, as they sought out venues to watch and listen to their true hero, John Mayall, and his ever-changing band the Bluesbreakers. So we have to be very thankful to them.

Anyway, where was I? I got distracted there, as I was going to list for you this ever-changing list of Bluesbreakers members, people like Eric Clapton, Mick Taylor of the Rolling Stones, most of Fleetwood Mac… but if I keep on with this you'll start to think I was a duffle coat, aka a trainspotter, myself, which I most definitely wasn't.

Jean was looking at me again, and I couldn't tell if she was looking at me, as in feasting her eyes on me (okay, okay, I hear you sighing again, but as they say, stranger things have happened at sea), or if she was looking at me to see if I was looking at her. Or perhaps she was just looking at me to see if I was going to respond. (Wow, it took a long time to get there with that one, didn't it?)

'You see,' she continued, after a few seconds, 'they lull you into a false sense of security with this "You've got a job for life" business, but it's only because they suck all the life out of you. And they do pay reasonably well, I know, but that's also part of the plot. No wonder working for the Civil Service is driving our Jean to distraction. But I can't get John to listen to me. He looks at me in disbelief, he really does. He looks at me as if to say "Are you mad or something?" But he never does of course. He never says that. He's in love with me and he'd never say that. I know he's thinking it but he'd never say it.'

'Listen,' I started, trying to sound like the voice of reason, 'you know there is something to be said for doing your hobby as a hobby. I think the enjoyment factor is so much greater when you're doing it because you want to, rather than having to do it to make a living. Turning your hobby into the thing that earns you money puts a different kind of pressure on things, Jean. Pressure can take the enjoyment out of something you once loved. Pressure also leads to compromise. What I'm saying is, I wouldn't push him too much.'

'God you're such a romantic! You're meant to be saying "Yeah, that's right, he's boring; get rid of him and jump into my bed!"' Jean gushed, as she finished another half pint of lager – her third of the evening (those northern girls sure knew how to knock it back. It didn't show on their figures though. Well, I'm referring to Miss Simpson and not Miss Kerr. Miss Kerr could have done with a few extra laps of the track, if truth be told).

'My round,' Miss Simpson gasped, and off she went to the bar.

I watched her up there – the barman tried to strike up a conversation with her, but she just nodded, ordered our drinks and dropped her head. A Welsh duffle coat, obviously attracted by her exquisite legs, also moved in for the kill – three of his best chat-up lines all shot down in flames. She ignored him completely as she paid, put the change away in her purse, lifted the drinks, turned from the bar and walked back towards me, all in one synchronised movement which gave out the 'I don't want anyone talking to me!' signal. So although she was chatty and friendly with me, part of her was still as shy and retiring as the girl who'd hidden behind Jean Kerr the first time I'd met them in the residents' lounge of the hostel.

'You'll never believe what that Welsh git just said to me!' she began, as she handed me my drink. Before I'd a chance to guess, she continued, 'He said, and get this, with a Welsh accent and all, "I may not be the best lover in the world, but number seven isn't too bad, now is it?" Can you believe that?'

'What did you say?' I replied, laughing because I did think it was rather funny. Mind you, that could also have been because I'd a rather limited repertoire of chat-up lines, as in zero, none.

'I ignored him,' she beamed proudly. 'Our Jean says that's the best way to deal with these gits. Ignoring them is also the most painful treatment you can give them; it makes them look really small in front of their mates and then maybe they won't do it to another girl.'

'Mmmm,' I replied, not quite getting a word out. I was trying to work out whether or not it was better to keep quiet on the subject. You see, it was a subject I had thought about a lot.

'What? Mmmm what, David?'

'Well, you see, there's another side to that isn't there?'

'I believe I'm about to hear it,' she said, laughing good-heartedly.

'Well for starters, just look at yourself – you look amazing,' I said, a little self-consciously. 'I mean, all the observations I'm about to make here are made only for the point of this argument, but you do look absolutely gorgeous. There's not a boy in the bar who hasn't stolen a few glances of you. In fact, even if Ray Charles himself came in here I bet he'd sit down in our corner of the bar.'

'Oh, I just love Crying Time – with a voice like that he can sit next to me any time he wants to!'

'There's the trap. I bet you if we went round and talked to every boy here, they'd all say "With looks like that she could sit beside me any time she wants to."'

I paused, took a sip of my wine – a cheeky little number, I'd say a French nail varnish remover, late sixties perhaps even early seventies – and collected my thoughts.

'You see, when someone looks as amazing as you do, well, it's obvious men will be attracted to you, we simply can't help it. However, our attention is not always wanted. It's like a signal is being sent out but it's not a very selective signal, everybody is able to tune in and receive it. So when the poor Welsh boy goes up to you and tries, in his cumbersome way, to make a verbal connection, he's only reacting to his instincts.'

'Flattering, Mr Buchanan,' she replied, 'very flattering. But I don't seem to remember you coming on to me or Jean within five seconds of clapping eyes on us. Correct?'

'But that was different,' I replied, sheepishly.

'Well, maybe you were more calculating about it, but there's also a good chance your brain was closer to your ears than your trousers. You had manners, you were polite, and you didn't treat either of us like a hunk of meat. Don't you see? That's why both of us took to you – not because you didn't have a good reserve list of chat-up lines, but because you showed us the courtesy of good manners. Our Jean says that the boys who want to jump on your bones the minute they see you are also the boys that will get bored with you and drop you just as quickly. Do you think that Welsh git wanted to get to know me? Do you think he wanted to know what I think about politics, about love, about music, about my parents or about life? No, of course he didn't, he just wanted me to use my pants to warm my ankles while he performed some primeval ritual to get his rocks off. I bet he wouldn't even know what it meant for a girl to get her rocks off.'

She must have seen the look of bemusement on my face because she stopped talking, picked up her drink and, before moving it to her lips, she said, 'Goodness, all of this on four half pints and I don't even know you properly yet, David Buchanan!'

'No honestly,' I protested, because I was really interested in all of this, 'I'm really interested in all of this,' I said. 'So let's see; would it be safe to say that you agree that women are created as such beautiful creatures to attract the opposite species?'

'Possibly David, but there's much more to it than our looks,' she replied, looking slightly disappointed.

'Exactly, which is what brings me to the second part of my theory. So the looks are there for the first hit, the initial attraction, but before you react to that reaction, there must be some additional interplay where both boy and girl get to know each other better.'

'Well I would hope so, otherwise we'd both be copulating on the pavement within seconds of meeting each other. Now that would never do, would it?'

'Quite. I think I'm with you so far. Now for the next part – it seems to me, though, that in this exchange the woman comes off the worse.'

'How so?' she asked, as I noticed most of the crowd making their way through to the music room. Bad timing, this was just getting interesting and we would have to find our place in front of the stage any second now.

'Okay; we, the men, get to interact with beautiful women and apart from anything else it's a very pleasing sensation. But can you honestly tell me that women experience the same feeling?'

'You mean do I look at a man and get turned on merely by his looks?'

'Yes, I think that's what I mean.'

'Well yes! Probably not to the same degree men seem to get turned on by looking at women,' she replied. She was now looking deep into my eyes and she was, I thought, revealing a bit of mischief in her own, 'But yes, David,' she continued very seductively, 'that can definitely happen, David.'

She'd just delivered an earthquake-sized shiver the whole way down my spine.

And then it was Jethro Tull's turn.

I can't remember a time before that night at the Toby Jug when I didn't get lost in the music or the performance at a gig. For once I wasn't thinking 'How come Rory Gallagher uses a simple VOX AC30 amplifier and sounds tonally perfect, and here's Mick Abrahams using a Marshall 100 Watt stack, with four 4x12" speaker stacks and whatever other gadgets and foot pedals and what have you, and he's continually fighting his sound? In fact, the only time he doesn't fight his sound is when he's lighting up another ciggy. That Wednesday night I was swaying with the music, shaking my head to the beat. However, when Ian Anderson took a flute solo standing on one leg, I didn't clock how dirty his overcoat was, because I was totally intoxicated by the scents of Jean Simpson. She was standing directly in front of me and was very close, so close that when either of our sways went out of sync we bumped into each other. She didn't seem to mind us bumping into each other. And, as I was behind, it was easier for me to orchestrate our bumping into each other. Pretty soon we'd bumped into each other and stuck and moved together as one, but only very subtly where nobody but ourselves was even aware of what we were doing.

And you know what? Yes, of course you're right. But I couldn't help it. Honestly, Jean seemed to be positively pushing into me. Gently, mind you, but firmly – in other words, she seemed to know exactly what was happening and she seemed to be physically encouraging it. She seemed to be charged. All of this could have been in my mind of course, I'll give you that, and she could have been just totally lost in the music, as I had been on numerous occasions before. I'd never know for sure because there was no eye contact and neither was anything said. But then again, she must have been pretty lost in the music not to notice what was developing between us. I just hoped that she wasn't going to go off to the toilet leading me standing… alone.

As Ian Anderson announced the last song of the set, coincidentally, 'Ode to a Jean', Jean moved away from me ever so slightly. I could still smell her perfume – mind you, that might have been an accumulative intoxication, but she had moved just far enough away so there was no longer any direct physical contact between us.

By the time the Tull's performance was concluded twenty-two minutes and three encores later, I found walking was possible, despite being a little tentative at first. We didn't have a lot of time to hang around and let me practice though, as we'd a last train to catch.

As I walked her home, we talked a lot about Jethro Tull's performance but not a lot, not anything at all, in fact, about the performance on her brightly lit doorstep, I'm sure I saw her wink at me as she quietly closed the door.

Chapter Fourteen.

Girls never cease to amaze me, though. Two days previous I thought I was having… well, I don't really know what I was having, but I was experiencing some kind of relationship. A relationship with two girls. Then I heard nothing for three weeks, not a peep, out of either of them for three whole weeks. I even rang Mary once and left a message, but no response. Explain that one for me, could you please?

A full nineteen days later – I wasn't counting, honest! – the doorbell rang in the Rostrevor Road, SW19 flat. I reluctantly went to answer it, convinced it was either Jehovah's Witnesses or a salesman (I'd have been pretty thrown if it'd been Hank Marvin selling guitars, wouldn't I?). I nearly didn't answer; my flatmate was out and if the caller hadn't persisted in continually pressing that wretched bell, I would've ignored it and continued on with what I was doing, which was reading while listening to music, of course.

I looked out of the bay window of my ground floor flat in hopes that the person who was annoying the hell out of me had taken a few steps back from the door, the way some do, because then I could have sneaked a peek at them before answering. But no, the porch hid the determined ringer from my view. I suppose I kind of went to the door with a bit of an attitude, you know, 'What kind of fresh hell is this?'

Thank goodness for the anger, or whatever else it was, that got me off of my backside and to the door on that dull Monday evening.

'Hi,' said Jean Simpson.

She was standing on my doorstep and smiling as if we'd just been to the Toby Jug the night before, and not the long nineteen days ago that I knew it to be.

'And how are you?'

'I'm good and you?' I replied in shock. I opened the door wider. 'Do you want to come in out of the cold?'

'I'm not sure I should. You've been mean to me. You haven't been in touch with me since we went to Tolworth to see that horrible dirty group.'

With that she kind of stormed past me, leaving nothing but a trail of perfume in her wake.

I followed her indoors as I said, 'Well, I thought, you know, because of Jean and John, it might not have been appropriate for me to get in touch.'

'You're my friend, right?'

'Of course!' I replied. She'd already taken off her long black coat and black French beret, and I could now see what she was wearing beneath them: black stockings; black calf-length boots; a black miniskirt; and a black Beatle-style polo neck jumper. She looked more like Johnny Cash's English daughter than the northern lass who'd only moved to London several months previous. She'd even taken to wearing some black eyeliner.

'And both Jean Kerr and John Harrison know you're my friend, right?'

'They do? Yes, I suppose they do,' I admitted, none too convincing. I doubted if they knew we were really friends and if they did, neither of them would have approved.

'Well friends are supposed to keep in touch with each other, right?'

'Right, so I'll remember that for next time. Okay?' I pleaded, and chanced a distraction course. 'So both of them know you've come around to see your friend tonight?'

'Jean knows – I've told her I wanted to listen to some of your records. But I made her promise not to tell

John and to cover for me. Talking about John, what do you think about the outfit?'

'Stunning, in a word,' I said, chin still on the floor.

'Good! I knew you'd approve. Am… if you meet John, ah, it's probably best that you don't mention this outfit; he'd never approve of the money I spent on it. Nor my other extravagance,' she said, as she fished in her black canvas bag for something. She eventually pulled out a bottle of wine. 'But I figure he spends more on cigarettes in a week than I do on wine. You uncork this and I'll select the music,' she ordered, as she made her way to the record player where Dylan was spinning needle-free at thirty-three and one-third revolutions per minute. You see, I'd raised the needle so as not to spoil my enjoyment of the album when I went to answer the doorbell.

I trusted Jean with my records. She very carefully, using only forefingers and thumbs, raised the record from the deck, expertly placed it back in its dust jacket and slid it gently into the sleeve. She then placed it back in the proper position, in the Dylan section. (I always flag the record-being-played's location on the shelf by pulling the neighbouring record out an inch or so from the pack.) I watched as she then made her selection, Mr. Fantasy by Traffic, and lowered the needle onto the record carefully.

Some people play a bunch of records and leave the evening's playlist scattered all over the floor until the following evening, or even the weekend, before tidying them up. Some even leave the records scattered around the floor and record deck, still out of their dust jackets. Not me; I find it better to put the current record away before selecting the next. Not only does it save on time, but it prolongs the life of the records. Jean Simpson, independent of me, had adopted the same procedure with her own records. She said she filed her albums alphabetically though, whereas mine were filed randomly by artist; it was always more impressive, I felt, when you could go into the middle of your record shelves and miraculously pull out the intended record on the first attempt. This would've been the first time I would have put that theory to the test, and I have to admit that Jean Simpson seemed far from impressed.

The sound of Traffic was filling my speakers to stretching by the time I returned to the bed-sitting room with the wine and two recently washed wine glasses. I gave her the bottle and held the glasses as she poured us both a generous serving.

'You don't like this skirt as much as you like the tartan pleated one, do you?' she said, as she sat down on the bed – sorry, I meant sofa.

'Well, I like them both…' I started, 'for different reasons.'

'And you like this one because…?' she inquired, sounding all innocent.

'Well because… ah… am, because it's black and it fits with the rest of your outfit.'

'Sneaky! I'll let you away with that, but only just. And you like the other one because…?'

'Because it's…' I struggled.

'Because it's pleated and when I spin around and give you a wee twirl it flows out and you get to steal a quick eyeful,' Jean Simpson said, no messing around.

It would appear that we were getting to be friends, if only because she knew exactly what I was thinking. I didn't admit it though. I didn't deny it either, for that matter.

'Poor David, no such treats so far tonight.'

I wasn't sure what she said next because she did it as her wine glass disappeared into her lips, but it sounded like she might have said, 'We'll see what we can do for you later though.'

Wishful thinking perhaps, because the next hour or so was taken up discussing music, groups, clubs, clothes, looks, and then we got to talking about Jean Kerr. I had to ask how she was doing, out of politeness.

'I know you've got a major downer on her,' Jean said, after another swig of wine, 'but it's sad, you know; it's all gone horribly wrong for her over the last couple of years. When we were growing up in Derby she was the envy of everyone. She was the best in the class, she looked great, was the first to wear make-up, the first to snog a boy, the first to pick a career, the first to go steady and… the first to ride a boy. She was so competitive, but as long as she was the best and the first she was always dead good with everyone else, with all of us. She'd help you with anything, she'd lend you clothes, she'd tell you what to do and what not to do with a boy, she'd give you her homework.'

All this talking was obviously making Jean dry because she waved her empty glass under my nose, encouraging me to give her a refill as she continued with her story.

'The only time she doesn't react generously is when things are going pear-shaped on her – when she's behind in her studies, when she's the one without a boy, when she's frustrated with her look, or when she's not the leader of the pack, then she is a right royal pain in the ass. Now, for the first time in her life, she's under pressure from all sides and she's not reacting well to any of it. She's not making the progress she thinks she should be at work, and she can see her planned career disappearing just because she says her superior has an anti on her. Her love life is a mess. She's putting on weight. She loves to look glamorous but she can't get it together at the minute, with her make-up or her hair, or her clothes, what with her current figure.'

'It can't help that there, right before her eyes, you're blossoming into the belle of the ball. Not to mention the fact that you seem happy enough at work. And you and John are going to marry.'

Jean Simpson grimaced as I said this.

'Yes, David, I've been thinking that as well. But what am I meant to do, wear sackcloth?'

'No, the little tartan number will do perfectly, thank you very much.'

'Yeah, which reminds me; I was watching you at the party, David Buchanan.' The look on her face clearly showed that she was remembering something.

'What? When?' I said, noticing that we'd already drained the bottle of wine between us.

'Remember the wrestling match at the party when there was me and Mary and John on the floor and you were in your beanbag, catching an eyeful?'

'Oh that. I think there was more than just me guilty on that occasion,' I offered in my defence as I went off to try to find some more wine.

I knew my flatmate always had two bottles of wine stashed away for such emergencies. The problem was, he was as unlucky in love as I was and so the wine had probably passed its sell-by date by now. But a bit of hooking around in the bottom of the fridge and I'd found it. I opened it quickly and took a brief swig. It was okay. Yes okay… just, but luckily for me it would definitely benefit from being the second bottle of the evening, rather than the first.

I returned to the other room just in time to see Jean lie down on the floor.

'It's more comfortable down here,' she said, 'come sit down beside me, but not at my feet to cop a view, you perv.'

I poured us two fresh glasses of wine then did as I was bid, sitting cross-legged, around about her waist. Do you know what the first thing about her lying down that I noticed was? No it was nothing pervy – well, at least nothing too pervy.

It was her breasts. They didn't fall! You know the way that when women lie down on their back their breasts tend to pretty much fall into their chests? Well Jean Simpson's didn't; they were firm, I thought, very firm. I mean, I'd been too preoccupied with her legs before now, barely paying any attention to her breasts. I mean, I'd kind of been working on the theory that girls with brilliant legs, who do everything in their power to draw your attention to their brilliant legs, did so because they had a weakness in the other department. But now I was very much intrigued by the sight of the other department. Or should I say, by the shape they appeared to be taking beneath her sweater.

You know all the rules you learn about girls when you're growing up? You know, things like if you make them laugh nothing will ever happen between you? But then again, now that I think about that rule, I'm sure Alfie, in the shape of Michael Caine, always said make them laugh and it's your first foot in the door, so to speak. What were the other rules? Oh yeah, treat 'em mean to keep 'em keen. Then there's girls who smoke are more inclined to let you cop a feel; never talk to anyone about what you did with a girl – if a girl knows you don't talk, there's going to be a better chance of you getting somewhere with them. You know, all those rules? Well, I followed them religiously. And you know what? I never got anywhere with a single one of them! I'm not even sure that I wanted to. The one time I had gotten anywhere with anybody was with Jean Kerr and, as far as I was concerned, all that happened by accident and equally, as far as I'm concerned, I really wish nothing had happened. It was such a non-event... well it kind of put me off it altogether.

The night in the Toby Jug with Miss Simpson, however, had had the complete opposite effect. Not that anything was going to happen. She was going to marry a boyfriend whom she saw twice a week and they (well, one more than the other) were feverishly saving up for said marriage (not to mention, saving themselves).

Anyway, I've gone off the beaten path a wee bit here, but on consideration, what I'm about to say is actually connected. See, when I was at school in Castlemartin, the word going around was that girls have firm breasts until they have sex, at which point gravity takes over. Once we'd been let into this little secret about how virginity and firm breasts were connected, we'd all run around the town, confidently predicting that so and so wasn't a virgin based on the pertness of their breasts; mind you to make sure our theory held up we'd usually play safe and point to women who were fifty, married with at least five children. QED.

The Jean Simpson lying on my floor at that moment was living proof of this little theory. Assuming, of course, she was still a virgin. She'd only said that she'd never slept with her husband-to-be. The assumption, born out to some degree with the aforementioned physical evidence, was that she'd never had sex with anyone else and by virtue of her pledge to her husband, he was the only one in her life she was going to share unchaste knowledge with.

'Remind you a bit of the party, does it?' Jean said, as she raised her head up a little from the threadbare red carpet to drink.

'I have to ask you something and it's to do with the party and I've been thinking about it ever since…' I hesitated, knowing that I could break the mood in a split second. But the other wee voice in my head kept reminding me that there was no mood, and there was no need for a mood. This girl, squiffy though she was, was committed to marry another. So what was there to spoil? Spit it out, David!

'Yes? For heaven's sake what's the big question you want to ask?' Jean replied, appearing to grow as impatient as I was with myself.

'Well, I couldn't help thinking at the party that you and Jean had been in a fight together before. Had you?'

'What, you mean her using her boot as a weapon?'

'And the rest, like her screaming her head off and putting the fear of God into everyone,' I said, feeling the first twangs of cramp in my leg muscles.

Jean laughed and kept on laughing.

'I thought you were working up courage to ask me some kind of sexual question,' she eventually managed to say, looking slightly disappointed. 'No, David, we'd never been in a fight before. I do think Jean had gone to some self-defence class; she's always going to some class or other. She keeps saying that what we make of ourselves in these few years is what we'll be for the rest of our lives, and so we better pack it all in now rather than regret it later on.'

My legs were growing stiffer by the second. How had Geronimo managed to sit around in this squatting position for hours on end? Jean noticed my awkwardness. I stood up to stretch and after a few seconds of doing so the blood started to flow in my legs again and the numbness disappeared.

'Come on,' she said, 'lie down beside me; it's much more comfortable down here. I love doing this – I used to do it all the time back home in Derby. I used to lie in our back garden, watching the clouds drift by. There's a big hill behind Jean's house and we used to climb up there – brilliant, totally brilliant. Come on, closer. I won't bite. Don't think you'll make me nervous either 'cause you won't, young man. I'm well able for the likes of you.'

Once again, I did as I was told, only this time I lay beside her – well, there was a six inch canal of red carpet between us. I started to giggle.

'You think that's funny do you? You think that just because you're a man and I'm a wee helpless girl that you could overpower me?'

Pride wasn't playing any part in this for me. I was happy to let it go; if that's what she thought, fine with me, but not for her. She had to prove it; she had to prove she was stronger than me.

Before I could say another word she had rolled over and was sitting on top of my waist, pinning my hands to the floor above my head.

I looked up at her. She was challenging me with her eyes and bracing herself against my counterattack. I looked down between our two bodies and any thought of a fight disappeared the moment I laid eyes on the vision of Heaven before me. Her miniskirt had ridden up on her hips and I could see her black stocking tops and just the white triangle of her knickers. To me, that's the biggest turn-on a man can ever see – I'm not greedy, I don't need everything, just suggestions of what might actually be there, hints of what might happen. That'll do it for me. Mystery is the magic word in all of this.

And it was a mystery to me, all of that, and that's the way I loved it to be. I hated it when it was functional, basic, like it was with Jean Kerr. You know, more like a mechanic under a car hood than two people sharing the most magical moment God created for us. I like it all to come together naturally, in the heat of passion. Well, I thought that's what I liked, but the truth was I didn't know – it had never happened, had it. But maybe…?

Hey come on now, David, you're getting a bit carried away here, she's only showing you that she's not scared of you and that she's happy to take you on in a wrestling match.

'You're not giving in that easy are you?'

I nodded, stealing another glimpse as I did.

'Now you're just playing, David. You genuinely think you can get out of this position but you're pretending that you can't so as not to hurt my feelings.'

I felt her press her hips down harder onto me, 'Come on, move me, David, move me if you can.'

I tentatively pushed up against her, testing her strength. She resisted and pushed back, but firmer this time.

'Ah, some stirrings in the nether regions,' she said, mocking my feeble movements.

Her mini had ridden up the whole way now and I'd a clear view of her knickers.

'Don't let yourself get distracted, David, you'll lose the fight,' Jean uttered, gritting her teeth and summoning up all her strength for what she anticipated was going to be my big attack.

There's no point in disappointing the girl is there? So I arched my back up against her, hoping to throw her off with the surprise of how high I could go.

'That's better, a bucking bronco! That's much better! But still not good enough,' she said breathlessly, gripping my waist with her thighs and holding on for dear life as she pressed down against me again.

I remained in the arched position and she took another three attempts at pushing me back down onto the carpet. On the third occasion I think she felt me because that's when she started to rock on me gently, moving her hips now, backwards and forwards, as well as up and down. She closed her eyes and I thought I heard her purring a little.

'Mmmm,' she whispered, 'so you want to fight unfair.'

Me, I was doing nothing. I just continued to brace myself against her as she gyrated above me, her eyes closed, and I imagined she was back on that hill, watching the clouds pass above her. I started to match her movement: when she pushed, I pushed, when she pulled, I pushed a little bit further. Her head had now dropped down towards me. Her eyes were still closed and she still had my hands pinned to the carpet.

'Oh, is that a little bit more resistance I feel?' she whispered, as she continued to rock against me. For some of her movements I closed my eyes and enjoyed it, for the other moments I opened my eyes to look at her and her mini, and her pants, and her thighs, and her stocking tops, and I enjoyed it even more.

Her breathing grew a little heavier and her thrusts seemed to be deeper and getting more and more desperate.

'Oh, I'm going, I'm going,' she whispered. All the time she kept up this gentle movement. This was different to her standing in front of me at the Toby Jug. That could have been an accident. This couldn't be an accident. She was pleasuring herself on my body and it was the most amazing thing I'd ever witnessed.

I grew a little anxious, though. I didn't think I was going to last much longer. I couldn't possibly last much longer. I closed my eyes tight; I knew if I caught one more glance of her white knickers, which were now beginning to grow darker where the damp was making them slightly translucent, I'd be gone for definite.

Her thrusts became more powerful, on and on, building up. I could hear her breathing very clearly now. It was more panting than steady breathing. She bucked against me and held herself there. I gave one final push, took a final glimpse at where our bodies met and she collapsed on top of me, her head falling beside me.

She lay there for a time, silent except for the beating of her heart, and eventually when she'd got her breath back she whispered in my ear, 'You got me, David Buchanan. You got me.'

Now the secret of Jean Simpson's planned two year celibacy was clearer to me. It appeared I was to be her eunuch. I mean, the great thing about it all was that she wasn't embarrassed in the slightest about what we had just done. Her exact words were: 'That was enjoyable, wasn't it?' as she smiled and raised her eyebrows.

We didn't kiss. She just went to the bathroom and by the time she'd returned, thanks to a quick change, I'd rearranged myself back into a well-known person.

I had to collect my thoughts on the experience. Yes, it was enjoyable – truth be told, it was the most enjoyable sexual experience of my life to date. I suppose it was surprising, particularly after what had just happened, that of the two of us I was the most sexually experienced. In fact, Jean said she'd never shared what we'd just done with anyone before in her life. She said, and I believed her, that she certainly hadn't meant for it to happen, it had just happened, naturally. More important, she was glad that it had.

'For as long as we can keep this a secret,' she said, with a twinkle in her eye, 'it'll be just our little secret, and if you can keep it a secret, it'll be a secret to cherish, I can promise you that.'

I thought that was a very diplomatic way to put it. Basically, what she was saying was that she wanted me to keep my mouth shut about it, but she suggested it in such a way that the onus was on both of us to keep quiet. Obviously she'd a lot more to lose.

She started to put her coat on.

I offered to walk her home.

'Flippin' sure you're going to walk me home! If you think I'm wandering the streets of Wimbledon on my own and without any knickers on you've got another thing coming, David Buchanan!'

'And when is this other thing coming?' I said, knowing I was probably chancing my neck.

She gave me a playful clip along the ear before saying, 'Well, it must soon be time for us to go and see another group. Maybe we'll go to the Marquee Club again.'

I walked her all the way to her door, though we didn't kiss. Not even a goodnight peck on the cheek.

PART TWO

DURING

Chapter Fifteen.

If Jean Simpson was the girl from the North Country far, then Mary Skeffington was the sad-eyed lady of the lowlands. Where Miss Simpson, the last time we met, seemed to have an inch to her step – and that might have had something to do with the cold night air – Mary Skeffington seemed to be getting bogged down in a rut over losing John Harrison.

When I think about that – you know, Jean walking home that night without any underwear on – it brings another thing to mind. Actually, it brings lots of things to mind like, for instance, how difficult it was for me to walk home afterwards, but that's not what I want to discuss with you at this particular time. What I want to discuss with you is about how you girls go out in the middle of a freezing cold night with next-to-nothing on. Now, lads, I'm not suggesting that we all put our mother's, sister's, wife's or girlfriend's dress on for this little experiment – a towel will do. Just wrap it around you – you know, like you do when you first come out of the shower… okay, it's fine to put your underpants on first. Okay so far? Now go out to the back door of your house (I should point out that it is not wise to carry out this experiment on your front doorstep, as you're sure to garner some funny looks, and maybe even a few weird and unwelcome invitations). When you're out back, I want you to see how long you can stand there before you start to freeze your whatsits off and have to run back to the heat of your living room. Well, don't you see? That's what girls must feel like every night they're out on the town bare-legged? Or sometimes even bare-bottomed. How do they do that? Why do they do that?

Anyway, we were talking about how happy Jean Simpson was and how sad Mary Skeffington was. You could say that Mary was in closed-lips mode. You might even say 'Well, that's obvious isn't it? Jean won the boy and Mary lost him.' But that's not how I would see it. I'd look at it and say that Mary was now free to decide what she wanted to do with the rest of her life; she'd got a clean slate. Don't you see, she'd committed to a boy who had subsequently been proven to have a roving eye? Don't you think it was much better she found that out now before marriage, houses, babies and mortgages complicated matters? He'd have been able to walk free, he's the man; she'd have had to pick up the pieces and the wains, and keep everything going, and try to get her own emotional life back on track.

No, she was better off – I genuinely believed that.

On the other hand, as I saw it, it was actually Miss Simpson who had the problem. And not one, but two at that: the first, John Harrison's roving eye; the second, much closer to home. Being perfectly frank about it, I'd hate to think that someone I was about to marry was off doing what she'd done with me on Monday last.

Yes, it might have happened accidentally. But then what about all the little twirls, how do you explain those away? And while we're on the subject, what about all the subtle flashes? More accidents? Perhaps, but then what about her bump and grind at the Jethro Tull gig? Yes, you could say it was safe sex – very safe sex; nothing happened, if you want to really get down to it. We both gave each other relief. She'd once mentioned solo sex as being a good way to avoid getting too 'horny' – her word (I think mine had been 'frustrated') – and, in an oblique way, you could possibly describe what we did on Monday night as solo. But solo, successful only by being together. Confused? Well spare a thought for me then; I was right in the middle of this scenario and I hadn't a clue what was going on.

But my main point would still have to be: Is what we did on the carpet something you would want to be caught doing behind your future husband's back? As one of the principals in the act, I'd have to say I'd prefer not to do it anywhere near her future husband's back, or in front of him. For that matter, anywhere within the same village might still be too close. But I wasn't exactly about to have a go at her about it, was I? I mention it only as justification as to why I thought Mary should be feeling better.

Yes, the same Mary who'd said that she thought she might want to be more than good friends. What exactly did that mean? Of course I know what it means, generally speaking. But what did it mean in this instance? Did she plan to get it together with me some time in the future? You see, it's not as clear as you first think. I remember when I was growing up whenever I asked my father for something, anything, he would either say 'no' or 'I'll think about it'. Now when he said 'no', that was obviously the end of the matter, but when he said 'I'll think about it', he actually meant yes. Whenever he'd said those words to me, he'd always meant yes. However, should anyone not have known him and our repartee then they'd be forgiven for thinking that when he said 'I'll think about it' I was wrong to get excited. And when he had thought about it, he could come back with a 'yes', but he could equally come back with a 'no'. Do you see what I'm getting at? It's all about how people personally use language. I didn't know Mary Skeffington well enough to know what she really meant when she said that she thought she might want us to be more than just good friends. But I certainly knew what I wanted her to mean.

Does that surprise you?

I'm being honest with you. I'm not hedging my bets, so that if and when something happened, I could say 'You know, I'm glad we got it together.'

But what about Jean Simpson, I hear you say?

That was exciting, that was thrilling. But it wasn't really a relationship now, was it?

I can also hear your next question. Something along the lines of: So if you get it together with Mary, what happens to Jean? Are you going to be guilty, like you've accused Jean of being, by having a proper relationship with a true love and having an improper one with someone else? Great question to be sure but hey, that's way too complicated for me. I suppose I'd better get on with the story and then you can judge for yourself.

Mary Skeffington rang me up at work Tuesday after the Monday, if you catch my drift. I had to keep it brief: we're not encouraged to take personal calls at the office just in case we accidentally let something slip, or in case something is going on in the background which is definitely not meant to be overheard.

Anyway, back to Mary. She apologised for not contacting me sooner and we arranged to meet later that evening. Conscious that it was my turn to stand the meal and equally conscious that she'd object to me doing so, I said I'd cook and invited her round to the flat.

Now my absolute favourite at that point was Safeway's hamburgers, baked beans (Crosse & Blackwell, of course), fried eggs and chips. That was possibly the single biggest thing I enjoyed the most about being independent from my parents: the biggest, no-longer-living- with-them benefit was that I could eat whatever I wanted, whenever I wanted. It's not that I could even claim that I didn't enjoy such meals with my parents, for if I asked my mother to cook me my favourite, she would have, and gladly. However, there were other times where I'd be faced with things that weren't quite so appetising, say for instance cabbage, turnips, carrots, beetroot. I still haven't figured out how people eat those things so willingly. Desserts were another example. Desserts are meant to be treats, right? Well then can you please tell me how anyone can sit down to a bowl of rhubarb? Agh! Even the thought of it turns my stomach.

Anyway, I'd prepared this meal (burgers, beans, egg and chips) so often that I was now an expert at it, which was all well and good but at the same time, it was hardly a meal to prepare for a girl you'd like to impress, and that didn't change whether she was a friend or more. I could hardly place a plate of that in front of her and then go about building my favourite chip-and-baked-bean buttie now, could I? (Homemade chips are so brilliant though, aren't they? If you get it right you can still taste the fullness of the potato and hardly any cooking oil. The chips you buy in fish and chip shops always taste secondhand to me. I tell you what, let me make you a chip-and-baked-bean buttie one time and I'll guarantee you'll soon see – and taste – what I'm on about. I could make chips that Alf Tupper, the Tough of the Track, would break the four-minute mile for!) The only problem was that any points I'd scored with Mary, if in fact I'd scored any points at all at this stage, would soon disappear as fast as the buttie vanished down my throat.

In the end I played safe, as opposed to Safeway (sorry…), and did her cod in butter sauce (courtesy of Birds Eye), boiled potatoes and peas, followed with Bakewell tart and custard. I didn't mind the cod really; it was quite tasty, but the fact that I'd Bakewell tart for afters made it all okay for me.

What about poor Mary though?

She enjoyed it as well, she said, so there. I think as much as for the fact that I'd actually taken the time to prepare it. John, according to Mary, could hardly open a tin of baked beans, so there again! Yet still there were all these beautiful girls running around after him, saying he couldn't do this and he couldn't do that, and he'd jumbo ears, but you know what, they were still chasing him. He must have been doing something right.

After dinner we drank the wine she'd brought around and listened to Bob Dylan. She seemed to be taking a lot of solace in Dylan's words. Have you ever listened to his words? I mean, really listened to his lyrics, and closely? Well, you should, because they are purely and simply nothing short of amazing. I'm continuously hearing something he says that is so simple, so logical, and wishing I'd thought of it. But I never did. Just listen to any of his songs and see if his lyrics don't inspire you in the same way.

You could tell they were inspiring Mary; she was letting his lyrics wash right over her. I thought she was hoping they would heal her. And you know what, they probably were capable of starting the healing process; all she needed to do was let them in.

'It's just that I'd resolved to accept that it was over between me and John,' she started, after I'd cleared the dishes away. 'I thought that was a big point, a big conclusion to reach, a resolution, which I thought would bring me some peace.'

She stopped talking to take a drink from her wine glass. I had a feeling it might be because she was about to cry, so I gave her the time to dip back into Dylan's music. Unfortunately, the song in question happened to be 'It's All Over Now Baby Blue'. No doubt it's a classic, but undoubtedly that wasn't the best moment for it to roll round.

But thankfully Mary didn't seem to be dwelling on those hearts bared lyrics, choosing instead to take solace in the beauty of the melody. About halfway through the song, she started to talk again.

'I thought the big point was me accepting that it was over. I thought that when I could accept that, I'd be fine, I'd be able to get over it. You see, up until we last spoke I'd harboured a thought that we might get together again. But the specialness of what John and I had has been ruined; we'd never be able to put it together again, not the way it was. So it was just going to be continued heartbreak. Now I think I'm grieving the loss of our love, and I never ever dreamt it would hurt as much as it did over the weekend.'

'You shouldn't be sitting in, moping about it,' I offered, hoping to encourage her.

'Well, I thought that too, but then I kept thinking that the last time I'd been out was at Tiger's party and look what happened there.'

We both shared that thought for a moment and then she spoke again.

'But I do enjoy being with you.'

It was spoken in not much more than a half-whisper, but I could tell that she meant it.

'But I must be a bore to be with when I'm like this,' she said, before smiling at me apologetically.

'Not at all – anything but, in fact,' I said.

I tried not to go too over the top; I mean, I didn't want her to think I was so morbid that I enjoyed being around her when she was depressed.

'I'm not usually like this. I'm usually much more fun. But I feel like I'm getting back on my feet again. I feel like I want to hang out with you and get to know you better. But I'm worried that I may just be on the rebound and I'd hate... well, I like you David, and I'd hate us to get together just because I've lost John, and then, because that was the basis of our relationship, for us to split up just because we hadn't taken the time now to make sure things were healed before I move on. Does that make sense?'

'Yes, that makes perfect sense,' I replied.

'I can't believe how easy it is to talk to you. I was thinking about you last night and I was thinking all these things and then I suddenly got a violent shudder. I had this flash. What happens if he meets someone else while I'm taking my time to get over John? What happens if he meets someone else? And, I know that this might sound a bit weird, but I thought that by even having that thought, well, in a way that showed me I was getting over it; my instincts were starting to click in again. You know, it's all fine lying around crying and feeling sorry for yourself, but equally, I might lose something special. That's when I decided to ring you.'

'I'm glad you did, Mary,' I said. I was lying back, basking in my glory, feeling great and allowing myself to believe that there was a chance that this beautiful girl might be attracted to me and all this might not be as complicated as I'd feared.

'You're not seeing anyone else at the minute are you David?'

My glory fell down around my throat and nearly choked me.

Let's consider this question, italics and all, for a moment or two: '*You're not seeing anyone at the moment?*' This in itself – and word for word – was perfectly correct. I wasn't really seeing anyone at that moment. I've got a few friends, very few, as you're already aware. I could have said, 'One of my friends happens to be a girl. I see bands in clubs with this girl, and we occasionally (once, to be exact) wrestle each other until we get our rocks off. Oh, and by the way she's also the same girl who stole your intended.'

That doesn't sound anywhere near as good as my actual answer.

'Well, you know I was kind of seeing Jean Kerr but she dumped me just after Tiger's party.'

Now, not even the very closest examination of this answer will reveal a lie, a porky pie. And the reason is because it was the truth. Not the full truth, I'm sure you'll understand, but it's also very important to note that there are no actual lies contained within those nineteen words.

'Well, I wouldn't blame you if you were, but all I can say is I'm glad you're not,' Mary Skeffington said.

And we both let it lie there.

But that wasn't the end of the evening. No, not by a longshot. You see, I walked her home and we loitered on her doorstep up on the long, straight for as far as the eye could see, Gladstone Road. This was the third time I'd walked Mary home. We stood talking about this and that, nothing heavy. We weren't resolving anything. Nor were we trying to.

She didn't invite me in for a coffee. I can't abide the stuff anyway.

'You're freezing,' she said.

'Just a little,' I lied.

'Let me give you a hug,' she said.

'That would be nice,' I said.

And so we hugged.

Tightly.

We were close and still looking into each other's eyes. Both smiling. It was a shame to be so close to her lips and not be able to taste them. That's what I thought. And I'd also like several other offences to be taken into consideration.

'I'd really like to kiss you,' I admitted, fearing the worst.

'That would be nice,' she said, and we kissed.

It was a great kiss. What can I tell you? It was passionate but not desperate; it was gentle but not wimpy. Her lips were full and soft and very kissable. We explored each other's mouths for a while. But the nice thing about the kiss for me was that it was never a prelude to something else, to something more, something intimate. It was a kiss for a kiss's sake, and those are the kind of kisses I absolutely adore and treasure the most.

At the end of the kiss we continued hugging and she rested her head on my shoulder. Eventually she whispered, 'I've never enjoyed a moment as tender as that before. Thank you David.'

As I walked home I thought that was quite a magical thing for her to have said. Like, she didn't say 'You're a better kisser than John.' Maybe she meant that, maybe she didn't; maybe she didn't want to get drawn into it. Maybe she wanted to say something and that was the best she could come up with. Maybe she realised after the kiss that I wasn't John and how much she missed being with him and having that kiss proved it to her for once and for all and that was just her way of letting me down easy.

Or, maybe she just said what was in her heart. Yes maybe that's what she did. She said what was in her heart.

That'll do for me.

Chapter Sixteen.

Jean Kerr was my next visitor. Honest. I'm not kidding.
The next day at work I received a very businesslike call from her.
'I need to see you, it's urgent. Can I come round tonight?'
My instincts told me to ask, 'What's this all about?' My boss hovering in the background told me to get rid of the call.
'Okay, tonight at eight, gotta go,' I said, but she was already gone. I'm sure I heard her disconnect following the word 'eight'.
Chronologically speaking, I realised the progression of my romantic life was definitely not in the correct order. First night should have been Mary: we'd kissed but hadn't got physical. Second night should have been Miss Simpson: we'd got physical but hadn't been intimate. Then the third night should have been Jean Kerr. We'd already been intimate, but I certainly didn't want to be intimate with her again.
Is that cruel?
It's not meant to be.
Fast-forward six hours and Jean Kerr is standing on my doorstep, not giving a fig about chronological order.
'We need to speak,' she just blurted out, still on the doorstep. 'We need to get back together again.'
And with that she rushed past me into the bed-sitting room. I closed the door and followed her in.

'I'm sorry, David. I was rash. I know I've hurt you. I know it wasn't your fault. But it's okay, we can make it better by getting back together again.'

Okay. My first instinct was to say, 'Get real Jean. It was the happiest day in my life when you dumped me, if only because I couldn't pick up the courage to dump you.'

Second instinct was to realise and accept that Jean Kerr was Jean Simpson's best friend. I liked hanging out with Miss Simpson, and that's putting it very mildly. So making an enemy out of Jean Kerr at this point wouldn't have been the best idea. Yes, I'll admit to it coming across as a bit scheming, but I was driven on by that image of Jean Simpson on top of me on the very red carpet, the very same carpet that now separated Jean Kerr and me.

Go with your second instinct, David.

'Well Jean,' I began cautiously. Please don't forget I was swimming upstream here. 'You kind of threw me. I mean, I was just helping the girl out of a bit of trouble. Then you went and got very mad at me. And I started to wonder why you got so mad at me. And the reason you got so mad at me is because you wanted so much more from me.'

Are you with me so far? Good, because I was struggling.

'And that made me think about us, you know, and I thought that maybe we'd taken things a wee bit too fast, you know, in getting to know each other. I'm really a country boy at heart and I like… I need to take time to get to know a girl, and we didn't really take that time, did we?'

'No Pet, but we still managed to–'

'Yes, yes, I know,' I said cutting her off at the pass, I really didn't want to go there, 'but, and I'm equally to blame here, but maybe that happened a wee bit too quickly as well.'

'For heaven's sake, David, I didn't notice you objecting much!'

I suddenly felt very sad. Not for Jean Kerr, but for myself. I had suddenly remembered another saying on the boy/girl front: they say, and they did repeat this one a lot, they say that you never ever forget the first girl you make love to. Jean Kerr would, for the rest of my life, haunt me with that memory. Does that make me a cad? It does? Oh, in that case I won't finish telling you exactly what I was thinking.

I smiled at Jean. I hope my smile suggested 'You've got to forgive me for that one.' But 'gift horse' and 'mouth' were two words that sprung from the darkest corners of my mind.

'Guilty, Jean, guilty!' I said, holding my hands up in surrender. 'But the thing I've been thinking is that we didn't go about our relationship properly. I thought that if I could turn back the clock I would go about things differently. I would certainly take things more slowly.'

'But it's just that we could be so super together!' she said. 'Everybody thinks you're really nice for what you did for bloody Mary Skeffington. Even John said, no matter the troubles he and Mary were having he was glad someone had the bottle to stand up for her when everyone else was against her. Our Jean thinks you're marvellous as well – she's always going on about what great fun you are and what a gentleman you always are when it comes to… you know.'

Yes, I knew!

'So, with you being so popular and all with my friends, Pet, I thought if we got back together we'd be a super couple and they'd all love us,' Jean said, a hint of desperation creeping into her voice. I also noticed that she taken to using the word 'super' quite a bit, that being the very same word she'd not long since stated she loathed whenever her supervisor used it.

'Jean, I now realise that in relationships it's so important you take it slowly. I'm not very good company at the moment. I'm still getting over the shock of breaking up with you, but I really feel that we should be friends and leave it like that for now.'

'For heaven's sake, if I ever hear anyone say those fockin' words again… "Let's just be friends!"… I'll fockin' swing for them, I swear I will! What with this and my supervisor at work – I just can't believe the way he treats me. It's true, David. He acts like he doesn't even see me. He just dishes out his orders to me and he always gives me all the complicated jobs and then gets on my case, just because I can't complete them for him. Why me? Why him? If it weren't for him I'd be in his position; my career would be taking off! I'd be a lot more attractive to you.'

'Jean, come on, it's not you,' I interrupted, 'it's me. I've just got to get through this part of my life and I think it's probably going to be best if I'm just a friend. Of course, I don't mean just a friend. But I do really think I'm going to be a better friend than I was boyfriend.'

I made her a cup of tea and she went on about her boss for a while and we generally talked around the houses a few times, and you know what? I don't think she really was interested in getting back with me. I just think it would've made things a wee bit cosier in her mind, you know; her & me, John & Jean and John & Yoko, all being cosy together. It was a bit like that Gordon Lightfoot song that was popular at the time: 'John loves Mary, does anyone love me?' In this instance switch Jean Simpson for Mary and have Jean Kerr the voice in the song and you've got it down pat. But I wondered; could there even still be a little bit of truth in the original line, 'John loves Mary'? Could that be the reason behind the farcical relationship he was having with Jean Simpson? Or was that, once again, just wishful thinking on my part?

Of course I walked Jean Kerr home. My poor corduroy shoes seemed to be pounding the silent Wimbledon streets a lot these recent nights. When we arrived at the flat, Jean Simpson and John Harrison were in and they invited me in for a tea.

That made Jean Kerr perk up and immediately announce, 'I've forgiven David and we've made up! I mean, made up as friends, of course. We've decided that it's best if we're just good friends. Isn't that right Pe… isn't that right David?'

'Yes,' I said, raising my cup of tea, 'to friends.'

They all joined in the toast and perhaps it was only my imagination but I could have sworn that Jean Simpson said 'To friends!' with a lot more volume and enthusiasm than the rest of us.

It was still relatively early at that stage in the evening and John suggested going down to the pub. Both the Jeans pooh-poohed the idea and so, as a compromise, he and I were dispatched to fetch some wine and cans of lager.

'So. You and our Jean are going to be friends now,' John began, as we set off into the cold him puffing away on a half-smoked Player he'd retrieved from his pocket.

I wasn't sure which of the Jeans he meant. Using the old reliable process of elimination and deduction, I assumed he was referring to Miss Kerr.

'Yes, I think it's for the best. The blow-up at the party brought it all to a head. I mean, we're not really right for each other and in a way I suppose we just drifted into it in the first place.'

'It's for the best,' he replied, shaking his head positively, 'on top of which she really is a right old battleaxe,' he continued candidly.

I was surprised, and relieved, that he wasn't one for toeing the party line. There was more to come.

'Even our Jean was surprised that you and Jean got that close.'

'Well,' I began, picking up my pace – John Harrison turned out, amongst other things, to be a speed-walker. He'd an awkward smile, which I liked. It was kind of a 'Don't you think so?' smile, very tentative. He still seemed hesitant over direct eye contact. Then, as previously in the Jeans' flat, he let his whole body rock with laughter, but even at that point he didn't make a lot of laughing noises. 'It was awkward there, to be honest. I was quite happy when she dumped me

– I felt major relief, to be honest, and then tonight, that whole thing.'

'Yep, my Jean told me what was happening. She advised her to just let it be, you know, just try to be friends again. But not our Jean, she was back to her old bull in a china shop again. She went on about how it would be super if we were both couples, doing couple things together and all that. I mean, I sometimes feel sorry for the girl but other times I think, well, she's only got herself to blame. It's all going horribly wrong for her and she still doesn't realise that… Well, my mum always said, "You have to walk before you can run". Things keep getting out of control for her and she keeps running back home to get better again.'

'Yeah, what exactly does she suffer from that she has this miracle cure for up in Derby?' I asked, as we turned the corner into Wimbledon Hill Road.

'Nervous exhaustion is what she gets written on her sick note for work,' John said, and then started his silent laughter routine again. 'I know it's unfair of me but when I saw her take her boot off to Mary at Tiger's party I thought I could see another nervous exhaustion trip to Derby coming up. And that's exactly what happened.'

Then he suddenly remembered something, 'Oh, and you'll never guess!' he started, grabbing my arm and nearly stopping us in the middle of the street. I was thankful of the rest, 'the morning after the party, just before she left for Derby, you know, I was around at the Jeans' flat and she takes me to one side and blames me for the whole sorry scene the night before! She goes on this complete tirade! I don't know what Jean was doing at the time or where she was, but Jean Kerr – eyes bulging out of their sockets – tells me to get my shit together, clear up the mess with Mary or she'll make sure my Jean walks. She also told me not to get any ideas about moving into the flat while she's away. You know, like she's Jean's mother or something, and having a right old go at me. I was just waiting for her to give me one of those "are your intentions honourable?" talks.'

We'd arrived at the off licence and we chipped a few bob each into the pot.

'Let's see,' John began, 'our Jeans like their lager and I like cider, what about yourself?'

'I'll have cider as well,' I said. I wasn't a great cider man myself, but beer and lager I could leave alone and I'd have a nice pint of Guinness now and again as a treat. Apart from that I liked wine or even orange juice, so cider I could get by with at a push.

'Jean Kerr's problem is that she thinks that if my Jean marries before she does, then she'll have no one. The two Jeans have been very close, you know, since their early teens. Jean has tried to explain to her that I'm not trying to separate them. That'll they'll be friends forever. Two married women with lots of children.' John Harrison stopped there for a second. He was wearing another of his 'Don't you think?' smiles. 'I'm not so sure about all that, you know, about kids and all that. Our Jean's got such a beautiful figure and if she has children, well, that's all going to go to hell, isn't it?'

'No, not really – I mean, after a little time it'll all be fine,' I offered, in encouragement.

'Besides which,' he continued, choosing to ignore me, 'would you really want to bring a child into this world at this time, with the Russians and all that kind of stuff going on?'

'Agh, you know, when you think about it there's never been a perfect time. There's always been a war or a depression, or a recession, or a strike, or a crap government, or a shortage of something or other. But people have always got by,' I said. I thought I was starting to sound like the PR person for society's reproduction department.

'Yeah, but that's if you want to just get by. I don't only want to get by. I've been saving for ages, you know – I want to enjoy my life. I want a beautiful wife. If our Jean starts to have lots of kids she won't be beautiful any more, you know. I'd like us to have a great house, a car, go away

139

for holidays. I want to lie on the beach with my beautiful wife, in her bikini, lying beside me. You know what, David, I'm not sure I want a pile of kids running around me, screaming and spilling ice cream and lemonade all over the place, and making a scene. I love a bit of peace and tranquillity. You need a lot of peace to do your drawings, you know.'

'They're good, your caricatures. I like your stuff,' I offered in genuine praise, hoping to get off this bizarre topic.

'Thanks, yeah, I enjoy it. But don't you see, all that would go out the window if we'd children.' He was obviously obsessed with this issue and I wondered why he'd chosen to discuss it with me. Not for much longer though – we were fast approaching the Jeans' flat.

'Have you discussed this with Jean?'

'Well, we talk around it,' he replied hesitantly.

'And what does she feel about it all?'

'Well, she says we should "never say never". She says, "Let's wait and see how we'll feel." You know?'

'Sounds fair to me.'

'But I know how I'll feel, David: I don't want kids. I'll never want kids. The sad thing is, the woman has the final say in this, doesn't she? We don't know if she'll take the pill all the time or not, do we?'

'Mind you, John,' I said, as we walked up to the front door, 'they say that the old pill plays havoc with a woman's figure.'

'Do they really?' he said, arching his bushy eyebrows. 'Oh well, we're here. I've enjoyed our conversation. Not a word to the girls though,' he added as he rang the doorbell.

I was very interested to note that he didn't have a door key. Probably a Jean Kerr rule, I thought.

Forty minutes later Jean Kerr retired to her bed claiming that she was exhausted. John and I looked at each other as she made her statement. Neither of us inquired if she was also feeling nervous. But I bet we were both simultaneously thinking it.

And so it was left to Jean Simpson to entertain us for the next hour or so. She was very witty when she wanted to be, when she was enjoying herself. I made my exit shortly thereafter being assured by Jean, quite unnecessarily I thought, that John would soon be out on his ear as well.

Being the perfect hostess, she led me to the door – we didn't kiss though, not even a peck on the cheek. However, as I turned to close the gate, she was still standing in the doorframe. She was wearing a long, flimsy housedress. The kind of garment girls like to flop out in, you know, about their flat. She stood there waving at me, her feet apart, and the hall light shone through the material of her dress, cutting the shape of her perfect legs. I bet she knew exactly what I was looking at and the exciting thing was she didn't seem to care.

Even when I heard John's voice shouting from inside 'Come back in Jean or you'll catch your death out there' she still stood frozen in the pose. I know this because I kept looking back and staring at her. So much so in fact that I stumbled and fell over a dustbin. I was sure I heard her giggle as she closed the door.

Chapter Seventeen.

'I saw you staring at me. That housedress is so thin, and what with the light and all it must have looked like I'd no clothes on at all,' Jean said, next time we met. It was a week or so later, a Wednesday night, and we were on a tube going up the West End to see the Savoy Brown Blues Band in the Marquee Club.

This time as we entered the Club, Jean Simpson took a lot more time to familiarise herself with her surroundings at the famous address of 90 Wardour Street, London W1. The shop frontage and adjoining double doors of the previous tenants, Burberry Raincoats, was still intact and slightly to the left of the small, white neon sign, which stuck out at right angles to the wall. The sign proudly, and simply, proclaimed the name – Marquee – in black letters. Jean Simpson stood around the door reading the coming events poster, which included Soft Machine, Renaissance, Brian Auger's Trinity featuring Julie Driscoll, Blossom Toes, Atomic Rooster, Yes, and she let out a little squeal when she read that Taste were returning in a fortnight's time on October 24 (we're still in 1969).

She leaned over my shoulder as I was collecting our tickets and was amused by my membership card and wanted to know had I ever met the club secretary Jack Dee, whose name was on my card. As we wandered through the corridor to the club space, she pestered me about all the band's names she'd picked up from the poster. She wanted to know who they all were, and what they did that was different from the others. She pleaded with me to bring her back in little over a fortnight's time for the Taste gig. She even used the word 'gig' rather than 'concert'.

While we excitedly chatted away, we made our way to the performance area, which was still scented with the previous night's mass perspiration. Jean said she hadn't notice the circus style, striped canopy above the stage when we'd been there to see Taste the first time. I felt I would've been just that bit too much of a trainspotter if I'd told her that the Angus McBean Circus decorations had been brought from the Marquee Club's original spot, in nearby Oxford Street. The numerous large mirrors around the club made it feel a lot bigger than it actually was, so that when you first walked into the club you were confused. I'm told it's an absolute nightmare to try to get out of if you've had a few drinks too many. Some nights (The Taste, Jimi Hendrix and Led Zeppelin) the audience was packed so tightly it looked like the club had sold out the mirror image space as well.

But here we were, Jean Simpson and me, back in the Marquee Club, and she was more relaxed and looking like she wanted to savour every actual microsecond this time.

It was rather chilly out that night as I seem to remember. Jean was wearing her wine duffle coat and goodness knows what underneath. I mention this only because I didn't know, even though it was, as usual, incredibly hot in the venue. But she still kept her favourite coat buttoned up the whole time.

I guided her to my usual spot, by the back wall facing the middle of the stage – I always thought that it was the best position because there was no one behind you, pushing into you, and you'd pretty much a good view of the stage due to its height and the distance you were away from it. But only if you were happy seeing the musicians from the waist up. I leaned against the wall and Jean followed suit directly beside me. In fact, she leaned closer to me so that our heads were nearly touching and she looked like butter wouldn't melt in her mouth as she said, 'I wish John looked at me the way you look at me. There's always hunger in your eyes. You'll never know how much that turns me on.' She smiled, and casually nodded at a girl who made her troubled way past the both of us before taking the empty space next to Jean.

'We'd never last the two years until marriage if it was you and not John. You see, I knew you'd be trouble. I knew you'd be the kind of trouble I liked, and I don't know how I knew because I've never experienced any of this before. But it is just so deliciously wicked,' she continued, all the time retaining a polite smile on her face. To any of our fellow audience members it looked like we could have been discussing the current Brian Auger & The Trinity – featuring Julie Driscoll – hit single 'This Wheel's On Fire', which was another classic Bob Dylan song, or the weather, or The Prisoner, which absolutely everyone was talking about that winter, or even Coronation Street, heaven forbid.

I'd developed another theory as to why John found it easy to keep his hands off Jean. He got his rewards with catching his fantasies of her in his drawing book. I thought he was a fool, but I now knew the reason he was abstaining – protecting her figure and his peace and quiet to draw – so it definitely wasn't the same reason Jean was abstaining. Not that she really was abstaining. Though, equally, to say she was 'cheating' might be too strong a word. Yes, cheating was too strong a word. Let's just say they were both attending to their own agenda while remaining under the umbrella of being an about-to-be-engaged couple. So what if we 'bumped' against each other to varying degrees on two separate occasions; for all I knew, that might have been the height of it. Maybe she was enjoying the drama going on around her but she no longer wished to participate further. But what did I know? Her signals were all over the place: she didn't want to sleep with her husband-to-be until they were wed, but that image didn't exactly coincide with that of the lady sitting on top of me on my well-worn red carpet, skirt up around her waist. An image I knew was branded into my brain for eternity.

You see, and you'll have probably noticed this from my story so far, that boys – single boys, single men – are preoccupied with sex and the fairer sex. In fact, we spend the majority of our time thinking about it and them. Jean Simpson was young and healthy, why shouldn't she be just as preoccupied with it? But there was no way she could look at a man and feel the same charge I felt when looking at a woman. But that was based on my physical attraction to the female form. Perhaps her mental charge was even stronger. She had just recently whispered into my ear 'This is just so deliciously wicked.' She'd said those words with the same sense of adventure I felt when lusting after her. And I have to say that, for me, the thing that made her words such a turn-on was that she wasn't a tart; she wasn't crude, or someone who used dirty language. I was convinced that she had not used those words before. I was equally convinced that she had never before done what she and I had experienced on the red carpet. She looked wholesome and innocent. Hell, she was wholesome and innocent. But at the same time she had an air of authority about her that convinced me she knew exactly where this was going, or where she wanted it to go.

I knew where I wanted it to go: I was intrigued by what she had on under her coat. All I could see were her black boots, which disappeared under the hem of her duffle. My mind raced forward through the evening; it was going to be 11.30 p.m. before we returned to Wimbledon. It was a Wednesday night; we were both working the following day. So nothing was going to happen, simple as that. Hey and you know what? That was fine, totally fine, because on another level I really enjoyed being out with her. She was great fun to be with if she knew you; around strangers she'd be very quiet, but when it was just the two of us she could be vivacious, upbeat, excited and exciting all of the time. She couldn't be more different from Jean Kerr if she tried.

Still though, she was going to marry John Harrison.

That was fine to a degree; he was a decent enough chap all right, but I believed they'd discover that neither was what they were looking for in a partner.

The Marquee was full – not quite as packed as the Taste gig, but still full by normal standards. It was a great night with the blues, and Jean in her wine duffle coat fitted in perfectly with the blues freaks. And just like that evening at the pub, any time any strange man came up to her, she just blanked him. Well, she didn't need to deal with any of them did she? First off, she'd already picked her husband and second off, she'd an escort. I've deleted a few of the adjectives I was going to put before escort – it's not that I don't feel they were apt, but in the circumstances perhaps we should wait and then you can fill in the missing words yourself.

We'd a quick, easy journey back to Wimbledon, arriving back at 11.25 p.m., five minutes ahead of my prediction. As we left the tube station we headed off in the direction of both of our flats. At the junction she guided us to the right, away from Wimbledon Hill Road (before it became steep), up Alexandra Road (with its overview of the railway and underground tracks), past her flat and in the direction of Rostrevor Road.

I think that once we were definitely heading in the direction of my flat I subconsciously picked up the pace a bit. I didn't really know why. I mean, yes, now I was once again expecting something to happen. But it wasn't like we were dating and we'd start with a kiss. She'd a regular boyfriend – her future husband, in fact – to take care of all of that kind of stuff.

I suppose that had to be a regret. You know, I just loved kissing so much you wouldn't believe it. But I couldn't really kiss Jean. You see, I'd this feeling that if I took the wrong step, or even the first step, I'd scare her off. Now, I didn't really know what I was scaring her away from. Our previous encounter – yes, encounter… I think that's the best thing to call it (in fact, Encounters is a rather apt thing to call them) – hadn't really happened, except within ourselves. We barely acknowledged that anything had happened. She had whispered 'You got me' and 'That was rather enjoyable.' I on the other hand had said nothing and I suppose if I hadn't had to change an item of clothing, it would have been difficult to take it as anything other than a wrestling match. But I was hardly going to put her in an armlock or a full Nelson the minute we arrived in the house in hopes that someway, somehow, we'd end up in an interesting position on the red carpet. You have to admit it was an awkward situation.

As we turned into Rostrevor Road she interlinked her arm with mine and pulled herself up close to me, just like Susi & Dylan on the sleeve for The Freewheelin' Bob Dylan.

'I bet you've been wondering what I'm wearing under my coat,' she announced out of nowhere.

'Mmmm,' I replied, a man of not too many words, hoping that she would take that as positive response.

'What do you think I'm wearing?' she teased.

'What do I think you're wearing or what do I hope you're wearing?' I asked, joining in the spirit of things.

'Well, they both may be connected,' she said. She was staring at the pavement in front of her as if she was deep in thought, another thought, that is, apart from the conversation she was having with me.

Do you ever find yourself doing that? Sometimes both thoughts are connected, as in you are answering a question and at the same time you are answering, your mind is off running, two stages ahead on the same topic. Was she wondering how I was going to react when I eventually found out what she was wearing? Was this thought giving her as much of a thrill as me wondering what she'd been wearing this whole time?

'That might have been too big a clue; I'd have to guess that you've got your tartan miniskirt on.'

'I like surprises, David – I've been roasting myself in this coat for the last three hours to give you a special surprise,' she said as we arrived at my front door. 'Hurry up with those keys; I need to see if you enjoy your surprise.'

Inside the flat she wasn't quite so confident. I liked that though; I liked that she wasn't so brassy that she was about to perform a strip tease. She shyly took off her duffle coat, knowing my eyes were glued to her every move.

'Wow!' was the only word I could find to say. 'Wow!' I said again.

She had a black crew neck sweater on and the famous Black Watch tartan pleated miniskirt. The only difference was that she had either taken it up by two inches or, more likely I guessed, she'd hiked the top of it a couple of inches above her belt, the effect being that the malleable tartan material barely covered her bottom. This meant there was about two inches of naked leg visible between the stocking tops and the skirt.

I am not a pervert, I believe, but I was struggling to catch my breath. Yes, I was undergoing a truly breathtaking experience.

'David, I love it that you're not crude. That's why I've the confidence to do this. I can see in your eyes how much you're enjoying your little surprise,' she said, and then winking at me she added, 'Maybe there'll be another surprise later. I love the hunger you have for me, but you never get all rude and crude on me. I couldn't stand it if you did that… it's like… it's clean. Your lust is pure and so, in turn, my lust is more intense.'

She did her twirl and my heart skipped a beat. I mean, it's not as if her mini was hiding much but seeing her standing there, her magnificent legs proudly supporting her torso, was just such an absolute turn-on as I'd never before experienced. Boys are always looking for that great figure, that's why we seem to be staring so much. But as far as I'm concerned the perfect figure is a full figure; which means perhaps just two or three stages before falling down the slippery slope to being overweight. Which also means it must be a very hard stage to keep. So what I'm saying is that Jean Simpson must have shown a lot of self-restraint so that I could enjoy a visual feast. It's like the complete, perfect package: Jean Simpson was the complete, perfect package. Most of us aren't blessed in the complete, perfect package department: our hips are too wide, or our legs are too short. Perhaps our bottom is too low or our head too large for our body, like someone in the Creation Department upstairs appears to be having a good bit of fun, mixing and matching.

Now, I'm just as guilty as the next person for searching for the perfect figure. But is what I consider to be the perfect figure in fact the perfect figure? Do you see what I mean?

Think of two people now, please. We're talking ordinary people here – you know, as opposed to actresses or models, because they're a different trip altogether (and what I'd like to know, is where do they find them all, all those perfect people?). Okay, now one of those two people is to be your idea of the perfect figure; let's call her Barbara. The second person is to be someone whom you consider, shall we say for the sake of politeness, to have a less than perfect figure. She's Lesley. Okay? Now, my question is this: Why does Barbara turn you on and Lesley doesn't? Why do we think, why do I think, that Barbara's figure is better than Lesley's? Why does Lesley's shape not do it for me? And equally, why will another man be turned off by Barbara, but at the same time he'll gladly run straight to Lesley? Does he think, 'Barbara is never going to go with me – she can have her choice of any man – but Lesley, well, Lesley will never turn me down because I'm probably the only one who's going to ask her out'? Is that the issue here, the fear of rejection? Or will he be genuinely turned on by Lesley and not get what all the fuss is over Barbara?

And it's not just the women, it's the same for men, too. To me, men are mostly ungainly; for every Paul Newman or Steve McQueen there's a million of the mismatched rest of us. Stomachs seem to be the issue with men, like you're either behind the belt, on the belt, pushing the belt, or appearing to be twenty-two months pregnant over the belt. Yet boys of varying shapes seem to find girls who'll treat them as special.

Why?

I'm afraid I don't know the answer to that question. I don't know the answers to any of these questions, and that is why they continue to intrigue me.

Not that any of the above troubled me as I sat on my bed-sofa, drinking in the delights of the body known to me as Jean Simpson. In doing her twirl she was exposing her underwear; they were white, as the last time I experienced them, albeit in briefer glances on that particular occasion. Even then, they were perfect – for me that is – and they covered her bum as opposed to being caught up in it. Her stockings, without the benefit of a garter belt, seemed to be defying gravity as they clung to her upper milky-white thighs, a few inches below that curvy overhang that gives the bum its voluptuous shape. I was staring at her in wonderment, at how all her curves seemed to flow together, helping in no small way to create this wonderful creature.

Jean stopped twirling and had her back to me. She leaned forward to undo her boots. The vision reminded me of her boyfriend's sketch of her. As I'd suspected, he'd managed to capture all of her curves perfectly. She realised what she was doing a second too late and, I think, became a little embarrassed – she didn't say a word, it was just my instinctual reading of her body language; she visibly tightened up a little. I put it down to the fact that she might have thought she was now being a wee bit crude and hadn't meant to – she was fine to give me a twirl but she didn't want to lose her decency. To defuse the situation I very quietly sneaked over to the record player.

'I just can't find anything I'd like to play. Have you any requests?' I said, suggesting that I'd been over there for some time, searching through my album collection. By being there I was (hopefully) suggesting that I'd missed the view I think she felt embarrassed about.

It seemed to have worked because she visibly relaxed and said, 'I fancy a bit of your blues, would you put on that John Lee Hooker album for me, for us, I mean?'

Hooker worked for me, too; I loved his earthy sound and it could be a brilliant mood setter.

It was.

Her boots now successfully removed, Jean stood two inches shorter on the carpet, moving slowly, sensuously, unconsciously to the blues.

I watched her for a few minutes, realising that my fears of what we were going to do when we got to my flat were unfounded. I'd been thinking, what could we possibly do after our encounter on the red carpet that would come naturally, without any awkwardness. But, in fact, this, this was enough. This was more than enough. She whispered for me to join her in her dance.

Now I'm no great dancer by any stretch of the imagination. I'm probably too self-conscious by far. Apart from anything else, on a purely selfish level, the closer I was to her the less of her I could see. Equally, however, I didn't want to lose the mood, so I moved towards her and when I was up close, still about six inches away from her, I fell into the sway of the music. We moved around slowly like that until the end of the song and then when the next song started, a very slow blues number, she moved right into me, so that our bodies were touching and now moving as one and I felt the fullness and comfort of her breasts against my chest. I'd my arms under her arms and around her back, while hers were draped over my shoulders. She rested her head on my right shoulder. What I was missing out on by not being able to look at her, I was more than making up for by the mixture of aromas created by her clean body scents, topped off with a hint of patchouli.

We didn't kiss, of course. It would have been forced, awkward, probably rejected. In this dance – or whatever it was we were doing and had been doing on the red carpet – she was the leader and I was more than happy to follow her lead. I'd closed my eyes and I was happy to follow her lead blindly.

I was tempted, I will admit, to lower my hands down to her bum, but it might have been interpreted as being crude. Does that seem weird to you? Here we were, dancing close, and although it was more than a dance – I could feel her heart pounding as fast as my own – whatever it was that was working was working because I wasn't pushing it. I had this feeling that it would only continue to work if I could suppress my animal urges. It would work because she'd continue to feel relaxed and natural and clean enough about following her instincts in this… this journey of discovery… That all probably sounds a wee bit too grand, even a little pompous, but that's exactly what I felt it was.

However the other view on it was I'd taken a friend to see a band. It was late at night, we'd stopped off at my flat on the way back and put on a record and we were both so moved by the record that we were enjoying a close dance. Nothing more. Yes, my friend was dressed in a very short miniskirt; yes, she had said she'd enjoyed the surprise she had in store for me by wearing the mini; and yes, she'd given me a thrill with her twirl. And yes, both our hearts were beating faster than the engine of The Flying Scotsman on its way home. But still, we were just two friends enjoying a dance. I'm not even sure anything more was needed. This surely was as good as it got.

Or so I thought.

As I've said, I was following her lead and when she led us over to the sofa, I followed. Of course, I didn't realise this until she'd fallen back into the sofa and I'd landed on top of her. It could've been an accident; equally, it could've been deliberate. Either way it didn't matter, because that's where we landed. She continued to hold me around the neck and over my shoulders, her head neatly, perhaps cleverly, tucked away in the nook of my neck.

I made to move to one side to try, I thought, to make her feel more comfortable. But she refused to budge, holding me fast on top of her. We lay like that for a time – it could have been seconds, it could have been longer – but when the next track came on and the Hooker was howling a more upbeat song, she started to pulse her hips, ever so gently, against me. When I was convinced the pulses were not accidental I tuned into them and pushed against her to the same beat. Her hold around my neck tightened a little and very gradually I felt her legs part, both of us still pushing to Hooker's hypnotic beat. Very shortly I was lying amongst her. She raised her knees on either side of me, to steady me. As she did, I could feel the swish of her nylons against my trousers.

I'd planted my elbows on the sofa so that I could rest my upper torso on them and not crush her. It didn't seem to matter because her grip around my neck tightened again. She pulled me closer into her and she, in turn, pushed closer into the nook of my neck. Both of us were silent except for our breathing. She was now pushing her hips against me and I was responding, matching her pulse, all the time with Hooker egging us on. I swaggered my hips a little to find a more comfortable position. I felt her softness.

In my mind's eye I was trying to imagine the view of our hips working against each other. I could see and feel the whiteness of her pants. I imagined how soft the skin of her thighs felt. I could feel more and more of her bare skin against the fabric of my trousers as her stockings worked their way down to her knees. No matter how strong the temptation was to free up my hands and feel this beautiful skin I continued to let her lead this dance. I was happy to let her lead this dance.

I could hear her purr ever so softly now. Her rising to the beat gained a bit more desperation now and I matched it. She was moving her hips in a circular movement, as well as up and down. The more she did this, the more she purred.

Jean Simpson was holding on to me for grim life. As well as tightening her grip around my neck, she'd also caught up a bunch of my t-shirt in her right fist. Her purring was definitely audible now, and she added a few 'aghs' and 'oohs' to her repertoire, and her breathing was heavier now. I pretty soon realised that mine was as well. Then she wrapped her legs around me and pumped her hips even harder. On and on she pushed, on and on to Hooker's beat. I knew I was going to listen to this record with different ears next time; that was, of course, if I could ever bear to listen to this record again if Jean Simpson wasn't there.

'Oh!' she panted, now nearly breaking my neck her grip was so tight, and I was convinced she was going to rip the t-shirt from my back so fierce and frantic was her grasping for more material. She held the 'oh' out for about ten seconds and then gasped, 'Oh... David Buchanan you got me again. You got me!'

This whole thing of Jean's about me getting her: what exactly was I getting? What does it mean to be got? Why do we try to be got? Why do we need to be got? Why do some people never need to be got? With Jean there was never any hidden agenda, she wanted to have an orgasm. There was nothing deviant about it; she just wanted some good, clean sex without, of course, having full sex. As you know, I wasn't objecting – it was also a new toy for me, not to mention my entire generation. I think the thing we were enjoying the most at the beginning of this so-called sexual revolution was that we were using sex not as a currency or as a weapon, but as pleasure source we could dip into as often as we wanted. It had transformed from being a seldom-performed body function merely for procreation. In fact, one of our biggest discoveries of the sixties was that a by-product of the act of continuing mankind was the pleasuring of the human body. I think we actually believed that, you know, that in the sixties we discovered that fact. Obviously the secret had been discovered since the beginning of mankind (literally), the only problem being that no one seemed anxious enough to pass the secret on down the line.

Jean kept rising and falling to our beat until about fifteen or so seconds later she got me as well. She got me good.

When she felt me tighten against her she rose to me and held that position, clinging to me tightly with one hand and patting my head affectionately with the other. We lay together for a couple of minutes. Then she manoeuvred both of us onto our sides until we were looking at each other. Both our faces were flush and dripping with sweat. She smiled and brushed the hair back from my face. It seemed appropriate that I do the same, so I did.

'That's twice you've got me, you naughty boy,' she whispered. 'That was just absolutely delicious. I knew you'd know how to do this.'

I thought that the reality was that she'd got herself twice. I hadn't a clue what to do apart from push against her and, well, just be there. However, I wasn't about to admit this to her.

'You should have been where I was,' was all I could find to say, my heart now returning to its regular beat.

'I was, dear boy, I was,' she replied in a half whisper as she continued to brush the sweat-soaked hair back from my brow. In a way this gesture was the most intimate she'd shown me thus far.

I stopped stroking her face and started to fondle her ear. Jean Simpson seemed to enjoy this because she started purring again. We lay like that for about ten minutes, to the end of the record in fact. Then she said: 'You didn't guess my surprise. Not really.'

'I thought I had?'

'Not quite,' she said, disentangling herself and leaping up from the sofa, which I suppose had really become a bed again. She ran across to her duffle coat, held it up and searched through the pockets. Eventually she pulled out a little piece of snow-white cloth, which I assumed might be a handkerchief.

Surely she hadn't bought me a handkerchief as a present?

I have to be honest and say I was just about to cringe slightly in embarrassment when she opened up the white cloth to reveal a fresh pair of pants.

'I thought something like this might happen this evening, so I came prepared. However, if you'd known I'd brought these with me it would have ruined the surprise!'

I suppose there was a bit of logic there, and perhaps even a bit of a clue as to what was now going on between me and Jean Simpson.

Chapter Eighteen.

The following day was Thursday, and I'd received a call from Mary Skeffington at work, wanting to know could we possibly meet up again that night. She'd wanted to return the favour and cook me a meal. This favour returning could go on forever!

'Come around about eight,' she said, before I'd a chance to risk my luck by even considering it.

I arrived at exactly eight o'clock with a bottle of white wine, and she greeted me at the door with a big hug and a kiss on the cheek.
She was wearing a cream off-the-shoulder satin blouse, supported only by two spaghetti straps. She had on a loose-fitting, knee-length, floral skirt that flowed with the contours of her body as she moved barefoot around the room. It suddenly dawned on me how tall she was; I was wearing shoes and we were eye-to-eye.

She'd a great flat, which she invited me to look around as she put the finishing touches to the food, the smell of which was mouth-watering. She'd stripped pinewood everywhere; doors, window frames and floorboards. The large living room was in two sections, clearly divided by a counter, with her cooking area to one side and her living space to the other. The cooking area was absolutely packed with pots and pans and utensils hanging all around her. There were two large silver pots on the cooker and whatever was inside was providing that delicious smell. Mary had a cookery book opened at some recipe and, try as I did, I couldn't make out what she was in the middle of preparing. The living section of the room had a light blue three piece suite forming an 'n' around the fireplace. She'd a few pictures of flowers scattered around her walls and on the mantelpiece she'd a large framed photograph of her and John Harrison, laughing away for each other and not the camera. Next to the photo was another of John Harrison's excellent caricatures. This one wasn't saucy as appeared to be his take on Jean Simpson. He'd made Mary Skeffington look like the woman with long flowing blonde hair who'd been trapped for years in a castle tower waiting to be rescued. In Harrison's original her long blonde hair formed a rope ladder scaling the length of the tower.

To one side of the fireplace she'd a television and to the other a bookcase, the latter of which was packed with paperbacks, although I didn't recognise either the titles or the authors. There was no sign of a record player or records. But on the mantelpiece beside the photograph was a radio, which she'd turned down to a hum when I entered. I re-tuned it to Radio Caroline on 199 and turned up the volume a bit. This brought a knowing smile to her face. She had two pink rugs, one in front of the fireplace and the other between the counter and the back of the sofa.

I stepped back out into the small hallway of her first floor flat and opened one of the two other doors. The one on the right led into a fair-sized bedroom, which was at the back of the house. It was very girly, with lots of soft colours and a double bed. It was also very tidy. The door on the left led to a small bathroom, which again was very feminine and smelled of the countryside. There was something I was gradually finding out about: the main difference between a boy's flat and a girl's flat. A girl's flat nearly always appeared like a home, a place to stay, to live in. A boy's flat, on the other hand, always seemed so very temporary to me, mostly somewhere to stop off at until your next move.

By the time I returned to the living room, Mary Skeffington had opened the bottle of wine and had poured us both a glass. I think since our kiss we'd spoken twice on the phone, once earlier that day when she invited me around for dinner. The first time had been five days ago, when she rang me up at home for a chat. At first our conversation had seemed forced, somewhat laboured, as we both tried to find things to say to keep the conversation going. Then we got talking about a movie, I think it was, and the chat just flowed from then on. I think we ended up talking for about thirty minutes. She said it was the longest conversation she'd had on the phone with anybody except her mother.

Despite that progression, I got the feeling that she was still struggling with her feelings. You know, getting over John Harrison and wondering was she interested in me only because I was there and John Harrison wasn't.

'I love your flat,' I began, as we raised glasses, 'it's very cosy.'

'I'm very happy here – it's my hideaway, my haven,' she said. I was still getting used to her posh accent. I loved the way she used her words and how I always knew exactly what she meant. On the other hand, my approach was to spout out as many words as possible in something that could be best be described as a degree sharper than a mumble, in the hope that somewhere there in the middle of this almighty mess the listener would pick up the thread of what I was trying to get across. I was never conscious of doing this back home in Ireland, so I think it must've been an indirect result of people in London always saying 'Pardon?' to me.

'I mean, I'm not house proud or anything like that and no matter how much cleaning we do back at my flat, it never looks much more than a doss house,' I said, feeling myself push up a subject for conversation.

I had a feeling that I was going to get to know this girl better but I felt that it was important at this stage to make an effort to converse with her. Because I was so physically and mentally attracted to Mary Skeffington, the temptation was to think that this in itself was enough, that talk would eventually follow naturally. Do you know what I mean? On the other hand with Jean Simpson, who I didn't need to make such a connection with, I never once thought about what I was going to say next, in spite of the fact that we had, on a couple of occasions, spent over five hours together. But, as I say, with Mary I knew I also needed to make that other vital connection. Two people can meet, be attracted to each other, and bonk each other's brains out, but what then? There still needs to be more. In another way, I suppose I was also trying to make Mary feel comfortable with me.

'I like my home to be orderly,' she announced, as she stopped stirring the contents of one of the pots. She leaned one hand on the counter and took a sip of her wine with the other, 'And I like that when the rest of the world is going crazy – just like with all that stuff with John and Jean – I know that I can come back here and close off all of that madness on the outside, leave it all behind me and retreat to the peace and tranquillity of my flat to recharge.'

'Talking about John,' I started, knowing that I was taking a stab in the dark here but thinking that if we were to discuss John Harrison that night, we might as well get it out of the way. At the same time I knew it could explode in my face, 'How are you doing?'

'Great,' she said proudly, rolling her head from side to side, ruffling her fringe, 'I'm finding myself not thinking about him much at all.'

'Good,' I replied, encouraged.

'In fact,' she said cutting into the end of my 'good', 'I find myself spending more and more time thinking about you, David.'

What could I say? I think I've told you that I'm not great at taking compliments. But hang on here for a minute; was it a compliment? Could she have spent a lot of time thinking about me only to decide that I was a rebound? Perhaps inviting me round was her polite way of letting me down easy?

'And?' she said.

'Sorry?' I said, shaking my head vigorously, trying to dump my last thought.

'You're meant to say, "And, what have you been thinking about me?" I mean, at least that's what a girl would say.'

'Aye, but then again, don't the solicitors always say "Never ask a question unless you want to know the answer." Or perhaps "You shouldn't ask the question unless you already know the answer" might be more accurate.'

She seemed slightly taken aback at that.

'Well, David, that could either mean that you know what I'm going to say and you want to avoid it or–'

'It could be good news or it could be bad news,' I said, realising where she was going and that I had nearly put my foot in it.

'But then my good news may not necessarily be good news to you, so you wish to avoid it. Goodness, this is getting into a wee bit of a muddle. Oh, I see what you mean. Look, I'm not very good at these coded conversations. What I meant to say was that I spent a lot of my time thinking pleasant thoughts about you, and wondering about you, and that surprised me because I thought that no matter how much I wanted to forget John, I would be thinking about him for some time to come. And I'm surprised that I haven't been. That's what I was trying to say. Goodness, that deserves a drink,' she said, and she took a large swig from her wine glass, replaced it on the counter and started stirring the pot again.

I smiled.

'Yeah,' I started, apologising by hiking my shoulders, 'I was worried that it might have been bad news, as in you letting me down gently with all this,' I said, gesturing around the kitchen.

'Well, that's nice; I mean, it's nice that you didn't want to be let down. Full stop!'

I think I knew where we were. I think we had reached the point when as Mary found herself thinking about me and not John, then she must genuinely like me. Don't you think?

'Good. Great to get that out of the way,' I said.

I liked this girl. I liked her a lot. That surprised me. I felt there was something special about her and if I didn't make the connection I'd regret it, mainly because there'd be a whole queue of people wanting to ask her out.

Do you think it's possible for that to happen? You know, miss out on somebody just because of the timing? What if I'd left Mary alone to get over John? Would she have met someone else, taken up with him instead? And then I'd come back into the picture only to find that I'm too late and she's gone off to live happily ever after with this new chap? Do you think that's possible? If I'm destined to live happily ever after with Mary, is it really going to happen just because it's written in the stars? In which case, I could just laze around and let her have her fling with John Harrison, or whomever else comes along, safe in the knowledge that eventually I'm going to get it together with her.

You see, this is one of the weak points of my theory of being a romantic. It could turn out any number of ways – she could end up with me, she could end up with him while I'm preoccupied staring into my navel. But in all of this the big question has to be: Would she be as happy with him as I thought she was going to be with me? Conversely, would I be as happy with someone else as I thought I was going to be with her?

'Okay, David Buchanan,' she said, as she ladled out some of her cream sauce onto two chicken breasts she'd been cooking in the oven. When I saw her set several spoonfuls of plain rice on the side of the plate, I felt like running to the phone box at the end of the road and ringing my mother to tell her I was about to eat a healthy meal for the first time since I'd moved to London.

'What's the catch?'

'I'd say... chicken?'

She either caught something in her throat or she laughed in disbelief at what I'd just said and some food went down the wrong way, but either way she started a fit of coughing. Dr Buchanan sprang quickly to the rescue with a glass of water and a couple of gentle pats on the back. This seemed to be having little to no effect, so I chanced my arm and gave her a bit of a whack with my hand in the middle of her back. This did the trick and whatever it was that had been causing the discomfort moved on.

'Goodness, Mr Buchanan,' she said, fluttering her eyelashes, 'you just saved my life for the second time! I guess that means I'm yours forever.'

'It used to be great on the television when that happened,' I started, trying to downplay how important her last statement had been to me. 'When the Lone Ranger saved some damsel in distress, he would ride off into the distance, promising to come back for his betrothed when he'd done whatever bravado-filled stunt he had to do. I watched it for ten years and, don't you know, he never, ever came back once, and I'm sure he promised at least three other ladies the same thing.'

'You're not getting off the hook that easy, though. You're not the Lone Ranger – you may have just saved my life but I've a few questions to ask you before we go any further,' she said regaining her composure. My first question is – and it's one I keep coming back to – what's the catch… with you? You seem so… perfect. You seem to be a nice guy, you've got good manners, you don't mind looking after people and you don't ask for anything in return. There must be a catch?'

'What, just because there was one, a catch, with John Harrison, there has to be one with me?'

'In a word, yes,' she said and then thought about it for a few seconds. 'Yes,' she continued more confidently this time, 'I thought he was the one. He led me to believe that he was the one. Don't forget that what John and I had was not a whirlwind romance; I've known him half my life. And it was he that pushed the romantic issue in the early days; I was just as happy, at that stage, to continue as friends, but he kept on and on about if it was right it was right, and just because we were already good friends we shouldn't rule it out. What can I tell you except that the man spoke with a forked tongue? So here you come along. Again, we make some kind of connection and we get on well. You behave like the perfect gentleman with me. You have things you're passionate about, like music, films and books. You might even be the ideal boyfriend. But the last thing I've been wanting is to get involved with another boy. However, something deep inside of me told me to follow my heart again. I know it's soon and I know I was hurt last time and I know I should be cautious and I've spent lots of time thinking about it, but this voice in my head just keeps telling me to follow my heart. Could that be because I'm not a good judge of character? As I say, I was totally convinced John Harrison was my man for life and look how that ended!'

'What can I tell you? I'm certainly no saint but that doesn't mean I'm going to turn out to be another John Harrison. Yes, Mary, I'd agree 100 per cent that it's early for you to be seeing someone again. But at the same time, if there is something there, something between us that seems natural, then maybe it's wrong to ignore it just because of the timing. Hey, nothing is guaranteed in the world – who knows what will happen between us. Worst case scenario, we're both going to make, at the very least, a good friend out of our relationship, and on top of which I'm going to enjoy some great food.'

'I like it that you don't push me – you're there, I feel you're there, but you're not putting any pressure on me. And so I wonder: is that you just being very clever because you know that that is what will work with me?'

'I'm not that clever! I enjoy your company. We met by accident. No matter what you were going through, no matter what was happening, you have to admit that there was something that happened between us. We got on great from the start. Now I didn't think that this was it and I needed to chase you. I just… liked you. I liked you a lot and I wanted to get to know you better.'

'And how much better do you want to get to know me, David?' she asked coyly.

'Is that the modern-day version of "Are your intentions honourable?"' I asked, enjoying both the conversation and the food.

I spared a thought about when I was younger and growing up in Ireland, setting off on my first romantic adventures. I'd been taught then that when you find yourself interested in a girl, a particular girl, you start by talking to her for a few minutes. Then you wait a day, then you talk to her for another few minutes. Then you get your mate to tell her mate that you like the girl. Then three or four days later, you talk to her again for a couple of minutes and you either ask her would she like to go out with you, or, if you don't have the bottle to do that, you get your mate to ask her mate would she like to go out with you. If she says yes, you're now officially going out with her. It seemed funny to me that you rarely went 'out' anywhere with each other. But that was the key word, and it would become common knowledge: 'David Buchanan is seeing Margaret Hutchinson!' Then you'd write each other wee notes and only then might you actually step out. Stepping out, in my case, usually meant going to Agnew's Café for a cup of coffee or a coke and a KitKat. You'd both pay for your own on early dates or, if you were a real scallywag, you'd get the girl to pay for the both of you. You'd sit in the corner while a few wee girls would stand around the jukebox and glance over at you every now and again, and start sniggering. Most disconcerting I can tell you, especially when you are trying to come across as the master of cool with the young lady in question.

After your date in Agnew's, you'd then walk your date to the end of her street, being very careful to bypass your own street. This would go on for a few weeks, and then you'd maybe take her out for a walk in the countryside and you'd go up a lane, away from prying eyes, and have your first wee kiss.

And things would develop from there – or not! Mostly, though, it was harmless fun. Although I seem to remember on one occasion that it wasn't much fun: it was quite cold-sweat scary, in fact. You see, I'd been following the 'User's Guide to Dating' with a certain ginger-haired girl. After about three months we were behind the bike shed of the Castlemartin Technical College, established in 1812. We'd shared a few explorative kisses and all of that stuff, each time venturing a little further than the previous date's exploration. Then all of a sudden, on the evening in question, this wee girl, as bold as brass, says that she'd like to go further, she'd like to do more.

She'd like to go the whole way!

Now you may think that those words are the words that every young boy wants to hear. Not so. I panicked. I claimed I needed to be home early. I left her standing there.

I never asked her out again. I liked her and all of that, but I just wasn't ready for it. Apart from anything else, she had three big bruisers for brothers. I knew I could run fast but not that fast.

Oh and by the way, I should tell you that Margaret Hutchinson was the most beautiful girl in my class – no, make that in my entire school, maybe even in the whole of Castlemartin. And I never picked up enough courage to ask her out. (The other point worth noting, and probably equally important in the grand scheme of things, is that Agnew's made the best ice cream in the world!)

Anyway, what I mean to say is that, in general it was all good, clean, carefree fun, and the procedure to get nowhere took forever.

All this contrasted enormously with the Mary Skeffington situation, where we were basically talking our way into each other's arms.

Now, even though I still wasn't worldly wise, I knew that my charged encounters with Jean Simpson were nothing more or less than that. Number one, she was promised to another. Number two, even if she wasn't promised to another, you couldn't base a permanent relationship on a sexual charge. I mean, how many hours a day can you spend lusting after someone? Not that I wasn't lusting after Mary Skeffington, too, of course. But that was a different kind of lust. That lust, the lust with Mary Skeffington, was more magnetic, part of a package, and potentially that package was love.

Are you still with me? I hope so, but I need you to know that in no way did either of the relationships interfere with each other. You don't believe that's possible? Okay, fair comment. From my point of view, and I realise this is not a point of view which can be shared by everyone, I couldn't possibly have cheated on, or with, Jean Simpson. She was getting married to someone else. She kept reminding everyone, including me, about this fact. And I was okay with that. Totally. As a friend, I advised her that she should watch John because she'd caught his roving eye when he was with Mary and who's to say the eye wasn't going to start roving again? (All of which reminds me that both his eyes seemed to have a (roving) life of their own.) I knew for a fact that Jean Simpson and John Harrison both had a different agenda on the no-sex issue, not that I ever discussed my theory with Jean; I didn't feel it was fair to do so. In short, though, I didn't feel any sense of loss that she was going to be riding off into the sunset with John Harrison, or anyone else for that matter. That's it as far as Miss Simpson is concerned. Okay?

Now, Mary Skeffington; well, how could I possibly be cheating on her when we hadn't started on anything yet?

So QED.

We used to write those letters at the end of complicated algebra questions in maths class. It was Latin for something or other, but our translation was Quite Easily Done. Or, as Laurie Anderson put it, 'Let $X = X$ you know it could be you.' The X's in the equation could be the fact that both Jean Simpson and Mary Skeffington could be out of my life in a heartbeat if they ever wised up to me.

I hear some rumblings in the one and thruppennies. Look, that's it, that's all I can tell you, and you're going to have to believe me. Now get over it, okay? That was exactly how I saw it. You do what you do. We do what we do. If we ever knew while in the eye of the storm that we were going to be called to task later to justify our actions, how different would our actions have been in the first place? Not a lot, I fear. We do what we do!

So, was Mary asking me whether or not my intentions were honourable?

'I suppose I could be,' she replied, after some hesitation.

'I suppose they could be,' I said with a smile.

'How did you get to be such a gentleman?'

Time to shatter the illusion. 'Look,' I said, putting my fork down on my plate, 'I'd really hate for you to think that I'm a Goody Two-Shoes. That's simply not the case. But, if my parents taught me anything it was never do to anyone what you wouldn't like done to yourself. My mum brainwashed me with "In your dealings with girls, never do anything you wouldn't be comfortable with someone doing to your sister." That's pretty much it, I think – I try to stick to that. It's not always possible of course, but I'm always conscious of it.'

'That makes sense,' she said, smiling ear to ear as though she'd made a decision. 'That makes a lot of sense.'

We'd finished our dinner at near enough the same time.

'That was just absolutely delicious,' I said. The mind's a funny old thing, isn't it? I mean, as I was saying those words I flashed back to Jean Simpson saying them during our red carpet wrestle. I flicked my head quickly from side to side in an effort to shake the thought out.

'I've got some ice cream,' Mary said, as she took both our plates to the sink, 'if you'd like a dessert.'

'No thanks, that was just perfect.'

'Some tea or coffee?'

'No, I'm happy with the wine.'

'Good, me too,' she replied. 'Let's go over to the sofa.'

So we did.

For the first time during the evening she tuned into the fact that her radio wasn't on the usual station. She seemed intrigued and she turned it up a little. They were playing 'Brown Eyed Girl' by Van Morrison, which sounded really amazing: uplifting, fresh, honest, original and even, dare I say it, commercial. Do you remember when we used to sing?

'It's Radio Caroline – I tuned your radio to it,' I said, when the song had finished. 'I hope you didn't mind.'

'No, not at all,' she said. She had taken up what I imagined to be her favourite pose on the sofa, both feet tucked up underneath her and her wine glass cupped in both hands. Her skirt fell about the curves of her legs. Mary Skeffington had a slightly fuller body than Miss Simpson and she seemed happier, confident even, with her sexuality. Whereas Jean always hid her breasts, Mary didn't exactly flaunt them but their full shape was clear above and through the blouse.

She looked cosy, comfortable and happy as she said, 'I can't believe that I nearly didn't meet you.'

'Here's to Tiger!' I said, raising my glass.

'To Tiger,' she echoed, and then paused before speaking again. 'You don't look very comfortable, David,' she said. The clink of the wine glass on wood as she set it on the floor chimed perfectly with the sound of The Beatles' 'Strawberry Fields Forever', which was majestically filling the puny speaker of her radio. I was sitting at the opposite end of the sofa so there were about two feet separating us. I was sitting upright, legs crossed, body facing forward, head turned to my left to speak to her. To an outsider, and on paper at least, it looked like there was more than the gap on the sofa separating us.

'Why don't you take your shoes off? Do.'

Does a bear do a do-do in the woods?

Then you realise as you start to undo your shoelaces that perhaps you socks aren't clean, perhaps they'll smell, even. That's the normal first reaction. But luckily I'd had a bath and a complete change of clothes before I'd left the flat. I don't know why I'd gone to such trouble; maybe I wanted to impress her. My mother had always encouraged me to take a bath and get a change of clothes, but I don't think her reasoning applied to this particular situation ('Just in case you get knocked down by a double-decker bus!').

I continued unlacing my shoes and confidently removed them before aping her shape in the opposite corner of the sofa.

We enjoyed the music and the wine for a couple more songs, whereupon she straightened her legs out on the sofa, to about a foot away from me, so I started to massage her feet with my free hand. Nothing professional you understand, just a bit of pressure where I like pressure applied to my own feet.

'Excellent,' she said, 'you've got the touch. Can you do my neck? Oh please, I'll be your best friend.'

How could I refuse? If I can bluff a foot massage, I could just as easily bluff a neck massage. I kneeled on the sofa while she sat in front of me, and I began working my fingers around her neck, applying varying degrees of pressure, pushing, kneading along her shoulders and up her long, elegant neck. There was something quite regal about the way she sat in front of me. She'd bunched her hair up out of my way with her left hand and she was breathing slowly, as though she had floated away somewhere. My fingers went automatically to her ear lobes. A split second later she jolted upright.

'Oh,' she said, 'no more of that please.'

'Sorry.'

'No, no, it's okay. It's just that… it's just that that is such a turn-on for me – you know, my ears. Touching my ears, kissing my ears, anything like that, well it just… am… well to be perfectly honest, it just turns me on.'

Good to know, I thought, but didn't say.

'Where did you learn to do that?' she asked, if only, I imagined, to draw a line under the last topic of conversation.

'From an old Indian, a member of the Kowitirie Tribe.'

'Sorry?' she said.

'Just kidding,' I confessed, hoping I hadn't ruined the mood. I went back to caressing her neck and she seemed to allow herself to drift off again. I kept away from her ears this time though.

Eventually she turned towards me.

'That was wonderful, David,' she whispered, 'I feel totally refreshed.'

Then she kind of just fell into my arms and lay there. It felt like she was committing herself to my care and it seemed that she was prepared to do so unconditionally. I put my hand under her chin and turned her face up towards mine. And we kissed. I'd really enjoyed the previous kiss with Mary, but this one was so much better. It seemed in that kiss that we were finalising a bond between us. Without breaking apart, we stretched out side by side on the sofa and lay kissing for what seemed like ages. It was not a kiss of sexual intent. It was in its own way the main course. It was totally, as in totally, enjoyable.

Then the kiss finished just as naturally as it had started and neither of us was disappointed, or longing for any more. I felt, I really felt, that something special had happened between Mary Skeffington and me.

It was after midnight.

'I'm afraid I've my reputation to think of, Mr Buchanan,' she said, as she rearranged herself, 'it's time you were on your way home.'

We had one more, much shorter kiss on her doorstep as I left.

'I can't begin to tell you how happy I feel,' were the last words I heard from her as I headed out into the cold.

Chapter Nineteen.

Jean Simpson and John seemed to be having problems around this time. I don't really know what the main issue was, and Jean would never really fully explain their difficulties. She'd say, 'Oh, he does make me mad sometimes, he really does. His head's in the clouds most of the time, clouds that are most likely a product of his own terrible habit of smoking. The rest of the time, he's in Cloud Cuckoo Land.'

And that was as specific as she would get. She said she didn't want to spend our time together discussing John Harrison so we didn't. We'd one such conversation a few nights after I'd seen Mary. Mary rang me, too, on the same day – in fact, they rang within minutes of each other. But I'll tell you about Mary's call later.

I wasn't meant to see Jean Simpson that night. It was a Friday. I mean, it wasn't that we had a 'usual night' or anything like that. It's just that she saw John on Tuesday and Thursday, and she and Jean went out for a bit of fun every Friday and Saturday. If they were going to a party on Saturday, they'd sometimes take John. So I got to see her on Wednesdays, sometimes Mondays. So Friday? This was a new one on me.

'Can I come round tonight?' she'd said. I could hear a wee bit of desperation in her voice.

'Of course,' I'd said and meant it, feeling another encounter coming on.

'I'd like us just to stay in and play records if you don't mind – I'll pick up some fish and chips on the way.

Will your flatmate be in or will we have the place to ourselves?' she'd asked, appearing to place extra emphasis on the last part of the question.

'I think he's off to see Nucleus tonight.' It was a safe bet. My flatmate was a fanatic of Ian Carr's jazz band and spent every waking minute and every penny he earned following them around the country.

'Good, then see you at eight,' she'd said, sounding a wee bit happier.

Six and a half hours later she was on my doorstep, large as life and twice as pretty, but without the fish and chips.

'God, you're so uncomplicated, David,' was her opening remark.

I'd worried that we were going to have a down-in-the-dumps kind of evening. Not so. Whatever it was that was getting her down, she left it on the other side of the doorstep.

She was dressed all in black again, although without the tartan miniskirt this time. Which was great, you know – I've always thought it boring to see a magician perform the same trick twice. Her current mini was short enough for me to ascertain the minute she sat down on my sofa that she was wearing black stockings and white underwear. No sooner had she sat down than she sprang up again and shouted, 'Oh, can I choose the record?'

'Please, feel free,' I said.

That may have sounded like a throwaway, but, as I've mentioned before, there were few people whom I trusted with my records and record deck. Jean Simpson was as caring and considerate of the records, their sleeves and the needle on the record deck, as I was. She always filed the records away properly when she'd finished playing them and, at the end of the session, she would always secure the arm in its position and turn off the power to the amp to avoid the dreaded speaker hum. Just like I did. So, yes, I was more than happy to allow her at my records.

This time, she picked an unusual one, unusual for her that was – The Spencer Davis Group's very fine album Autumn '66. I didn't think she'd like it because she was more into the poppy Stevie Winwood stuff and Autumn '66 was mainstream R'n'B.

It might have been that it suited her mood

'Agh, that voice!' she said, as the music burst into the room. The volume was up to weekend volume – it was a social kind of thing; we played our records louder at the weekend than we did midweek.

Then she did the strangest of things.

She started fiddling around with the zip on her skirt before saying, 'If you think you're going to crease and crumple up my skirt again you've got another thing coming, David Buchanan.'

And with that she dropped her black miniskirt to the floor and stepped over it. She bent over, modestly this time, by hunkering, picked up the skirt and folded it carefully over the back of a hard chair by the stereo. More comfortably attired, she went over and sat down on my sofa bed.

'Would you like a glass of wine?' I asked, literally unable to find anything else to say. I was sure she could hear the desperation in my voice. Perhaps desperation was too strong a word and anticipation too keen a word, but somewhere right in the middle of the two would probably be spot on. I mean, here she was in my room, on my bed (okay sofa), stripped down to her knickers and stockings. She'd kept her polo neck jumper on. Yes, I'd a few brief flashes of her legs before, but mostly they were stolen glances. Now that I didn't have to steal a look at her perfect legs, I found myself self-consciously looking everywhere else but her legs.

'David,' she said shooting me a lopsided smile, 'why don't you pick your chin up off the floor and come and sit beside me on your bed?'

Did you notice that, that little Freudian slip? She called my soda a head! I'm sorry, of course I mean she called my sofa a bed – can you see how out of sync my brain was?

So we lay side by side on the sofa, listening to the music; well, actually I was taking as much enjoyment from looking at her beautiful legs as I was from the music. In fact, I was so close I could have touched the skin of her thigh just above the stocking top. It looked so soft I reckoned on it being exquisite to the touch, although I felt it was prudent not to try.

'David,' she said, 'I feel totally safe lying here beside you, dressed like this.'

'Don't you mean undressed like that?' I replied, and added as an afterthought, 'I'm not quite so sure that's a compliment.'

'Oh, but it is! You don't know exactly how big a compliment it is; I can only do this because I feel totally comfortable with you. On the one hand it feels so absolutely wicked, yet on the other I feel that I can totally trust you and that nothing will happen that I don't want to happen.'

Miss Simpson put her arm under my neck and used her other hand to stroke my hair. We lay like that for a time. Then she rolled over on top of me, her head returned to her favourite position in the nook of my neck. We lay like that for a time and then she rolled the opposite way so that I was lying on her. Precisely flat on top of her, as her legs were closed. She didn't move. I didn't move. It was as if she was testing me.

That seemed likely to be the case, for her next words were, 'If I let you take your trousers off, will you behave?'

'Yes,' I replied, perhaps a fraction too quick.

'I mean, I don't want you to behave yourself altogether. In fact, I need you to misbehave a little. You know what I mean?'

'Yes,' I whispered.

'Okay,' she said after a few seconds' consideration. You could tell that she was nervous about this move, but she was obviously also having fun making it. As I've said before, it was her dance and she was leading it – if I'd ever, even once, tried to lead the dance, we'd probably never have progressed beyond the first encounter, enjoyable though it was.

She released me from her arms and turned to face the wall, thereby, I believe, inviting me to remove my trousers. I'd seen the movie so I knew that men are meant to look ridiculous in their underpants, shirt-tails and socks. Luckily enough I had on a short-sleeve, green granddad shirt and dark blue boxer shorts. I quickly removed my socks.

I lay back down on the sofa and she rolled over onto her opposite side so that she was facing me again.

Unlike myself, who was taking every available opportunity to look at her legs, she didn't once look at any part of my body, preferring instead to bury her head in my neck. Then she rolled me over on top of her and very slowly opened her legs. Stevie Winwood had started to sing 'I Washed My Hands in Muddy Water' and as I fell in between her legs, I felt her rise against me. Now the softness of her skin pressed onto my bare legs. The sensation was mind-blowing, no other word to describe it. The skin on her thighs was as soft as velvet, it really was. I could have lain there forever.

As she pushed into me, now, less the hindrance of trousers, I could feel her dampness. To be honest I was surprised at how wet she was. It kind of disproved my theory that girls can only get excited through physical contact down there.

Not that this contact wasn't pretty wild – we knew each other a little and I could feel her buckle against me, searching for that one final scratch to push her over the edge. I was losing control and I feared I was going to leave her behind. So I pushed further against her and ground my hips in a circular motion as she had done on the previous occasion. Her grip tightened on my neck. She was taking larger and larger, louder and louder gasps of air.

Then she screamed out at the top of her voice, 'Oh David Buchanan!' and she bucked against me aggressively, aggressively enough to look after my pleasure as well.

I rested myself on my elbows and disentangled our heads. Her eyes were barely open and she was still drinking in the last gulps of air. She continued her heavy breathing, her eyes bare and vulnerable.

'You got me. I can't believe how often you've got me.'

What do you say to that? I certainly didn't know. We didn't usually talk about it much, you know, our encounters. Though it appeared that this time she wanted to.

'No, I'm serious,' she started, smiling up at me, 'I can't believe I'm discussing this with a boy, but it's part of the excitement to be able to be candid with you about this. I… I find it hard to do that myself. I mean, I've had a lot of practice…'

I pulled my head back a little from her in surprise.

'No, no, I don't mean I do it all the time of course, but when I do, I rarely get there.'

'And you're trying to tell me that you're going to abstain from sex with John for two years. Who do you think you're kidding?'

'This is nothing to do with John, David! He'd never bother with any of this. I think he's strictly a missionary position kind of guy – a few pumps and he's not going to be interested in anyone but himself.'

'Do you ever discuss it? You know, sex?'

'No. Never. To be honest, I'm really not that sure how interested he is.' Then she started to wriggle around a bit. 'Oh, you're wet! Oh, you're very wet, David.'

I made to move away from her but she pulled me back to her with her arms and legs.

'No! No, please stay there for a little while more. I just love this feeling. I love doing this with you. I don't really know what it is exactly that we're doing but I love it. I knew when I saw you that this could happen. I knew it the second I saw you. This could only happen because I met you, no… more because we met each other. I don't want this to sound big-headed but I never thought much of myself until I saw you looking at me. It's even given me the confidence to try out some make-up. I'm still working at it and I'll get there. I don't want to develop the decadent look of some of the Marquee Club girls though, you know, like I'm wasting away because I'm taking all my pleasure in drugs. I want to continue to look as great as I now feel, thanks to you. It's important to me, David, that I help you to maintain that look of hunger you have for me in your eyes, your beautiful green eyes.'

She snuggled her bottom in closer to mine. I was embarrassed by my dampness but she seemed fine with it. She pushed a little more against me, having felt me pulling back a little from her. She pulled me back by tightening her grip with both arms and legs.

'It's okay, David, I like it – it shows me the pleasure I've given you. And after what you've done to me I'm happy to know you're pleasured as well.'

I resisted no longer and fell back against her. I don't know whether it was her candid talk (as I've said before, candid but never dirty) or what, but I felt stirrings in the nether regions. She obviously felt them too because she tucked her head back into the nook of my neck and started pulsing against me again.

This time it was truly wonderful; the best sexual experience I'd ever had in my life. It lasted quite a long time and we went around and around in circles, sometimes in the same circle, sometimes in the opposite direction, until eventually, both of us drenched in sweat and with the sound of her panting and the needle sticking on the centre groove of the record, we both spent our pleasure in nearly, but not quite, the same moment.

I'd just about picked up the confidence to tell her it was the best I'd ever felt when she beat me to it.

'I can't believe it! You got me again! That was just the bestest feeling ever,' Jean said, between her gasps for breath.

'I was thinking exactly the same thing.'

'What's it your man Dylan says in 'Ballad Of A Thin Man'? "And something is happening but you don't know what it is, do you Mr Jones"? That pretty much sums up what's going on here.'

Jean Simpson stayed until about 2.00 a.m. We enjoyed one more encounter, at just after midnight, but I don't think it was as enjoyable as the second one for either of us. I think she did consider staying the night but she said something about having fewer tracks to cover, and being worried that perhaps things would get out of control. She assured me she meant as much from her side as mine, and so I walked her to her front door in the early hours of Saturday morning, we said goodnight and guess what, we didn't kiss.

On the walk home I considered what we'd done and were doing. What I was doing. I was admitting to myself that I was having feelings for Mary Skeffington, as in serious feelings for her, yet here I was being got by Jean Simpson – not once, but three times in the one night. So if I sat down and thought about both relationships, I knew there was something wrong in what I was doing. I knew I was doing something that I shouldn't really be doing. I'm not even sure. But you look at it; you look at the crime, and assess how big it is. And then you decide that, okay, it's wrong, and I'll accept the consequences if there are any. But the truth is, you don't actually have these thoughts. You are with Mary Skeffington and you feel the feelings you have for her and then you are with Jean Simpson, and she is who she is, and she does what she does, and it happens. It's not even something you consider: is it right or is it wrong? None of this comes into it: you just do it. Yes, afterwards, you do consider it and you convince yourself that you're not cheating on Mary because you and her are still in the process of deciding whether something is going to happen or long term it's never going to go anywhere because she's just a rebound, which was certainly still the most likely scenario for her interest in me.

    I considered all of our relationships as I walked home and when I got home, I stopped considering them.

Chapter Twenty.

Right, remember I mentioned earlier that Mary had rung me around the same time as Jean on that Friday? And in a time of my life where surprises were falling fast and furious, Mary still managed to shock me with her request.

'What are you doing for the weekend?' she inquired, down the telephone. (Where I grew up, that question would've been phrased "What are you doing at the weekend?" But in Mary's set, where weekends are a viable currency, everything was different.)

'Not much,' I replied. I'd kind of considered refilling my records on Saturday afternoon assuming, of course, that I'd picked up a few rarities from the stalls on my Saturday morning walkabout. But that was about the height of it: Jean Simpson had gone up to Derby to see Jean Kerr and there were no gigs worth going to see, so it was shaping up to be a dossing-about kind of weekend.

'Good! Do you fancy coming to Bath with me?' she asked, all matter-of-fact when it clearly wasn't matter-of-fact.

'Am…' I stuttered, 'what's happening?'

'Well, I promised a school friend of mine, Susan, ages ago that I'd go to her party, and I was leaving it to the last moment to ring up and cancel with an excuse of the flu or something equally contagious because I didn't feel like I'd be in the mood to be bothered with it. But I feel absolutely great now, thanks to you, and so I thought why not? It'll be great fun and I'd like to take you.'

Can't get any plainer than that, can you?
'Where would we stay – with your friend?'

'No, actually, my mother's boyfriend keeps a suite of rooms at the Regency Hotel and I've checked, we can have them for the weekend.'

I was about to ask about the sleeping arrangements in said suite of rooms, but I was in the office and walls have ears. I just didn't want any last-minute embarrassment with, you know, her expecting us to sleep in the same bed whereas I wanted to insist, at this stage in our relationship, that we had separate rooms. Just kidding, perhaps I switched those around there... I needn't have worried, though.

'We'll have separate rooms of course,' she said, most likely reading my mind. 'I just thought I should point that out now, to avoid any potential problems later.'

'Of course,' I said.

'Well David?' she pushed.

'Well what?' I said in puzzlement.

'Will you come?'

'Sorry, yes of course! I thought I'd already said so. Goodness, I'd love to.'

'Perfect. I'll meet you outside Wimbledon train station tomorrow at ten forty-five.'

And with that she was gone. Thirty seconds later, Jean rang, and you know what had happened, and happened, and happened, as a result of that call.

Now I was bound for an adventure in Bath, via Paddington. We arrived into Bath at about 1.30 p.m. and took a taxi – a taxi, nonetheless! – to 16 Royal Crescent and walked into an unmarked house. I thought it must have been someone's house, a very grand house I grant you, but still a house at that. But this, in fact, was the hotel. They were so discreet they didn't even have to have a sign on the door. The staff recognised Mary immediately and we were taken through a grassed courtyard to some buildings at the other side. We took the door to the extreme right and one flight up and we were in Mary's mother's boyfriend's suite of rooms. We'd a bedroom each and Mary seemed to make a fuss in drawing our porter's attention to the fact that our luggage was to be placed in the separate bedrooms. I tried not to look disappointed; I'm not sure I carried it off. I mean, I certainly knew that we were to have separate bedrooms, so was I guilty of my ego being bruised because the porter now also knew I wasn't to be sharing her bed? Sad to have to admit it, but the boy Mary Skeffington considered to be 'the perfect gentleman' was just yet another flawed human.

Between the two bedrooms was a sitting room, with a television and tea-making facilities, complete with a couple of micro-packs of shortbread. The room enjoyed a spectacular view of the courtyard, which in turn let you see exactly what these grand crescents looked like from the rear.

Mary stuck straight into brewing us up a cup of tea and I sank back into the sofa, enjoying the comfort and the change of scene. I'd hate to think what any poor soul must have to pay for a night in a place like that. And what about Mary's mother's boyfriend, how rich must he have been to afford to keep a permanent suite of rooms like that? Mary seemed completely in her element in this setting and quite happily busied herself as I soaked up the affluent atmosphere.

'I'd hate you to think that I…' she began, as she poured the tea, 'that I do this a lot. It's just that Mum and Rob have been pestering me for ages to use the rooms. It's a little treat. He works down here a lot in the family business, something to do with cars, and his father has always had rooms here and so Rob seems to have inherited them.'

'What does he do with cars?' I asked, wondering how many cars you'd have to trade just to stay in the hotel for one night.

'Oh, I think his family manufactures them,' she replied, and in the blink of an eye added, 'how many sugars?'

'Oh,' I replied, dumbstruck. 'Yes, two would be perfect, please.'

Anyway, I'd hate you to think that she was a spoiled brat, for she wasn't. She'd been born into a rich family, but her father had run off with his secretary, forcing Mary's mother to survive on a barely tolerable allowance. She'd found a job with a publishing house, just so she and her daughter could enjoy independence. When Mary's mother first met Rob, apparently he'd wanted 'to take you and the little one away from all of this.' Forget, of course, that the little one was Mary and she was a beautiful twenty-year-old woman. Anyway, Mary's mum continued the relationship, but she kept her job, and her independence.

Mary seemed proud of her mum, particularly the bits about having to support both of them by her own means and still refusing, when she would have been forgiven for putting her feet up, to be anyone's woman but her own.

On the train journey earlier that afternoon I'd been telling Mary how my parents had just always got on with things. The reason they'd never split up, apart from loving each other, of course, was that it was never an option. They came from a time and a society where a marriage is union for life and you never have the option of splitting, you'd just never consider it. Consequently you always worked your way through your problems.

She said she thought I'd a wonderfully simplistic view on relationships, and that she loved me for that, and that if you really were in love that's fine, my way would work.

We talked the whole way from London to Bath about this and other subjects relating to love. She said she loved the fact that for one so young, I was so positive about the possibilities of love. She said that because of John Harrison she should have been cynical about them but, she thought, because she'd met me, she was growing to become a believer again.

And as I saw her face – her signature mid-lips open smile below her blonde fringe and dark eyebrows – I saw that I was a believer too.

The party was okay. I mean, I knew no one but Mary Skeffington, and by the way she was dressed that was just fine by me – she was easily more than enough to hold my attention. (She wore a black matador-style outfit. Her eye-catching ensemble comprised a pair of high-waisted, figure-hugging trousers, a white blouse and an open-bum freezer jacket. The overall effect was completed with calf-length, high-heeled, black boots. She looked stunning.)

Mary Skeffington, on the other hand, knew absolutely everyone who was there. She introduced me to everyone as her friend, which was fine by me. A few of them blatantly sniggered in front of her, not quite but nearly implying: 'Friends, yes of course, who do you think you're kidding?' Or maybe once again that was just wishful thinking on my part, knowing that they didn't know what the hotel porter knew.

But by and large they were a great group of people and the music was brilliant, although if I never hear 'Hi Ho Silver Lining' by The Jeff Beck Group again it will be too soon. It's a floor-filler all right, but the problem with such songs is that they also fill the floor with those who can't dance as well as those who can. I'm speaking from experience here, being a paid-up member of the former of the two. Usually I can find a way to sit out most of the dances but then when something like 'Hi Ho Silver Lining', or The Beatles' 'Twist And Shout', or the Stones' '19th Nervous Breakdown' comes on, the place seems to go ape and I'm invariably dragged onto the dance floor. It seems that when these three-minute classics are spun, no excuse, short of permanently being in a wheelchair, will suffice. I've never been able to fully understand this phenomenon. I just don't understand what's going on in the idiot dancers' minds. I suppose it says a lot for those songs, in that they make people who clearly can't dance, want to dance. But do these people not realise that they have to at least listen to the music they are supposed to be dancing to? You know, at least try to clock in to the beat? That's usually that dull thud that you hear pulsating under the floor.

Mary, on the other hand, was a good dancer. Quite deceptive, really; I mean, she's not really loud in anything she does, but when she's dancing she gets into this sensual little groove of hers and genuinely immerses herself in the music. On the smoochy numbers she's positively a sensation to be with – she literally glues herself to you, or at least that's what she did to me, Guv.

There were a couple of chaps at the party from Ireland; friends of the hostess. Two chaps from Dublin and they were invited along because they were musicians! They sat on the sofa most of the night, singing and accompanying themselves with their guitars. They'd beautiful voices with very close harmonies, which made their renditions of Dylan, Beatles and Simon & Garfunkel material stunning. They performed such a beautiful soulful version of 'The Mountains Of Mourne' that I'm sure there wasn't a dry eye in the house. I was equally sure that if I hadn't been with Mary, then the interpretation of the classic song would have been enough for my winning battle with homesickness to falter.

Besides the music, the food and drink were plentiful and the atmosphere entertaining. The only slightly sour note was when this toff tried to chat up Mary. He'd known her before, when they were at college, and Mary had always been with John Harrison and apparently this chap had viewed her from afar. Now that she was Harrison-free, of course, he moved in for the kill. The only problem, as far as this chap was concerned, was that Mary wanted to at least be allowed to have a say in the matter. And her say was, 'No!' and although she said 'no' in the politest of manners, still he persisted.

Most girls I know don't like you to interfere on their behalf in public. It was just a sign of the times, I assumed – equality and all of that – and I'm fine with it, honestly. But I've never thought a six-foot, ugly rugby player and a beautiful, five-foot-nine girl to be equal, in any sense other than mentally and spiritually. So when this chap wouldn't take the hint, I politely inquired if he'd either like to visit another room or stand aside so that we could. Problem is that when you're a bit drunk (or very drunk, as was the case in his case), you don't really want to listen to reason, do you? You've had your one good eye on this girl for years and now here's this Irish intruder from nowhere getting in your way. So, he – that is to say me – becomes the object of your frustration. You remove him – me – and you remove your problem and you claim your prize: the beautiful young woman. Logical, isn't it?

By this point a wee bit of a crowd had gathered and people were saying things like, 'Now Roger, steady on old chap', 'I say, Roger, that's enough, let it lie.' Then a high-pitched female voice pipes in with, 'We don't want any trouble here, let's all go back to the music room, boogie and enjoy ourselves.'

But Roger wasn't having any of it. Luckily, for me, he was drunk. He took one wild swing at me and I could see it coming a mile off, so I literally swerved to the left – a trick I'd clocked Paul Newman doing in The Drowning Pool. Roger noticed my swerve too late and although he tried to recall his troops, his brick-sized fist went smashing into the doorpost I had been leaning on just one and a half seconds previous.

The humiliation obviously hardened his resolve, if not his other fist, and he lined it up for another poke at my head. They say never hit a man with glasses; use your fist instead. I used a variation on this and positioned myself and my glasses in front of the other doorpost. Once again my radar was working loud and clear, and he took another flying swing at me, muttering something about how he was going to hit me so hard he was going to hurt my parents. I waited until the last possible second and ducked this time, figuring he might be expecting me to swerve, so he'd be prepared to swerve his fist to a new target. The sight of me simply ducking must have looked quite comical but it was effective, very effective. His left fist came crashing into the doorpost. I had now unmanned the missile, or whatever they call it. I had one final trick up my sleeve, which luckily enough I didn't have to use, and I won't tell you about it now – you never know when it might come in handy; surprise is the secret of the deadliest weapon.

Anyway, the lack of apparent aggression on my part won me the praise of the hostess and the two singers from Dublin who were 'right there' for me if I needed them. But apparently I looked like I was 'well able' for the troublemaker myself, or so they said. I wonder what they all would have said if they'd needed to scrape me off the wall?

Mary Skeffington, on the other hand, was beaming with pride, and she pulled me into a darkened corner and whispered, 'That's thrice now you saved my life, so that settles it.'

Settles what? I didn't dare ask. Hey, you've got to keep your dreams alive some way, haven't you?

Back at our suite of rooms at the Royal Crescent Hotel (did you notice there how the suite of rooms had changed from her mother's boyfriend's suite of rooms to our suite of rooms?). Anyway, back at our suite of rooms, we settled into the living room for a nightcap. I must admit, I'd had quite a bit of wine at this stage and so as well as accepting her offer of a glass of brandy, I also requested a glass of water. As we snuggled up in the sofa in front of the dying embers of the fire, I sipped from the water and barely wet my lips with the brandy.

'This is good,' she said a few minutes later, 'and if it's this good, it must be right.'

'Why do you say that, are you scared that it might not be right?' I asked, because that was exactly what I was thinking.

'Everyone worries that you've maybe caught me on the rebound. If I was watching someone else go through the same as us, I'd probably think the same thing,' she confessed.

'Everyone?'

'Oh you know, like tonight Susan said, "Of course he's more than a friend." She said she could see how much I liked you. She just said to be careful in case I was on the rebound.'

'Well, I suppose you have to accept the fact that you could be on the rebound,' I offered, trying to be sympathetic.

'Do you think I am?'

'No. I think there's something happening between us that's very natural, and we can take all the time we need to make sure it's correct – there's no rush here, Mary.'

'Why are you so patient with me David?'

'I'm not really patient, Mary. I just want to make sure we do this right.'

Whereas that was correct to a degree, I'd also have to admit that I knew if I tried anything more at this stage it would surely backfire and I'd be out on my ear. There was also a part of me, a growing part of me I will admit, that felt I was really out of my depth with Mary and at some point, maybe whenever she finally got over John, she'd realise this and be off (politely, of course), seeking one more suited to her station. For now though I was keeping my niggling doubts at bay and taking the time to readjust to this new concept of being in a relationship. I've already told you what my ambitions for Mary were, but if this relationship should've turned out to be as serious as I'd dreamed then I was afraid that going to gigs with other girls – no matter how beautiful and desirable – was going to be an unacceptable lifestyle. Other goals and dreams would come in to play. Other goals and dreams needed to come into play.

In the ideal world, I would have preferred to do a Lone Ranger on her. You know, ride off into the sunset, putting our relationship on hold for say five or six years and then return to claim my prize in hopes that she would've been content to spend those six years gazing out of her window with that faraway look in her eyes, waiting for my return. ('Get real, David!' I hear you say.) The other thing to consider – and this is perhaps the real reason why the Lone Ranger never returned to claim any of the four brides – is that perhaps the four brides, content in the fact that they had snared their man, spent the entire six years stuffing their faces with chocolate, as well as glaring out the window longingly. Consequently, that slim-line wedding dress which the Lone Ranger's advance people arrived with in order to set up the television event of the century would no longer fit the bill, and so old Kemosabe would've been tipped off to keep on riding into yet another sunset.

Likewise, I knew I'd be a fool to let a girl like Mary Skeffington pass out of my life now that I'd found her. But it was important for me that Mary be equally convinced, rather than caught on the legendary rebound roundabout we keep hearing so much about.

Time for another admission, I feel. Mary was the kind of girl I dreamed about meeting. However, I'd figured that I'd have to wait at least half my life to meet her. One of my main worries was, when I eventually met this perfect lady, as I knew I should, would either of us already be tied up in something that made the whole thing far too complicated and messy?

That was nearly the case, wasn't it? You know, with Mary Skeffington and me, thanks to the (not unwanted) attention from Jean Simpson?

But not quite. Correct?

That night in our suite of rooms, as I held Mary, I genuinely felt we were meant to be together. I felt I had found my soul mate. I was totally at ease with Mary Skeffington. I was falling in love for the first and possibly the last time. I remember verbally and audibly chastising myself for that one, fearing that such a thought was surely damning the budding relationship. But I crossed my fingers as I hoped and prayed that none of her doubts about the past and John Harrison were hindering her from doing the same.

I was content to snuggle up close to her in the sofa in front of the fire. Six months previous to this, if someone had told me about that situation, alone in a room with a stunning girl, romantic atmosphere, etc., and then asked the question, 'Would you be able to keep your hands off her?', the answer would not have been 'no', it would've been 'NO!' And of course you can say 'That's easy for you to say, you're getting your rocks off with someone else, you cad!' Not true. I mean, yes, true that I was enjoying my encounters with Jean Simpson, but that certainly wasn't the reason behind me being happy to take things as they came with Mary Skeffington. It was simply the right thing to do and if something was going to happen, it was going to be all the more special if it happened in its own good time.

Nonetheless, I will admit, that I'd packed a spare few pairs of boxer shorts, just in case.

'It's time I went to bed,' she said, breaking a few minutes' silence, 'I could lie here all night like this, but I'll look terrible in the morning.'

So we bid our goodnights and that was that.

Come on, David, admit that you were just the slightest bit disappointed, I hear you say. Well of course I was, but please read the above again – we had enjoyed a lingering kiss at the door to her bedroom and that sent me to bed with a smile on my face and a pole for my tent.

But there's more.

Of course there is, you say.

But not what you think, I say.

In the middle of the night, 2.20 a.m. to be exact, I heard a tap on the door – they'd funny plumbers in those days (sorry about that, I tried it before, didn't I?). At first I thought I was dreaming, maybe even wishful thinking, but the gentle rapping on the door continued, then through my half-sleep I could hear, 'David, are you awake?'

'Yes,' I mumbled.

The door opened and this form walked into my room. I lifted my head from the pillow and tried to get my eyes to adjust to the dark. The next thing I heard was Mary.

'I couldn't sleep,' she said and I felt the mattress tilt ever so slightly as she sat on the edge of the bed beside me.

'It's okay,' I said, sitting up and taking her in my arms.

'I just feel so close to you, David, and I wanted to be near you. Could you hold me? Could we just lie together with you holding me? I'd like you to hold me.'

'Sure,' I said, as I held up the bedclothes, 'of course.'

I heard some more rustling as she climbed in beside me. She snuggled up close and she eventually fell asleep in my arms and that, I promise, was it! We woke up the next morning in the same position and I realised for the first time that she was wearing nothing but the flimsiest of nighties. We kissed, another lingering kiss, a very enjoyable lingering kiss. We were lying on our sides and her body was against me. I tried to move my hips away from her to avoid embarrassment.

'No, it's okay,' she said, in a shy voice a little above a whisper, 'it lets me know how much you want me. I need you to know that I want you just as much.'

'I do,' I said, but spoiled it for myself by remembering Jean Simpson whispering similar words.

Her lips parted in the middle slightly to reveal that heart-warming smile of hers and we kissed again, this time our full bodies tight against each other.

She broke free suddenly.

'Okay,' she announced, 'that's all for now. I need you to go to the bathroom first so that I can protect my honour and decency by stealing back into my room.'

'Fine with me,' I said and off I trotted.

'We need to hurry,' she announced, just as I was departing the doorway, 'we're having breakfast with mother in forty-five minutes.'

'Oh,' I said, stopping in my tracks, 'right then, I'll put an inch to my foot!'

As I showered I wondered if last night had been a test. A test first of all at the party, to see how I reacted to socialising with her friends, and then later a test in bed, to see whether I could show self-restraint. And now that I'd hopefully passed both tests, came the biggest test of all as we were off to see her mum.

But I needn't have worried. Her mum was great!

'I hope you weren't doing anything with my daughter last night that'll you regret,' were her first words to me.

'Oh Mum!' Mary complained, good-heartedly.

'We were angels, to be sure,' I said, moving towards Mary's mother to take her hand. She caught it firmly and she used her grip to pull me towards her and presented her cheek for a peck. I obliged. To anyone looking on it would appear that I was sophisticated and knew what I was doing.

'Well, legend has it that the devil is an angel who misbehaved,' she offered, as she moved back. 'But I don't see any regret in my daughter's eyes, so I'll give you the benefit of the doubt on this occasion.'

We were in the restaurant downstairs one hour later, enjoying a hearty breakfast. Mary's mum was like an older version of Mary. It was uncanny. I felt like I was being given a flash preview of how Mary was going to look when she was older.

It's funny that – the way children will occasionally grow up to look just like their parents. Sometimes it's pitiful, you know, when they're in that in-between stage and they're not yet old enough to be comfortable with their parents' faces, and they just have to hang on in there for a few years until they grow into them. The lucky ones are perfect right the way through, of course, at every stage of life. Then there are others who are either waiting until they can put on a few wrinkles for the look to work, or wishing for a kinder mirror. Saddest of all must be those daughters who inherit their father's looks. It occasionally happens, believe you me, but it certainly was not the case with Mary Skeffington. She was truly blessed with her mother's stunning looks. They didn't quite look like sisters but it was pretty close.

Mary's mother wore a grey trouser suit and a brilliant red shirt, which matched her shoes. Unlike Mary, though, she wore her fine blonde hair up in some elaborate contraption at the back of her head. The whole thing looked very precarious, I'm sure.

Pretty soon we were just three people enjoying a friendly chat over breakfast, as opposed to a wee boy from Castlemartin being interviewed by his potential girlfriend's mother.

'God, I'm so glad she's stopped seeking that John Harrison boy.'

'Mother!' Mary pleaded, forcing a smile. 'Hello, I'm right here with you.'

'I've never trusted a boy who can't look you in the eye,' she continued, choosing to ignore her daughter. 'And those eyebrows! They're much too bushy and nearly joined up. Yes, I'm afraid to say the overall effect is much too devious for my liking. David here, now his features portray an open and honest personality.'

I do like the way people sometimes talk about you as though you're not there. She addressed me again, this time directly.

'John Harrison took advantage of Mary, you know, and I just had to sit by and watch it happen. We've got a close relationship, Mary and I. She keeps me informed about everything that's happening in her life; mind you, at the same time she never pays any attention to my advice.'

'That's just not true, Mum!' Mary complained.

'When have you ever listened to me?'

'Okay,' Mary said, seeming very happy at a discovery, 'with David here, for instance. I told you I was scared because I might just be on the rebound from John.

And you said if there was the slightest chances my feeling were genuine, I shouldn't let him get away.'

Mrs Skeffington smiled.

'I understand you know the young lady John Harrison has now taken up with?' her mother said to me, equal parts changing the subject and displaying selective memory. The fact that John had now taken up with Jean implied that John and Mary had finished their relationship at the point he met Jean Simpson.

'Yes I… Jean Simpson's her name; I was at a party with her friend…'

'Yes, your ex-girlfriend, also called Jean, I believe,' Mrs Skeffington announced, letting me know that Mary really had filled her in on all the details.

'Mmmm, not really what you'd call a girlfriend,' I ventured; I didn't want her thinking I was a fickle as John Harrison.

'Yes, I've also heard about that emotional blackmail. Tell me; would you consider Mary to be really a girlfriend?'

'I'm hoping so,' I said quickly, but not too confidently. It's just the way it came out.

Mary didn't offer anything but she… well, I interpreted her look as one of pride, on top of which she took my hand across the table. But I still figured she wasn't quite 100 per cent there.

'Good,' Mrs Skeffington said with a warm smile and she gripped my free arm, 'Mary doesn't have a father, you know, but if you mess with her, well, you'll have me to deal with and I can tell you, I'm no pushover. Right, that's that settled. Now, what's this I hear about Roger having to be put in his place again last evening? You know, Roger's been pining over Mary for years.'

So there obviously was an effective bush telegraph in the area and I imagined Mrs Skeffington was probably at the hub of it.

Chapter Twenty-One.

After Bath, things kind of got a wee bit awkward. For a start, Mary Skeffington and I had crossed some imaginary line in our relationship. Neither of us had declared our undying love for each other or anything like that but, at the same time, I had acknowledged to myself that I was falling in love with her. Well, what was there to not fall in love with? This meant, of course, that at the very least we were sure to spend more time in each other's company. However, I'd at least a week's grace to tidy up the Jean Simpson Affair, since Mary decided to stay on in Bath for the following week.

Jean Simpson, driven partially by the fact that she was having a hard time with John, partially by the fact that her mate was as batty as a fruit cake, wanted to get out of the flat. On top of which, her sexual inquisitiveness was getting the better of her – well, the better of both of us really – so she was becoming a regular round mine, both before and after the Bath visit. I used my flatmate as an excuse when I didn't want her around or when I was due to see Mary. Luckily enough, Jean always had the good manners to ring me up to see if it was okay to come round. This was not a quality her mate, and my ex, Jean Kerr shared. She'd just turn up on your doorstep out of the blue, wearing out the doorbell until you could take no more and got up to let her in.

Just like she did the Tuesday night following my weekend in Bath.

'What's going on David?'

I started to feel guilty, I didn't know why. Was it because she knew what Jean Simpson and I had been up to? Was it because she knew I was seeing Mary Skeffington? And if she did know any of this, was she annoyed because she was a mate of Jean's or annoyed just because, well, Mary Skeffington was Mary Skeffington, and the two Jeans and John had a history with her?

You can see my dilemma, can't you?

Take it on the chin, just face the music, David. Okay, right!

'What's going on with what, Jean?' I said, emphasising a slight impatience, thereby appearing to have nothing to hide. Was this a clever ploy or what?

'With our Jean of course, dumbo?' she shrieked, as she pushed passed me and tore on into my flat, her blonde mane shaking like the leaves on a tree on a stormy night.

'Hello Jean, good to see you too.' I said to the space where she'd just been standing but which was now filled with nothing but her perfume. (A funny kind of scent for a perfume, I thought. I'd always been led to believe that if you were going to cover up your own smell, you should at least do it with something a bit more pleasant. But Jean hadn't followed that advice; she smelled like a hospital ward after the cleaners had just been round.)

It's funny how at times like these, you experience flashes of your childhood. As I closed the door and followed Jean Kerr into my flat I felt like I was back at school and I was following the headmaster into his study. You know, that mixture of butterflies in your stomach and wanting to be physically sick? Now Jean Kerr had summoned me in a similar fashion. Why did I give a fig what she knew or thought she knew?

There's a very easy and obvious answer to this question. Don't you see? I cared about Mary Skeffington and I didn't want to see her hurt. It was that simple.

'Okay Jean,' I said, 'calm down and tell me what this is all about.'

'Something's going on. Jean is always complaining about John. Yet on the other hand she doesn't seem to care. In fact, she seems positively happy. What's that all about? And then she's taken to wearing make-up and seems a lot more conscious about her clothes. Now, Jean Simpson has always been a clean girl, but you know what, she never, ever seems to be out of the bath these days and... and... when I go in the bathroom after her, there's always lots of funny smells wafting around. Do you think she's on drugs, David?'

'Of course not, Jean!' I said, before laughing, part from relief and part from the fact that there was a very funny side to thinking that Jean Simpson was taking drugs. I couldn't think of one person less likely to indulge in drugs. 'She's probably just taken to using patchouli, and one can perhaps be forgiven for mistaking it to be the musky aromas of dope.'

'The musky aromas of dope, for heaven's sake!' she lampooned, 'Hark at you would you, Mr Cool!'

The last time I'd been referred to as 'cool' was when I figured out how to lodge a lollipop stick between the brakes of the back wheel of my bicycle, so that the other end of said lollipop stick just about touched the wheel spokes. The end effect I was after was the faster I pedalled, the more my bike sounded like a motorbike. The reality was that my so-called endeavours to 'be cool' never sounded much more than a bumblebee on (a different kind of) speed. If that really was the definition of cool, I was happy to leave it behind.

'She's definitely on something,' Jean barked. She sat down on the sofa in her full regalia, which tonight was topped off with a pink overcoat. She used her umbrella to prop her hands up in front of her and she looked as if she was a cocker spaniel begging from its master. 'I can tell you, the way she's wandering around all the time, always with a wee bit of a smirk on her face. It's as though she knows something I don't.'

'What's this thing with her and John, what's the problem there?'

'Oh they've had a few blazing rows about you.'

'They have?' I asked. Maybe I wasn't going to get away so lightly after all.

'Yes. He thinks she spends too much money when she goes out with you to the clubs. He also thinks that if you weren't going out to see all these groups she wouldn't be spending anywhere near as much on clothes. He said, if they're saving to get married they should be saving to get married.'

'Really?' I said, hoping the relief wasn't visible in my voice.

'She told him to take a running jump. She said that she wasn't going to hang around waiting like a nun for two years on bread and cheese just so that she could fit into his plans. And then he said why doesn't David pay for you when you go out. He said he's the man, isn't that what men do.'

'He did?'

'He did.'

'Wow!' I said.

'She said that you weren't her boyfriend so why should you,' Jean reported, with the beat of a poem. 'She said that you were good enough to let her tag along in the first place, she wasn't going to get you to pay as well. She said that if anything he, John, should be paying for you to be entertaining his girlfriend.'

'She did?'

'She did.'

'What did John say to that?' I said.

'John Harrison just blew a gasket at that point, for heaven's sake! I was sure smoke was going to come out of his nose. His face went bright red. He started to say something several times but couldn't get it out and he had to leave without saying another word. It was hilarious. Our Jean and I cracked up the minute he left.'

'And how are you these days, Jean?' I asked. She was a bit puffy around the cheeks and I'm sure she'd put on a bit of weight since I'd last seen her.

'Oh,' she replied, hiking her shoulders, 'I've been better. I'm going home at the weekend for a week's sick leave. I'm just hoping I can wait it out until my supervisor leaves, then I know I'll get on better at work. Once I get my career back on track, everything will fall back into place for me. Just you wait and see, David Buchanan. You'll be begging me to come running back to you.'

Noticeably she didn't say 'But you'll be too late then.'

'My loss,' I said. I said it to try to make her feel a little better, but I had miscalculated. She visibly picked up in her mood.

'Well, of course you don't need to wait until then if you don't want to!'

'Ah Jean, I've resigned myself to the fact that it's not to be.'

'I bet it would be easier if I was into all these weird groups of yours. But then you wouldn't be interested in having a relationship with me, you'd just want someone to talk to about your music.'

As she said this she started to eye my extensive record collection, which was directly opposite her and just behind me. I clicked my teeth in an 'ah well' expression.

'Tell me; what do you and our Jean talk about all this time you're together? Don't you ever get bored just talking about music?'

'But look at all these records, Jean,' I said, swinging around by gripping my hands around my knees to use my bottom as a pivot. 'We have to work our way through these. I think we're only as far as The Spencer Davis Group and Autumn '66. In fact, we were only examining in detail a song from that particular album the other night – 'I Washed My Hands In Muddy Water.'

'Oh well,' Jean said, without missing a beat, 'at least you're making progress if you're already up to the D's.'

Chapter Twenty-Two.

'Jean Kerr is definitely behaving very strangely, dear boy,' Jean Simpson announced, as she entered my flat

'Really?' I said. I was getting a bit of a system together: just sit back and say 'Really?' – make sure you mean the question mark though – and it'll all come spilling out for you.

It was the following Friday. I was missing Mary – that's not an excuse, that's a fact. She was due back at work the following Monday and we'd planned to meet that evening.

In the meantime it was, as I've already said, Friday. 7.45 p.m. to be exact, and Jean Simpson had just walked in as per the arrangement we had made the previous Wednesday. Interesting to note that she had started to give me more notice about her arrivals. Not that it really mattered, because when she did turn up I have to admit it, she was stunning, absolutely, breathtakingly beautiful. She was getting the make-up stuff together, particularly her work around her eyes. She'd clear blue eyes, which sparkled, and so she had to be careful that her eyeliner didn't make her look like Piccadilly Circus. She was wearing her wine-coloured duffle coat, which she allowed me to remove by standing about five inches in front of me and shaking her hands like she was a runner doing their warm-up. Okay. The next bit was too much for any man to resist, I promise. She was wearing a satin minidress that clung to her bottom and the tops of her legs like it was second skin. For a change she wore a white blouse, which was slightly transparent – well, transparent enough for you to be able to see the shape of her white bra and the contrasting white of her breasts immediately above it. Over this she wore the briefest of cardigans, black with three buttons all undone. Finally, to complete the ensemble, she wore white stockings and black lace-up ankle boots. I looked back up to the blouse; until now she'd never drawn any attention to her breasts. In fact, the only way I had any reason to suspect that they might be as marvellous as they now appeared through the thin white material, was the night I hugged her. That night I suspected. Now I knew.

'Yes, David, she's behaving very strangely. She's always following me around, looking at me funny and scurrying off somewhere, muttering when she sees that I notice her.'

I decided not to dig and I decided not to mention Jean Kerr's visit.

'You look amazing, Jean,' I said, changing the subject to a subject I preferred. My tact seemed to have worked because she dropped the Jean Kerr topic like a ton of hot bricks.

'Oh, I've been so looking forward to this evening,' she said, with such conviction that I accepted the statement as truth and not mere politeness. I mention that only because people use the funniest of words to describe things. For instance, people are prone to say 'I could murder a cup of tea' or 'I'm dying to go to the toilet' or 'I'd kill for a bacon buttie.' And so forth. But they don't actually mean that literally now, do they?

Besides, I don't know if you noticed it there, but she didn't say 'I've been so looking forward to seeing you, David.' Yes, I know it's kind of implied. But at the same time it's not. Not really. That one little omission probably spoke volumes about our relationship. The vision before me, however, without even uttering a word, spoke volumes of every man's fantasies. Well, at least my fantasies.

That Friday, Jean was up for some wine and she had brought a couple of bottles of her own, the first of which we made short work of.

'Good, I needed that,' she said, as she drained the final drops of the first bottle into her glass. 'I was a wee bit tense. Now I'm relaxed. I need to feel loosened up. Why don't you go and open the other bottle, David?' she said, as in issuing an order she wanted obeyed. I'm a good soldier when I have to be.

But as I opened the second bottle in our sparse kitchen, Mary Skeffington jumped into my mind. I thought of our time in Bath. I wondered what she was doing at that particular moment. Was she still troubled about what to do about us? Had she already made a decision? Should I tell Jean? But tell her what? Tell her that someone was thinking about having a relationship with me? That didn't seem to make sense. Then I remembered Jean waiting for me in the other room and I grew preoccupied by her again.

I was thankful I'd been a good soldier, because when I came back into the room she had removed, from the floor up, her boots, her miniskirt, her jumper and her white blouse, leaving her standing – feet apart – in only her stockings, bra and knickers. I should tell you here that her underwear was functional underwear, and all the more erotic for being so; I really can't abide all this lewd, whimsical lingerie. I find it rude and crude, and, as I've said before, rude and crude is not a turn-on for me. Now, that probably makes me an L 7 (write the letter and number down. Still don't get it? Okay, this time write them very close together).

Jean just stood there – not especially brazen, but not especially shy either. She stood there, I believe, in a position she felt would give me the most pleasure. Then she took my hand and led me to the sofa bed. The difference being that night that this time she pulled back the covers, revealing the white sheets. Thank goodness they were clean.

Then she threw the blankets on the floor and said, 'We'll be more comfortable tonight between the sheets.'

She lay down. I made to lie down beside her. Well, you would wouldn't you?

'Aren't you forgetting something?' she said, and then let out a little chuckle as she continued, 'or should I say, aren't you forgetting to forget something?'

I calmly removed my shoes and socks and trousers. After careful consideration, I also removed my waistcoat.

'I think we can do a bit better than that,' she said, pointing to my green t-shirt.

So I joined her in the bed wearing only my green boxer shorts.

As with previous encounters, we snuggled up closer to each other and I felt a shiver flash down both our bodies. I knew mine was from the sheer excitement of her cold flesh next to mine. Hers, I suppose, could just have been from the chill of the night, but from the look in her eyes I wouldn't have said so. This time, though, it was different. Every inch of her skin was next to mine. I could, for the first time, feel the fullness of her breasts. That's one of the things that I loved, you know, that she could have such absolutely beautiful breasts but that she'd kept them hidden from me all this time, even after all the things we'd done together. I was dying to remove her bra and feel those breasts.

But don't forget, this was her dance.

She turned her back to me and manoeuvred her bum into my hips, forming the classic two spoons. Another first during our series of encounters was that we'd both been so excited to lie with each other that we'd forgotten the music. But it didn't distract us. In fact, we lay like that for a time, very, very close. I didn't want to push, though I did want to get her again. That was a big part of the thrill for me, 'getting' her, or at the very least her pretending that it was me who was doing the getting.

She turned around to face me and lay on her back. She took my hand and said, 'Look... feel how wet I am already.' This was the first time any physical contact with hands had taken place. I think she did it as a test – you know, to see how much would I feel? Would I try to grope her, would I be rough and hurt her? I intended to stick with what I'd done up to this point, and that was to follow her lead in this dance. Around and around, gently holding my hand in a position where my fingers could only brush the damp cotton. Then she pushed my hand tightly between her legs and gripped my wrist between her thighs to hold me there. After a few seconds she released my hand and turned me over on my back, before straddling me. She was now on top, riding me horseback style, as she had done in our fully-clothed first adventure. She was steadying her hands on my shoulders and I had an amazing view of her breasts. I was itching for them, quite literally itching to just touch them.

Jean Simpson must already have been quite excited because about a minute later she went rigid, pushing firmly down on me. Her eyes were shut, her hair was behind her ears and her head was tilted back. She had such a perfect body. The entire combination made for such an incredible view that I could gladly have stayed in that position all night.

'David!' she screamed, at the top of her lungs, 'Agh David, you got me!'

She bucked a few times and collapsed on top of me where she lay panting for a couple of minutes.

'That was incredible, David,' she whispered. 'Let me put on a record – I know you're not in a position to walk very comfortably. Just wait there, dear boy, I've got another little treat for you.'

As she went about selecting her music, Otis Blue by Otis Redding, I tried to work out what her little treat for me was. Had she made sure I hadn't spent first time around because she'd something else in store?

I was soon to find out. Otis was blaring out of the speakers as she returned to the bed and vanished under the sheet. Ooh la, la! She seemed to be fighting and twisting around beneath the sheet for a few seconds before she made any actual contact with me. It appeared from the shape of the sheet that she was on all fours and now she leaned over on me, so that our bodies would soon touch again. I could see her move closer and closer to me. Then her breasts came into contact with me somewhere about my midriff. The effect was electrifying and I quite quickly realised why: she'd removed her bra and her nipples were on my skin. That realisation sent the shudder the whole way down my spine.

'And now for your little treat, for being such a good boy to me,' she said, at least that's what I think she said – you see, her head was under the sheet and her voice was muffled. I thought I'd already enjoyed the treat, but I gave myself the benefit of the doubt and assumed that's what she said.

With that, she raised her body back up from me and rested on her knees. I could feel her hands interfering with my boxer shorts.

'Now I'm going to take you out, David, so you must promise to be very good,' she ordered.

I muttered, 'Okay.' By this point we were both shivering with excitement.

She cupped me in her hands, then leant over to rub me between her breasts. The sensation sent waves of shudders up and down my spine – nearly unbearable, just nearly, mind you. I was prepared to force myself to enjoy it.

Jean Simpson must have considered me to be a very good boy because my treat didn't stop there.

She took me in her mouth.

I mean, I should, I suppose, have been expecting something like that to happen but I can honestly say I never dreamed that she would do such a thing. I was so excited at that point. I was clinging on for dear life. I mean, I knew if I should let her get me, then the sensation would be short-lived. But how do your resist the inevitable when every nerve in your body is no longer under your control? Jean Simpson now controlled the horizontal and she definitely controlled the vertical.

I stretched my hand full length down my side and then worked my way up to find her breasts. I could feel her whole body tense above me. She held me in her mouth but stopped her magic. She froze in that position for a few seconds. I gently kneaded her breasts with each hand. She seemed to relax. I assumed it was because I wasn't grabbing handfuls of flesh and squeezing the life out of her. She held her position, still not moving. I continued caressing her breasts, working my way to her nipples. They were already hard and I gently rubbed them. I didn't know what else to do, I just wanted to do something to her in return for all the pleasure she was giving me.

Panic over, she started up her magic again. I'm glad I persevered, though; I thought that someone must have been very rough with Jean Simpson in the past so now I needed her to know that I wasn't going to be rough too. As I said, I always remembered being told by my mother never to do anything to a girl that you wouldn't like someone doing to your sister. I wasn't exactly sure that this was what she meant, but forget my sister, I'd hate anyone to grab handfuls of my chest and maul me. (I assure you I wasn't having this exact thought right then, just the much quicker version of it.)

Then, as if there wasn't enough going on, Jean added her tongue to the mixture. It was cool – not cold, just cooler than everything else going on around me. I was happy to say that this was it for me, I couldn't resist any longer. I didn't even want to try to resist any longer, I just went with the flow. I started following her in her dance again. I was happy that I did, as my entire body gave an uncontrollable shudder and I exploded. No other word for it, just an almighty eruption, and she contained it all. I suppose that in itself made it all the more exciting when I realised what she was doing.

Otis Redding was singing 'My Girl' and as I tuned into the lyrics, I got a quick flash of Mary Skeffington.

But here was Jean Simpson, making herself comfortable beside me. She'd just given me the treat of my life – no exaggeration – and guess what she said?

She said, 'I really loved what you were doing to my breasts there. Do it some more please.'

And I did.

'Mmmm,' she purred, and drifted into a trance-like state. She was lying on her back, I was lying on my side leaning over her, touching her full but sturdy breasts and I might as well have been in Heaven. And get this; she said she loved the treat I was giving her.

Then, after a few minutes she said, 'Would you kiss them please?'

Would I kiss them?

I did!

She started to purr some more. The more I caressed her nipples with my tongue the harder they got, and the harder they got the more she purred, and the more she purred the more I got in the mood again. That's the way it worked.

Otis had finished and she whispered into my ear, 'I don't really want you to stop what you're doing but it's your turn to put on a record.'

I rearranged my boxer shorts to make me look semi-decent and went over to the record deck, took off Otis Blue, put it back in its sleeve and replaced it in its section, and then took out a Muddy Waters album. That kicked up the mood a bit as I returned to the bed.

She flashed a bit of an impish smile as I got under the covers. Pretty soon, I realised why: I was about to fondle my new toys – my new favourite toys, her breasts – again when she gently took hold of my hand and lazily pulled it away from her breasts, down over her naval. She circled her naval a few times, using her hand to chaperone mine, and then she pushed it down even further.

I genuinely got the shock of my life when I realised Jean Simpson had removed her pants when I'd been putting on the new record.

I'd been told that some women have a little hair, some have a lot, and some are badly thatched and flimsy, just like someone who is going bald. But Jean Simpson, well, she was soft and silky and it felt, to my finger, like it was lovingly washed, shampooed, brushed and combed at least once a day. Jean Simpson's private hair was exquisite. I just loved that.

She took my fingers in her hand now and caressed them ever so gently, before tentatively combing her bush with them a few times. She was putting more and more pressure on my fingers, which were in turn putting more and more pressure on her. As she did this she spread her legs further and further apart and raised her knees. She gave out a little gasp as she finally pushed a solitary finger of mine into her.

She'd been looking away from me towards the wall but she turned to face me and whispered, 'be very gentle, David.'

Then she pushed my finger further into her and took her hand away from mine, leaving me free to explore. I'd never done this before with anyone and it felt so far out. It's difficult in the middle of experiencing all of these new sensations to pull words out of the air to describe exactly what I was feeling. I was as gentle as I knew how to be and eventually another of my fingers followed the first. The word was obviously going back down the line of how brilliant this new sensation was, because some of the other wee fingers wanted to find out for themselves. She was purring louder and louder now, pushing herself against my wrist. I was happy just to feel inside – it was as soft as velvet, and I caressed her, inside and out.

Jean's breathing was growing louder and she took my hand again in hers and directed me to places inside her. Every time she found a new spot she purred louder and let out a few 'oohs' and a few 'ahhs'.

'I can't believe how good you are at this,' she said, seeming to forget that she was directing my hand. 'God, this is so gorgeous I want it to last forever. I want you to do this to me forever and ever. Yes, just there. Yes, yes, a wee bit harder, David. Oh yes. Oh yes. OHHHH YES.'

She was wildly grinding herself against my wrist and I began to get a bit of cramp in my arm, the last thing I wanted to happen in the middle of all this heaven. She released my hand again to its own devices and used her own to caress her breast.

She tried with her other hand to free me from my boxer shorts but before she achieved this she screamed at the top of her voice: 'David Buchanan, you dear boy, YOU FLIPPIN' GOT ME AGAIN!' After that, she groaned and purred and moaned for at least a couple of minutes.

We were both drenched in sweat from head to toe. While she was enjoying the last of her convulsions I took the opportunity to lift the top sheet up and steal a glimpse of her body. I was seeing her in the nude for the first time: she was positively glowing from our latest encounter. The mixture of all of her scents and the sex was totally intoxicating. I hungrily took several deep breaths to truly wallow in this new sensation. No one had ever described this to me, no one had ever let on how just how naturally addictive the mixture of aromas of a passionate woman would be, and how they would ignite senses I'd never before dreamed of experiencing. She turned and cuddled up towards me, burying her head in its favourite resting place, the nook of my neck.

And that's how we fell asleep.

I woke up a couple of hours later, at midnight. I think I would've gladly slept the whole way through the night were it not for the fact that she was stroking me, ever so gently, using the tips of her thumb and forefinger.

When she saw that I had awoken she said, 'Okay, I want to try to put one of your theories to the test. You know you keep saying that you think I'm beautiful and that I've a beautiful body.'

'Never more beautiful than now,' I said, risking her wrath and modesty by lifting the sheet and viewing her in full again, and not bothering with what she continued to do to me. As the sheet fell it expelled another whiff of her unique collection of fragrances.

Unbelievably that was nearly enough for me.

She flashed me a playful chastising look and said, 'Well my question, David, is – are you reacting like this because of something within you or because you are looking at the body and the face which goes with the hand that is doing this to you?'

I closed my eyes to prove my point and my immediate reaction in her hand surprised her. 'That's definitely because of you, because of the you inside,' I said when she was convinced, 'and of course the body, and the face, and the mind, and the person that goes with all that makes you. You!'

She looked at me like she was considering something and her eyes betrayed the fact that she was hovering this way and that over her decision.

'I can't for one moment imagine it could ever be this amazing with anyone else,' I whispered, and in that hallowed moment I meant it. In moments like that you do believe that, don't you?

She let go of me and snuggled up close again. I was lying on my back; she was on her side, her mouth right beside my ear.

'Okay,' she sighed and took a deep breath. 'There's something else I'd like to try to do but I need to know that I can trust you, David.'

I nodded.

'I want to take your shorts off so that we can be close to each other but you must only do what I want you to do; you must not try to enter me. I want you close, David, but I don't want you inside me. Are you okay with that? I'll be okay if you feel that you can't do that. If you think that you might get carried away and lose control then it's okay; we can continue to have our other fun. But if you can promise then–'

'I promise Jean,' I said. On reflection, I was happy to promise. She obviously didn't want to have full sex before she got married and if she felt that by doing this she wasn't being unfaithful to John, then by the same logic I wasn't being unfaithful to Mary. I mean, Mary and I certainly weren't as far down the line as John and Jean were, and I had an inkling that Mary had decided to stay in Bath for the week so that she could make her final decision as to whether or not she was going to give me a try. I have to admit most of those thoughts came afterwards. For when I said, 'I promise, Jean,' I was bursting with nothing else but excitement.

Jean was nervous and I suppose that was probably adding to her own excitement. She tentatively removed my shorts after a few false starts.

'Now; don't forget what you promised,' she said, as she threw them on the floor.

Now we were both completely nude. And then she lay on top of me. She had her legs tightly shut but had placed me between them first. I could feel her silky hair brushing against me as she moved up and down while locking me between her legs. She was shivering with excitement. I nudged my head around so that I could get one of her breasts to my mouth. I grabbed her nipple between my lips and trapped it there as I used my tongue to caress the tip of it. I felt it grow harder against my lips. I could feel her growing wet between the legs at the same time. I was hardly able to contain myself and probably wouldn't have if we hadn't already enjoyed two encounters thus far that evening.

She rolled over on to her side, keeping me trapped between her legs. It was as though that was her final method of control, the fact that I couldn't move unless she wanted me to. I kept kissing her breasts, moving from one to the other, and she started to groan a little and her body visibly relaxed.

I pulled my hips back from her, freeing myself. She didn't react – I mean, she didn't react negatively. I nudged her over from her side onto her back, letting her breast go. I placed my hand between her legs, and she was a lot more welcoming to my hand than she had been to another part of my anatomy, and I used it to explore her silkiness, while the other I used to massage her nipple.

She brought both her hands down to my hand, the one that was between her legs, and lovingly caressed it, pushing my fingers deeper into her. Her eyes were closed this whole time.

'Oh David, I love what you do to me with your fingers. It's like they've known me all my life! That's so beautiful,' she said. Then she took my hand away from her and brought it up to her lips and kissed it. She then pulled me over on to her.

'Oh please be careful, David,' she pleaded.

I was above her, supporting myself on my arms. She cupped me gently in her hands and gingerly pulled me towards her. She carefully used my tip to caress her through her silky private hair. She groaned. I could feel her wetness along my length. It felt lush. It felt wonderful. I was now positioned between her legs, our private hairs messing, and she was pushing herself along me. The more she did it the wetter she got, the wetter she got the more I pushed against her. She relaxed a little more as she realised there was no way I could accidentally slip into her while we maintained this action. To be honest, the pleasure I was experiencing at that moment was so beautiful, I doubt it would have felt any better even if I had entered her; she had already formed a sheath for me, using her hands beneath me and her silky bush above me.

She seemed to accept the fact that I was going to be careful because she wriggled and snaked beneath me, pushing harder and harder against me all the time.

'Oh David, you're getting so hard, it's so delicious – please be car…' she said. She either didn't complete the last word because she cared or because she no longer cared, you choose.

I leaned down on her, resting on her bountiful breasts, squashing them between us. I pushed one of my free hands between our bodies and soon came into contact with her hands. Then I pushed two of my fingers deep inside her. She opened her eyes wide, felt around for a couple of seconds with her hands, and when she realised that it was only my fingers inside her she grinded against me for all her worth.

'Oh David, you're going to get me again!' she panted.

This was the first time she had given me advance warning, but she had her reasons.

'Please, please, please let me get you at the same time.'

She tightened against me. I pushed for all my worth against her.

'Oh God, you're going to get me, you're going to get me, I need to feel your cum on me, David,' she said. 'Please, all over me! Please!'

She manoeuvred me so that a certain part of my anatomy, the object of both her desire and her fear, was now placed between us, up between both of our navels. She wrapped her legs around me and pushed and pushed.

'Oh David, oh David, you're going to… agh! You got me!'

And right at that precise moment I spurted between the both of us.

We collapsed into each other and lay there, allowing our body sweat and other liquids to mix naturally. I thought she would have wanted to clean off, but she seemed happy to put her hand between us and rub my spurts over her. Perhaps it was just her way of knowing that none of me had gone inside her.

We dozed off again. This time we slept for about three hours. The next time I woke up first, and I returned the favour, caressing her between her legs as she slept. I think she awoke from her slumber quite a bit before she acknowledged this because she gently repositioned her hips so that I'd have better access to her. She surrendered to my fingers immediately this time, making them feel very welcome, and then as she sighed out of her sleep, she took me in her hands. She was very gentle – playful even – and she seemed content for both of us to concentrate on her pleasure. A few minutes later I 'got' her again and then she returned the favour by taking me in her mouth again.

She showered, I showered, our energy completely spent. Then we dozed for a while until Saturday broke with the dawn and I walked her home. We passed my flatmate just before we reached Jean's flat on the graveyard quiet Alexandra Road. He nodded at us in a nudge, nudge, wink, wink kind of way. Jean and I both continued on our way, managing not to smirk.

'I'll tell him I just met you when I was out to get the newspaper,' I said.

She nodded her agreement.

Again on her doorstep we bid our goodbyes, but didn't kiss. Before I left, though, she hugged me and whispered in my ear.

'Next time, David, you have to decide what to do. You can do anything you want to do to me, except… enter me.'

Before I could say 'Pardon?' she'd let herself into her house and closed the door behind her.

I walked home aching, but not aching so much I wasn't reliving details of the previous hours' encounters. And as I reached Rostrevor Road, a combination of guilt and tiredness made me realise that Mary Skeffington would soon be returning from Bath, and when she returned with her decision, I'd have to face up to resolving the Jean Simpson situation once and for all before everything blew up in my face.

Worst-case scenario (for me) was that Mary Skeffington and Jean Simpson could both end whatever it was they had with me and resort once again to a physical fight; they'd already proven back at Tiger's party that they were both well capable of symbolically rolling up their sleeves and getting stuck into a bout of fisticuffs for their man.

Chapter Twenty-Three.

Jean, Jean Simpson that was, contacted me next. It was that Sunday morning. It wasn't that she couldn't keep her hands off me. No, it was bad news. Well, at least it sounded like bad news.

'Our Jean's taken a turn for the worse,' she started, omitting the niceties.

'Wow!' was the only word I could find to say. I mean, I wasn't going to say, Really? as in I didn't believe her, was I? 'What's happened?'

'I've just got a call from her mother,' Jean continued, a little quaver noticeable in her voice. 'She says that unless Jean improves a lot by the beginning of the week, the doctor wants to check her on to a psychiatric ward.'

'Un-believe-able!' I hissed.

'Can you believe it, our Jean in a flippin' loony bin?' she gushed, down the phone.

I'm sure if I had been the one to make the comment she'd have had my guts for garters. I let it go, as you do in such circumstances.

'What happened?'

'I don't know, David. I told you she was acting strange. Her mum says she was acting very strange at home and eventually she had to send for a doctor, who sent her to a specialist.'

I was in shock. I mean, we all have the occasional weird thought, don't we? Well, I certainly do and you know from your own counsel that you certainly do as well, so the next time I say, 'Well, we all have the occasional weird thought', you all shout back at me in unison: 'Yes we do, David!' Otherwise I'll start to think I'm only weird one round here.

Now, we all have the occasional weird thought, don't we?

'YES WE DO, DAVID!'

Thank you, that was much better. Much better. But even when you're thinking these far out thoughts, of course, you keep them to yourself and all that, but you never go as far as to think you're truly mental. Now, I know Jean Kerr. I knew her quite well in one way and I wouldn't say she was entirely by-the-book normal, but neither would I say she was genuinely crazy. Mary Skeffington on the other hand, well in my opinion, she was as close as you could get to normal, to the normal that I knew and trusted.

Jean Simpson was going on and on, down the phone about how bad she felt about Jean, and how shocked she was, and she eventually said, 'Her mother wanted to know if I could come up to Derby with a few friends, see if we couldn't cheer our Jean up.'

'Sounds like a good idea,' I offered supportively. I assumed she was telling me this because she was letting me know that I shouldn't spend too much time dreaming up the details of our next encounter, since she'd be out of town for a while. Mind you, if Mary Skeffington returned from Bath having made her decision to give it a try (and I have to admit, as the week progressed and there was no contact from her, I was now having severe doubts that there would ever be a Mary & Me), surely there would be no further encounters with Miss Jean Simpson.

'Good. Will you come then?'

Now that one I hadn't expected. 'Hasn't she got any other friends?' I asked, ignoring my roots. 'I mean, it might be sending out a mixed signal if I go up.'

'David,' Jean said in a schoolmistress voice, 'she needs us.'

The thing about the Irish is that they can never say no to people in need.

'Yes, you're right. When do you want to go?'

'There's a train leaving Euston in about two hours – we'll make it easy. Oh and by the way, David, Jean's mum is insisting that she looks after the train fares and will put some of us up.'

'Which of us are going?' I asked, breathing a sigh of relief. My trip to Bath and my recent frequent visits to the off licence were starting to tell on my pocket.

'Well, for now there's me, you and John,' she replied, matter of fact.

'Jean!' I said stretching her name into three syllables as my relief disappeared. I had this vision of Jean lying on my bed after our last encounter, rubbing my juices onto her stomach. I wasn't so sure that now was a particularly good time to be spending a three-hour train journey with John Harrison.

But Jean Simpson, reduced to two travelling companions to support her sick friend, was not about to drop her numbers by one.

And that is how we came to be on Jean Kerr's doorstep five and one quarter hours later. The Kerr's didn't actually live in Derby, rather they lived in Matlock, a village on the other side of Derby (if you were on your way to Manchester) so Mrs Kerr picked us up at the train station. She insisted on giving Jean our train fares there and then.

Jean Kerr was neither surprised to see us nor did she look crazy. But then again, how would I have known the difference? Something must have been wrong with her for the doctor to be acting as serious as he was.

First thing we did was to listen to Jean's new record on her new record player. She'd bought a Donovan album, A Gift From A Flower To A Garden. I'd always considered Donovan to be a poor man's Dylan but with the hippy, flower power direction he'd taken on this new work, he was making his own mark at last. A Gift From A Flower To A Garden was a double album and the first I'd ever seen released in a box. It had a very distinctive mauve-coloured sleeve with a psychedelic photo of the man himself on the cover. Overall, it was a very enjoyable album. To be honest, I was glad to be able to have a musical distraction. After the opening track, the gentle whispery, 'Wear Your Love Like Heaven', Jean Kerr ignored me and instead started talking to Jean and John about me, as if I wasn't there.

'That's him gone for the next two hours. He just loves his music doesn't he? It was awfully good of him to come up and see me,' she said.

At this point in the conversation I tuned out completely and joined Donovan on his astral travels.

After the first disc finished we had tea and then Jean Kerr said we should go for a walk out the back of her house. She said I'd enjoy it, which I did. We climbed this steep, grass-covered field and when we reached the top, we'd a clear view for 270 degrees. There before us was the most amazing countryside I'd seen outside of Donegal. Jean Kerr was so proud that I loved it so much. We all sat down crossed-legged, just like the hippies do, and absorbed the wonderful views.

I don't really remember much about the rest of the day; it was getting dark by then. I remember John Harrison being a little put out by the sleeping arrangements, as Jean Simpson had quite clearly stated that John would stay in Jean Kerr's house and I would sleep in her house. John's response was to make long and plaintive faces.

'John, we're to wed. Around these parts it wouldn't be considered decent for both of us to sleep under the one roof.'

'Oh!' John replied, obviously downhearted.

'Oh!' said Jean's mum, 'I thought it was the other one you were getting hitched to anyway. Sorry, I must have picked it up wrong!'

'Oh,' was all John Harrison could find to say, for a second time, and his shoulders visibly dropped another two inches.

Jean Simpson's mum was a very jolly lady and she made me feel very welcome. If I'd any thoughts, though, of enjoying any encounters under her roof with her precious daughter then I'd certainly another thing coming. Or, in Jean Simpson speak, I certainly didn't have another thing coming.

Her mother eventually left the two of us alone at about 11.00 p.m.

'I've got to be heard to be going upstairs pretty shortly, David. I don't want my mother for one second imagining what we might be up to down here.'

I had forgotten to mention to you that she was wearing her famous tartan miniskirt, although at a much more respectable length this time. I was still sitting at the table and Jean stood up beside me. She took my hand from the table and placed it on her knee. Then she pulled it slowly up the stocking until it vanished under her mini. And I could feel the cold skin above her stocking, the cold, smooth skin. (I love the feel of cold skin; it sends a shiver down my spine. Is that morbid or sick or anything like that?) Next, I touched her pants. She cupped my palm into her axis. She removed her own hand and started to stroke my neck.

My fingers quickly found their way into her pants and amongst her silky hair. Jean bent slightly at her knees to give me more room to manoeuvre, and I rubbed her gently with the tips of my fingers. She bent her head towards the ceiling and moved her hips sensually around my hand. It seemed like a dream as two of my fingers slipped into her.

'Oh,' she whispered, 'naughty.' She winked at me and added, 'Naughty but scrumptious.'

We stayed in that position for a time then she pulled her hand away from my hair, dropped it down to her knees, and then up and under her skirt, where she gently removed my hand.

First she kissed my fingers then she placed them up to my nose and said, 'Naughty boy, that'll have to do you for tonight. Perhaps this little taster will keep you awake long enough to help you dream up something very naughty to do to me next time we meet.'

She did a quick twirl for me at the door, flashing her beautiful bottom. She made a bit more noise than she needed to as she went up to her room.

Then she was gone.

Chapter Twenty-Four.

If the trip to Derby seemed a bit blurred to you that's perfectly understandable, because that's the way I remember it. I still can't really fit it altogether in my mind. I remember enjoying listening to Donovan. I remember sitting in the field, loving the view, and I remember going to bed, Miss Simpson's fragrance still lingering on my fingers. And that's it. I kind of remember the two Jean's mums but not anywhere near as clearly as I remember Mary's mum. I do remember how John Harrison looked at me as I left with Jean to sleep at her house. Thank goodness looks couldn't kill.

Meanwhile my thoughts were with Mary Skeffington who was due back in town. In fact, I was dining at her house that evening.

Jean and John and I caught the dawn train back to London and we didn't speak much because we slept for most of the journey. We bid our goodbyes at Euston and departed for our respective offices. I was only thirty minutes late, and I told my boss what had happened and he was thankfully sympathetic about Jean Kerr and unconcerned about my lateness.

The first thing I did after I walked through Mary's front door was to tell her about the Derby trip. Well, actually it was the second thing; the real first thing was a lingering kiss. She particularly enjoyed Jean Simpson's plans for the sleeping arrangements, claiming she probably was protecting me against an attack from Jean Kerr late in the night.

'I loved your mum,' I said, as she started the cooking. As on the previous evening in her flat, I retuned her radio to 199 and Radio Caroline and turned it up a bit.

'She loved you,' Mary replied, 'she really did.'

'Did you have fun the rest of the week?'

'We had a great ride above Bath in an air balloon,' Mary said, as she peeled the potatoes. 'I've noticed something about you, you're not really good at taking compliments are you?'

'Augh, you know,' I said. The worst possible answer I could have given was one of agreement.

'Well, if you want to know the full truth, what my mother really said was that I should make sure I didn't let you slip through my fingers.'

'Oh,' I replied, simply because I couldn't believe that I was so lucky. But that thought was still worrying me. So I came right out with it. 'What did you decide in your week's thinking time?'

'I decided that I cared for you very much. I decided that I was totally over John. I decided that there was no part of me still longing for any part of a relationship with him. I decided that if we're both careful we could make this work, and I decided I'd be a fool not to try to make it work with you if you're still interested.'

God, I couldn't believe I was here with this woman in her flat and she was saying all these things, all the things I'd been dreaming about, and there she was, twice as pretty and saying them to me. I walked across to her and pulled her towards me. Then I kissed her and we clung on to each other as if our lives depended on it.

'Nothing's guaranteed, David,' she said, 'we're going to have to work at it. You know, not take each other for granted or anything like that and–'

'Don't worry, we'll be fine,' I said as I patted her on her back. I admit I was being a tad naïve – I knew that this was what I wanted more than I'd ever wanted for anything in my life. It meant that I was going to have to completely re-plan my unplanned life from scratch. This wasn't meant to happen for, say, at least another ten years or so; but now that it had, I would fight tooth and nail for her, I would sweat guts to make sure this happened. I also knew that I had to resolve one massive issue before I started anything as serious as this.

We'd a great evening. The food was great, Radio Caroline was, as usual, excellent, and we kissed a few times. She asked me if I minded if she turfed me out early; she'd been away for so long she was way behind on her work and she wanted to spend the rest of the week getting back up to speed with it and seeing her friends (who seemed interested in her again, now that she seemed to be over John). She did say, however, that we should do something special on Friday, spend the weekend together.

I was glad of the early night, to be honest; I'd still some sleep to catch up on. Plus it gave me the time I so desperately needed to resolve, or more appropriately dissolve, this thing with Jean Simpson before I moved to the next stage with Mary Skeffington. Maybe in hindsight I'm making it sound a wee bit too neat and tidy. But I don't think so. I don't believe it's selective memory on my part. I remember thinking that Mary's time in Bath and the decisions she'd made about us during that time were vitally important. I figured up until then I might have been a bit casual about it, maybe preparing myself for Mary shooting me down. Now that she'd come to the decision that I wasn't a rebound, from that point on it mattered to me how I behaved. You could say, 'Augh, come on David, you were just playing out this fantasy kick with Jean and you wanted to see how far it would go while at the same time building up the budding relationship with Mary!'

And you might even be correct, but I would have said if that was the case.

Chapter Twenty-Five.

The Jean Simpson Problem was really a much bigger problem than I'd first imagined. I came home from work on Tuesday to find John Harrison sitting on my doorstep.

'How's Jean?' I asked, thinking that Jean Kerr might have taken a turn for the worst.

'There's something going on, David,' he said. The way he said it implied that he was referring to the other Jean.

'Come on in,' I said,

As you do.

I made him a cup of tea – he didn't want anything stronger. I felt like something stronger, I felt I was going to need it.

'Okay, now give it to me from the top,' I said.

'Look, it's not fair. I mean, when you're going with someone and you're in for the long haul, well of course a little bit of the excitement goes out of it, doesn't it? Stands to reason, doesn't it? We'd all look like bleedin' fools if we followed our girlfriends round all the time with our tongues dragging on the floor.'

'Yes, I suppose so, John. But at the same time you've got to feel it's special,' I said, trying to play devil's advocate.

'What am I supposed to do? I mean I gave up Mary for her. Maybe I shouldn't have given up Mary. You see, with Mary the situation was reversed. I was the one who thought, God is this it for the rest of my life? And I felt bad about thinking that. And then Jean came along and she was exciting and she was interested in me. I mean, I didn't even know if girls were attracted to me in the first place – Mary and I just grew up together and kind of drifted into our relationship. It felt right, you know? I knew her and I supposed because I'd deflowered her I had a responsibility towards her and her family. But then I thought there's got to be more. There's got to be more than moral obligation. Mary has strong opinions about certain things, you know.

'So Jean came along, and she's buzzing all the time and she seemed happier to go with my flow. She wasn't as sexually inquisitive as Mary was – she had this thing about wanting to be pure on her wedding day. I liked that and I thought, okay, that's a way of dealing with this.'

It's just amazing how you can be with two girls and get them both so wrong. I mean, according to John Harrison, Jean Simpson was supposedly sexually un-inquisitive? If that wasn't hard enough to take, he then topped it off by implying that Mary Skeffington was physically boring? Where was John's head at anyway? Maybe his ears were just too big a target for the wind. Mary Skeffington took my breath away every time I looked at her! She was so stunning I could hardly keep my hands off her! Not that I didn't feel it wise to keep my hands off her, at least for the time being. But I'd always a great time with her; she was always graceful, intelligent, entertaining. Recently I found myself reaching the stage where I felt I wasn't out of my depth with her, that she might not be out of my league. I could actually talk to her and be around her for hours on end without getting bored, but more importantly without her getting bored.

And then of course there was the impish Jean Simpson, I mean to say, I'd great fun with her. Yes, perhaps the encounters were the big part of my attraction to her and, let's put our cards on the table, it was too large a part of the attraction to ignore. We've discussed this before, but I'll never work out why John wasn't knocking on her door every single night, with his tongue dragging on the floor.

And what's the main difference between the two girls? Well, I suppose the easiest way to describe it would be that I loved to look at and lust after Jean Simpson in her various stages of undress. I'll admit it here and now, even though I'm getting uncomfortable sitting here talking about it. But with Mary it was different, there was just so much more. I'm saying that, having little to no knowledge of Mary and that's not to say it's easy for me to keep my hands off her because it's not, it's just that there are other priorities and the other priority is the importance of doing everything right with her, getting it all properly in place. And I felt if I did… well, all of the other stuff would also fall into place.

'David, I think Jean is seeing someone else,' John said.

'What gives you that impression?' I asked, trying to come across like I was dismissing his fear.

'Well, Jean Kerr says she been staying out late at night. One of the girls in the top flat told Jean that my Jean got home in the early hours of the morning. Apparently one morning she got home after eight!'

'They must be mistaken,' I said, 'she's always talking about getting married to you.'

'When you take her out to see these groups and bands, what time do you get back by?' he asked, ignoring my encouragement.

'I'd say around midnight? Yeah, maybe just before midnight.'

'Yeah, that what my Jean says, but that's not what Jean Kerr says, David.'

'Jean Kerr must have picked it up wrong, John – she's a bit, you know… she's not beyond winding any of us up. You know, she's got her own wee agenda going on as well.'

'Aye, maybe,' John offered, 'but then again the girl upstairs also swears my Jean has come home one morning at 2.00 a.m. and another morning at breakfast time.'

'Really?' I offered in lieu of nothing else worthwhile.

There was deafening silence.

'One of our Jeans is telling lies, David,' he eventually said.

'Why? Have you asked your Jean about this?' I inquired, going out to make him another cup of tea.

'I'll take something stronger now, David,' he shouted after me as he lit up a Player. 'I mentioned it vaguely, you know – she's spending all of our money buying clothes and all of that. You know, you can dress yourself just as well with words. And then there's all this wearing new make-up and things. I kind of thought that–'

'You know, John,' I said, 'our Jean is a beautiful young lady. She's spent the last five or six years in Jean Kerr's shadow and now, for the first time, thanks to you, she's gaining a bit of independence and starting to stand up as her own person. But you can't expect her to be hiding herself away under a bushel for the next few years while you save up to get married. It's not meant to be a prison sentence, you know; it's meant to be the start of a great adventure together. It's not meant to be about denial, it's meant to be about enjoyment, fulfilment.'

I was surprised at how forthright I'd been, but I found myself thinking about Mary Skeffington and my relationship with her, and not about Jean Simpson and John Harrison for once. The reality was that John had better get his act together and get it together soon or he was going to lose Jean. I still didn't know what she saw in him in the first place. Perhaps it might have been that because he'd been with such a beautiful woman (Mary) he was, in Jean's eyes, a bit of a catch? And so when he'd shown interest in her, she'd jumped at the chance as a way of getting out from behind Jean Kerr's coat-tails? Maybe that was it.

Now that she was free from Jean and she was enjoying her encounters with me, free of any emotional involvement, perhaps she felt she was even outgrowing John Harrison? Better now, I thought, than in three years' time when they'd been married for a year. I saw Jean Simpson as the beautiful body blooming before all of our eyes. Without wishing to be rude, I thought that emotionally she certainly had a bit to go, and she had better address that side of her life before she even started to think about making any lasting commitments. I hope that doesn't all sound a wee bit amateur-hour analyst, but that's what I thought, and her behaviour did seem to fall into that particular pattern.

I also had a wee theory about how Jean Kerr's downfall was directionally proportional to Jean Simpson's rise. But we'll leave that for later.

Needless to say, I didn't take John Harrison into my confidence on either of my thoughts.

'So you think I need to loosen up a bit?'

'Well...' I didn't want to be negative on him.

'Jean Kerr keeps telling me I'm too stiff, that I need to let my hair down,' he spouted, and then he went quiet for a minute.

I felt he had something more to say so I just kept looking at him, saying nothing. It's funny the way that always works, you know, just looking at someone, demanding they speak to you without actually having to say a word. It always seemed to work.

'Jean Kerr actually said to me that I should be a bit more like you.'

Then just before I got a bit too big-headed he continued, 'She also said that you were a waste of space in bed and that the reason she dumped you was not because of the fight at Tiger's but because you were so interested in your music you'd no time whatsoever for girls.'

Thank you Jean Kerr. I owed that girl a couple of Dexy's.

'Well, that's me put in my place John, hasn't it?' I started, smiling as falsely as I knew how. 'You know, I think it's all to do with people who are unsuitable for each other trying to get involved with each other. Case in point – it didn't work out between you and Mary Skeffington, but that doesn't mean that you're a waste of space, does it? It just means that Mary wasn't right for you, and vice versa. You've met Jean and Mary will meet someone as well, I'm sure. She seemed like a very nice girl to me, John. I'm sure it's just that it didn't click with you and her, but I bet you she'll get it together with someone else. And Jean Kerr and me, well, we weren't really made for each other. Yes, it would have helped if we'd both liked the same music, but it was more than that I'm sure. She'll go off and find someone once she's sorted out her illness and of course I'm hopeful of finding someone as well at some time in my life. You know, I might have even met her already. Perhaps I'm just too blind to have noticed it.'

I was trying to give him as many hints as possible about Mary as a potential partner, so that when word got out, it wouldn't be so much of a shock. Tonight, though, he was only listening out for the words concerning him and Jean Simpson; everything else was swishing right over his head. In the future, though, should Mary and I actually get it together, this conversation would replay in his memory and he'd twig what I'd been on about.

John kept looking at his watch then looking back at me.

'So, you also think I should let my hair down. I mean, could you turn me on to some groups? Who does our Jean like? Which of the groups that you've taken her to see did she like the most? Which of your records does she like to listen to?'

Was this a trick question? Judging by his face, it wasn't anything of the sort, so I decided to go with the flow.

'Well, I think she's very partial to the blues. She likes The Spencer Davis Group, John Lee Hooker, Traffic and Otis Redding on record. And she liked Taste live.'

'Sorry, what's her taste live?'

'No, it's a group called Taste – they're from Ireland, we saw them in the Marquee Club once and she loved them. I think they're her favourite live group. They're certainly one of mine.'

'Right,' John said, like I'd just been speaking a foreign language. 'So, do you have any records here that she likes?'

'Yes,' I answered, looking at my wall of albums, 'just a few.'

'Could you play me one of them?' he said, as he looked at his watch again.

'Certainly,' I said, this time unconsciously checking my watch. It was 7.53 p.m.

I found Traffic's Mr. Fantasy and placed it on my record deck. I dusted it with my record cleaner. 'The thing you should know about Traffic is that the lead singer of this group is a chap called Stevie Winwood and he's about twenty years old but he sounds like he might be fifty, and he used to sing in a group called The Spencer Davis Group.'

I put on the record.

He stared at me.

I stared at him.

I hate playing records for unbelievers. It's a bit like people smoking cannabis for the first time: they keep looking at you to see if it's kicked in with you yet, just because it hasn't kicked in with them yet, and then they start to wonder if there's something wrong with them. Yes, there is something wrong with them – they're too uptight!

John Harrison didn't get Traffic, and he didn't get them in a big way. I defy anyone with a soul to listen to 'No Face, No Name and No Number' and not be moved. Stevie Winwood sings this song like his heart is breaking before your ears. He makes you want to cry.

But John Harrison was far from moved. He wasn't in the slightest bit moved. That's a fact, and there's no denying it. How was someone like Jean Simpson going to spend the rest of her life with a person who wouldn't be moved by 'No Face, No Name, No Number'?

There was one more chance for him. I stood up and placed the needle at the start of the final track, 'Dear Mr. Fantasy'. There was still no sign of movement from the sceptic. He kept staring at me, waiting for me to go all funny on him. It wasn't working, all this energy I was spending on him. He really was a hopeless case.

I tried yet another tack.

'The magic thing about Traffic is that they have two amazing singers and songwriters in the one band. The first is Stevie Winwood, the one singing this song; and the second is Dave Mason, and he's also got a brilliant voice and is a good songwriter to boot.'

'To boot what?' John Harrison said, 'what does that mean?'

'It just means "as well",' I said.

John looked at his watch again. It was now 8.03 p.m.

'Is this the music that you and my Jean listen to?'

'Well, we talk about it, and I think one night when the two Jeans were around we played this album. Jean Kerr, she doesn't like any of this stuff. She doesn't even pretend. But your Jean, she's got a good ear for music. She loves her music does your Jean. Did Mary, Mary Skeffington like music, John?'

He surprised me. A large, warm smile came over his face as he said, 'Ah Mary, she loved her classical music. She wasn't a big fan of this pop music but she and her mother used to go to a lot of classical concerts and I also believe they went to the occasional Latin music concerts. Her mother, well now, there's a strange one. She's too independent for her own good, if you ask me. She could be living off her rich boyfriend by now but she insists on holding down her own job. Everyone knows she's loaded. You know I walked away from a fortune there, David? Yes, a fortune, and all for the love of Jean. And then she's accusing me of being a penny-pincher. Humph, I could have been set up for life with the Skeffingtons.'

He looked at his watch again.

'Do you have to be somewhere?' I asked. Then the penny dropped. 'It's Tuesday, of course – you're meeting Jean.'

'No I'm not, David. She blew me out for someone tonight. And to tell you the truth I thought it was you. Jean Kerr said it was you my Jean was going see. She was delirious in Derby but she told me to watch my Jean now that she wasn't going be in London. She said to watch David Buchanan. And I have, David, and I'm convinced that you've been hiding nothing and I'd bet whoever it was she was going to see tonight, it isn't you.'

He set his glass down on the floor and got up to leave. He walked into the kitchen area and doused the butt of his Player under the cold water tap and threw the damp remains in my bin.

'There's something else I should tell you, David. This taste music, I can't stand it, all the Dave Winwood and Stevie Mason and Traffic, what a silly name for a group! But come to think of it, they do sound like a load of vehicles roaring along the road. What an almighty racket!'

And with that he staggered out of my flat into the cold winter night. One glass of wine had him staggering. The boy definitely needed to let his hair down a bit. I do think he felt very good about putting me in my place once and for all about my music.

That wasn't what was troubling me though.

What was troubling me was if Jean Simpson wasn't seeing me and nor was she seeing John Harrison on this particular Tuesday night, who the feck was she seeing?

Chapter Twenty–Six.

I'd like to say that when I received a call the next day from Jean Simpson looking to know if my flatmate was out that night and, if he was, could she see me, that I'd replied 'No, he's not but I'm not really into us messing around any more.' But I said none of the above; in fact, I agreed to see her immediately. Maybe I was intrigued with finding out who she'd been out with the previous night and maybe I was intrigued by the fact that she'd said I could do anything I wanted to her the next time we met. Anything, that was except enter her.

Hang on there, hang on just a minute, David; weren't you meant to be dropping your encounters with Jean and concentrating on Mary now that she had made a commitment to you? Well, yes, I suppose so, but in another way one scene had to end before the other one could begin properly, don't you think? That may all just be justification after the fact because when she rang up, no matter what my brain was thinking I ought to say and do, I heard this familiar voice, which I recognised immediately to be my own, inviting her to come straight on over.

Jean Simpson streamed straight into my flat without saying a word. She was nervous – this was to be my dance after all – but still I'd have to say, for all of that, her nervousness somehow made her even more attractive.

Her experiments with make-up were proving effective. She'd used blood-red lipstick, added a bit of colour in her cheeks and added a few subtle dark colours around her eyes. Her hair was slicked back and held in place with some kind of shiny gel. She stood in the middle of my floor on the very same red carpet where we'd experienced our first encounter no more than a few months previous. In that short time a magical metamorphosis had occurred. This transformation had perhaps taken place at Jean Kerr's cost or perhaps it was always destined to happen no matter what was happening in the other Jean's life.

She allowed me to come up behind her and remove her wine-coloured duffle coat. Was this coat now the only remaining link to the mousy girl from Derby? Who knows? Underneath her favourite coat she was dressed all in black. New black pleated miniskirt, black stockings, black high-heeled shoes and a black satin, clerical-type shirt with a high collar.

I placed her coat over the chair and put on a Dylan record. I knew it wasn't her favourite, but it was mine, and this was to be was my dance after all. She was still standing in the middle of the floor when I returned to her and again I approached her from behind. I couldn't resist putting my hand on the inside of her thigh and running it the whole way up to her stocking tops, where I felt what I knew to be the smoothest skin on her magnificent body. I felt her relax a little as she leaned back against me with just the slightest hint of her weight. I caressed her skin for a few seconds more before pushing my hand further up until it was between her legs. She was already damp.

For one who had led the dance so well she was enjoying not knowing what was going to happen.

Neither of us had spoken since the initial greeting on the doorstep.

I walked around her so that we were facing each other. I removed her shirt and then her miniskirt. She was wearing her usual white underwear. I would have been devastated if she hadn't been. Miss Simpson was staring at me, a hint of apprehension visible in her eyes but at the same time she was willing me on, willing me to take the lead in our dance. I led her over to the bed and lay her down. I brushed her eyelids shut with the palm of my hand. I knelt over her and kissed her eyelids. I pulled her hands up over her head, kissing the full length of her bare arms as I did so. Next I kissed my way down her body, bypassing her glorious breasts, down past her naval and straight to her milky thighs. One by one I removed her stockings, rolling them down very slowly, kissing the newly revealed skin as I went along. I pulled her legs gently apart and gently kissed my way back up her entire body, omitting only her lips. As I was using my lips to caress her I was positively drinking in large dollops of her aromas. I adored the smell of Jean Simpson, she just smelled so darned lusty!

I reached under the bed and pulled out four neckties and tied two of them around her wrists, pulling them to the opposite side of the bed-head. I repeated the process, and completed the sensual X, with her ankles at the bottom of the bed. All the time this she was obediently lying still, her eyes closed. As she felt my weight move up off the bed she opened her eyes and pulled against all her restraints as if testing their strength. She seemed content that she could not free herself.

I sat on the chair opposite her, drinking in every inch of this incredible sight. All her curves, the multitude of little nooks and crannies, which formed this… this perfect body. There is no other way for me to describe the vision for you. Jean Simpson's body was my idea of perfection. She wasn't exactly struggling but she was moving against her restraints and as she did so her breasts would rise to fullness and then her thigh would rise into my view, and then her long neck would strain to rise from the bed to see what I was doing. She'd wriggle her bum to find a more comfortable position and that sensual action would nearly be enough for me – she nearly got me with her every move. The thing that I keep going back to about Jean Simpson, and perhaps the single biggest turn-on for me, was the fact that she never once acted brazen or flaunted herself in anyway. Her tentativeness was, to me, a large part of her charm.

I slowly removed my clothes, not slowly in an exhibitionist kind of way, but more so that I could continue to feast my eyes on the sight before me.

Just then Dylan's 'She Belongs To Me' gently caressed the speakers of my stereo system, his distinctive, compelling, talk-along voice singing:

She's got everything she needs. She's an artist, she don't look back.
She's got everything she needs. She's an artist, she don't look back.
She can take the dark out of the night-time and paint the daytime black.

I swear to you Dylan was singing about Jean Simpson. She was an artist, and her art was sex. She was never more the complete artist than she was that night, as she lay restrained, reticent, tempting and exquisite upon my bed.

All my clothes removed, I lay beside her and caressed every part of her body. She moaned gently. She was wriggling quite a bit now, encouraging me by her movements to where she wanted to be caressed. When I touched between her legs she did as best she could to pull her legs together to trap my hand there. No further encouragement needed, I continued to explore her softness. I was now kneeling between her knees and started to kiss her softness as well.

It was all too much for her and after a few seconds she screamed, 'You got me! Oh, did you get me!'

These had been the first words spoken between us since she'd entered the room.

She examined me up and down as she recovered and relaxed into a more normal breathing pattern. Her eyes widened as they focused on my midriff, or somewhere thereabouts.

'Oh my goodness, David you'd better kneel above my head and lean over me, quickly,' she ordered. It was my dance, and of course I could have said no. I didn't. I did as she bid, and she took me in her mouth, and it was so sensational, she got me immediately.

We lay there for several minutes. Me beside her, she still restrained and not asking to be untied. I caressed her breasts this time and she was so responsive that I was in the same instant responsiveness again. I lay on top of her and we started to grind against each other.

'Agh, this isn't fair,' she whispered breathlessly, 'I can't feel you properly. I need to feel you close to me, David.'

All the time she was saying this she was rising to me and falling away from me. I have to admit, in my mind's eye, the vision of her in her bra and pants was much more appealing than her completely unclothed. I was happy to continue as we were, so I did. It was my dance after all.

'David, I can't feel you – I need to feel you next to me, please!'

'I'd have to untie you first,' I said, resisting and offering the first excuse I could think of.

'Tear them off, flippin' rip them off! Oh please, David!'

I pulled feebly at her pants. The cotton wouldn't give. So I worked out a compromise; I pulled her pants down as close to her knees as possible. But now they were digging into her skin and making her uncomfortable.

'Take them off completely,' she pleaded in a whisper.

I tried again to get them to give and couldn't, so I made to undo one of the ties on her leg.

'No, no, don't untie me! This is too delicious. Get some scissors or a knife, David. Yes, David… get a knife.'

So I did, and I cut her pants on the thin sides so I could pull them off her. I was about to lie on her again when she asked me to do the same with her bra. So I did, and now there was nothing, absolutely nothing between us. Very soon we were comfortable again and I was lying between her legs and I was using what's referred to in the dictionary as 'an instrument of copulation' to touch her. I wondered, what was the dictionary term for what we were doing? As per my promise, I never entered her – just touched her, and daringly caressed her. Her eyebrows would rise when we got a little bit close. Eventually she seemed to stop thinking about it and just started to follow her pleasure, and so I followed mine, and very soon we got each other and it was the best it had ever been. We both told each other this, our bodies completely covered in sweat. We'd no reason to lie.

I untied her and as I did so I kissed where the ties had marked her skin.

She sat up in the bed and started to rub her wrists. 'You dear, dear boy, you. That was just the best,' she eventually said, in a near hoarse voice, 'I can't remember a time I ever felt as thrilled or as excited as that. It was painful for me in that you had control over me and you had the power to keep this liaison going between us, because if you had entered me, you'd have most certainly ended everything. But the fact that it was so close and you had the power to ride me, but didn't, well, that just made it all so flippin' unbearable. You could have entered me at any time and you didn't. The fact that you didn't means that we can continue doing this, this thing that we do to each other, forever. I mean that. Nothing or no one will ever change that, ever! Feel me, feel how every part of my body is just buzzing. We can keep doing this just as long as we never consummate a fully physical relationship.'

I mean, I really had no response to that. What was I meant to say to her? Did she really expect me to say that no matter who I might be with in the future, Mary Skeffington or otherwise, I would still be up for our encounters? Did she believe that I would? Did she even believe it when she said it herself?

I did what most people who like to eat their cake and keep it too do; I went to make a cup of tea as Jean Simpson started to try to fix her bra by tying the straps together. By the time I'd returned with the tea she'd succeeded and was pulling on what was now becoming her regular spare pair of pants. She omitted her stockings, shirt and skirt and just put on her duffle coat as she enjoyed her tea.

'You know John came around to see me last night?' I said, as I put on a new record, Spooky Tooth's, It's All About.

She ignored my statement, choosing instead to focus on the music. 'I don't think I'll ever be negative on a Dylan record again,' she said, breaking into a grin, 'particularly that Dylan record.'

'John thinks you're cheating on him,' I continued on my original line, if only to warn her of the conversation we'd had. And then I insisted on telling her everything that had happened the previous evening. 'He only left,' I concluded, 'when he'd convinced himself that I wasn't meant to be seeing you myself.'

'Oh, he's getting to be such a flippin' bore,' she said with a sigh.

'So where were you yesterday evening?'

'Oh, it's all getting so complicated, David,' she said, wrapping her duffle coat tighter around her. 'Why can't it all be so simple, like this? Why can't we just lock the door and throw away the key and do naughty things to each other forever?'

'Because then I'd be the next one to be a bore,' I offered, with a hike of my shoulders.

'Oh no,' she protested, 'not if you're going to dream up little treats like that for me every night.'

I didn't bother to protest and tell her that she'd now received my entire bag of tricks – she clearly wasn't in the mood for that reality on that particular evening, so we dropped the topic and about ten minutes later got back to a much safer subject: pleasuring each other.

It wasn't as great as the one we'd just experienced but then it's always the averages that make the peaks the peaks.

Chapter Twenty-Seven.

Refreshingly my relationship with Mary Skeffington was somewhat less complicated and, it has to be said, all the more rewarding for it. I hope that doesn't sound disrespectful to Jean Simpson, or even Jean Kerr for that matter, because it's not meant to. It's just, as I've said before, Mary came along at a time in my life when I was least expecting her to. You know, you're always wary when you see friends and relations and their wives or girlfriends arguing and you just think what's the point? If they obviously dislike each other as much as they appear to, then why are they spending even a day together let alone potentially the rest of their lives?

One of the things I've never been able to come to grips with is husbands and wives, or even boyfriends and girlfriends, belittling each other in public. It shows neither of them in a good light. It's like advertising their mistakes and flaws in the most effectively public way possible. I'll let you into a little secret here. The reason I'm considered to be a romantic, I suppose the reason I'm happy to be a romantic, is because I buy into all of that happily ever after stuff. Equally, and because of that, I felt that it would take me a considerable number of years and a bit of living before I either met the right person or knew what to do about it.

I've always thought the biggest mistake I could make in my life was to have a failed marriage. I don't know why I shared that with you. I don't really know why I thought that. It might have something to do with the fact that my parents are enjoying a great marriage. Notice I didn't say there 'enjoying the perfect marriage'. Another recipe for a potential disaster is to think that you are in the middle of the perfect marriage. You're only tempting fate. But back to my parents for a minute, the reason I feel their marriage is so good is that they met and felt they were right for each other and embarked on the wonderful adventure of sharing the rest of their lives together. Now, they may have been lucky in that at the time they met, breaking up, separating or getting a divorce was never considered to be an option. Come good or bad, for either or both of them, it didn't matter: they had committed to be together for life. When troubles came along, and I'm sure troubles did, they would work their way through them. But, and here's another important bit for me, neither of them worked it out in front of either my sister or me. I'm sure it wasn't always a bed of roses, but as far as we were concerned there was that major bit of stability: our parents were a team for life and were always there for us.

I suppose in a way I did know why I told you all of the above; when I met Mary Skeffington and it seemed we might have a chance, a chance of making it work well, all of the above was a constant backdrop in my mind.

Equally, I know I could be accused of setting a bit of a double standard here. You know, at the same time as I was embarking on my dream romance with Mary Skeffington, I was helping to wreck another potential marriage between Jean Simpson and John Harrison. But it's not quite as simple as that, is it?

'Oh it's not, is it not?' I hear the gallery shout.

Well, actually no, it's not.

Chronologically speaking, I met Jean Simpson first. Jean Simpson and John Harrison were going to suffer their problems whether I was a catalyst or not. If it hadn't have been me then it most certainly would have been someone else. Not very flattering for me I know, but nonetheless a fact. The more serious Mary Skeffington and I grew, the more I resolved that I would have to stop seeing Jean Simpson.

'There, you knew it was wrong!' I hear you shout, 'Otherwise why would you feel the need to stop the encounters with Jean Simpson if you weren't doing anything wrong?'

Okay, good point.

At a time in all our lives, we're preoccupied with sex. In my particular case, I will admit I was totally preoccupied with it. That particular time in my life was the time I knew Jean Simpson. And the same applied for Jean Simpson, I'm sure, hence the reason for our encounters and experiments. Now, where we differed was that Jean was happy for us to continue our encounters, she claimed, just as long as I didn't consummate the physical relationship, even potentially (I have to believe after what she'd said the other night) after she and John Harrison had married.

Are you with me so far? Good.

Now, Mary Skeffington was, I believe, trying to decide what her true feelings were for me. Up to now, you could hardly say that we were boyfriend and girlfriend, so you could hardly imply that I was cheating on her with Jean Simpson.

I hadn't even kissed Jean Simpson, for heaven's sake!

Anyway, it's time I got back to the story and told you what happened next.

As you know, I saw John Harrison on Tuesday night. I saw Jean Simpson on Wednesday night. I went to the Marquee Club on Thursday night by myself to see The Nice (they were very nice, in fact). I suppose apart from anything else I wanted to be out of the flat in case anyone else felt like popping around. Friday night I went to Mary's for dinner. I spruced myself up, trimmed my moustache and bought a good bottle of wine on the way. Things got off to a great start when Mary greeted me with a long kiss on her doorstep.

Mary was a more confident dresser than either of the two Jeans. Jean Kerr dressed in a wannabe glamorous style, very forced, pretty expensive and a wee bit too mismatched for my liking. Jean Simpson was literally just finding her legs and loved to show them off. She left the eye-catching to the quality of her legs, and not to the quality or class of her clothes – her clothes complemented her rather than helped to create her, if you know what I mean. Mary Skeffington, on the other hand, dressed classy and casual, yet she was always elegant, very elegant – like, you never felt it was a show or a statement.

For instance, on the evening in question she wore an ankle-length dress with a high neck and no sleeves. It was a deep blue and, to my eyes, worked brilliantly with her blonde hair, which she'd done up from her usual Cathy McGowan style. The fringe remained, though. Her skin was clear and benefited from only hints of make-up. Mary Skeffington's mid-lips were parted, she looked happy, if slightly frail, as she whisked around the room, her free-flowing dress betraying the rich contours of her body, a body I longed to hold as close as I had during our night in Bath. You see, that was another important thing for me, I would be happy just to lie with her again, you know, holding her close like we'd done on that night.

The more I watched her happily going about her cooking rituals the more choked up I became. Up to that moment I had been happy to leave events up to her. If she decided that she wanted to give it a try, I would be happy, but if she'd decided that she'd mistaken her emotions and wanted to let it pass, to let this pass, well, then I'd have been content to move on as well. But at that exact moment, the moment I studied her fighting to return a few strands of her blonde hair back to the top of her head while adding flour to a bowl, and brushing some from her cheek with flour-coated fingers, well, I knew I couldn't just let her go, would not let her go.

I felt a resolve to fight for this relationship.

'Mary,' I called out, almost involuntarily, 'I need you to know that I need you.'

'My hands are full, David,' she replied, playfully.

I went over to her and rubbed her back as she regained control of her various tasks.

'I just meant,' I started to say and was surprised to find that my voice was barely above a whisper, 'I need you to know how much you mean to me.'

I hadn't planned to say that, it just came out. I wondered if it had anything to do with the fact that I had resolved not to see Jean Simpson again.

'I know, David,' she replied, turning to face me, 'I've seen it in those green eyes of yours.'

I forced a smile.

'I just feel this force pulling us together,' she continued, brushing my nose with her floury hands. 'It feels strong to me, like everything is meant to be this way. I'm sorry it's taken some time for me to accept it. I hoped it wouldn't scare you off or, worse, away for good. I just felt it was important–'

'It was,' I offered, I suppose to try to let her know I understood. 'If you went into this doubting your reasons it would never have worked. It was better this way.'

She grabbed me and pulled me towards her and hugged me. We both clung on to each other as if our lives depended on it. On reflection perhaps, they did.

I pulled back from her and looked at her face. Her wisp of hair had broken free again. This time I tried to replace it but after a few unsuccessful attempts I decided that she looked better with it hanging freely anyway. She took her towel and brushed the flour from my face, then she used the same towel to shoe me over to the sofa and away from her cooking castle. My turn in the kitchen was later, with the dirty dishes.

About thirty minutes later we were eating chicken in a mushroom sauce with potato gratin – a personal favourite – and a few vegetables. All washed down with a nice, crisp and dry Chablis. We talked about everything under the sun – nothing important and nothing unimportant – and we laughed a lot. We had released all of our reservations and were now getting to know each other, and enjoying doing so.

She was very proud of her mum and of how well she had done for her. Mary Skeffington was the first person I'd met in my life that was ambitious. I don't mean she was ambitious in terms of longing for a successful career or enjoying financial rewards. She was ambitious because she wanted to enjoy a fulfilling life. Her career, her money and her home were only a very small part of this. The major part for her was to be in a successful relationship and to build on everything from there. As you know, I believed that neither of the Skeffington women would be a slave to their work, or their money. I just hadn't come up with an alternate priority. She had, and she said it was thanks to her mother.

We cleared away the dishes – mine for later. I retuned her radio once again to Radio Caroline just in time to hear Dylan's 'Just Like A Woman', and if I'd requested it myself I couldn't have picked a more apt song. I particularly found myself focusing in on the line:

And she makes love just like a woman.

And then, and this is true, this is exactly how it happened, Mary rose up from the sofa, took me by the hand and led me into her bedroom.

And we made love.

It's important that you know and accept that that is exactly what we did. We made love. It's not important to describe here how we did so; love-making is precious and private. But it's very important that you know that is exactly what we did. There was one point that maybe I should mention, though: I have never seen anyone look so glorious, soulful, spiritual or beautiful as when I stole a glance at Mary Skeffington during our love-making. She was in that state, like she was midway between Heaven and Earth. She was lost in the celebration of her and her partner's pleasure. Her hair was a mess, which made her look wild. Her eyes were lightly closed; the middle third of her lips was slightly apart, as ever; her face was slightly flushed, coated in a fine film of sweat, which testified to the sheer physicality required to achieve our joint bliss. But you know what? In that moment, that very moment, I was so overcome by the enormity of the whole picture, really… of the vision of Mary Skeffington and the light and the angles of her long, slender, elegant and sensual neck… it was enough to make one believe in a God or some special creator, to make me believe in something capable of creating an image so inspiring, so exotic, and yet so pure.

We made love.

We declared our love for each other and by our actions and reactions and feelings and deeds and words, I believe we formed a bond that evening that could never be broken for as long as we both should live.

It was as simple and as complicated as that.

Mary said, 'I just knew that first night, the night I cooked you dinner for the first time, you remember; the time you massaged my feet and neck and then the things you did with my ears? I mean, you turned me on then more than I'd even been turned on in my life, and you didn't even know that you were doing it. I knew then, David, just how brilliant this was going to be. And then that night in Bath; that meant so much to me. I really did need for you to hold me, just to hold me, and that was enough for you. It was like you could have been behaving like a gentleman but at the same time there could have been this slight feeling of regret from you as to what didn't happen. But there wasn't, not even in the slightest – it was as though you were just as happy as I was to lie that way as well.

'I was,' I replied, 'I was totally happy.'

'I lay awake most of that night in Bath,' she said, and paused again, perhaps so that she could re-live the memory. 'The feeling was so potent and so strong that I just didn't want to waste any of it by sleeping. For the first minutes, maybe even as much as half an hour, I felt that you would turn over and start to kiss me and want to make love, and I wouldn't have resisted, I couldn't have resisted. Yet I just preferred that we didn't do it then, and you instinctively seemed to know that.'

It wasn't a great big decision for me, you know – 'will I, won't I?' It just wasn't... I mean, I'd just felt... waiting was important and it was. Because that night in her flat after Dylan, well, it was how you dream it should be, it was how you dream you should feel. It's not even that; the intensity of the feeling was really so much more than that. It was perfect. I didn't even want to try to put it into words for her there, that night. It's not even important who did what to whom and how, and how many times this, that, or the other thing happened. The course of the whole series of events and feelings and actions all added up to those three magical little words.

We made love.

And the whole point was that if we'd had sex before we'd made love, it would have been wrong and we could have ruined it. Don't you see that's how close we all are in our lives to getting things wrong? Wrong is never always at the completely opposite end of the scale to right. It's just they are so close sometimes you can't even see the join. Hey, maybe there isn't even a join; maybe they're the same thing in the end. But when you discover that there is a possibility you might, just might, really click, you realise how absolutely important it is to hold out and get it right.

And that was the start of Mary Skeffington and me.

Chapter Twenty-Eight.

Have you ever wondered what happens in the movies just after the end credits roll and they're all meant to go off and live happily ever after? You know, boy meets girl, boy loses girl, boy goes through the wars of life, comes out of his battles a better person, returns to the girl, girl looks at the boy with different eyes, boy wins girl back again and in the dying seconds of the movie you see them drive off into the sunset? Have you ever wondered what happens when the screen goes to black?

I have.

That's the film I'd really like to see. This film would start with our loving couple waking up the following morning and then they would get into it from there. Yes, our male hero did know how to look after himself in all those battles, and yes he does cut a mean silhouette against the orange sundown, but then he opens his mouth and he sounds more like Michael Crawford in Some Mothers Do 'Ave 'Em than Clint Eastwood in Dirty Harry. Not only that, but he starts to talk about horses or cars or his top ten rodeos or the top ten acres, and if his talking doesn't drive her to distraction, the combination of his bad breath and yellow teeth might. And then our lucky lady, our heroine, perhaps she's got nothing at all to say the following day. Perhaps her role has just been to sit and look pretty for the camera, and he discovers she's as deep as the cardboard cutout that represents her in the cinema foyer. Yes, that's when the real story really starts.

I moved in to the Gladstone Road flat with Mary a couple of weeks later. We didn't labour over the decision, we just did it. Neither did we talk in detail about marriage; we just knew that we would marry. Her mother knew that we would eventually (Hermione's word and pronounced – like her daughter – in italics) and she seemed totally fine with us living together. Although, having said that, every time we visited her, she'd always make up two rooms for us – she'd never insist we use them, but she'd always have them made up.

The next time Jean Simpson rang it was the middle of the week before I moved in with Mary, I think. I told her simply and honestly that I wouldn't be up for any more encounters, as I had started to see a girl. I told her that 'Yes, it is serious' and 'No, it wouldn't be a good idea for us to go to the Marquee Club together any more.'

She sounded shocked, as in dumbfounded, at the other end of the phone. I mean, it was probably down to the contrast. She came on the line so positive and the call ended with her being as down as I'd ever heard her, and I felt totally responsible for that and guilty for the same. It was such a horrible feeling. It's at times like these when you realise why some people avoid break-ups; there's nearly nothing you wouldn't do to avoid making someone feel as bad as that.

No, I didn't tell her that the girl I was serious about was the very same Mary Skeffington she'd stolen John Harrison from.

Why didn't I?

Good question. I suppose the honest answer was I just couldn't bring myself to do so. Maybe I was just scared or maybe I didn't want to hurt her any more than I already had. Or perhaps I was, pure and simple, just scared she would tell Mary Skeffington about our encounters. It appeared Miss Simpson had already taken the trouble to map out our next one. Either way I figured that she and John and the other Jean, for that matter, would find out through the grapevine about Mary Skeffington and I, and when she, Jean Simpson, did, she'd surely come to the conclusion that it'd be much better that all parties involved ceased communications.

Did I really think that was the case? I don't know. I was too up on my relationship with Mary Skeffington to give it too much consideration to be honest. Was I guilty of wanting some time to pass so that the lines between: (a) Mary Skeffington saying she wanted to try to make it work with me; (b) Jean Simpson and I having our final encounter; (c) Mary and I having our memorable dinner and making love for the first time; and (d) Mary and I moving in together, became clearer? Of course I was, but maybe only subconsciously. Even if I wasn't admitting it to myself, I was certainly aware that if I could just put some time between those four monumental events and people catching on to the fact that Mary and I were a couple, I could certainly avoid some awkward questions. In my defence, I will say that after Mary and I made love for the first time, I never for one second considered another encounter with Jean Simpson.

But, as I say, I did keep my head down and willed the time to pass.

And then before I knew it, some time had passed, possibly as much as six weeks, and I'd heard nothing directly or indirectly from that camp, and you know what they say about sleeping dogs? Let them lie. Yes. Oh how I wished the sleeping dogs had been allowed to lie.

Why?

Because exactly seven weeks to the day after Mary and I made love for the first time, I received a telephone call from a very agitated John Harrison.

'I don't know exactly what's going on,' he wheezed down the line, 'but I felt you should know that one of our Jeans is missing!'

PART THREE

AFTER

Chapter Twenty-Nine.

You know when you hear something – it could be bad, it could even be good, or, it could be nothing – but you invariably always immediately start to think the worst? Well, that's what John Harrison's declaration did to me.

I felt physically sick in the very centre of the pit of my stomach.

The scene of my meeting Jean & Jean for the first time in the residents' lounge, in the Wimbledon hostel, flashed into my mind. Very melodramatic, I know, but I was overcome by what we'd all been through, separately and in our various duos, trios and later, with John Harrison and Mary Skeffington on the scene, quartets and quintet.

Then I started to think 'Poor Jean Kerr.'

She'd obviously let all of her problems with her boss, her work, her romantic life, her illness get the better of her. Maybe she'd run off somewhere and taken her life. I wondered who would discover her body and in what state it would be.

I admit I felt guilty, very guilty. I tried (alas in vain) to convince myself that it had nothing whatsoever to do with me. Yes, she had led the way through our brief relationship-of-sorts. But I could have very easily said no at any time. But I didn't; I just went with the flow, no matter how much I claimed it to be an unpleasant experience. I should have said no the first time, and if not the first time then most definitely the second time, and double that for the third time. First time, shame on her; second time, shame on me; third time, an even bigger shame on me.

Then I thought that Jean Simpson must be beside herself with worry and, like myself, fearing the worst. They'd been friends for fifteen years and though it had certainly been rocky lately, they were still each other's nominated best friend.

My mind flew off on another tangent: if Jean Kerr really was missing then there had to be a chance she'd been murdered. You immediately chastise yourself for entertaining such thoughts though, don't you? You know, fearing the very worst. But then, statistically speaking, there must be similar occasions when people fear the same worst only to discover that their fears were founded.

Jean Simpson must have also been having that thought, and probably at that exact moment.

'How's your Jean reacting to this news, John?' I asked, voicing the words fresh in my mind.

He'd been muttering away in the background, mostly to himself, I thought, as I was living through my worst nightmares.

'David,' he shouted down the phone at the top of his voice, 'you haven't been listening to a word I've said! I'm not talking about Jean Kerr. I'm talking about my Jean. It's my Jean who's gone missing!

Good God, Jean Simpson! I instantly had this flash of her lying across a bed somewhere, dressed in her undies, as she had been during our last encounter. Of course, I should have said there during our final encounter. I didn't recognise the location in my vision and I suppose she could have been sleeping, but she seemed quite lifeless to me. I remember reflecting on how great her legs looked for a split second longer than I should have. My next thought was of the two Jeans together, the simple solution to the mystery being that Jean Simpson was up in Derby, cajoling Jean Kerr into getting her life back on the rails. I figured that the latter was the more likely of the two scenarios.

Not that John Harrison seemed unduly concerned. That just might have been a performance for me, of course; you know, trying to appear casual in case I was going to say something like, 'Oh, didn't you know that Mary and I are shacked up together?' Totally bizarre I know, but these were the things floating through my mind. Those facts I eventually did manage to garner from John were: 1) He hadn't seen Jean Simpson for a going on a week; 2) She wasn't at her flat; and 3) The girls in the flat above them hadn't seen her for going on a week, either. And in response to John's phone call, Jean Kerr assured John that his Jean wasn't in Derby; in fact, just that very day, Miss Kerr had visited Miss Simpson's family home.

That was about it.

Except it wasn't.

Except it was troubling me.

Okay, as I saw it, the Top Five things that could have happened to Miss Simpson were:

1. She'd got bored with John – she'd predicted just as much last time we met – and she'd returned to Derby and had sworn Jean Kerr to secrecy.
2. She was still in London, also hiding out from John Harrison.
3. She'd had an accident.
4. Someone had done her harm.
5. She'd found a replacement for me in her adventures. We know for a fact there was that one night where she wasn't with either me or John.

Yes, the whole thing troubled me and it troubled me because, if something had happened to her, had it happened because I'd stopped seeing her? Had she gone to ground to regroup, commence planning her attack on Mary and I? If Mary ever found out what Jean and I had been up to, surely it would signal the end of our relationship. So could the reason behind Jean's disappearance be as simple as getting me to sweat a bit?

But what about an accident? I'd forgotten to ask John if he'd checked with all the hospitals in the district. I hadn't forgotten to ask him if he'd checked with the police – he hadn't – I'd just forgotten to ask him about the hospitals, and he just hadn't offered. I was going to start making a few calls myself, but then I thought I would wait until Mary came home. She was at night class in Twickenham and I wiled away the hours (two) trying to read (impossible), trying to listen to music (even more impossible) and eventually spending the time walking around her flat (yes, I still referred to it as her flat even though I was living there now) thinking about what could have happened, fearing the worst.

My heart leapt up to my throat as I heard her key in the door.

'God, you're white as a sheet, David!' she said, as she dropped her bags to the floor and ran over to me. 'What's happened?'

'John Harrison rang two hours ago.'

'Oh?' she said, and meant it.

'Jean Simpson has gone missing.'

'Oh!'

'And there's more,' I said, hearing a faltering in my voice, 'there's something else I need to tell you.'

'Oh?' she said raising her eyebrows.

'Well, I should have told you this before, and I would have! I mean, there's no reason not to have told you, only that I hadn't told you and the longer I hadn't told you the harder it was to tell you.'

'Oh?' she coaxed. I could tell by the look in her eyes that she wasn't sure she wanted to hear what it was that I was having such great difficulty telling her.

I started several different ways, and all of them sounded terrible to me, so in the end I just went with: 'First off, nothing has happened since you and I started going out together. But I had a bit of a relationship with Jean.'

'You fool' she said, visibly relaxing, 'of course you told me that! You told me that you and Jean Kerr had had a bit of a fling when the Jeans moved into the hostel.'

'Ah. No. I mean, yes, I did tell you that, but what I hadn't told you was that I'd also had a bit of a relationship with the other Jean.'

'What!' she began, a bemused but cautious look creeping across her face, 'you mean John's Jean – Jean Simpson?'

I nodded.

She took my hand and pulled me over to the sofa, leaving her bags still standing by the open hall door.

'Okay, you had a scene with both the Jeans. Both before you met me. That's fine, I went out with John Harrison – you know I went to bed with him. I don't see where your concern is coming from. Did you date her after you'd finished with the first Jean and before the second Jean had started with John? Goodness, with all these Jeans this is all starting to get incredibly confusing.'

I knew she'd said that as a comfort to me. I knew she was not one bit confused by any of this. You'll have also noticed that I let one little bit of inaccurate information go uncorrected in her last statement. She'd said, when referring to my relationships with the Jeans that they had been: 'Both before you met me'. Technically speaking, that was not strictly true, as you well know. I returned to my mother's words of advice when I was much younger: 'Be careful because your lies will find you out.' I wasn't actually lying, but maybe I was being somewhat economical with the truth.

'Not exactly,' I continued.

'Okay, I think you'd better explain. But can I just say, that from what you've just told me, you'd stopped seeing her when you started seeing me. In which case, we have nothing to worry about.'

You see, that sentence right there showed how generous Mary Skeffington was. She hadn't said, 'In which case you have nothing to worry about.' She'd said, 'In which case we have nothing to worry about.' We were a team and we were in this together.

However, just in case I was in any doubt as to whether or not she would follow me blindly while chasing a pack of lies, she then asked me, quite firmly and looking deep into my eyes without letting go of my hands, 'You haven't being seeing her since we started going out together, have you David?'

'No,' I said, emphatically shaking my head.

'So what's your concern then?'

'I was seeing her when she was dating John.'

'Oh,' she said blowing the 'oh' out to a full block-bursting word, 'I see. She was seeing you behind John's back. Omigoodness! Were you sleeping with her?'

'No! Just… messing around,' I admitted allowing myself, I suppose, a very liberal interpretation of the phrase 'messing around'.

'How long did this go on?'

'Until you and I started going out together. Then I stopped it immediately.'

'And was this a regular thing or what?'

'I took her out to the clubs, you know, to see some of the groups. We sometimes went back to her flat or my flat and… messed around. That was it.'

'Define "messing around", David.'

'We never had sex, we never kissed; we just messed around. There was no love mentioned or even considered. She was going to marry John but she just wanted to have a bit of fun. I wasn't seeing anybody, I was up for a bit of fun as well; I suppose we were just using each other.'

'I believe it's referred to as dry humping,' she said, very matter of fact.

Only someone like Mary Skeffington would have a word to describe what Jean Simpson and I had been up to. And here I was thinking we'd invented it.

'The pair of you sound just like Mrs Wallis and Jimmy Donahue,' she said, smiling for the first time since she'd sat down. I noticed a bit of the colour return to her cheeks.

'Sorry?' I asked. That one had gone completely over my head.

'Oh, it's not important, I'll tell you another time,' she replied, dropping her smile and getting serious again. 'Look. When you and I started going out and you told Jean that you didn't want to see her any more, did you tell her it was because of me?'

'No, I didn't. I told her I was very serious about someone. I didn't particularly want the two Jeans and John running around behind our backs, gossiping about us.'

'But she would have found out.'

'I'd say for sure that she's found out,' I replied.

'And now she's missing,' Mary sighed. She walked over, closed the door and brought her bags into the flat, as I replied,

'And now she's missing.'

'So what are you going to do about it?'

'Well, the first thing I wanted to do was to tell you about her, about us. I mean, John said that no one had officially told the police yet because everyone was expecting her to turn up at some point,' I said, at the same time thinking what should we do next?

'So all the time you were seeing her, what was she saying about her relationship with John for heaven's sake?'

'Well, she kind of compartmentalised it. She was still going to marry him, and she always made it clear she was just messing around with me.'

'It all sounds frightfully simple when you say it like that, David,' she said.

She'd stopped unpacking her bags and was standing, mid-job, staring at me. I couldn't quite make out her stare. It worried me slightly to be honest.

'Well, in a way it was – like I said, we were only messing about. I mean, it was definitely never anything serious,' I offered, in hopes that she wouldn't play my bluff and say, 'Define messing about more exactly?'

'That's all very well for you and Jean but what would John have said if he'd found out that you were dry humping his wife-to-be? How would you feel if I was messing about with someone else?'

'That's different, Mary,' I complained. I could see where this was going and whereas I had escaped one trap, I'd walked straight into another.

'Oh yes? And how so, David?'

'Okay. Number one, we're in love. Number two, we're not in a part-time, two-nights-a-week relationship. Number three, we're totally involved in each other's lives. Number four, we care about each other. Number five, we're not saving for John Harrison's future. Number six, you're not saving yourself for when we get married. Number seven, I'm not trying to avoid at all costs having a child. Number eight, you don't have a mad friend called Jean Kerr. Number nine, we have a full physical relationship and number ten, and this one's worth repeating, because it's the most important, I'm in love with you. I've never been so sure about anything in my life.'

Mary Skeffington softened a bit at that, though I decided not to bask in my newfound glory and pushed on. For some reason unknown to me, I found myself rubbing my neck with the fingers of my right hand. 'It's because of that and how I feel about us, that I wanted to tell you everything. When John rang about Jean, there was a split second when I had this terrible flash that something awful had happened to her. Hopefully it hasn't. Hopefully she's fine and she's just been off having fun with someone else. But I thought that if something bad had happened to her, then all of her past was going to be examined carefully and then I'd be questioned, and in the middle of it all, the details of our relationship, if you could call it that, would come out. Now, although all this happened before you and I came together, I felt it appropriate that I tell you everything.'

'David, would you have ever told me if Jean hadn't gone missing?'

'Yes, I can honestly say that most likely I would have. There was no reason not to, really. I suppose because of all the things that happened between you and John, and John and Jean, that although there was no reason not to tell you, equally, there really was no reason to tell you if all it was going to do was hurt you. I saw this situation developing in my mind's eye where I kept delaying telling you, waiting for the right moment, and the right moment never came along, and now Jean's disappeared and it would've been too late to tell you because it all would have blown up in my face.'

'In our faces, David, in our faces. I'm glad you told me,' she said, as she came over and kissed me and ruffled my hair playfully like she does when she's happy with me. She stopped mid-ruffle. 'Goodness David, I've just thought. Do you think it's possible that John found out that you and Jean were messing about and he... killed her? No, no, of course not, that's just too silly. I know him. Augh,' she shrugged and shivered violently at the thought, 'that's just too weird. I've slept with him. Augh, I can't even think about that!'

Chapter Thirty.

And there we dropped the conversation. It was an interesting thought though, wasn't it? Let's take a murderer, any murderer. For the sake of this discussion, let's assume our murderer is male. Now there are people in our murderer's life, who will have had a normal relationship with him – friends, lovers, wives, girlfriends, parents, brothers, sisters, will all have had a normal relationship with our murderer. Just because he's murdered once, doesn't necessarily mean that he'll murder again or that all of the people in this list are in mortal danger.

But Jean hadn't been murdered, had she? She'd just found someone else to enjoy encounters with. Good luck to her. Good luck to him. They were probably off somewhere, each busy dreaming up games for the following day's entertainment. What about the other twenty-one hours in the day? If Jean Simpson sat around in her honest-to-goodness underwear all day, day after day, it would surely cease to be a turn-on; because surely the reason it's a turn-on in the first place is that you're stealing glimpses of something you're not really supposed to see. By doing what we'd done, she had actually gone as far as physically joining me in my fantasy of her; she had encouraged me to live out my fantasy of her with her.

And that was fine to a point, but surely it would have worn a bit thin when we started to repeat ourselves? There needs to be something other than mere lust to maintain human attraction. Boredom will most definitely set in with any routine.

That's why one of the things I loved about Mary Skeffington was that she kept our physical relationship fresh by avoiding routine. When we went to bed at night, I didn't know whether we were going to make love or not. In other words, just because we were in bed, didn't mean we were going to make love. It was never guaranteed. You see, certain things have to be correct; a relationship is not a prison sentence, where one partner has to submit to the other's whims. When you're not in a relationship, it has to be special before the love-making situation arises, so why should it be any different when you are in a relationship? If anything, I would've thought it's more important to make it even more special in that case. And so it was with Mary and me. She kept the mystery, the intrigue, as it were, alive, so that when we made love it wasn't a mere physical function in reply to our animal urges. Because if you want to think about it, it's a pretty basic act really, isn't it? Yes, and it will continue to be so unless you put a bit of romance and a lot of love into it.

Jean Simpson was going down that road very quickly. Our encounters really finished at the perfect time. We hadn't been doing it long enough to repeat ourselves and it was still a buzz every time. And that is why I can report to you – and this is no disrespect to Jean – that it wasn't difficult to stop the relationship with her. I can honestly say I didn't have one pang of regret, not even the slightest. Well apart, that is, from the guilt of making her feel so bad. On the other hand, as you know, if anything should have happened to Mary Skeffington and I, well I'd have been devastated, truly I would.

I held on to that heart-warming thought. In fact, all my thoughts turned to Mary and I forgot all about Jean for a time.

A week later, we hadn't heard anything else on the Jean matter so, prompted by Mary, I called John.

Still no word from Jean Simpson.

And John definitely seemed more concerned than the previous time we'd spoken. So you'd think he'd have reported the matter to the police by now? Well, you'd think wrong – he still hadn't.

'What? Isn't Jean's mother beside herself with worry?' Mary asked me when I came off the phone.

'I don't know. I suppose when people first leave home to begin their lives, it's very hard for the parents. They're probably desperate to find out how their kids are doing every hour, on the hour, but they bite their lip and stay in the background so that they don't appear to be fussing, for fear that the child will react further by cutting them out of their lives entirely.'

Mary thought for a few moments, then said, 'I spoke to my mother yesterday. When did you last speak to yours?'

'Over the weekend.'

'How long has Jean been missing now?'

'Must be coming up to two weeks,' I estimated.

'I think you should ring her mum. I think you should ring Jean Kerr. I think you should check this out and if you can't find out where Jean is, then either you or one of them should inform the police.'

'Isn't that overreacting?'

'Perhaps. But it's better to overreact than not to react at all. I can't believe that John Harrison is not out searching the streets at this moment!'

So I did as I was bid. Well you do, don't you, particularly when you know it's the right thing to do.

Jean Kerr banged the phone down on me just after she spat out the words, 'How could you fockin' take up with that Mary Skef-fockin'-ton?'

It took me a while to get hold of Mrs Simpson. She didn't have a phone in the house so I had to ring a phone box in her street and wait until someone answered the phone in hopes that they would go and get her. In the meantime, I was standing in the hallway of the house that contained Mary's flat, feeding pennies into the communal phone box.

Jean's mum gave me more time than Jean Kerr did, yet she grew concerned only because of my concern.

'Well, it's coming up for two weeks now since she was last in touch. She usually writes to us every other week. I dropped her a letter in the post yesterday evening. Is she not in her flat?'

'Apparently not,' I replied, hopping from one foot to the other to try to keep the blood circulating. 'It's probably nothing; I'll check with John Harrison again.'

'I'm so glad our Jean's got friends in London who would go to this much trouble to look out for her,' Mrs Simpson offered, before disconnecting.

'Now what?' I asked Mary, after I'd relayed the details of my conversation with Jean's mum.

'Okay, simple,' Mary said, 'let's go round to her flat.'

I found myself agreeing, betraying the fact that I was more worried than I was letting on even to myself.

'Do you think it's wise that you come too?' I asked.

'I'll risk it, David!' she said, before laughing. 'I'd be happy to meet Jean, if only because it'll mean she's come to no harm.'

It would have to be a wet dank night, wouldn't it? It would have to be a night that ninety-nine per cent of the population would have shied away from my chosen task for the alternative of staying put in their cosy houses until first thing in the morning. That ninety-nine per cent of the population didn't include Mary Skeffington and whatever didn't include Mark Skeffington, didn't include me.

Once we'd gone to the trouble of preparing for the blustery and showery night it was quite invigorating battling the elements in the company of the one I loved. We put our heads down, interlinked our arms, nuzzled up close together and headed off into the sheet rain. It was so dark and we were so physically close that, to any others on the street that evening, we would have looked like a four-legged creature of the night. If this mythical creature was in search of prey then

I can tell you that the pickings were very slim that night, very slim indeed. We tried running a few times, but we found it difficult to be so close together and to run at the same time. Instinctively we both seemed to have come to the conclusion that it was more important to be slow and together, than to be fast and apart. So following a few intermittent unsuccessful attempts at running together, like we were in some bizarre three-legged race through a wind- and rain-swept, slippery obstacle course, we settled for the best version of team speed-walking we could muster through Wimbledon's ghost town-like streets.

As is frequently the case in life – while trying to avoid things we'd rather put off until tomorrow – it didn't take us as long as we expected to make the journey from Mary's flat in Gladstone Road to the Jeans' flat in Alexandra Road which was, coincidently, just four streets away from my previous accommodation in Rostrevor Road.

There was no answer to the two Jeans' doorbell, so we rang the bell of the girls in the upstairs flat.

They both answered the door.

Mary spoke first.

'Look, sorry to disturb you at this hour – I'm Mary Skeffington and this is my boyfriend, David Buchanan. The two Jeans are friends of David's and we're worried about Jean Simpson; apparently no one has seen or heard from her in nearly two weeks?'

'Augh, sure of course we recognise David – come on in won't you?' the taller of the two girls said in a thick Glaswegian accent.

'Sure she's up in Derby,' the little one said. She was quite plump and rather jolly.

'No, the other Jean, Jean Kerr – she's the one who's up in Derby,' I explained, 'but we've just spoken to Jean Simpson's mum and she hasn't heard from her daughter in two weeks.'

'Well, it has been awfully quiet recently, I would agree,' the Scottish girl admitted. She then shook her head from side to side several times, before saying 'But we haven't a clue, really, do we Doreen?'

'No sorry, I wouldn't even know where to start – they pretty much keep to themselves. I think we've spoken to them maybe twice? We hear their music though; it's terrific, if a little loud.'

'Am,' I began, unsure of how my request would go down, 'I wonder, would you have a key so that we could have a look? You know, to make sure nothing has happened to her?'

Both the girls looked at each other.

'We don't have a key,' they replied in unison.

'We could burst the door down,' Mary suggested.

Doreen raised her eyebrows at Mary's suggestion.

'Oh, I not sure that would be a good idea,' she said.

'I think we're going to have to,' Mary said, forcefully, 'I also think we should phone for the police.'

Mary was in effect taking charge of the operation.

Doreen came with us. Her flatmate returned to their flat to phone the police. I kicked the door in. Mary eyed me with newfound admiration following my feat with my feet – I didn't admit how easily it had given way.

We walked around the living room and then the bedroom and then looked in the bathroom. No sign of Jean Simpson. It was a relief for all of us, to be honest; I think we were all expecting the worst. I know I was, but then when you think about it, if Jean had been there she'd have been there for getting on two weeks and, well, the place would have ponged a bit. But in reality the flat was neat and tidy. I returned to the living room to see if I could find something, anything, which would give us a clue as to Jean's whereabouts.

I walked over to her stereo unit. The power was still on and the speakers had developed the dreaded hum. I replaced the needle arm in its rest and secured it as I struggled to see the name of the record on her deck. It was a CBS record in fact, Bob Dylan's Bringing It All Back Home. I couldn't help smiling. She'd clearly got over her original aversion to Dylan. I looked around for the sleeve to check the song titles on this particular album. I was convinced 'She Belongs To Me' was included. I knew for a fact it was included, but for some strange reason I found myself looking for the sleeve to confirm this fact.

But I couldn't find it.

I checked her record shelf; she'd about 100 albums, all filed alphabetically by artist. But the empty Dylan jacket was not in the D section – only The Doors occupied this space, and she'd aped my trick by pulling her Doors album out about half an inch from the rest of the albums to mark the space of the album currently gracing the record deck.

A bit more of a browse and I eventually found the offending sleeve amongst her Beatles section. The colour sleeve featured Dylan and Sally Grossman – Dylan's manager's wife – caught in a fish-eyed lens shot, lounging in a lounge amongst, coincidentally, a pile of records, one of which, Dylan's first, seemed destined for the fireplace located directly behind Mrs Grossman. Perhaps the vivid red of her dress (or was it a trouser suit? Hard to tell from the photograph) was meant to symbolise the absent flames.

I was about to pull the sleeve fully out to check the song titles when I suddenly realised that Jean Simpson hadn't replaced the record sleeve. She would never have left a record out on the deck overnight and she certainly would never have filed an empty sleeve. She'd even gone as far as marking her space, for heaven's sake, with the trick I taught her. True, if she'd been in a hurry there was a slight possibility that she might have misfiled the record. But I was having a hard time accepting that as a possibility. She would still have taken the time to return the record to its white and cellophane liner, which protected the precious vinyl from getting scratched in the cardboard album sleeve, which itself would be protected, for life, in a clear, polythene, snuggly fitting sheath. And she never would've left her record player in such a state; she'd most certainly have turned it off and returned the needle arm to the rest, as I had instinctively done.

Suddenly it all came together: someone else had made an attempt to 'tidy up' the record area. And whoever this person was, they'd also misfiled her Dylan sleeve.

And left their fingerprints all over it.

I felt quite proud of myself. I'd come up with a clue as to the perpetrator's identity.

I left the record exactly where it was and then immediately became depressed by my next thought. Let's take the worst-case scenario, okay? Jean Simpson is dead, right? Someone has done her harm, right? Now let's fast-forward to a possible list of suspects. Okay? Please bear with me. Any police list, after an initial investigation would, have to read:

1. John Harrison. Motive: Either Jean was going to leave him or he'd discovered what Jean and I had been doing behind his back.
2. Jean Kerr. Motive: Jealousy. She'd also found out about Jean and I; she couldn't abide the fact that Jean was having her cake and eating it and adding insult to injury, unlike herself, was not putting on an ounce of weight in the process.
3. Mary Skeffington. Motive: She'd found out about me and Jean before I'd told her about me and Jean. Added to the fact that Jean had stolen John Harrison from her, and was now setting about stealing her current boyfriend... well, the whole thing would have been unbearable for her.
4. David Buchanan. Motive: Jean (I suppose) could have threatened to tell Mary about our illicit encounters, so I had to silence her.

I know number four is a bit far-fetched – well, totally far-fetched in reality – but I had to think like the police would think, didn't I? So, apart from that, are you with me so far? Good. Now do me up another list, please, only this time include the names of the suspects whose prints would be most likely to be on the Dylan sleeve. Suspects for whom it would have been normal to be in Jean Simpson's flat. Okay?

1. Jean Simpson herself
2. Jean Kerr
3. John Harrison
4. David Buchanan
5. Harvey Lee

(You'll note that I also threw an additional name in there, a mystery person. I hadn't a clue who he or she may have been, but I called them Harvey Lee – you know, after Lee Harvey Oswald?)

'But what about the shop assistants at Musicland?' I hear you say. 'Wouldn't their fingerprints be all over that album? And what about anyone who'd picked up that album while browsing the racks in the record store?' And you'd be right to ask, of course you would. But then you could never have known that Musicland sold every album shrink-wrapped, could you? So their fingerprints would be nowhere near that album sleeve, would they? No, they wouldn't.

So, that left only one person whose fingerprints would have been out of place on the album sleeve. My Mary. And if Mary Skeffington's fingerprints happened to be on the sleeve she'd have been the most likely suspect, wouldn't she? She was never (meant to be) in Jean Simpson's flat.

Equally, if the sleeve contained only the two Jeans', John Harrison's and my prints, and no prints from any stranger, then that meant either Jean Kerr, John Harrison or I was the culprit.

Can you see my dilemma?

Chapter Thirty-One.

The police were none too happy to be called out. The only crime that had been committed, as far as they were concerned, was one of breaking and entering. WPC McGinley advised me of my crime in no uncertain terms and her colleague PC Jackman grinned devilishly in the background. So, I didn't advise them about my fingerprint discovery. I thought I needed a bit more information before I could do that. I could always discover it at a later date and then tell the police.

As McGinley and Jackman carried out a search of the premises I noticed Mary standing in the middle of the room, looking like she was a million miles away, lost in her thoughts. She appeared composed to a degree; I couldn't work out whether she was trying to figure out what had happened or she was merely trying to look like she was trying to figure out what had happened.

Had there really been a murder here? And could Mary really be the murderer? What did I feel about that, about the prospect of Mary Skeffington being the murderer? We're talking here about a girl I was going to spend the rest of my life with. I was in love with Mary Skeffington; I knew with her that I had found my rainbow. Was I now to accept that she had taken out the person she'd considered a competitor for my affections?

So how would it work if she was the perpetrator? Was I morally obliged to protect her? I couldn't possibly shop her to the police, could I? Let's say she had murdered Jean Simpson. Then she'd obviously done so because of what had happened between Jean and me – so I was partially to blame, wasn't I? Besides, when you marry someone, don't you take him, or her, for better or worse? At least now I knew what the worst could be. Whoops, I couldn't believe I'd even just thought that.

I really didn't know what to think. I mean, was I actually considering covering up for a killer?

Please don't just gloss over those words – please read them again,

Was I actually considering covering up for a killer?

On top of which, I was planning to spend the rest of my life with this murderer. You see that's the thing, isn't it? Murderers are also people. Of course that's an oversimplification, but my point is that they also have feelings, they also have parents, they also have lovers and they also have lives. Just because they murder someone doesn't mean that they've spent their entire life thinking about killing people. Even though they've just broken the biggest law in the land, Thou Shalt Not Kill, I bet they still get annoyed at people breaking the rules. Take stealing, for instance: Do you think that just because you're a murderer and someone breaks into your flat and steals your records or jewellery or television or whatever, that you're not going to be annoyed by that? Perhaps even so annoyed that you would seek out the perpetrator to kill them?

I think not. I think most murderers are themselves victims of circumstance. Yes, of course you get the premeditated murders, but think of all the crimes of passion, or frustration, where you just get so mad with someone that perhaps you shove them and perhaps they fall over and, as they fall over, perhaps they accidentally hit their head on the hearth of your fireplace, and then perhaps they die and then perhaps you panic.

Is that what had happened between Mary and Jean? Had Mary discovered our encounters and come round to Jean's flat to warn her off? Had things got out of control and

Mary shoved Jean, and Jean fell and hit her head, and Jean died, and Mary panicked? And disposed of the body?

So how did she dispose of the body, David?

Good question, very good question, in fact – glad to see you're still paying attention. Let's just think about that one now. How would she have disposed of the body? The two Jeans' flat is on the first floor. This meant that their accommodation benefited from neither a loft, nor a basement, nor a garden, which in my book ruled out three of the best possible avenues of hiding or disposing of a body. I could hardly see Mary Skeffington throwing Jean over her shoulder and brazenly wandering up to Wimbledon Common to bury her there or even just dump her in the pond! There's always the chance that one of those horrible Wombles would be lurking around, tidying up, and would shop you to the local bobby on the beat. Sorry, I hate to be facetious at a time like this, but… it helps me to keep my mind wandering. The more it wanders, the more likely it is that I will stumble upon the truth.

So what would Mary have done? Had there been a fight, was there any telltale blood? I wandered around all the likely spots where an accident could have happened and I couldn't for the life of me find a spot of blood. That pretty much ruled out the flat. But then if it wasn't the flat – I mean, if Jean hadn't met her end in the flat – then that pretty much ruled out Mary, didn't it? I mean, Mary wasn't going to ring on Jean's doorbell and just invite her out, was she? Jean certainly wouldn't have gone willingly and she was quite feisty, as proven in our red carpet wrestling match. I doubt Mary could have easily overpowered Jean.

I was grasping at straws here, but Mary and I hadn't spoken much since we'd broken into Jean's flat. She'd infrequently catch my eye and try to shape an open-lip smile for me. What was she thinking as she wandered around? Was she having the same dark thoughts about me?

Could she be thinking that maybe Jean had been threatening to tell her about our encounters and because I so desperately didn't want her to, it was me who killed her? Was she thinking why on Earth had he waited till now to tell me about his messing about with Jean Simpson? What exactly did he mean when he said they were only messing about? Was she now considering whether or not she could help me get away with it? Was she also thinking what it was going to be like, living with a murderer for the rest of her life? Try as I might to decipher what she was thinking, her eyes were giving nothing away.

Could she be thinking: How did he kill her? How did he dispose of the body? Okay, so let me help everyone out a wee bit here. Let me put myself in the frame for a minute.

Say, for instance, Jean had rung me up and said she was missing me? Say she said she couldn't live without our encounters and unless we resumed play she would spill the beans to Mary?

Does that sound plausible so far? Please don't say yes too quickly!

But, taking this hypothetical scenario to the next level, perhaps I could have suggested to Mary that I was going down the Marquee Club on one of her college nights, so that she knew I was going to be out late. (She'd think nothing of it – she hated coming with me to the Marquee; we'd tried once and it was disaster. It didn't help that the main act (Terry Reid) didn't show up and that Jeff Dexter just spun some records.) Anyway, so I go around to Jean's flat. Do I take a bottle of wine? Yes, of course I take a bottle of wine – I want her drunk, don't I? She's going to be more controllable if she's drunk.

Now, when I'm in her flat, what do I do? Have I already decided that I'm going to kill her? No, I don't think so. You see, if I take you down that route, I know that it's going to be fiction because I could never plan to murder Jean Simpson, or anyone else for that matter. So, I have to go the accidental route, don't I? I bring the bottle of wine because I want her to loosen up, so that we can have a more honest chat. We start to drink the wine. At this stage she's probably going to want to enjoy one of our encounters.

Okay, here's a very important question, David: If she goes down that route – if she's dressed in her famous tartan miniskirt and gives you a quick twirl and a flash of those exquisite legs of hers – do you join in?

No!

No?

No!

'Oh, come on. What's the harm? You've said it yourself; you've only been messing around?' I hear you say. (I have to admit, that your voice is starting to sound a wee bit like Richard Harris right about now.)

And I say, 'No, no way, that was all before I got it together with Mary Skeffington and no one, not even Barbara Parkins, could interest me now.'

'Right answer. So far so good. So, what happens next?' you say.

Well, we have a few glasses of wine, I put Bob Dylan on her stereo and we play it through in relative silence as we sip our wine. Dylan is such compulsive listening – his imagery is so vivid, so vital, so stimulating, so real, you see, it's impossible for me not to tune into him completely.

'So, how's it going with you and John?' I'd have said, after a time.

'Oh, he's boring,' she'd say.

'But you love him and sometimes it's more important to find someone who is dependable and caring?' I would've said.

'But I'm only twenty, David. I want to have some fun. Why can't we have some more fun?' she'd say.

'Well, because we both have other partners and we did have some fun – some great fun – and I think it's important we keep that as a warm memory and don't soil it by–'

'By me running to your girlfriend and telling her about what we've been getting up to?' she'd tease.

'No, I wasn't going to say that. I was going to say that we shouldn't ruin it–'

'Soil it, you said, soil it,' she'd say, slyly correcting me.

'Soil it. Yes, soil it, by pushing on after we'd run out of steam.'

'Oh, we'd run out of steam had we, David?' she'd say, a hint of a tease in her voice as she'd rise up from the sofa to give me another twirl. 'I know how much you like me in my underwear, would you like to see it better, or do you actually prefer those little flashes I give you? You know, the ones you think are accidental?'

She'd still not be slutty or anything but she'd peel off her black blouse and miniskirt and she'd be down to her bra and pants, walking towards me.

'Isn't this the view of me you like? You said you liked the way I kept my treasures hidden didn't you? You were happy once that my hidden treasures were only seen and experienced by you, weren't you? You thought it was exciting that the man I was going to marry never got to see these, didn't you? You thought it was wicked he never touched or kissed what's in my pants, didn't you? Here, let me take this off so that you can see my breasts better. Remember how you once said you were amazed how solid they were and how responsive my nipples were? Look, they're still responsive. You don't even have to touch them; all I have to do is think of you. Here, let me take my pants off for you. I know how much you love to look at my bush. You always say how silky it is. I'm wet just thinking about you. This time it's going to be different, David. This time I'm going to keep you. This time I want you inside me. This time I need you inside me.'

She'd kneel down in front of me. I wouldn't say a word. She'd continue in her gentle northern voice.

'Here, let me undo your belt and help you off with your trousers – I can see how uncomfortable you are in them. Let me take off all of your clothes so that we're as close as it is possible for two humans to be. Oh, look at this! I told you that you wanted me, didn't I? This time it's going to be different, David. I can do things for you and to you I know no one else will ever be able to do. I should've realised after our last time that we could never continue with all that abstaining malarkey. You're right, they are such sweet memories, and we will both keep them and cherish them and have them in our hearts for the rest of our lives, and we shouldn't try to repeat them. We have to move on. We've passed the point of restraint, David. It's time to move on, David. You need to be inside me. I can tell. I need you inside me. I'm so ready for you, David. I don't want you pulling out either; I don't care what happens. I'm ready for you to really get me.'

She would take my hand in hers. I wouldn't say a word.

'Here, feel how ready I am for you, David.'

She'd lean forward to me to engage us in our first kiss. We'd be caught there in slow motion, my hand moving closer and closer towards her, to touch her again. Our faces moving closer and closer together, and she'd be so close that I would feel her breath on my face and our lips would be brushing, and I would feel the beginning of her silky curls with my hand when I'd shout:

'No!'

And I'd push her away with such force and hate and anger. And she'd be shocked and feel she'd done something wrong, or... or, there had been some kind of an accident, and she'd come back towards me whispering, 'It's okay, Pet, it's going to be okay. Everything will be okay when you really get me.'

And I'd stand up from my chair and she'd take that as a welcoming sign, and my entire body would tense up as she moved closer to me. Again I'd shout 'No!' at the top of my voice. There'd be tears in my eyes. I'd grit my teeth and push her back, and she'd stumble away from me and I'd follow her, pushing her again and again, making my point by cutting the air in wide arcs with my hands, like I was swimming, every time I pushed her.

'Get away from me!' I'd keep shouting, and for my last shove I'd summon up all the energy and power that I possessed and I would smack my hand straight into her chest so violently that, as she fell away from me, I'd see the white marks my hands had left on her red, flushed skin. There'd be a look of fear in her eyes as she'd lose her balance and start to stumble uncontrollably backwards. She'd be beseeching me with her eyes to do something to help her, but I'd be too angry to do anything other than smirk, as she fell gracelessly from her life. Even though her body would be falling one way, the thud of her head against the wooden mantelpiece would be so forceful and the thump so loud, that her head would deflect to the opposite direction.

I'd still be standing, tense and defiant as ever, my anger building and building, wishing nothing but harm on this body; the body that I once knew so well, the body of which I'd explored every single nook and cranny with my fingers, my lips. I'd wonder, seeing it lying there on the hearth, how this body had once held so many mysteries for me. How the quickest of twirls, or the briefest of flashes of forbidden skin, would arouse me way beyond a point I'd ever dreamed existed.

Now those magnificent proud breasts would be mere floppy bags of skin filled with meat and fat. Her glorious, graceful legs would be inert and gangly. Her once hungry thighs would no longer be inviting. Her once radiant, translucent, taut skin would now be billowing and ashen.

I'd stand there like a gladiator gloating over his conquest. My cheeks would be red as a rage-filled furnace. Not anger at what she had done to me, or wanted to do to me, or what she may or may not have done to Mary Skeffington; no, my anger would be at myself, because once again I had hesitated. It might only have been for a second, maybe even just a split second, but that was all it would have taken for me to betray my beloved. To betray Mary Skeffington.

Then my anger would subside and I'd confront the enormity of what I'd just done… and the consequences. Unless I did something quick to cover my crime, I'd lose my liberty. Worse, I'd lose Mary Skeffington forever. This would be my main motivation from then onwards; every single thing I'd do, I'd do it in order to protect my relationship with Mary Skeffington.

So what would I do? With the body, I mean? What would anybody do with an incriminating corpse? You see, if this was premeditated, then our perpetrator would have a contingency plan for disposal of the remains already in place, wouldn't they? But in a crime of passion, the murderer would have to think on his or her feet.

'Okay, David, you've just come up with a very plausible end for Jean Simpson. So accepting that we acknowledge this fate to be feasible, what did you do with the body?' I know you're thinking this – you're too reserved to voice it, but you really are thinking it, aren't you?

You're going to have to give me some time on that one. I mean in my fictitious account there. Let's see now… I've just killed her, so I'm going to have to wait until my heart stops trying to break through my rib cage, before I can start to think logically again and come up with a plan for disposing of the body.

Suddenly, I had snapped out of my musings and was back in the room, watching the police at their work. They seemed somewhat detached to me – you know, thinking that this was something and nothing. WPC McGinley hovered around Jean's record collection for a few moments. She was careful not to touch anything; she just stood and stared at the three lines of albums, their multi-coloured spines creating a unique pop art frieze.

I had a bizarre thought at that moment. I'm not proud of it, but I feel I should tell you.

I started to wonder who would get Jean's albums. She'd such a great collection and each and every one of them was in mint condition because, as you know, like myself, Jean took great care of her records. But to whom would they go? Jean Simpson was too young to have made a will, I figured. So did that mean the records and all her other possessions automatically went to her mother? And what would her mother do with those records? Would she give them to Jean Kerr or perhaps even John Harrison? Okay, I confess: I harboured the thought that she might even give them to me.

There, I've admitted it.

'So will you start an investigation?' I felt compelled to ask the WPC.

'It's an investigation you want, is it?' she replied in her quiet, charming Donegal accent. 'Sure, the only investigation we'd be interested in here would be the destruction of private property,' she continued, taking great trouble to eye the damaged door up and down.

'But what about Jean Simpson? She's been missing for ages now,' I protested.

'Would Miss Simpson be your girlfriend?'

I dithered on that one. I was on the verge of saying, well, she's a girl and she's a friend, but I'm not sure she's a girlfriend. If pushed by the police I'd have had to admit that maybe she was more than just a girl who was a friend, but thankfully, Mary Skeffington saved the day by walking across the room and confidently taking my hand.

'Actually, I'm David's girlfriend – Jean Simpson is a friend of David's; she met him on her first day down in London, in fact.'

'Okay, good to know,' WPC McGinley replied, writing a quick note in her wee black book.

She started to stare at me intently, as if waiting for me to give her some more information to put in her book. I mean, come on now – how are you not going to look anything but guilty under such circumstances?

No further information forthcoming she continued with, 'Miss Simpson's next of kin can report her missing, if they so choose.'

She saw I was about to protest once again and so she quickly followed up with, 'With regard to your destruction of private property, Mr Buchanan, in this instance I'm prepared to let you off with a warning.' I'm sure I saw her wink at her colleague before she concluded with, 'Mr Buchanan, you and you alone are responsible for making good the damage to the door.'

And with that, she and her colleague left us to meekly tidy up the mess I'd made of said door – no doubt full details of which were now also officially logged in her wee black book.

Chapter Thirty-Two.

Then what?

Then we left the flat, and Mary and I walked home in silence. And I started to try to figure out what you'd do with a body, say a body weighing eight-odd stone – how would you get rid of it? More importantly, how would you get rid of it without leaving any clues, or without drawing undue attention to yourself?

Wimbledon Common was an obvious bet but only if you'd a car. You could hardly hail a taxi and shout, 'Wimbledon Common, Guv – the darkest and remotest part you can find, I need to dump this suitcase.'

And he'd say, 'Now let's see, Guv; we're going to have to put this in the front, Guv. Cripes, heavy, ain't it? I'm going to have to charge you the rate for two regular suitcases. Now, where was it you wanted to go? Oh yeah, I remember, Wimbledon Common. Let's see, we'll have to go via Kingston. Oh, you know a quicker way do you? Okay, we'll go your way then, if you insist. Oh yeah, as it happens, I know the place you mean. Yes, I know the very place, up by the Windmill. We need to take a left just after the Vatican Embassy. You in a hurry, Guv? Did you see United over the weekend? Crap! They've been crap the whole ten years I've been supporting 'em! Now if they run their football team the same way Wilson ran this country they'd win absolutely everything. Harold Wilson, now he's the Guv, isn't he Guv? Oh, we're here already. I think you were correct, Guv, your way just might have been the quickest.'

I'm sure that's what he would have said, or words to that effect.

But you can see the problem, can't you? How disposing of a body is a tad tricky? Perhaps you could hire someone. But how much would that all cost? And surely you'd leave yourself open to blackmail?

What to do with a body.

Burn it?

Bury it?

Hide it?

Let it be discovered, just make sure there are no incriminating marks left on or about it? That way, of course, you could help with the inquiries yourself and by being very helpful, no one would ever doubt you, would they?

Thinking about it and running with the theory that we are each the best supporters of our own weight, why not have the body itself accompany you to the scene of the proposed crime? Say Jean Simpson had telephoned me and threatened me, threatened to inform Mary about our adventures. Couldn't I have said, 'Okay, you win, I've had a brilliant idea for an encounter – meet me tonight at midnight up by the Windmill on Wimbledon Common.' How brilliant would that be? She'd be helping me cover up her own murder! No taxi drivers, no one to witness me carting a body about the vast Common in the depths of night. I'd simply walk with her under the cloak of darkness, murder her there, and dispose of her body on the spot.

I dwelled on this idea for a time and then snapped out of it and returned my mind to the scene back at her flat. Could her flat be the last place she'd been seen? Had there been someone there with her? Could it have been the mystery person she'd been with the night she'd avoided both John and I? It had been tidy – no sign of a scuffle, and no sign of blood. Someone else had been there, though, on that I could be sure – they'd misfiled her empty album sleeve and not turned off her stereo system.

So did that mean they'd forced her out of the house? Or did it mean they'd returned to the scene of the crime to mount a cover-up?

Or perhaps the stereo system, the record left on the desk, the badly filed album sleeve were all deliberate clues left by Jean herself? If so, they were clues for no one else but me. Did Jean want me to notice that something was wrong?

Okay, now bear with me – let's go down this road for a few minutes. If the above scenario was, in fact, fact, then could I assume that the person in Jean's flat was someone she knew, someone who hadn't needed to force an entry? Either they had taken the trouble to pack away the record or they'd let Jean do it. So had things still been civil at that point? But surely Jean must have feared this person to go to the trouble of leaving so subtle a clue for me. Yes, yes, of course – great point! Yes of course, really a brilliant point, even though I do say so myself.

Next suspect!

Jean Kerr. See how quickly you can go from thinking someone is missing and feeling sorry for them to placing them front and centre on your suspect list? But seriously, could Jean Kerr have physically threatened her friend to the extent that she would obediently do as bid? Having seen Jean Kerr in action – you remember, at Tiger's party when she'd gone all Wild West on Mary – I wasn't so sure I could rule her out. Then, of course, there was that incident where Jean Simpson told me about Jean Kerr's old boyfriend, Brian. Do you remember, the one who apparently was into boys? The one who'd disappeared from the face of the Earth, just like another friend of Jean Kerr's had recently done?

What about Mary? Was Mary capable of physically terrorising Jean? Or John? I couldn't really see Mary physically overpowering anyone, but what about John? Surely he would have had the strength? Mind you, any of the above – any of us in fact – could have taken her from her flat at gun- or knife-point.

Yes, this certainly shone a different light altogether on the matter.

But why was I alone being left agonising over this? It's just that it seemed to me that the two local police were showing little to no interest in the fate of Jean Simpson.

As we arrived back at Mary's flat, soaking wet and weather beaten, I found myself wondering where Jean was at that very moment. Could she really be in some dark hole? How strong was the possibility that she had already met her Maker?

Another week passed. Still nothing happened. Jean Simpson's mother did, however, finally contact the police. This was due in some way, I think, to me bugging her. The bottom line was that Jean's mum just didn't want to believe that anything unpleasant had happened to her daughter. She told me this after she rang the police. She rang me back to apologise for burying her head in the sand – her words, not mine. She said that she felt that if she treated the situation as problem-free, then it would remain problem-free. Once she started to treat her daughter as a missing person, then and only then would it became a problem for her.

Two more police officers visited me and Mary, meaning that our names were now definitely in the Jean Simpson Missing Person File. The Derby Police had already spoken with Jean Kerr and apparently she'd not been in London herself for several weeks, so she didn't have any other information to give them. They'd also spoken to John Harrison; he'd elected to visit the police station, and apparently he was helpful. Mary and I didn't really have much additional information to give them either, apart from above that was.

They told us the number of girls who disappear in London each year – not quite as many as you'd think, but still in the hundreds. They also told us that their inquiries hadn't given them reason to be unduly concerned about

Jean's wellbeing. In short, they were confident that she'd turn up.

Despite their assurances, they kept asking me about the Marquee Club and the kind of people she'd met there.

'Did I think,' they'd asked, 'that she could have met up with a bunch of hippies and headed off down to Bristol?'

I told them I didn't think so, realising that John had obviously seen fit to take them into his confidence with one of his theories.

They said, 'Don't be so sure!' They said there were lots of communes starting up and down the country, but particularly in the West Country, and lots of beautiful girls were ending up in them.

I still didn't tell them about my Bob Dylan Record-Sleeve-With-Fingerprints-All-Over-It clue. You see, I hate to say it, but I hadn't entirely ruled out Mary. Is that an awful thing to admit about your intended? I wondered if I could find a way of getting back into Jean's flat to have another rummage. You see, I was hoping I could somehow plant Mary's fingerprints on the sleeve. Not to implicate her, of course, no – to set her free. If only I'd handed the record to her that night we kicked the door down to the two Jeans' flat; I could've given the record to Mary to pass to WPC McGinley. Don't you see? That way Mary's prints would've shown up for a reason other than murder. Clever, eh?

Yeah, very clever, but sadly just a week or so too late.

It's funny, the way we deal with the bad stuff when we have to. You know, Jean Simpson was missing and I personally feared the worst, yet everyone was just getting on with their lives, even her mum. Is that why we fear dying so much, because we know we're going to be quickly forgotten? Or is it because we fear the devil, or dread going to Hell?

I asked Mary and she said: 'Oh, I don't know. I think that the older we get the less we actually fear Hell. When I was younger I used to actually think that I could go to a place called Hell and that I would physically burn there.

That was probably my biggest fear – that was the worst thing in the world I could ever imagine happening to me. You know, being physically burned. But then for a period of about seven years I replaced my fear of Hell with my fear of the dentist. And then, after I'd been to the dentist about a dozen or so times and he'd thrown his worst – or maybe that should be his best – at me, and I got through it, then I started to think, well, perhaps there is something worse than the dentist.'

'So what's your biggest fear now?' I asked.

'Oh, it's no longer a fear. Because of us,' she said quietly. 'But for a time recently I feared a loveless life. But getting back to your original question, I do think we all fear dying because we fear we're going to be forgotten. But we have to be forgotten, don't we? The survivors couldn't possibly continue walking around, carrying the baggage of everyone they'd ever known to die.'

'Interesting, I'd never considered that before.'

'David, are all these thoughts of mortality to do with Jean?'

'I suppose,' I admitted. 'Do you think you get to Heaven automatically when your life is taken from you as opposed to being judged when you die of natural causes?'

'Oh David, don't get morose on me.'

Was that response just a tad flippant? Perhaps lacking in understanding?

'There are enough people worrying about Jean without you carrying it all on your shoulders,' she added, pressing home her point.

'That's part of the problem Mary; no one seems to really care about Jean Simpson at all.'

'One positive thing though is coming out of all of this worrying of yours,' she said, lightening up a bit.

'And what's that?' I replied, taking the bait, hook, line and sinker.

'Well, if nothing else, all your concern is proving that you at least had nothing to do with her disappearance.'

I basked in this newfound feeling of security. Not that I really know why it should have been such a relief for someone – even the girl I loved – to realise I was blameless in this Jean Simpson drama. The relief, however, was brief, because a few seconds later she added, doing her best to form her two dark eyebrows into a straight line, 'unless you're trying to throw everyone else, including me, off your trail.'

Chapter Thirty-Three.

Trail… now there is a word to get you going. It certainly got me going, as in, it was time to stop messing around and get on the trail of the person, or persons unknown who had, on or about July 20, 1969, caused the disappearance of one Jean Simpson.

You're up to speed with who my main suspects were: Jean Kerr, John Harrison, Mary Skeffington and my 'mystery person', the aforementioned Harvey Lee.

The more I thought about it the less far-fetched it became; I mean, Jean Simpson being assassinated. Could Mary Skeffington murder Jean Simpson with her bare hands? I'd have to say, most definitely not. But could she have hired someone – maybe even this Harvey Lee character – to do the dirty work for her? Now that had to be a possibility, didn't it? The same went for Jean Kerr; surely she could have stayed up in Derby and hired a hitman to do her dirty work for her? But even if Jean Simpson had died at the hands of a hitman, said hitman would've had to have been paid, so that brought us straight back to the people on my list.
Yes, I agree with you – I would have to include myself on the list. Well, it's only fair isn't it? But then what is truly fair in love and murder?

I started to think about police procedure at this stage. Would the police investigate all their suspects simultaneously or would they mark them off their list, one by one, until there was only one left – their perpetrator? Mind you, did that mean that, if you were the last person to be investigated, you were also the last and therefore the only person left on their list of suspects? Surely that would mean that by the process of elimination and deduction you were the only possible perpetrator, not to mention the only one available.

No, the police couldn't really afford to go up so many potentially blind alleys; they'd have to juggle all the balls in the air at once. But whereas they had the resources to do that, I certainly didn't.

Not that any of the police resources were on display. Should the Wimbledon CID have treated the case seriously and actually opened an investigation into the disappearance of Jean Simpson, I still would've been at least two steps ahead of them at that point. The first clue involved the Dylan record sleeve. The second clue involved my encounters with Jean Simpson. So, what I now needed to know was, which one of my suspects had discovered that Jean Simpson and I had been messing around?

And how could I find this out without letting the others know about it too?

I had to get deeper.

But why me? Why not her mum, or John Harrison? Jean Kerr was on sick leave again in Matlock so, well, she could be forgiven for not risking putting herself through any further strain. But surely John Harrison or Mrs Simpson Senior or the police, or even a combination of all of the above should have shown just a wee bit more concern? Did John's reticence put him under the spotlight? Did my desperate need to find out, throw the spotlight on me?

I just had to get back into Jean's flat and take that Dylan record sleeve. I then had to figure out how I could check it for fingerprints, and then I had to get fingerprints of my suspects, including Harvey Lee. Should there be a stranger's set of prints on the sleeve, Harvey Lee would jump right to the top of my list.

I think I reached this point on a Saturday morning. Luckily enough, Mary was off to Bath to see her mum that weekend, so I figured I'd take the Monday and Tuesday off work and use the four days to go about this investigation properly. I felt I should go to Derby as soon as possible. I needed to speak to Jean Kerr and to Jean Simpson's mum, and I needed to do it face to face.

Like the proper detective I felt I was becoming, I also believed a quick visit to John Harrison was in order before I left for Derby. I'd do it in person, and there was no time like the present, so I immediately left for his flat in the upper end of Worple Road.

The end of Worple Road away from Wimbledon Hill Road was interchangeable with any other London suburb. Like, as I walked up Worple Road that day, I could just as easily have been walking up any street in West Hampstead, Balham, Streatham, or even Dulwich for that matter.

John didn't seem very happy to see me turning up uninvited on his doorstep. I was quite intrigued to see the inside of his flat, since I'd never been there before.

'Aye David, I was just thinking of going for a spot of breakfast,' he announced, 'do you fancy joining me?'

'Good game,' I replied, 'good game.'

'Just give me a second to fetch my coat and I'll be right with you,' he added and shut the door in my face, denying me an opportunity to nosey around his living quarters.

Ten minutes later, we were in his local greasy spoon. He ordered the works: two super sausages, three rashers of bacon, two runny fried eggs, a tomato cut in half and fried, baked beans, three rounds of toast and some potatoes that had obviously been in the frying pan at least three times too long. I, on the other hand, took the more conservative approach: two poached eggs and baked beans on toast. We both washed down our belly-fillers with a mug of excellent tea.

'God I needed that,' he said. He wasn't a boy prone to exaggeration was our John. He'd hardly spoken a word during the time it had taken him to gulp down his food. I assumed he was finished because he soaked up the last bit of egg yolk and the last few baked beans with his one remaining corner of toast. He belched loudly, ordered another two mugs of tea and lit up his first post-breakfast Player of the day.

'Me too,' I replied and we both laughed. I stopped to consider how to best manoeuvre the conversation to where I wanted it to go. Only he beat me to the punch.

'Heard anything more from the police on Jean?' he asked.

'No, have you?'

'Nagh,' he replied. Then he did that very disconcerting thing with his eyes, you remember; he rolled them up whenever you looked him in the eye. He only ever looked you directly in the eye accidentally, you know, as he was moving them to avoid looking you in the eye. 'I went in to see the police,' he continued. 'Told them what I knew and that was it really.'

'You haven't heard from her since?'

'Who?' he asked, looking like he was going to start giggling at any moment. I had to remind myself that this was how he always looked.

'Why, Jean of course!'

'Oh Jean, oh no. I mean, she's probably,' he paused and looked at me (though being careful to avoid eye contact, of course), as if to ask whether he could tell me a secret, 'she's probably run off with one of your friends from the Marquee Club.'

I started to say no, but he immediately cut me off with, 'Look, the police seem to think that she joined some troop of hippies and she's happy on grass. What's it Timothy Leary said? "Drop out and tune in"? Or was it "Tune in and drop out"? Jean's very gullible, as you well know, and she'll go with the flow. Look how she stuck to Jean Kerr's coat-tails for so long. She can't think for herself. That's her main problem.'

'How do you feel about that?'

'What, that's she's run off with a bunch of hippies or that she's left me?'

'Either?'

'Well, at least she didn't leave me for you, like Jean Kerr said she would,' he said, as he rolled his eyes away from me once again. The split-second I caught his eyes, he looked sad, sadder than his words betrayed.

'Jean Kerr actually said that?' I asked, thinking that I probably should have denied it first.

'Yep.' His reply bordered on smugness.

'But you know that couldn't possibly be true?'

'What, because you've taken up with Mary?'

'No!' I found myself snarling, 'because you and Jean are going to get married! Because we, your Jean and I, are just friends, we share an interest in music.'

'Agh you see, that's just from your point of view. But take it from my Jean's perspective. She stole me from Mary, you're her friend, then you betray her by starting to go out with Mary and so she thinks I've stolen one boyfriend from Mary, maybe I can steal another.'

'You can't honestly think that – you're going to marry the girl, for heaven's sake!'

'David, David,' he said, laughing, 'Jean and I, we're al…' he seemed to think better about what he was going to say. He gritted his face up into an exaggerated smile and continued, 'We're… we're okay. How are you and Mary getting on?'

Did he mean they were okay as in it was over and he was dealing with it? Did it mean he knew where she was? And was he asking how Mary and I were getting on because he was thinking of making another move on her?

'We're getting on great, you know?' I said, simply and quickly. I wasn't going to be caught by starting to justify mine and Mary's relationship to her ex.

'Aye, she's a good girl,' he said expansively. 'We've been friends a long time. Mary and I were good friends.'

He must have spotted something awkward in my expression because he explained: 'No, no, David, nothing like that. We really were good friends, long before anything else happened. We'd been friends for years. I just thought we were going to be together forever and ever. That's the funny thing in all of this; we were like mates, and we discussed everything under the sun with each other. We were the first person each other turned to when the other was feeling down, and now… and now we don't even… we don't even talk. I find that bizarre. I mean, I know I hurt her and all of that. But we were friends before our relationship, why couldn't we have been friends after?'

'Probably too much baggage, too much pain,' I replied. Then I paused before adding, 'When Jean left, you know, when she disappeared, had you been arguing or anything like that?'

'Not really. She was acting a wee bit strange and all of that, but that was because she was going to leave me for you, according to Jean Kerr.'

'But no fights?'

'Nagh,' he said, before giggling, 'Jean wasn't really the fighting type. No not at all, she'd sooner sulk.'

'Was she sulking just before she left?' I asked, trying to open up the lid he'd offered.

'She was always sulking! Jean Kerr had taught Jean Simpson how to deal with a man. It was a pretty rural approach. "Reward rewards," Jean Kerr would say. Keep the man in his place by keeping control. "Once you lose control, you've lost the battle," she'd say. I'll tell you, David, she was convinced it was a war out here. "Total war," she claimed, you know, this thing between men and women, the battle of the sexes. The funny thing about it was that she hadn't a clue about any of it. Look at her, for heaven's sake; her love life was a mess, is a mess! It was only when my Jean started to say that you were really okay, that Jean Kerr wanted you back. When she'd heard you'd started dating Mary, well then, that was all it took to make her want you back again. She went absolutely ballistic at that one. I thought she was going to go round there and kill the both of you!'

'What, with her boots?'

'Now wasn't that a hoot?' John said, and began to laugh, before taking another sip of tea. 'You know, that battle was raging and all you could do was gawk at the girls' legs. Both the Jeans laughed about that. They wondered... they wondered, were you the kind of perv who liked to watch girls do it.'

'Ah, come on now, it was a pretty sight, wasn't it?' I was trying desperately hard to make light of my indiscretion.

'Each to their own, David, that's what I say. Each to their own.'

'I was wondering, John, how Jean – your Jean – reacted when she knew I was going out with Mary?'

'She was surprised you hadn't mentioned it to her before. She was surprised that you didn't want to see groups with her any more. Her point was that she had a boyfriend, as in moi, and it was fine for the both of you to see bands together, but then when you got a girlfriend you didn't want to see my Jean any more as a friend. I must admit, I was surprised as well. I've a question for you though, David: Did Mary think it was weird that you went out to the clubs with Jean?'

'Not really, I think I told her that we both pretty much liked the same kind of music the first time we met, you know before the battle...'

'Then why did you have to stop taking Jean out? I think that really hurt her, you know. I think that's the single biggest thing that threw her off kilter.'

'Sheer demands on my time, John; I was spending all my time with Mary,' I offered, hoping, praying even, he didn't notice how much I was squirming in my seat.

'Yeah, I suppose that's the other way to do it. Perhaps Jean and I planned things out a bit too much. It was a bit like, okay you're the one, let's hang around and save for two years until we can afford to be together and get married.

Perhaps your approach would have served Jean and me better. You know, just get it together and then figure out how to make it work.'

That's the big thing about men and women, isn't it? Making it work? Trying to make the perfect match, no… make that trying to make a match. Because needs must, and all that. But when we come across an obvious mismatch you can't help but wonder how they make it work. Do they see something in each other that no one else does? Have they actually discovered the real, secret magic of their partner? Or have they gone beyond physical attractiveness to a deeper, more spiritual attraction, arriving at that point because they needed to find a partner? Or did they really find their partner naturally?

It's all just so very precarious, so fragile really. Isn't it all a just a bit too hit and miss? Hit, and you're with the perfect person for life; miss, and (at least) two people's lives are a complete disaster. And when you miss, like John Harrison and Jean Simpson did, look what the fallout can produce.

Here we were – Mary, Jean, John and I – all young, all single, all in London in the Swinging Sixties, and instead of us going out searching for that famous free love, we were all actively involved in the politics of long-term relationships. I was about to say something about this, but John cleared the remainder of his tea, rolled his eyes again and asked me his final question.

'Did Mary know all about you and Jean?'

'She knew all about me and both Jeans,' I replied, trying to show that I'd no secrets at all from Mary. I didn't know what was on his mind, but there was definitely something. It would appear that both of us had been on a bit of a fishing trip that morning.

I had a feeling that our breakfast was nearly over and I'd run out of questions. Well, I hadn't really run out of questions – I'd a million questions to ask, I just couldn't find a way of working them into the conversation. Either that or

I was lacking the bottle for the more direct approach. You know, something along the lines of, 'So John, what exactly did you do with Jean's body?' I did, however, have one question I felt it important I asked before we departed.

'When did you first notice that Jean was missing, John?' I asked, feeling it was somewhat more palatable than, 'When was the last time you saw Jean alive, John?'

'Let's see now, it would have been three weeks ago last Thursday.'

'And did she seem strange, preoccupied or anything like that?' I knew I was pushing my luck, but if I could just get him to open up a bit I might be able to get a string of quick questions in and maybe that way he wouldn't be as calculating with his answers.

'As I said David, I seem to remember she was sulking. I seem to remember that she was sulking because she couldn't get her way over something. I mean, if I'd known things were going to turn out like they'd turned out, then maybe, just maybe, I'd have reacted differently. Perhaps I'd have taken more care in remembering the exact details of our last date. But at the time it was just another sulk. The simple answer is: I didn't know that it was going to become such a momentously important evening for me to remember. We met. She sulked. I drew – I enjoyed drawing her when she was sulking. I know that shows how sad I am. But there was something about her when she was sulking, like she built this wall around herself and she was defying me to try to enter it. I might have one here, actually,' he said, as he started to search in his pockets. He found his sketchpad and rummaged through the pages for a few seconds. 'Here it is!' he almost shouted. 'I knew it was here somewhere.'

He rolled the dead pages over on the spiral of his book and showed me a sketch. He had managed to catch exactly how pissed off Jean Simpson was with him on their final night together. She'd her head to one side and was looking at him out of the corner of her eyes, eyes that were willing him to leave her alone. He'd drawn her wearing a wedding dress, only in his cartoon version he'd made it not so much a mini-wedding dress but more of a micro-wedding dress that exposed her stocking tops. She'd her lips pursed up under her nose and her hands clasped in front of her knees. She was wearing a pair of black hobnail boots.

So had they been arguing about the wedding?

'This is brilliant – you've caught her perfectly. Are there any more here I can look at?' I asked, as I was just about to flick through the pages, as you do.

'No! No,' John chastised. He reached across and positively snapped the book out of my hand. 'I'll find you a few.'

The next sketch he showed me was a head-only view, a few pages into the book, which I had to assume meant it had been drawn sometime after their final meeting. It was a full face and she still looked annoyed. There were two large tears rolling down her left cheek and she was wearing the wedding veil from the previous sketch.

He showed me one final sketch, which was a variation on the very first of John's caricatures I'd seen. Jean was bending over, picking up something from the floor. Our eagle-eyed artist had caught the scene from the rear and his details were so accurate it was nearly possible to see what she'd had for dinner.

Once again, I feel myself needing to ask you, don't you think it was funny that a person would do that? I mean, yes, there was a cartoon quality to his work and some of it was quite amusing, but doesn't it feel like one step away from showing dirty pictures of your girlfriend to another man? I mean, never in a million years could I imagine sharing such private visions of Mary with anyone. The bottom line is, I suppose, that these photos – these dirty pictures that somehow find their way into the hands of dirty men – well, they're all of someone's wife or girlfriend or sister or daughter, aren't they? So I'm just not sure it's in good taste for a boyfriend to be sharing them, that's all.

And that was all I got out of John Harrison on that particular Saturday morning.

Chapter Thirty-Four.

Train train, going so fast. Were they the words to a song? Well my train was an hour late en route to Derby, and certainly wasn't going to break any speed records. Weekend trains you see, they're so much slower, aren't they?

I arrived at my destination at around seven o'clock that evening. I'd intended to find a cheap B&B but Jean Simpson's mum wouldn't hear of it; I was Jean's friend and as I was going to the trouble of looking for her daughter (her words), she'd not hear of me spending any of my own money.

Her bloodshot eyes and untidy house betrayed the fact that maybe she'd now started giving herself a hard time over not being more on the case of her daughter's disappearance. Saying that, she did cook me a great dinner and we spent the evening with her telling me tales about Jean's childhood. She said that her Jean always looked up to Jean Kerr.

'I always told her to be careful, David. I mean, I always thought that Jean Kerr – well, don't get me wrong, she's a nice girl and all of that, but she was always a wee bit too shaky on her own feet to be trying to prop up someone else at the same time.'

I fully understood what she meant. So I nodded my agreement.

'I was so happy when they moved to London and our Jean started to come out of her shell a bit. She liked you a lot you know, David. She was always talking about you. In fact, she talked more about you than she did about that John

Harrison. I could never work that one out – what was that all about? I told her, when she agrees to marry someone it should be the happiest day of her life. Harrison just seemed to make our Jean miserable.'

'Yes, it always seemed a bit strange to me as well. Do you think it could have anything to do with the other Jean?'

'You mean you think that our Jean was trying to stamp a bit more independence on their relationship?' she asked me, as she wiped her hands in her apron and fetched me another portion of her dangerously delicious Bakewell pudding and hot custard.

'Possibly,' I replied. I was trying to be helpful, but my answers were also tempered by the fact that I was talking to Jean's mum and she'd already suffered enough, what with her daughter missing and all that, so I didn't want to tell her what I really thought about John Harrison and Jean Kerr and their relationship with her daughter.

The thing is that having children must just be so continuously hard. It just never stops, does it? I mean, take a boy and a girl and they meet, okay? Maybe they met through friends, okay? Let's say they are shy and bashful and so they spend time circling each other until one invites the other out. Then they discover that they're fond of each other, so now they're actually dating. Next up, they get engaged and eventually they marry, and I know there's a ton of painful stuff in the middle of all that, lots of soul-searching and the like, but for one reason or another they eventually get there. Following the wedding (not too soon after the wedding, mind) the wife becomes pregnant and then a child comes along and maybe a year later another one.

And then it's time for the parenthood phase, and the amount of time, care, love, energy, teaching, chastising, praising, crying, laughing, worrying, beaming, gloating and pride that goes into that phase is incredible. I mean, it really is. Then the fun really begins: 'I hate carrots!' and perhaps a bit of 'Cabbage makes me sick!' or maybe, 'I know tomatoes are meant to be good for you, but it's just like eating blood.' And what about dressing them? 'I don't like socks when they come up to my knees! Jim next door, he just wears them to his ankles!' And 'Why can't I wear my skirt that short? My best pal Georgina wears her skirt much shorter!'

Then think of the grief that schooling brings? And by that point, we've nearly completed the cycle, because it's time for the children to start bringing home their own first boyfriends or girlfriends. Think of all the tears and impromptu counselling sessions the parents encounter during that phase! Mind you, by the time their kids are thinking about boys or girls, they're already far too old to ask for their parents' counsel anyway, of course preferring instead to cry on the shoulders of their fellow sufferers.

And then the children are getting married, and the circle is complete. I know it's only words to a song, but I bet you most people on this great big circle of life probably do cry a river as they travel its circumference.

So, consider all of this and then consider how it is all – all of it – wasted when someone is killed in an accident. Or murdered.

It's all such a waste.

I mean, Jean's parents probably wouldn't have brought her up any differently had they known in advance what was to happen to her. They'd never have let her off eating her tomatoes, or overlooked the length of her skirt. Well, they just wouldn't do that, even if they knew what Jean's future held, would they?

Having said all of that, Jean Simpson's mum was still convinced that her daughter was very much alive. Her theory was that her Jean and John Harrison had called off the wedding. She didn't care what John Harrison had told me – her daughter had called off the wedding, split up with John, was embarrassed at her failure and was now lying low for a time.

'If I could only find the wee pet,' she continued while fighting back the tears, 'and tell her that she shouldn't be embarrassed. She hasn't failed, David. She'd only have failed if she'd gone ahead and married the twit.'

'When Jean was growing up, Mrs Simpson, did you have any places you regularly went for holidays?' I thought I'd try falling in with the missing person theory for a moment.

'No, not really, son. We went to Blackpool a few times but sure that was always a disaster, sure it rained all the time. No, when her father was alive we'd always just head off and follow our noses.'

'In your travels, was there any place that Jean seemed to particularly like, you know, somewhere she'd a strong affinity with?'

'Hand on heart, no. She'd only recently said how much she loved being around here again. She said when she'd all the time in her life to spare she'd ignored Matlock entirely, but now that there were greater demands on her time she'd fallen in love with the hills of her hometown. Funny that. Aye, there's nowt queerer than folk.'

Mrs Simpson went on to show me some of her prized possessions; her photographs of Jean growing up.

Photographs, yes: why hadn't any of us thought of it before? Why not get a photograph of Jean circulated around the newspapers? That way, if she really was still out there, someone would be bound to recognise her? I mean, I suppose it would be part of the police procedure if and when they started to take the case seriously. But how many months did we have to wait until that happened?

I left the following morning after a good night's sleep and a hearty breakfast with a large envelope containing a photograph of Jean Simpson. I'd get it copied on Monday and get it out to all the papers with a wee note stating Jean's circumstances.

My next port of call was Jean Kerr's house. I'd rung her the previous evening from the Simpsons' phone. Surprisingly, she was happy that I was in town, looking forward to seeing me, even. In fact, she was so upbeat that upon setting the phone down on Jean Kerr I remember thinking that maybe she sounded just a wee bit too happy that Jean Simpson was no longer in our midst.

Chapter Thirty-Five.

So I'd dinner and breakfast with the Simpson's and lunch with the Kerr's.

Jean Kerr had even dolled herself up a bit for me. I knew this to be the case, because even by the time I'd got round there at midday, she'd already got her 'face' on. Quite amazing for someone on sick leave. Her hair was puffed up like the woman from Charlie's Angels – you know the one I mean, she was with Ryan O'Neal for quite a time? Yeah, that's her – the blonde one, Farrah Fawcett Majors. Given the choice though… no, no, we mustn't get into that.

Anyway, we'd a pleasant enough lunch and then Jean suggested that we go out for a walk and a chat.

'I'm looking for Jean,' I began simply. I know it must have been obvious, but I just felt it was important to state it, you know?

'I know,' she replied, 'our Jean's mum rang me to tell me.'

We walked on in silence for a time. Jean Simpson had been right to pine after the rolling hills of Matlock – they really were that stunning. I mean, half a mile from Jean Kerr's house and we were already in the wilds.

'Do you think she's up here?' Jean said, as she cast her eyes over the landscape.

'No.' I don't know why I said that. I don't even know why I thought it.

'So where do you think she is?'

'I don't know. I really haven't a clue,' I confessed.

'You think something has happened to our Jean?'

'Her mother thinks she's called off the wedding with John and gone into hiding until the embarrassment passes,' I replied, avoiding the question.

'But you don't think so,' Jean said, pushing for an answer. She could be forceful when she wanted to be. Perhaps she should maybe have been out and about looking for her friend rather than me. But then she was also on my list of suspects. So maybe she was pushing me to see how much I really knew. She might even have been cute enough to be trying to figure out whether or not I suspected her.

'I don't think so' I replied, staring at her face for a clue.

'Why?'

'I think if that was the case, at the very least she would ring her mum and you, you know, tell you that she was safe and she'd be back in touch when she had it all sorted out in her head.'

'She might ring her mum, David,' she began, her voice dropped to nearly a whisper for the second part, 'but she'd never ring me now in a million years.'

'For her not to have been in touch with anyone for over three weeks… well, it does worry me…' I continued, before realising what she'd just said. 'Why would she never ring you in a million years?'

'Oh, we'd a wee bit of a fight,' Jean Kerr continued, playing her cards very close to her chest. She rooted around in her pockets for a few seconds before producing a packet of Players and a cheap lighter, which didn't immediately strike me as strange.

'Oh? What was the fight about?'

'John Harrison,' she replied, over-dragging on her ciggie.

Things were looking up. Here we were only a few minutes into the conversation and we were already talking motives.

'Yes?' I said, wanting her to expand.

She obviously didn't want to because she just replied, 'Yes.'

'So what was the fight about?' I pushed.

'Look, I'd been telling her for ages that John was not the one for her.'

'Why?'

'Because I felt that to be so' she replied, matter of fact.

'No, I meant why did you feel that John was not the one for Jean?'

'Oh for heaven's sake…' she started and faltered. 'Well, let's just say I had my reasons.'

'Jean, this might be important – I really need to know everything that went on between you two. You see, it seems to me that she did listen to you and dump him, well, at least according to her mum.'

'I just used to think that there was something weird about him. I couldn't quite put my finger on it. To be very honest with you, Pet, I could never work out why he would leave a girl like Mary Skeffington for Jean Simpson. That's just being perfectly honest with you, David, that's no disrespect to our Jean.'

She had a point. I'd considered the same issue and the only thing I could come up with now that I knew Mary as well as I knew her, was that Jean was perhaps more malleable. Mary would listen to you, take into consideration what you had to say, yes, but she would make up her own mind as to the direction she'd take. I think that she regretted the only occasion in her life when she went against her instincts, which was when John had persuaded her that they should become lovers. Her instinct had been to keep the relationship on a friendship level. She'd proven to herself that her initial instinct had been spot on.

'So when you had this discussion with Jean, was it all very heated?' I asked.

'Yes, you could say that.'

'So what did you say to her that convinced her to leave John?'

'I told her that I'd slept with John Harrison.'

'You what?'

She looked beyond me, out into the hills. The wind was blowing her mane all about her face and she used the excuse to hide herself from me. Nonetheless, she held her head up defiantly.

'I slept with John,' she repeated, this time staring long and hard at the cigarette.

'I can't believe it,' I said, still in shock, 'you've just told me you thought he was a bit weird and then you go off and sleep with the future husband of your best friend?'

'Don't get all pious on me, David Buchanan, I know what you and Jean were up to when you were meant to be off "seeing your groups".'

I'd a feeling she was bluffing. I wanted her to be bluffing. So I played her bluff.

'She was a mate, Jean! I'd never as much as kiss her. I swear to you, I've never kissed Jean Simpson.'

She looked at me and smiled a knowing smile. 'Now that's funny, David. Because that's exactly what she said; she said you'd never even kissed.'

'Well, that's only because it's true,' I protested. 'But let's get back to you and John Harrison.'

'It was nothing, really. He came round to the flat one night, our Jean wasn't there. He'd had a few drinks already. He said he knew she wasn't out with you. I said she probably was, he said no, he knew for a fact that she wasn't. I'll be honest, David, I told him I thought you two were getting close. He opened the bottle of wine he'd brought round and a few glasses later we were at it like animals in front of the electric fire.'

'Really?'

'I was thinking about it afterwards, and I think she could have walked in on us, and in a way I think we both were hoping that might happen. In John's case, so that he could get his own back on her for running off with you all the time. She was seeing you a lot more than she was seeing John, David, did you know that?'

'I thought it was because he was busy saving to get married,' I started and then returned to her earlier threat. 'Why did you hope Jean would walk in on the pair of you?'

'What? Oh, well I just wanted her to see that he wasn't all he was making himself out to be. This "great husband-to-be" of hers wasn't exactly the great Almighty.'

'The cigarettes?' I said nodding at her Player, 'did John turn you on to those?'

'I used to smoke,' she began, taking a long drag as if she was trying to demonstrate the fact, 'then John reminded me they're good for losing weight.'

'So youse shared a ciggie after the sex?'

She just grimaced slightly but seemed happy I'd twigged.

'Did you continue the affair?' I asked.

'Affair!' she said, laughing as if she was quite chuffed that I'd called it that. 'For heaven's sake, David! It wasn't an affair! We just... it only happened the once. He wanted to continue. I was tempted because I have to admit he may look like a mountain man, but his lunchbox is well packed.'

His lunchbox is well packed! Please! Only someone like Jean Kerr would use a phrase like that. You remember what I was saying about all that education? Well, Jean's a perfect example of how it was wasted. It's the confidence she has, though, to get away with it. I don't know another person in this world, particularly a woman, who would ever dream of saying that without cringing and here was Jean Kerr, proudly beaming on as if it was the most natural thing in the world!

'I suppose I was upset about work, about being ill, about you, about everything and I just wanted a wee bit of comfort. I needed some comfort, David, we all do.'

'Yes, but you risk weakening the power of love by seeking it in all the wrong places.'

'Oh yeah, thus speaks the romantic. It's all right for you: you've slept with two out of the three of us for sure and I'd still bet good money you were riding our Jea–'

I made to protest.

'Don't even bother to try, David. It's not important,' she said, shaking her head. 'I just find it weird the way the three of us, our Jean, Mary and me, we are all in some way connected. Even though we don't particularly want to be. Even the five of us, you know the Fab Five, you and John included. God, think of who's been with whom and when and who did what.'

If only she knew the half of it. On second thoughts, hopefully she, nor anyone else, ever would.

'When you and Jean had this conversation about John, how was she about it?'

'She was quite casual, really; dismissive wouldn't be too strong a word. She said she expected it of both of us. But she said it gave her an easy out, and she'd been looking for an out.'

'Did she say why?'

'I honestly thought she'd set her sights on you, David. She'd go all gooey when she spoke about you,' she said, now staring at me as if she was waiting for me to give her a hint at whether she was on the right track.

'Look Jean, she knew I was totally into Mary. I told her.'

'You told her that you had a girlfriend, but we had to find out for ourselves that it was Mary Skeffington,' she butted in, correcting me.

'Either way, she knew I was only interested in being her friend. We were good friends.'

'Such a good friend you dropped her entirely when you started going out with Mary.'

'Jean, there was a history there, you must realise–'

'I do,' she said, interrupting me again. 'I just don't want you pretending that everything was nice and sweet in your wee corner of the world where you and Mary were getting cosy.'

'Did Jean tell you that she was going to pack up with John after you'd slept with him?' I asked. I didn't want to let her off the hook either.

'I guessed she was going to, but she never actually said as much. I haven't spoken to her since. I thought all this might have been because she was pissed off with me. That would account for her vanishing act but, like you, I thought even if she was pissed off with me she'd still contact her mum to let her know everything was okay.'

'Yeah, you're right,' I muttered.

'But then I thought if she'd vanished because of any harm that had come to her, perhaps John would be back in the frame as the main suspect. If only because she wanted to dump him.'

We'd stopped walking and were looking out over the hills. Perhaps because we didn't have eye contact, she said, 'I've also considered the possibility that you could have harmed her, because of Mary.'

'Sorry?'

'Well for that one to work I'd have needed you and Jean to be having an affair, but you've nipped that one in the bud. Haven't you?' she smirked awkwardly, leading me to believe that she still wasn't convinced otherwise.

Thank goodness I'd played her bluff. But before I'd a chance to get too smug about it she continued: 'Then, of course, I considered Mary. Mary had two reasons: 1) She'd lost John to Jean; and 2) She might have felt that you two were getting too close. Does Mary know you're up here by the way?'

'Yes she does. But I should also point out that I haven't seen Jean Simpson since Mary and I got it together, so that dumps Mary off your list. She's had nothing to be jealous of. But talking about lists, since you've been so honest with me, I should also tell you that you were on my list, and after what you've just told me about you and John perhaps your name will move up said list a bit.'

'Perhaps, perhaps not, David; don't forget, I've been up here in Matlock most of the time.'

'Yeah that's true,' I said, as much to myself as Jean Kerr.

We stopped talking for a time, just walking in silence, either enjoying the spectacular views or going over our thoughts.

'So, you really haven't heard from either John or Jean since you confessed to her about sleeping with John?' I asked, sensing that the conversation, and walk, was coming to a natural end.

'That's correct, David. All of this aside, I do care for her and I want to make sure she's okay – I'll do anything else I can to help,' she said, making a dog's dinner out of trying to stub out the remains of her cigarette with her boot.

Finally I asked her the same question I'd asked Mrs Simpson Senior: Was there anywhere Jean liked to go, any place at all she was fond of? Jean Kerr concurred with Mrs Simpson about Jean Simpson's newfound love for Matlock.

Next on my list was to check in with the local police station, without either Jean Kerr or Mrs Simpson knowing. I wanted to know if there'd been any unidentified bodies turned up recently matching the description of Jean Simpson. Thankfully, the response was to the negative.

So, armed with my few new bits and pieces of information, and Jean Simpson's photograph, I caught the mid-afternoon train back to Wimbledon. About ten minutes into the journey I opened the envelope to find paper-clipped to the top of the photograph a wee note from Jean Simpson's mum. She just wished me well, asked me to keep in touch, thanked me for my efforts and enclosed fifty pounds towards my expenses. I thought it was a terrible lot of money – I wouldn't need anywhere near that amount to cover my expenses. Well, I hoped I wouldn't need it, anyway. I resolved I would return as much of the stipend as possible to her. However, I have to tell you that for a few moments, a few precious moments, I did feel very good about the whole affair. It was now on a professional level. I was officially investigating a missing person and I was being paid expenses-plus to do so.

Yes, it made me feel good. It was a contentment I'd never experienced before. I should have enjoyed it more while it lasted, because that feeling of purpose wasn't going to last much longer.

Chapter Thirty-Six.

When I got back to London, I went immediately to Mary's flat. She was due back from her mother's about 7.00 p.m. so I figured I'd at least two hours to collect my thoughts. I'd like to say that I'd some kind of handle on the Jean Simpson case. Would you just listen to me? Here I am acting the big shot detective already. Did you hear what I'd just said there? I said, 'I'd like to think I'd some kind of handle on the Jean Simpson case.'
Here was I, 'not long since, knee-high to a packet of Surf,' as my father had a habit of reminding me, perfectly happy to blast off all this bleedin' television jargon. Tell the truth, David, what exactly was your handle on the case so far?
Okay, since you've asked, I'll tell you.
Jean Kerr had told Jean Simpson that she'd bonked Jean Simpson's future husband, John Harrison. Jean Simpson had told John Harrison that the marriage was off. Finito, the end, whatever you want to call it, it was over. John Harrison didn't want it to be over, for lots of reasons, maybe even because his first ex was now set up very cosily with yours truly. We know John had a few demons of his own: he didn't want children, and (maybe because of this) he didn't want to have sex with his wife until they were married, and he liked to control his women. Hell, even Jean Kerr suspected that Jean Simpson and I were more than friends and she'd suggested as much to John. Perhaps John had brought this up in the argument with Jean Simpson about Jean Kerr, and perhaps Jean Simpson had admitted it, admitted every sordid little detail of what we'd got up to

behind his back. Perhaps she did this to get her own back on John for bonking Jean Kerr. Perhaps she was even madder due to the startling fact that in all the time she and John had been betrothed to each other, he'd never once tried to make love to her. Added to which, Jean Simpson knew that John had definitely done the wild thing with his ex (and my current) girlfriend, a certain Miss Mary Skeffington, who herself may or may not be more annoyed than even I thought at John dumping her in favour of Miss Simpson.

So in our big pot we've got two people, Jean Simpson and John Harrison, and we've got all of the above crazy mixture going on around them. You leave that brewing long enough and eventually it has to catch fire, doesn't it? I mean, come on! This is all very flammable stuff. Perhaps it was an accident, perhaps it wasn't, but the end result was that Jean Simpson was no more.

Yes, there was still a slim chance that Jean had gone to ground until the whole John Harrison thing had blown over. But that option was becoming slimmer by the hour. Jean had been missing now for just over three and a half weeks – that's exactly twenty-five days since she'd last been seen – and my money would have been on Jean contacting her mother, or her place of work at the very least, if only to secure her financial future. She'd been in touch with neither and so the signs were ominous.

I had taken out a fresh notebook and I was jotting ideas down, nothing of consequence, nothing at all, as a matter of fact. My mind was wandering away from the case: I was looking forward to Mary Skeffington returning home. I was thinking of the last time we'd made love.

There's something very magical about the way a woman will sometimes give herself to you totally, unselfishly, completely, while having no interest in their own pleasure. This special magnetism is so powerful, so overwhelming, that a part of you knows that you should wait, you should be conscious of her pleasure. But that's only a little part of you, the other part – the major part – pushes you selfishly on and the fact that your partner is so giving, so available and so willing, makes it unbearable to try to stop or slow down.

That was the way it had been the last time Mary Skeffington and I had made love and even thinking about it three days later made every part of my body tingle with excitement. Not that I wanted to enjoy it the same way again immediately; no, not at all. In fact, if anything the complete opposite was the case. I wanted to try to be as preoccupied with her pleasure as she had been with mine. But it wasn't even that; I just wanted to be with her again.

Seven o'clock passed and no Mary. Trains, you can set your watch on them always being late. I fell asleep shortly after eight, I guessed. I must have been pretty tired because I woke just after ten o'clock. This was very unusual for me; I usually couldn't sleep during the day if my life depended on it. Mary must have been tired as well because when I woke up she was nowhere to be seen. She'd obviously missed me sleeping on the sofa and gone straight to bed. I crept into the bedroom hoping to find her asleep.

No Mary.

Surely the train couldn't have been three hours late? Three hours was a bit ridiculous. I wanted so much for Mary to be there so that I could share all the new information I'd discovered over the weekend. Equally I wanted to find out what kind of weekend she and her mum had had. Now I'd been to their home, I could imagine Mary and her mother, two very English people, having a very elegant English weekend in a very English house.

I was tired. I was fighting sleep. I just wanted my Mary back with me so that we could cuddle up in bed together. She'd say, 'No monkey business, Buchanan,' as we were both about to fall asleep. I wouldn't have considered any monkey business up to that point, but once she'd planted the idea in my mind and what with a wee bit of strategic wiggling, well, who knows.

At 10.40 p.m. I rang Wimbledon station to find out what had happened to the train. They let the phone ring off the hook; either that or they were at home safely tucked up in their own beds, not all together, mind you.

At 10.45 p.m. I rang her mum.

'Hello David, how are you?' she said, in a very polite voice while I knew she was thinking what the hell was I doing, ringing her up at this time of night?

You see, I'd figured that Mary had stayed on an extra night and I just wanted to check in with her so that I could go to sleep. I'd be a bit sad about having to go to bed by myself but tiredness would win that battle.

'Ah, is Mary in bed already, Mrs Skeffington?'

'David, how many times do I have to tell you? My name is Hermione, please – call me Hermione. Now, what was it you were ringing about?' she said sheepishly. I'd obviously woken her up.

'Sorry Mrs Skeff… sorry, I mean Hermione. Is Mary already asleep?'

'David,' she said, a sharpness entering her voice, 'Mary left here just after lunchtime. She caught the earlier train; she wanted to be home when you arrived.'

'Ah. Well, it's just that the information line at Wimbledon station is shut for the night. I assume they're carrying out engineering works.'

'Not for six hours, David, let me make a call. Stay by the phone box, I'll ring you back presently.'

Three and a half minutes later the coin box in the cold hall of Mary's flat rang.

'God David, the train got in on time! She would have been in Wimbledon by 3.20 p.m!'

A lump climbed straight from my heart and stuck in my throat. 'Is there anywhere she'd go?' I asked, trying to keep the panic I felt growing up through my chest at bay.

'No, she was so desperate to see you! That John Harrison bugged her a few times over the weekend, though.'

'He did? Was he down there?'

'No, but he was never off the phone,' she answered calmly; she was dealing with this better than me.

'How did he know she was down there?'

'He rang the flat and when he didn't get any answer, he rang here.'

'What was he annoying her about Mrs Sk... sorry, Hermione?'

'She said he was saying horrible things about you. He told her you were in Derby. She said she knew. He said, cheeky as you like, "Ah, but did you know that he was up there to see the other Jean?" He said one Jean wasn't enough for you.'

'Agh.'

'Listen, David, now listen to me closely David Buchanan: Mary didn't believe any of it. She knows what John's like. We both know what he's like, David. She gave him an earful and sent him on his way. She said she couldn't believe how lucky she was to have met you, she said she was starting to have nightmares thinking about the fact that if she'd have married him, the saddest thing would have been that she would never have met you.'

'Hermione–'

'Listen David, I'm telling you this not to give you a big head, but so that there are no doubts in your mind about you and Mary. Doubts are the seed of the devil, David – they can destroy you if you let them.'

'Thank you, Hermione,' I said. I always felt weird calling her by her first name. You see, to me she was a real lady and I felt like I should respect her by calling her Mrs Skeffington, because that's the way I'd been brought up, and the older I grew the more I found that my parents lessons and manners always stood me in good stead. 'Thank you, and I need you to know that I have absolutely no doubts whatsoever about my Mary and I. I've rarely been more convinced about anything in my life.'

'Good.'

'Now, is there anything else you can tell me about what John said to Mary?'

'Let's see now. Oh yes, he said that he and Jean Simpson were finished. He suggested that he and Mary should get back together again. Mary said that whenever she said something to John it wasn't just like he hadn't heard her – it was more like she hadn't even spoken.'

'Did Mary ask him about Jean?'

'Yes, she did. He told her something about how Jean had got married sooner than she wanted to. Do you think that means she has run off and married someone else? Mary was beside herself with worry; she didn't know what to think! Have you any idea what's happening, David?'

'Tell me, Hermione: Did John know when Mary was due to come back to town?'

'Well, I heard her telling him not to come round because you'd be there. I don't know when she was referring to. Should I ring the police David? Is Mary okay?'

'Look Mrs Skeff… Hermione, I've got to go out and find Mary. If you don't hear from me by the morning, ring the police. Now, try to get some sleep.'

'David…' She started to say something but she obviously thought better of it and stopped before starting again, 'Look David, I'll wait up for your call. Please ring me. Please ring me even it's just to tell me that nothing has happened.'

'Don't worry, Mrs Skeffington, everything is going to be okay,' I said, just before I set the phone down. I don't know whether I was trying more to reassure her or myself.

Either way, I hoped it was working better on her than it was on me.

Chapter Thirty-Seven.

The tiredness had vanished completely from my body. I felt tight and taut with adrenalin and I was bursting to do something, anything really that might help Mary and Jean. I was so up for it, for a bit of action, I just hoped that I wouldn't peak too quickly.

It took me about fifteen minutes to reach John Harrison's first floor flat at 36 Worple Road. The yellow hue from the lights of the second floor cast a large rectangular beam of light onto the darkness of his unkempt lawn. I'm sure I could hear noises coming from above, but the problem with a house of flats is that anything you hear could be coming from any of the apartments.

I rang the doorbell. I didn't have a plan. I just knew I needed to move forward, in any direction. I just needed to do something.

There was no reply, so I looked through the letterbox into the hallway and as I did, I remembered the line from Dylan's song: 'You will wind up peeking through a keyhole down upon your knees.' Dylan had Miss Simpson better pegged from the beginning than I ever had.

I rang the doorbell once more, same response as last time. I was now starting to panic. What was I to do, burst the door down? Was Mary inside? If so, what was he doing to her? How had she got inside? Had she merely gone with him, you know, had he turned on the old charm again?

I walked out into the rectangular light beam in the garden and started to pick up stones, pebbles bits of mud, anything I could get a handful of to throw at John's window.

I started to shout, as loud as I knew how. I was going to get a reaction, someway, somehow, anyhow in fact.

Two minutes later the front door opened and the very sheepish head of John Harrison peeked out from behind the eight or so inches he'd opened the door.

'Buchanan, what the feck are you doing at my house at this time of night?'

'I'd like to come into your flat for a minute and talk to you,' I tried. I could hear the nervousness in my voice. I did wish that I hadn't sounded so feeble, so wimpy. No disrespect to your burgers, Mister, but you picked the name!

'Come back tomorrow, I'm just about to go to bed! I've been drawing all day.'

If the stale whiff of tobacco and lack of daylight was anything to go by, I'd say he definitely hadn't been out of his flat all weekend. There also was a little pong of sick coming from him. The combination was quite vile to be honest, and I stepped back a bit.'

'I'm sorry, John, it won't wait. I need to come in. NOW!' I was happy I'd finally managed to get a bit of authority in my voice.

'Come back tomorrow, Buchanan,' he hissed and started to shut the door.

I tried to protest and at the same time as I stuck my foot in the door, I also stuck my chin forward, just like a sprinter might while trying to nudge at least some part of his body past the winning tape.

That's when he slammed the door and it connected full on with both my chin and nose. The last thing I remembered was the metallic smell of blood. I don't think I'd even worked out it was my own blood I was smelling as I slumped into a heap on his doorstep.

I don't remember how long I was unconscious for.

I do remember taking comfort from the ice-cold, red-tiled step, in an effort to reduce the heat in my flushed face. I thought I could hear footsteps coming from inside, I thought I'd better try to struggle to my feet to face John Harrison as he came to finish me off.

I thought he must have opened the door again, because I imagined I felt a warm draft from within.

'I know you took Jean from her flat! I know you know where she is! If you don't let me in right now I'm going to the police!' I believed I said.

'What are you on about?' he'd said, dropping back to the Scottish accent he usually hid so well.

If he didn't close the door on me then that was a good sign, wasn't it? A little hesitation would have showed something, wouldn't it?

'What's all this crap about Jean?' he said.

'Look John, I know that you're involved with her disappearance,' I heard my voice say, working up to my bluff.

He rolled his eyes, laughed and replied. 'Oh yeah?'

That would be another positive clue, you know, the fact that he wanted to hear my evidence.

'Yes, I know you were the last person in her flat,' I continued. I'd try not to act. The way to make it work would be to believe it, genuinely believe in this scenario I was creating. That way, he wouldn't see through my scam. You see, I have this theory that all great actors don't act, they don't pretend; they really make themselves believe they are the character they are playing.

'Right, of course you do,' he said, smirking.

He was giving nothing away. His previous two answers, however, encouraged me to lay out the information I'd gathered, in order to flush out any proof I thought I might have. But he wouldn't once even hint at.

'And how do you know that?' he asked.

Ah ha! So he was implying that my accusation was correct!

'Okay, John,' I said, voice still sounding shaky, fuzzy even. If I was attempting to go for bust, it was vitally important that he believed I knew something, 'I know you were in Jean's flat just before she disappeared because of the way you tidied away her records. You put her record sleeve away and left the record on the deck.'

'But anyone in the world could have done that, Inspector Holmes! I'm afraid you've come up with nothing elementary old chap, more of a lemon entry, if you ask me,' he replied, enjoying a right old chuckle at my expense with his weak attempt at humour. He started to close the door again.

'Perhaps so, John, but you... you and Jean Simpson were the only two people in the world whose fingerprints were found on the record sleeve,' I bluffed.

'Fingerprints? But surely there'd be loads of fingerprints on a record sleeve?' Again he allowed himself a bit of a chuckle, but this time it wasn't be quite so hearty.

'Possibly, but the difference on this occasion was that it was a brand new record, John – Bob Dylan's Bringing It All Back Home. Mary had just bought it at Musicland. Yes, John, that's right – Musicland. Do you know what they do at Musicland, John? They shrink-wrap all their new records. So that Bob Dylan record would have been untouched until she got it home. The only prints on the sleeve would have been Jean's and the person who filed it away when they tried to tidy up after abducting her.'

John countered that with, 'Fingerprints? What do you know about fingerprints anyway? Did you get your magnifying glass out and examine the bloody thing?'

'No John, actually that's what I do professionally,' I lied, 'that's why I've never been able to tell you guys about my work – it's all secret work, for the government.'

For once in my life, my not being allowed to admit what I did at work had worked to my advantage.

He stood in shock, still managing to give very little away. But I was on a bit of a roll so I continued down on this shaky road.

'Yesterday, when we'd breakfast, at the end of the meal? I stole your knife. Yep, that's right, and your prints matched up exactly with those on the record sleeve,' I said, not even bothering to cross my fingers behind my back. Well I could have, couldn't I?

That's the thing about lying isn't it? You've got to keep going. You've got to keep on with the lies, layering and layering them, and the lies have to get bigger and bigger in order to cover up the flaws of the previous ones. By this point, then, I definitely had him interested, as he seemed to be considering his options.

'Oh sod off home, Buchanan, I'm off to bed,' he'd said, playing my bluff.

'I'll get the police out. I'm serious.'

'Yeah, right, and remind them to bring a search warrant won't you?' he said, as he rolled his eyes and disappeared behind the closed door once again. This time he was more cautious or I was less adventurous but either way, his green door and I avoided contact.

It's funny how in your fantasy, you always know the correct questions to ask your adversary and they always know the correct answers to give. I wondered whether the police really need a search warrant. Surely if they thought something untoward was going on they could just burst the door down? But if they needed a warrant that meant it was going to take until tomorrow morning, and by that time Mary could be… well, it didn't bear thinking about, did it?

I decided to go with Plan B.

The problem was, there was no Plan B. There hadn't even been a Plan A. Then I started to think; if I did work for the government on secret work, what would I do?

Simple: I'd try to gain access by another route.

John Harrison's flat was in a terraced street so I counted the houses down to the first break and hopped over the hedge. Then I nipped into the back garden and counted the number of gardens back down again until I reached Harrison's. I knew it immediately; it was as overgrown as the front and I took some comfort in that, because the additional foliage offered me shelter should anyone, including my chief suspect, happen to look out of their back window.

All the houses were identical and lucky for me they had a single storey extension built out into the garden. Some people used this for a kitchen, some used it for a dining room and some kept them for their original purpose, which was a washroom and a coal shed. The ground floor flat had converted their coal shed into an extension for the kitchen, forming an L-shaped dining area.

I needed the owner of this house to: a) be in bed; and b) be considerate enough to leave me a dustbin in the garden. Which, to my great delight, they had. I climbed onto the dustbin and then up onto the single-storey roof. It creaked, like what sounded to my ears, like thunder as I tiptoed across it, to what I considered to be John Harrison's back window.

I spent quite a few minutes trying to work out the best way to open it. James Bond would have a diamond glasscutter and he'd scratch a perfect semi-circle close to the latch on the frame, but not before sticking a rubber suction pad to the piece of glass he wished to remove. He'd then very gently tap the glass, tug the rubber and the glass would come effortlessly with it. He'd stick his hand through, open the latch, step into the room, dust himself down and proceed to save the heroine.

My initial idea was somewhat less ingenious than James Bond's. I'd take off one of my shoes and break the glass with the heel of my size eight and a half. It would cause a bit of a racket, I know, but I've been in houses on numerous occasions where people hear things and they go, 'What's that?' and everyone goes silent for a few seconds and when they hear no further disturbance, they all continue talking as though nothing had happened, perhaps even assuming the disturbance was from next door. So I knew that it was vitally important to remain totally motionless for that period, you know, just after the 'What's that?'

On second thought, perhaps better not to risk that approach and have John Harrison coming to investigating the disturbance immediately after the 'What's that?' point.

I then started to think that if I'd a knife or something I could stick it between the gap – you know, where one window frame slides up or down past the other, which would allow me to flick the catch open with my knife. The problem being that I didn't have a knife. Well, that wasn't the only problem. It was very cold and Mary Skeffington was in danger. There had to be something I could do to gain access. And then I had another idea.

I placed my hands on the wooden cross of the window and tried to push it and guess what, the window slid up – freely and quietly! The catch had been open the whole time. Eat your heart out Sean and Sherlock.

I'd pushed the window up to its full height and instantly I wished I hadn't. The smell that escaped into the fresh air, nearly, quite literally, knocked me off my feet and back down off the roof. The stench was totally unbearable, like an open cesspool. I had to sit down on the roof to catch my breath and some fresh air. I ventured back towards the open window again. Same thing happened. I took a handkerchief and placed it over my bloodied nose, which for some reason or other had mysteriously stopped bleeding, and tried again. This time I made it into the room.

I moved across the floor on my hands and knees and infrequently I'd drop my handkerchief hand to make a wide arc in front of me in the darkness, to ensure I didn't bump into anything and give the game away. I heard some muffled sounds from the next room and I made my way gingerly towards the vertical stripe of white light, which signalled, I hoped, the bottom of the door.

I wasn't quite able to hear what was going on, but I was sure I could hear someone giggling.

When I reached the stripe of light I dropped on to my stomach and put my ear to the door. The idea was to see what I could hear, but again the sour, sickly stench nearly got the better of me. I put the handkerchief back over my nose and I tried again to position my ear next to the crack where the light had been coming from.

I was now able to hear a little more clearly this cycle of sound.

First there was a click, like someone clicking his or her tongue, sounding a bit like tetc. Next there was a hissing sound and then another little chuckle.

I would have been happy to find one of Dylan's keyholes to peek through, even down upon my knees. I didn't want to burst through into the other room if there was a chance I would endanger Mary's life. At the same time I realised that I needed to do something.

I raised myself up onto my knees and took the door handle in my free hand. I'd turn the handle as slowly as I possibly could; stopping every time there was even a suggestion of a noise. I tried to time my sounds to the cycle of sounds from within. As I did, I tried to figure out what the strange sounds were. I didn't like it, John's sinister laughter, not one little bit.

After what seemed like an age I'd worked up the courage to turn the door handle to its extreme. I waited for a few seconds and started to pull the door towards me. It came easily. Very slowly, I let the handle return to its regular position. The door was a couple of inches ajar now, but my view was obscured by what looked to be a high-back sofa. I eyed my way around the room as much as I could. There was a red glow of some sort rising from the other side of the sofa, lighting up the ceiling and shooting a few shadows around it.

'This is such fun, isn't it?' John Harrison said.

I hugged the floor, then I realised he wasn't talking to me.

I strained my neck as much as I could, but I couldn't for the life of me see anyone else in the room. In my desperation to see something I accidentally dropped my handkerchief and I was sure I was going to pass out from the fumes clouding the room.

Those odd sounds were clearer now, still the tetc, then the hissing noise and then John's manic wee laugh.

I heard John say, 'I'll get around to you, Mary. It'll be your turn very shortly, I promise. I have to finish with Jean first – she's very jealous, you know. She's always been very jealous of you, you know. Even though it was me who left you. That was never enough for her, you know. Nag, nag, nag, every time we met, Mary this, Mary that. Sulk, sulk, sulk. If it wasn't Mary this or that then it was bloody David this and bloody David that.'

Okay, so Mary and Jean were both in the room with him. I thanked God she was alive. That must be what she foul smell was, I'd think, he must have locked Jean in this room for the last three weeks and not let her out for anything. But then I'd managed to get in, hadn't I?

Tetc, hiss, then the evil little laugh. On and on the sound circle continued.

'You know,' Harrison continued, after one of his laughs, 'we get married until death do us part. That's what I told Jean, anyway. I told her that when we had agreed to marry. We'd promised each other to marry and the only way to break it was by one of us dying. Now, I certainly wasn't going to lose my life over Jean dumping me. So I was fair, Mary, I gave her the option; she could either marry me or die.'

He wasn't going to kill anybody if I'd anything to do with it.

Tetc. Hiss. Laugh.

'She spat in my face and said "Not if you were the last person on this Earth." What a stupid thing to say! If I were the last person on this Earth, she'd be jumping all over me to keep the wild animals away from her. She'd be desperate for me to feed her, to house her. Mary, why do you think man is put on this planet? We're here to look after you. It's that simple. Jean didn't get that. She thought she could do without me and look what happened to her when she lost my protection?' he continued, as I tried to make myself comfortable and avoid a cramp.

Okay, he'd done Jean some harm but he kept saying he wasn't finished. What was he doing? Exactly how much time did I have left? What was I going to do? What would Bond or Holmes do, for heaven's sake? Somebody help me… please.

I'd do what I always do in times of trouble. I was about to say in 'such' times of trouble there, but I'd never been in such a situation before. But in any other troublesome situation I always do the same thing, and that is to say the Lord's Prayer. There, it's out. I know it probably doesn't do any good… I know, I know, but it's the only thing I was able to think of. It was as if was I was inviting a little bit of good to come onto this Earth from Heaven.

'From Heaven? Where exactly is Heaven, David?' you ask.

Okay, okay, enough already – I told you I was desperate!

Tetc. Hiss. Laugh.

What was he doing in there?

Tetc. Hiss. Laugh.

'It was simple after that really,' he continued, 'I was really shocked how simple it was, Mary. I mean, this big thing we call "life", this miracle we call a "human being", it's so frail really. It doesn't take much to topple it. Yeah, yeah, the scientists go on and on about how phenomenal the brain is, how miraculous the heart is, how incredible life is, but all it takes is a bit of metal to put an end to all that. You know what, Mary, talking about knives; I was surprised how easy it was to stick a knife into Jean.'

John stopped for another laugh, only this time it was a different sounding one, as though he was amused at himself.

'From the look in Jean's eyes I'd say she was also quite surprised at how easy the knife slipped into her. Funny that she should lose her virginity to a knife. And the skin, you know, it's not really all that strong. You'd think it would be made to protect you against all eventualities. But it was a bit like it is when you stick a fork into a walnut. You don't think you're going to be able to do it, you think maybe, you know, because of the strength of the name, walnut, even steel would never pierce it. Then you push your fork into it and it starts to give way, and you can actually feel your fork sliding right into it. That's exactly what it was like with Jean, Mary. I didn't think the knife ever would go in, but it did – on and on and on, and then I tried again and again, and every single time her skin couldn't resist the metal blade of my knife. I have to tell you, Mary, I've never been as turned on as I was when I was stabbing her. You should be flattered, because I'm turned on just thinking about how I'm going to wet my pants all over again when I do it to you.'

Tetc. Hiss. Laugh.

Part of my difficultly, frustration if you will, was that I still didn't know if he had a knife to Mary's throat. I would still have to be careful. But shit… I was clearly running out of time here. My heart got the better of my head and I stood up and burst into the room.

My element of surprise was lost immediately due to the sight and smell of the scene in front of me.

John Harrison was sitting on the sofa in front of the electric fire. He had Jean Simpson's decomposed head resting on his lap. He was plucking hairs – the tetc sound – from her hideous-looking head and throwing them onto the bars of the fire, thereby creating the hissing sounds.

Tetc. Hiss.

But he would stop laughing when he saw me.

Jean Simpson was dressed in a wedding dress but the once white, micro-dress would be odiously soiled by all of her escaping body fluids. The smells were unbearable, yet John Harrison would appear to be unaffected by them.

As I walked closer to John and Jean, Mary eventually came into view; she was lying, bound and gagged, at John's feet.

I tried to keep my eye on both John and Mary. I watched John in fear and I studied Mary for a sign of life.

I felt mutterings in my stomach. I remembered all the crisps and sandwiches I hadn't enjoyed on the train journey back from Derby. Derby, and the walk around Matlock with Jean Kerr, would seem like years ago. I had to try not to think of the food in my stomach. But I could feel a cold sweat starting to cover my body from top to bottom. I started to gasp for air.

'Ah Holmes! I didn't think you'd be troubling me until the morning,' John said, as he lifted the remains of Jean's head from his lap.

He stood up, leaned over the fire to the mantelpiece and picked up a stainless steel knife. The blade was about a foot long.

'Yes Holmes,' he continued, as he rolled his eyes, 'I've got another experiment you can help me with. I want to see if it's as big a turn-on to kill a man as it is to kill a woman. I mean, I know I'm not gay or anything like that, but I have this feeling that taking a man's life is probably going to be just as exciting. Too bad you're not going to be around for me to discuss the results of my experiment with you.'

'It's too late, John, the police are outside,' I'd lied. Well, I'd had to hadn't I. I couldn't believe how shaky my voice sounded.

'Oh, we're going for the pantomime version then, are we?' he laughed, louder this time.

Mary Skeffington moaned through her gag.

She was alive!

Halleluiah! Halleluiah! (Never ever knock the Lord's Prayer again, okay?)

John was edging towards me, knife tightly grasped in his right fist. From his grip, it was clear he was going to stab me from above. From his trousers it was clear that he was aroused.

My stomach started to heave; it cared not a hoot for either man or blade. The repugnant smells were not mixing well with the recurring taste of the sandwiches and crisps. John continued towards me. Now he was no more than a few paces away. The light of the electric fire element was glistening on the blade. I knew I should be embarking on some kind of campaign, but I felt like death warmed up. I couldn't summon up any energy to combat either John or my stomach.

Thankfully my stomach gave first. It offered up its contents, all of them, and all over John Harrison's face. For a man who had been spending so much time in such vile conditions recently, I was shocked at his reaction. He was repelled. He yelled and screamed and tried to get the sick from his head. My heaving had subsided so I took careful aim and landed one kick with all of my might, square in the middle of his goolies. It was an easy target, you know, his "well-packed lunchbox", as Jean Kerr had unselfconsciously labelled it.

'Confucius say never go to battle with your tent still up,' I'd said, more out of relief than anything else.

He toppled to the floor in agony. I found it a little bewildering that this person who had just taken life and was about to take another would now be crying in pain on the floor like a baby. His face was blood red and he started to froth at the mouth. I'd walked over to him, literally, to make sure the wind was completely out of him and also to rescue Mary Skeffington.

By the time I'd managed to help her out into the street, the police had arrived. Apparently I wasn't as quiet or as discreet as I thought when I was climbing over the neighbour's roof, and they'd called the police.

Time for the end credits, I thought – when the hero and heroine walk off into the sunset. That's really what I was expecting to happen but instead I found myself lying on a cold, hard surface. I was still lying on a cold, hard surface. John Harrison's doorstep, in fact, exactly where he'd knocked me out by slamming his door full force into the middle of my face. While lying unconscious on his doorstep, I'd dreamed that entire nightmare but please believe me, at the time it was most certainly my reality.

But you know what bad nightmares are like; sometimes they're worth having just to enjoy the relief, the bliss you experience when you regain consciousness and realise they're not real.

But what was real was that both Jean Simpson and Mary Skeffington were still missing.

Chapter Thirty-Eight.

Did you believe that? Do you think I've been hiding the truth behind that just-suppose story? It would make a lot of sense wouldn't it? It would explain John's behaviour.

You see, when you come across someone in your life and you see how they act and you think they are maybe a wee bit funny with their ways; as in drawing dirty pictures of their wife-to-be; as in never looking you in the eye; as in always saving, never spending; as in being a bit grubby; as in not wanting to have sex with their girlfriend; as in having eyebrows that are very nearly joined in the middle; as in not liking great music; as in having sex with their girlfriend's girlfriend; as in always planning for the future and not ever living in the present; as in having no obvious friends. When you come across someone like that, well, at the time you just think they're funny, not as in funny peculiar, but just as in funny, as in different, don't you? Well, you just let it pass, don't you? But afterwards, when you find out they've murdered someone, then you start to think that all their funny little idiosyncrasies were, in fact, very weird, and that you should have spotted them as clues to the fact that you were dealing with a potential murderer.

That night, as I struggled to my feet again on the doorstep outside John Harrison's flat, imagining the worst and trying to figure out what to do next, but never quite managing to, I knew something was amiss. I felt it in my waters. I had an intuition. I'd a second sight. I was convinced of his evil deeds and intentions. I recalled all the clues he'd given us over the last several weeks, clues I'd not picked up on at the time. Clues I'd been too blind to notice and now, because I hadn't being paying attention, John Harrison was up in his room with the decomposing body of Jean Simpson and, worse than that, he'd kidnapped Mary. If I didn't really figure out a way to get into his smelly flat, he would definitely do her harm.

However, what with my making a racket and my threatening that the police were on their way, he'd probably be in a hurry to dispose of her and Jean's remains before I'd a chance to make good on my threat. Taking for granted that John was probably mentally disturbed, would it be a worry to him that I was about to return with the cavalry? Or was he above all that? (In case you are interested, I tried the back entrance and there was no open door, neither was there a flat roof, let alone a flat roof with access to an open window.)

As I regained consciousness on the front doorstep that night I was convinced there was still someone behind the door. All the hall lights were off. I opened the letterbox ever so slightly and I swear to you I could hear his breathing. I shouted in through the letterbox – nothing coherent, just a loud scream.

No reaction.

I opened the letter box again and shouted in, 'I know you're in there, Harrison, and I'm not leaving until I get Mary!'

Still no reply.

'Harrison!' I repeated, 'come on out, the game's up!'

Come on out, the game's up. Sorry? Was that supposed to scare the life out of him, or the conscience back into him? I couldn't believe I'd shouted that. Obviously someone else agreed with me because I could hear laughter from the other side of the door. It was a quiet giggle at first but then it grew and grew until at last it had grown into full-scale laughter.

The hall light went on and I could hear footsteps on the other side of the door and then, slowly at first, the door started to creak open.

'What the feck's your problem, Buchanan–' Harrison started, but before he'd a chance to get any more out I'd smashed the door full welt into his chest and rushed past him and up into his flat on the first floor.

You can imagine my surprise when all I found was a very tidy flat, well, tidy that was, apart from lots of drawings lying all over the floor and pinned all over the walls. No evil smells, no decomposing bodies, no Mary Skeffington tied up and helpless on the floor.

Yes, as I looked around the flat I was happy I hadn't picked up on all of his clues. You see, in John Harrison's case it's lucky that I didn't make a connection between all his wee quirks, because they were nothing more than that – quirks. They might have made him seem a little strange but the one thing they didn't make him was a murderer. He was, quite simply, a fellow human who was trying to deal with the problems of life in the best way he knew how. That's all he was guilty of.

With all of my overreacting he could have been forgiven if he'd done me some GBH. But no, he sat me down, genuinely concerned about my wellbeing and, after he'd showed me through to his bathroom so that I could tidy up the mess that was once my face, he made me a cup of tea. My bloodied face actually looked a lot worse than it was and with cold water and copious amounts of toilet roll, I was ready for my close-up again, Mr DeMille, although hopefully it wouldn't turn out to be my swan song.

More importantly, I was ready to apologise to John Harrison for my actions and declare him totally innocent in all of this.

Me, well I was guilty of a lot more. And now is the time for my confession.

The pure and simple fact in all of this is that I was guilty.

If Jean Simpson and I had not been enjoying our encounters, she most definitely would not be missing and, as I feared, murdered. So yes, it was my fault that she was missing, presumed murdered. Absolutely. No doubt about it. Jean Simpson died because of our relationship. When we were enjoying our early sexual experiments, what we were doing had repercussions outside of our wee room with the ageing red carpet.

And now I was inside John Harrison's wee room, acting and looking like a fool. Jean Simpson was missing and now Mary Skeffington was missing as well. I think John was now beginning to wonder about me and whether I could have been involved in either or both of their disappearances. What was it about girls who were involved with me? Jean Kerr had (thankfully, in her case) beaten a hasty retreat to Derby. Jean Simpson had disappeared from the face of the Earth several weeks since and now Mary Skeffington, the last of the trio, had vanished as well. I didn't confess any of my fears in this area to John, but I would imagine he had reached a similar conclusion. Mind you, he wasn't off the hook completely, was he? He'd also enjoyed a relationship of one kind and another with our trio of would-be Miss Houdinis.

We sat talking, John and I, for ages, each trying to convince ourselves, and each other, that we were neither involved in this nor responsible for the ongoing mystery. Besides, he was still convinced that Jean would show up sometime, somewhere and when she did, she'd be wearing her trademark miniskirt. His theory, and his worry about marrying her, was that Jean had never really been excited about the prospect of domestic bliss, staying at home cooking and washing for him. He had ruled out having children. John thought that if there was such an animal as a clean and well-dressed hippie who hosted a commune in a self-financing and well-kept house, it would be hard to hold Jean Simpson back from it. He also felt that she was very easily swayed, so, equally he figured she could have been swept off her feet by some cult or another. He'd been reading about that quite a bit recently, he said, and if I could find out which cult had captured her, then he, with his newfound knowledge, would help me find her and he, personally, would re-programme her. All very encouraging for Jean Simpson, but he offered no such theory or offer of help for Mary.

I asked him, would he take Jean Simpson back should she turn up.

'No way José! She's flown the nest and the nest is no longer there for her to come back to,' he said, without a moment's hesitation, just like a politician trouping out one of their well-used buzz phrases, in fact.

'But should you not wait until you find out what's happened to her before you go making any rash decisions?' I offered, trying to be the voice of reason when in fact all my thoughts were preoccupied with Mary.
'No, I don't think so, David. We were growing apart before she disappeared. Maybe she was the one who'd the confidence to do something about it.'

I started to wonder, if John had already made such a definite decision about Jean did that also mean he'd made his decision to try to win back Mary again.

Perhaps he was reading my thoughts because he said, 'I've made such a mess of things with my last three girlfriends. I need to try to work out where I went wrong before I try it again with another one. It's just that, even when you find a girl and you think you love her, hey, and maybe even you do love her, it doesn't really matter how much you love her, or how much she loves you, because you're still going to be alone with your thoughts. No one can ever be as tight with you as you'd like them to be. We'd all love to know someone as well as we know ourselves, but that's just never going to happen.'

We made small talk for another twenty minutes or so and then it was time for me to head off back home.

I felt lost.

I was worried, would other people, including WPC McGinley, come to the same conclusion I had, you know, the one about every girl I had a relationship with disappearing? I mean, Jean Kerr hadn't really disappeared, sure – she'd left town but we knew where she'd gone to.

I took little comfort in the fact that, aside from John and I, no one in our weird little group was aware that Mary had even disappeared.

Chapter Thirty-Nine.

As I opened the door to Mary's flat I was going through all the possible answers I could give to McGinley's inevitable question, 'So, Mr Buchanan, can you tell me how it is that every girl you've been biblical with disappears?'

I was mentally preparing my argument that Jean Kerr hadn't technically disappeared when I heard sounds from within the flat.

I threw caution to the wind and burst into the living room expecting to see, and confront, the person responsible for both Jean and Mary's disappearance.

'Where've you been to this hour of the night you old stop-out?' Mary Skeffington said, barely paying attention to me as she continued to unpack her overnight bag.

It was all I could do to remain standing on my feet. It took me what seemed like ages to catch my breath.

'I could ask you the same question! I rang your mother to see where you were.'

'I know, I spoke to her when I got in; she was beside herself with worry, David; you really scared her.'

'But I hadn't a clue where you were! I didn't know what else to do!'

'Well, I rang you from Wimbledon Station when I arrived back this afternoon and you weren't in, and I didn't want to be by myself so I went round to a friend's flat and… well, I found a soft seat. We were chatting away for ages before I realised what time it was. I just got in, about twenty minutes ago. What on Earth has happened to your face?'

343

She was most amused when I told her I'd accused John Harrison of kidnapping her. She tried not to laugh when I told her about the dream, more of a nightmare, which I'd experienced while unconscious on John Harrison's doorstep.

'Who was this friend?' I asked her defensively, when that little bit of strangeness between us had vanished.

'Oh, just a girlfriend from work. Catherine.'

Catherine, I thought, she'd never mentioned a Catherine before. But she didn't expand further and I didn't ask her to. I tried to find a subtle question to get into it with her but I couldn't think of one so I let the matter drop, for then at least.

I went to bed with mixed feelings. You know, happy that she was back and safe but worried about the unanswered (and unasked) questions.

I woke up in the same state I'd woken up for the previous couple of weeks: preoccupied with the missing Jean.

Where exactly do you start in your efforts to solve a crime? In a way, I suppose it's like being a kid in a sweet shop: What do you eat first? The main problem would always seem to be that you would spend so much of your time looking from delight to delight that you'd hardly have had a chance to select something before a parent or a grown-up would come into the shop and pull you away.

I mean, in my case it wasn't as if I was exactly spoilt for choice with clues or anything like that. I did have a multitude of suspects but I didn't have a clue as to where to start with them. On the couple of occasions I'd gotten somewhere with my investigation, as in with Jean Kerr and John Harrison, I'd convinced myself not only of their guilt but also as to how they'd carried out the crime. What if it was someone I didn't even know?

This approach held a lot of water. I mean where exactly was Jean Simpson on the night John came round to my flat, expecting to surprise us in the act? Who had she actually been out with and why? Had she been with a hippie perhaps? Had she, like John suggested, already run off with said hippie to a commune in the West Country? I couldn't really see it myself. Jean Simpson – and Jean Kerr, for that matter – hated all things dirty. They hated, with a passion, boys who smelled bad. When Jean Kerr said that I had scrubbed up well, the emphasis had been on the word 'scrubbed'. Now hippies, while not being exactly what you would describe as dirty, certainly could be a bit musty. This probably stemmed from the fact that they would crash straight from their living room to their bedroom (usually the same space) without feeling either the need or the desire for a visit to the bathroom. Neither did they seem keen to celebrate the arrival of each brand new day with a change of clothing. No, I doubt Jean Simpson could ever have abided that.

But she had to be somewhere – she had to have been with someone. You just don't disappear into thin air. In telly-land the suspects are always a lot more considerate; they always hang around throughout the programme to allow you to build up a healthy suspicion of them. Yes, the writer and director will throw in the odd red herring here and there and they'll take you on at least a few trips up the proverbial garden path. But eventually the long arm of the law will always extend just far enough to nick their man or, in a few exceptional cases, their woman. Invariably at that precise moment you exclaim: 'I knew it was him (or her)!' and, at least on some of the occasions you won't have been fibbing.

I wondered just how many real life murders go unsolved. Just how many murderers get away with it, you know, just because the police haven't always managed to put two and two together? It would have to be a fair number, I assessed, if only by the amount of attention WPC McGinley and her colleague weren't paying to this particular crime.

If I could just think of the perfect crime, a perfect crime that fitted all of Jean Simpson's circumstances, then perhaps I could come closer to solving this mystery and avoiding all the red herrings along the way.

'How do the police trap killers?' I asked Mary the following evening.

We'd just enjoyed a meal I'd cooked and Mary, surprisingly, had opened a second bottle of wine.

'With evidence,' she replied quickly, through a very definite sigh, 'evidence is the vital source of justice.'

'What kind of evidence?'

'Oh, you know, a knife with fingerprints, or a gun with fingerprints? Or a gun that leaves incriminating gunpowder stains on the hand that held it in anger? Or perhaps even containers of poison which are found under the suspect's sink and the poison turns out to be similar to the type used to kill the victim?'

'Yes but we haven't found any such evidence of Jean's disappearance,' I offered, starting to clear away the dishes.

'David,' she called after me, 'if you're going to commit the perfect crime you want to make sure that you destroy all of the evidence.'

All was quiet for a time, apart from the sound of me running the dishes under the tap. After about thirty or forty seconds she called out again.

'Maybe you ensure there is no telltale evidence in the first place.'

'Sorry?' I said, returning to the living room.

'Well, you know, if you stab someone – well, it's messy isn't it? There'd be blood all over the scene and perhaps even all over the murderer. And then you're left with the knife and you can't burn it. You could never destroy it completely.'

'You could throw it in a river,' I offered.

'The police can drag a river,' she said.

'But they can't drag the sea,' I said.

'No... but you'd always risk the chance of someone seeing you if you threw the knife from a boat or a bridge or something similar. If you threw it in from the coast, you'd risk the current washing it back in again.'

I thought her answers and observations proved that Mary had also been playing her games of just-suppose. I decided to see just what kind of conclusions she'd reached. Perhaps I was even worried that I'd figured somewhere in her 'most likely' scenario.

'So, stabbings are out then?'

'Yes David, stabbing is out. So are guns – too noisy, too messy, and too easy to trace the sale of the gun. On top of which, it's much too complicated to get rid of the body. So is poison. Yes, poison is also out; it can take too long and once again you have to purchase the poison somewhere.'

'Which leaves… what?' I quizzed further.

'Well, think about it yourself. What would you do? How would you commit the perfect crime?'

'I'd probably come up with some elaborate plan whereby I was somewhere else, with several convenient witnesses at the time the murder took place; you know, thereby giving myself the perfect alibi.'

'Ah, the Agatha Christie approach?'

'Yes, probably.'

'But don't you see, David? That means that the body would have to be found, and the body always carries clues,' she replied, polishing off the remains of her wine. 'No, surely the perfect crime has to entail neither a visible body nor a visible instrument of destruction.'

'You mean as is the case with Jean Simpson, for instance, where most people, including the police, think that she simply ran off somewhere and that no actual crime has been committed?'

'Well I suppose so, yes.'

'Yeah, that's all fine, Mary, but even if she had just upped and run off surely she would still, at the very least, have rung her mother?'

'Not necessarily.'

'Oh come on.'

'Oh come on yourself, David!' Mary snapped, taking our game of just-suppose into one degree of anger. 'Sometimes people just want to go missing. Maybe they feel they've made an almighty mess of their lives so far, and if they're just allowed the chance to make a clean break, you know, get away from it all, they can start all over again in hopes that next time they'll do it better. But for that to work the break must be total, if only so that they can really make a fresh start. Say for instance Jean moved to Sydney: What would be the likelihood of her meeting up with someone who knew her?'

'Probably totally never,' I replied, obediently.

'Probably totally never?' she laughed, as she repeated my words and paused to eagerly empty her glass of wine again. 'Don't you mean more than a million to one chance?'

'Yes,' I conceded.

'And the odds drop a little, don't they, if say, she moved to America, a little less for Asia, a little less again for Europe. Even less again if she had moved to Scotland and further still if it was Newcastle. The odds would drop further and further, wouldn't they, the closer she moved to London? The odds would be down to something like ten to one if she just moved to the other side of London, say somewhere like Enfield.'

'You're not for one moment suggesting that Jean Simpson is in Enfield, are you?'

'No, no! We're not talking about Jean Simpson here, David. We're talking about the perfect crime. We're talking about what could have happened to someone like Jean Simpson. So say our particular victim had lived in the shadow of someone like Jean Kerr for most of her life. She moves to London and then she starts to find her own legs. She agrees to marry someone like John Harrison, she messes around with someone like you, someone like you would get it together with someone like me, someone like you would desert someone like her and then someone like her and someone like John would split up. Then someone like Jean

Kerr, her original and great protector and model, would do a mental loop-the-loop and look like she's about to head off to the nearest loony bin. So it would be quite forgivable, excusable and not exactly out of character if someone like Jean Simpson literally just took off and ran away.'

I was about to say something – I knew not what, perhaps something to do with I'd never imagined that it would suit Jean's character for her to run away, something along those lines, and I was struggling for the words when Mary held up the palm of her hand to silence my efforts. Then she raised her empty wine glass with her other hand. I was obedient on both accounts and so she continued.

'The police obviously believe that is exactly what has happened to Jean Simpson. We have to believe that they've already checked into her life. There are no drugs, there are no shady characters,' She stared at me at this point and broke into a warm smile before continuing, 'well, not too shady. You see, they say that in the majority of murder cases the victim knows their murderer and so the police have obviously checked out all her friends and obviously none of you were behaving suspiciously. There were no reasons for blackmail. And hey, it's the sixties – we're in the middle of a sexual revolution, so what's to stop a beautiful young girl just upping off somewhere to start a new life?'

'Maybe that's what happened then.'

'Perhaps David, but just for the sake of the discussion I'd have to disagree with you.'

I raised my eyebrows into a 'pardon'?

'Well, as you've already said, you'd have to think that she'd at least drop a note to her mother,' Mary, obviously on a roll, continued, 'if only just to put her mother's mind at rest. The police are probably ignoring this issue. I imagine they feel that as it took Jean's mum so long to report her daughter missing, a logical conclusion would probably be that mother and daughter were never very close. Jean's mum's actions, or lack of them, would've sent out a couldn't-care-less attitude, you know. Also, I imagine the police probably think only child, maybe even adopted child, so they wouldn't have expected the bond to have been as tight as, say it is with someone like my mum and me, or even Jean Kerr and her mum.'

'Isn't that a wee bit hard on Jean Simpson's mum?'

Mary closed her lips and smiled a sad smile. 'A mother's place is to always be in the wrong,' she quietly said, 'that's what my mum would frequently tell me. But please listen to me, David – once again, I repeat, this is not about Jean Simpson or her mum, it's about the perfect murder.'

I took a large sip of wine, hoping it would take the fast track into my blood stream, if only so that I could catch up with Mary; she was definitely getting a little merry.

'Okay,' I began, after the generous gulp, 'you've got a young girl who may or may not have disappeared. The police seem to think that nothing untoward has happened to her, besides which there are possible reasons why she just might want to disappear in the first place. I'm not sure that I agree with you 100 per cent on those, but I am interested in your method and motive for the perfect crime.'

'Agh, the penny drops, now we're making progress at last! Okay, let's address the motive; that's much easier, isn't it? Why would someone decide to murder someone?' Mary asked, pausing at her own question as she took another generous sip of wine.

My last gulp had started to take effect, so I used the old trick of merely wetting my lips in a vain attempt to appear to keep up with her intake.

'Well,' I began licking my lips, 'more particularly, why would anyone want to murder one of our Jeans?'

'You see, there's a point right there. Perhaps even a clue if you want. Jean Kerr and Jean Simpson are not our Jeans,' she began indignantly but not, I hasten to add, rudely, 'we don't live in the north of England and nor are we related to either of the Jeans. Yes, we both know them. Yes, one of them stole my ex-boyfriend, yes, one of them – the very same one coincidently who stole my ex-boyfriend – has been messing around with my current boyfriend. Yes, the other one of them bonked both my ex-boyfriend and my current boyfriend and, yes, butter wouldn't melt in my mouth, but then the one of them who stole my ex and was messing around with my current, wanted to more-than-mess-around with my current boyfriend.'

'Sorry?'

'Yes David!'

'No Mary!'

'Yes David!'

'I've already told you that by the time you and I started dating Jean and I had stopped messing around!'

'Yes, and I believed you! Although I have to say here that it's not you that I'm worried about.'

'But you know that I'd never–'

'Yes, yes,' she cut in quickly, with hurt now clearly visible in her eyes, 'I do, David, I do. But you don't tell me everything.'

'I'd never lie to you,' I said confidently, not sure where this was going.

'It's not lying I'm talking about. Sometimes not telling someone everything is actually worse than lying to them.'

'And what exactly are you referring to here, Mary?'

'Exactly what I'm referring to here, David, is the fact that you didn't tell me that Jean Simpson rang you up and told you that she would dump John Harrison if you'd dump me and go steady with her!'

I just managed (I hoped) to avoid grimacing. 'But I said no! I told her no way, that I was totally happy with you!'

'But you never told me about it, David. You never told me.'

And she was correct. It was true. I mean, it was true that I never told her, and I never told you, dear reader, but it is true that Jean Simpson did ring me up, and it is true that I didn't admit it to you before either. Well, if I had told you, and Mary, it just would have complicated things, wouldn't it?

I mean, it wasn't an issue, really. Okay, okay, I'll tell you exactly what happened, shall I?

Jean Simpson rang me at work five days before she disappeared, saying that she wanted to see me, she wanted to meet up with me again. I said, and this is the absolute truth, I said that I didn't think it was such a good idea for us to meet up again. I didn't mention Mary Skeffington, neither did Jean. Now I could have just said no, couldn't I? But I didn't. In circumstances such as those I've just described, we don't, do we? Why is that? I know it would have been easier to say no; I know by saying 'I don't think it's such a good idea' I was, to some extent, leaving the door open. Jean Simpson obviously saw the open door because she continued; she said she had something she wanted to talk to me about. I was about to say, 'Look, why don't you just say what it is you need to say on the phone now?' when my boss came into the office and started to give me the old evil eye about being on the phone. So that was when I reluctantly said to Jean Simpson, 'Okay, let's meet up at the Alex for a quick drink.'

So we did, okay? We did meet up at the Alex, that is, later that evening. She was dressed in her favourite tartan skirt and duffle coat and, as always, looked absolutely fabulous. We small-talked about groups, the Marquee Club, movies, and then I said I was really sorry but I didn't have much time. Then she just blurted out this thing about wanting to get back together again. She said she would split up with John Harrison if I'd get back with her. She implied that we wouldn't have to keep messing around the way we had been doing. She said that if we were going steady, we should live together and sleep together.

In all of this she never once mentioned the word love. She never once said that she cared for me, nor did she ask me if I loved or cared about her. I said that I was sorry, but I was already with someone. She asked me, was it because she was too late? I said no, it had nothing to do with that; it had to do with the fact that I had met someone. I also told her that she should leave John only if it wasn't right for her to be with him and not because it would make her more attractive to me or to someone else. I said she would meet someone else because she was special. She asked me if it was a definite no. She asked me if I would ever go back with her. I said, 'No, I'm sorry I can't, I really want my new relationship to work.' Then she packed away her stuff, rippled my hair with her hand and said she felt that she had let me slip through her fingers. She said that it was her own fault that she had lost me – she just hadn't realised at the time how special it had been between us.

And then she was gone.

There were no tears, nor talk of love, not even a goodbye kiss, nor even just a peck on the cheek; none of that.

We'd never, ever kissed, not even as friends.

As I watched her walk out of the crowded Alex, I perhaps realised why Jean didn't entertain kissing me. Or even need to kiss me. It had nothing whatsoever to do with our relationship. It would have been too affectionate, too tender, and what we had, what we enjoyed; had nothing whatsoever to do with affection or tenderness. Music, in fact, was one of the things – maybe even the only thing – that genuinely held us together, in that it allowed us to be together without being 'together'.

I'd also come to realise that I was really only a pawn in Jean Simpson's erotic endeavours, her need to experiment safely.

'That's all you're getting for now,' she had once said, after an apparent accidental flash. But when I thought about her words later I realised it had been a plan, her plan all along. At first I wondered what was so magical about me that she had chosen me for her little series of erotic adventures, or our encounters as she called them. But when I came to really focus on our relationship, I realised that she could've picked anyone to be her lust-buddy, anyone really would have done, just so long as they were clean and obedient. I knew she wasn't really going to be cut up about us not seeing each other again, because she certainly wasn't in love with me. In fact, she might not even have been attracted to me. She was most certainly attracted, or even addicted, to the lust, and I was most certainly helping her in her endeavours in that direction. People can't be preoccupied all the time about the big S. In order to truly live our lives we need to clear our mind and think and deal with the other things, ordinary things that come our way. Jean Simpson was behaving as if she'd time for nothing other than our carnal encounters. It seemed to me as if she was continuously preoccupied with her lust and, now that I think about it, she did look a bit like a junkie while in the throes of our passion. Yes, that was exactly it: she looked exactly like a junkie who was about to get their fix, every time we'd meet for one of our adventures.

But the body has to have other self-preserving qualities. The fact that we hadn't actually made love had, she said, meant that she would always lust after me; our fantasies were our bond, our special bond in lieu of some kind of love, as it were. So I felt it was really more a kind of drug for her. It was certainly a very successful drug for her, because it worked every single time, she got high every single time. So did I, for that matter. But her lust, no make that our lust, took her to where she needed to go. And you know what, if we had talked more about it, discussed it more than we did, that would only have served to weaken the grasp this illusion of attraction we were creating held over the both of us.

She disappeared through the crowd in the Alex and then five days later she disappeared altogether.

So perhaps you're thinking that maybe it didn't end there. Perhaps the conversation turned ugly and she threatened to tell Mary about all of our messing around – you know, how much, exactly how, where and, most importantly, when. You see, I knew you'd think that. And what's more, I knew Mary would think that as well. And that's why I didn't tell either of you.

'How did you know?' I asked Mary while trying to regain my composure.

'I found out from John.'

'You found out from John. When were you talking to John?'

'I wasn't.'

'But you just said that you were!'

'No, David, I said I found out from John – I meant indirectly, of course. He rang my mum's house asking to speak to me and he told Mum about Jean wanting to go back with you and Mum told me.'

'Oh,' I said, wondering whether or not to believe her.

'But let's not get bogged down in this, David. I trust you 100 per cent and so does my mother. No, that's not what we're discussing here; what we were talking about was developing a method and a motive for a murder, a perfect murder, in fact. So, with regards to the motive, if we continue down our little road and this tale of woe of me & you, and me & John, and John & Jean, and Jean & you, and then you & the other Jean, and then the other Jean & John.'

She started to laugh, softly at first, but quickly breaking into an infectious ripple. She was definitely getting a quite squiffy. I don't think I'd ever seen her that drunk before, or since in fact.

'What?' I asked.

'Well, I was just thinking there that fact really is stranger than fiction.'

'Sorry?'

'Well, when I was going through that list, as in who'd been with who in the biblical sense, if you read that in a book or saw it in a movie, well, you quite simply wouldn't believe it, believe all of it was possible! However, because we've all been involved in this five-ringed circus, we know it's not fiction. It's very much the truth, because John lay with Mary, who lay with David, who lay with Jean K, who lay with David, who lay with Mary, who was set upon by

Jean K, who lay with John, who was betrothed to Jean S, who completes the circle by messing around with David. Am I missing anyone?' she finally concluded, still looking – after all that she'd admitted to – like butter wouldn't melt in her mouth.

'Okay, okay,' I said, happy that we had appeared to cut at least one particular potential problem off at the pass. I was equally intrigued as to where we were going with this.

'Instead of establishing a quartet of motives, let's focus, if you will, on me. I have a situation where I lost my husband-to-be to Jean Simpson, who had no doubt been offered more than a little assistance by Jean Kerr. I get over that loss; admittedly you were there to help me pick up the pieces. Now I find that Jean Simpson is actively chasing my current boyfriend. It doesn't matter that he's saying he's not interested; she's proven in the past that she's not prepared to give up.

'So, I care about you, I care about you a lot and I don't want to lose you. Despite you saying no to Jean's advances, she's obviously not going away, she still wants you; maybe she's so fickle she only wants you because you are with me. I don't know, it doesn't really matter but, from my point of view, you have to accept that she's already been successful in her previous endeavours to steal a boyfriend of mine, so here's my question, David: What could I do to stop her? What would I do to make her go away?'

The bluntness of her question stopped me in my tracks.

Up until then I'd just considered that we'd been sitting around having a drink and chatting away, all very matter of fact. And now, if I'm not mistaken, she'd just admitted her motive for murdering Jean Simpson.

I needed another drink, anything rather than let my suspicions run away with her.

'So,' she continued, as if she'd just been discussing the weather, 'I suppose now we need to come up with some kind of method of murdering Jean Simpson.'

'Well, that's the bit that gets me you see, Mary,' I offered, slipping into the devil's advocate role just a wee bit too easily, not to mention a tad too quickly. 'How could you just disappear somebody? I mean, it's not that simple.'

'Really?' she said quietly, as she raised her eyes, but not her head, to gauge my reaction.

Chapter Forty.

'If I show you how it could have been accomplished, will you promise to let this – this Case of the Missing Jean – rest for once and forever?' she asked.

'Okay,' I said, not entirely sure of where this was going.

'Well,' Mary began expansively, 'the first thing you need to do is to be sure of your intentions.'

'Sorry?'

'Well, you need to be aware that once you have done it, once you have murdered someone, you can't undo it.'

'Of course.'

'You say "of course". And you say it very quickly, but it's not nearly as simple as that. Let's just stop and think about it for a minute: you are changing the course of your life and the course of the lives of all of those around you. You're not exactly going to be invited to all the best dinner parties if you or your partner is a convicted murderer.'

'Oh, in these celebrity-worshipping days I wouldn't be too sure of that,' I offered quietly, 'everybody wants to be famous for something or other; they'll try anything that will guarantee them their five minutes of glory. However, if your murder is the perfect murder, then no one is going to find out about it, so there's not going to be much glory, is there?'

'Absolutely. No one is ever going to know about it, so there'll be no glory nor guilt,' Mary agreed and then stopped to consider before continuing, 'but do you think you could murder someone and your lover not be aware of it?'

I couldn't work out whether what she was actually trying to say was, would I know if she had killed someone? Or maybe would she know if I'd killed someone? Could you sleep with a killer and not be aware of it? Are there things that killers do that give them away?

I didn't think so, and certainly not in every case.

As we've discussed before, I wasn't so sure that all killers had cold, dark, stony stares. I didn't have a mental picture of someone frothing at the mouth. Perhaps that was just because, personally speaking, I had already come up with a scenario where I could have accidentally killed Jean Simpson, you know, like I told you a few minutes ago? If Jean had come around to my flat and made advances towards me and I'd got mad at myself and pushed her away, and she'd fallen and hit her head – remember that? Would that make me a different person? You know, it's as easy to push as not – would you change as a person in that split second that you decided to push?

Do me a favour, please: just raise your hand to your ear. Okay, now in the time it took you to do that, that's about the time it would take for you to become a murderer. So, say that's what happened, does that mean you'll no longer love and respect your parents? Does it mean that you won't want to go to work each day? Does it mean that you – in this instance, I mean me – does it mean that I would no longer want to get naked with Mary Skeffington? Does it mean that I would never think that someone like Jean Simpson had a beautiful body? Does it mean that I would break the law in other ways? Would I suddenly turn to stealing? Would I not worry any more about not having a television licence?

Hey, would it mean that I wouldn't be able to get mad if someone broke into my flat and stole my records or helped themselves to something valuable of mine? You know, could I really be upset at someone who had stolen a record worth thirty-two shillings and six pence when I was guilty of robbing someone of their life?

Mary interrupted my thoughts with, 'You see, in my instance that's where it would all fall down, in actually having to murder someone. I'm much too squeamish; I wouldn't have the stomach for it. I couldn't just go and face them and stick a knife in them, oh no.'

She actually shivered at the thought. She kept on shaking her head as she continued: 'You know, some people can stick their hand up a cow's bum and from the midst of all that blood and gore they can pull out a sweet little calf. I love the end product. I'd love to come along when everything has been washed and tidied up and you have this sweet, cuddly little calf and it looks so vulnerable. But I'd need to miss out all the bits to do with blood and guts. Agh!'

'Well, I'm not exactly in love with all that myself,' I offered.

'I know, David, I know. But some people are totally comfortable with it. Some people can even cut open a human and stick their hands into the body and massage a heart back to life! Even the thought of it is sending shivers down my spine! But some people can do it just like it's second nature and then they immediately go off and eat a rare steak and wash it down with a red wine. They seem to be able to divorce the two acts, so I have to think that a murderer can separate the vile act from the rest of their lives.'

'Or they employ someone else to carry out the vile act for them?' I offered.

'No, no, David; you couldn't afford the risk of anyone else knowing that you were involved, no matter how directly or indirectly your involvement may have been. You see, to commit the perfect murder there must be no witnesses, there must be no alibi, there must be no lies to cover up. Yes, lies – they're another big thing. You tell the police a lie and see how long it takes them to catch you out. For instance, "Why were you not back at your house at six thirty if you say you left work at five thirty?" So you say, "Oh, I went to Safeway to do my shopping." "Well," WDC

McGinley would reply, as she snaps the handcuffs around your wrists, "how come your fridge and your cupboards are empty?"'

'Okay, I'm with you so far – no blood, no lies, no accomplice, no witnesses, no shopping, no knives. But to me that all adds up to NO MURDER!'

'And you forgot "and no body",' she said, before smiling.

I'd been going along with our little hypothetical just-suppose but every now and then she'd add a little line that would stop me in my tracks. And the 'and no body' was such a heart-stopping line.

Before I'd a chance to collect my thoughts Mary jumped up from the sofa in a high state of excitement and shouted, 'Let's go for a walk!'

Ten minutes later we were out in the cold night air, our cheeks flushed from a little too much wine. We were walking down the lonely and long Gladstone Road, down towards Broadway, left into Broadway, over Wimbledon Bridge Road on to Wimbledon Hill Road, and up as far as Worple Road on the left, and we stopped down at the corner. At first, I'd thought she was taking me to her office, which is in Mond Road, but then she walked on past her office and took a right into Mansel Road. At that point she broke into a canter, followed by a mere stroll as she came level with the hoarding which sheltered and secured a building site on the other side. She searched the hoarding for a few seconds, pushing here and pushing there, searching for something, I knew not what. By the light of the full moon she eventually found what she was looking for: a loose section. She untied a rope and the section of hoarding – complete with a Tolworth Toby Jug poster advertising forthcoming appearances of Free, Sam Apple Pie, East of Eden, Anno Domini and The Edgar Broughton Band – that functioned as a makeshift door with rope hinges.

Mary caught my hand and pulled me into the site, closing the makeshift door and retying the rope behind us.

We carefully picked our way through bricks, planks, scaffolding, a cement mixer, wheelbarrows, hods, mounds of sand, heaps of gravel, bags of cement and trenches – some of which were partially filled with water.

Kopace, flush with the success of their first superstore, had planned to add at least twenty per cent to their current floor space, a fact borne out by the grid of rolled steel joist's rising majestically towards the Moon. Mary stopped where one of the RSJs disappeared into the ground. There was an eerie silence, broken only by the occasional sound of cars passing by on the other side of the hoarding. Now and then we could hear our feet crunching through gravel.

'Don't you see, it's the perfect place for the perfect murder,' Mary boasted excitedly.

I didn't quite get it; I didn't get it at all, in fact.

'Oh David, where's your imagination?' Mary whispered, as she took my hand and led me to another corner of the site.

This time the steel joists were lying flat on the ground and they bordered a large pit, which I guessed, by the reflection of the water, was at least twenty feet deep. A crane towered lifelessly above us, ready, I imagined, to spring into action the following morning and raise the same RSJs one by one into the sky and then, when in perfect position, lower them into their final resting place in the depths of the pit, where they'd be housed for at least the next hundred years or so.

'You see,' Mary continued, with her moonlit lecture, 'if you really want to lose a body, you'd dump it into one of these deep holes. I've been watching the work continue here for the last several months – look, I can see the site clearly from my office window.'

She stopped and pointed towards the sky over my shoulder. There was no doubt about it, she was perfectly placed to observe the site. As she saw the penny dropping, she pushed on further.

'First they excavate the holes in the ground, then they fill in the bottom with cement and rusted steel rods, you know, to make a binded foundation, which serves as their base. Then, before it's fully set, they put in a steel plate with bolts sticking upright onto the top solid concrete base. They let that settle and sit for several weeks before they place the girder down into the hole and bolt it into place on the steel plate. Then they fill in the rest of the hole with more cement and again they let that settle before they start adding more and more sections and floors above the foundations. It's intriguing – I've loved watching the workers and working out what their system is.'

'Ok-ay.'

'So, what you'd do,' she continued, sounding slightly annoyed that I'd interrupted her, 'is you'd bring your victim in here–'

'What, they'd just obediently follow you in?'

'What, like you just did?' she said and then laughed. In a way I had proved her point.

I smiled but stopped the second that a vision of Jean Simpson at the building site hoarding flashed into my mind.

'Actually, if anything it would've been easier with Jean Simpson,' Mary whispered. 'All I would've had to do would have been to fix up a meeting with her at the Alexandra. I'd pretend I'd something important to tell her. I'd meet her at the pub; I'd be very friendly and girlie with her. We'd have a girlie talk about you, you know, comparing notes over a few drinks, all frightfully civilised. I'd tell her that you and I were going to split up and that the coast was clear for her to resume messing around with you. We'd have a few more drinks and we'd leave the pub the best of friends, and we'd come out of the pub, cross the road, and walk past here and I'd say to her "You'll never guess what goes on in there." She'd be intrigued, just like you were, David, so I'd bring her in here and bring her to the edge of a freshly dug pit.'

At this point I looked back up towards Mary's office window and followed the line down. I couldn't work out if I was trying to see whether all this was truly possible or if I had gone beyond that point and now was looking for the girder which would: a) be visible from Mary's window; and b) be the final resting place of Jean Simpson? It would have to be one of the older positions, I figured. I continued to try to figure out which girder we were talking about as Mary whispered on with her just-suppose.

'So, you'd bring her right to the edge of one of the freshly dug, deep pits and you'd say "Look down there!" And she'd lean forward, still not able to see anything, and so you'd say "Look – down there – at the bottom. Here, I'll support you so that you can look over the edge." And then, just right when she was on the brink of her balance, you'd just give her a wee push and she'd topple over into the pit. She'd be winded and stunned when she hit the bottom, so you'd need to take aim with a couple of bricks, you know, properly finish the job. If you don't manage to kill her with the bricks on the head you'd at least knock her unconscious and there's always at least enough water in the bottom of the pit for her to drown.'

'Mary!' I hissed

'David, snap out of it. I'm just telling you what I'd do to commit the perfect murder. Let me get on with it, please! The following morning the workmen would come along, our Jean would be hidden in the water in the bottom of the pit. The workmen would pour concrete into the hole – they never bother removing the water before they pour the cement. Within a day the corpse would become a part of the building foundations. Don't you see? It's so perfect! The body is never going to be found. What's more, there would be no evidence of any kind on or about your body. There would be nothing to connect you to the murder.'

'What if someone saw you come in here?'

'Well, first off, you'd be very careful when you came in, but the even more important thing is to be very careful when you leave. There's not a lot of people using the side street, anyway, since they started the building works. So, with a little care and attention you could come and go unnoticed. You'd dump your shoes in a dustbin on your way home, having brought a change with you, hidden in your handbag.

'Where is she Mary? Which hole is Jean buried in?'

'Oh, don't be so stupid, David! I'm just playing out this little game of ours! I just wanted to show you that it is possible to commit the perfect murder,' she said, as she took my hand and cautiously led me off the building site, 'and I needed to shut you up once and for all about what happened to Jean Simpson.'

Chapter Forty-One.

Had all that been Mary's way of telling me what had happened? Was it meant to be a warning? I mean, it was flawless – it all made perfect sense. I did find it hard to believe that Jean Simpson would have met with Mary, but I suppose Jean could have been intrigued with what Mary wanted to see her about.

I still couldn't accept it though; that Mary was capable of murder, even though, I had to admit, that it was murder once removed. Jean Simpson would have been several feet beneath Mary and a still target for whatever missiles Mary would have thrown at her.

Another important thing in all of this (for Mary) was that she wouldn't have had to look Jean in the eyes as she dealt the fatal blow. Perhaps Mary was even able to convince herself that Jean had finally died from drowning, or by being suffocated beneath several tons of concrete.

On the other hand, all Mary's main points were accurate: no body, no evidence, no witnesses. What about a motive, though? Could she have been convicted purely on motive? Assuming, that is, that Mary's actions were anything more than hypothetical.

She'd lost one boyfriend to Jean. She didn't want to lose another. Her exact words. Would she really have seen killing Jean Simpson as a solution to her problem? Did Mary Skeffington really have it in her make-up as a human being to take the life of another? You see, that's what troubled me the most: Could I really be head-over-heels in love with a murderer? As we've discussed, most murderers aren't likely to be bad people all of the time.

Like me, there might have been a moment, even just a split second, when Mary saw killing Jean as the only way to solve her problem. Unlike me, though, had she seen that opportunity and taken it? She'd opted for the final solution to her problem and in all probability would never resort to such drastic actions again. The alternate was that she was a serial killer who either enjoyed the act of killing or enjoyed the notoriety it gave her. Nagh, Mary definitely didn't fit into that category. But it troubled me that she could have been so cool and collected about the whole thing. She didn't seem to be suffering from nightmares – if anything she was sleeping better than ever. Mind you, she said she would tell me her hypothetical method of getting rid of someone only as a way to get me to shut up about Jean Simpson. I was living with Mary, and I didn't suspect her capable of anything as bizarre as her hypothetical solution. She was too… well, too normal for that. Yes, I would have definitely considered her to be normal, as normal as you could get, in fact. But at the same time we still had no Jean Simpson!
And you know maybe she did just really wanted me to finally shut up for once and for all about Jean's disappearance?

Every time I passed the Kopace Superstore – which was at least ten times a week – I thought of Jean Simpson and I thought of Mary. That lasted for about three months, then I started to remember that I was forgetting about Jean and then I'd feel a quick, albeit ever so brief, pull on my conscience.

By May, Jean Simpson's mother decided to have a party to celebrate not the death, but the life of her daughter. Mary and I both attended. It wasn't as sad a gathering as you'd expect it to be. I suppose that had something to do with the fact that at the time of the party, we'd all had nearly several months to adjust to the loss of a life from our midst.

Also, there was something quite comforting about the fact that we were celebrating Jean's life in such a beautiful landscape. Ironically, there was a graveyard at the foot of Jean's mother's garden. Every one of the guests, on at least one occasion during the party and mostly at varying times, stole at least a single glance into that graveyard, all of us privately wondering where Jean Simpson's final resting place was. Why do we all like graveyards to be as beautiful as picture-postcard scenes? I mean, it's obviously too late for the residents. Could it be that when we come to visit them, to visit the faithful departed, we need to be reminded that the reality in all of this, in the whole big scheme of things, is that we are really nothing more than knee-high to the packet of Surf called life, and that at some point in the future we'll end up in a similar spot to the dearly departed?

No, you don't think so? Augh, you know what, you're probably right.

Jean Kerr was at the celebration. She seemed like she was starting to get her act together. She'd started to lose weight and she was smoking a lot. These two facts may or may not be related. She'd cut way back on her make-up and was dressing more casually. She said she couldn't believe how much she missed Jean. She said the loss of Jean was the kick up the backside she'd needed to get her act together. She'd applied for several jobs rather than wait for the hopeless situation she found herself in with her present supervisor to work itself out.

In spite of what had happened to Jean Simpson, Jean Kerr was making a return to London. Her mother wasn't best pleased at that but, as Jean said, the alternative was to lock herself away forever.

'Life's for living,' she said, brushing her proud mane over her shoulders, 'it's time I started to do some living again. I feel I've got to live for two now.'

What, you think that's a bit over the top? Yeah, you're probably right, but that's always been our Jean Kerr for you.

Mary Skeffington and me? Well, our relationship is still getting better all the time. I suppose in a way it could have gone either way following our midnight stroll to the building site. I actually made a conscious decision to put all of the stuff behind us… you know… the stuff.

What stuff, David?

Okay, I'll say it: the fact that I knew there was a distinct possibility that Mary Skeffington could have murdered Jean Simpson. I put all that stuff behind me, and us, and we just got on with our lives. Even if I hadn't, Mary had a big enough heart and enough energy to pull both of us through it. You see, that's one of the things I've since learned about Mary: once she wants something, she goes all out to get it. Perhaps it's something to do with losing her father when she was young. Perhaps it's something to do with losing John Harrison when she did. I don't know, I just know her resolve is unfaltering.

You see, I knew she was something special the day I met her. I also knew that fate hadn't put us together; I knew we'd met by accident. We weren't meant to meet up at all, in fact, and because we did… because we clicked and then started to deal with the fact that we could be together if we worked at it, perhaps we threw things around us off the chosen cosmic track – you know, out of sync?

Maybe that's why all of the things that happened around us, happened. I've searched my heart and wracked my brain and I cannot for the life of me come up with any other reason.

I think of the night we all met, you remember, at Tiger's party? The first and possibly only time we were all in the one room at the one time. I think of the time I had with Mary before the others happened upon the two of us, you know, when we were sitting in our beanbags getting to know each other before the fight broke out. That was a very magical meeting. I can remember every single thing I was thinking; mostly, I remember thinking that it must have been a dream. I can remember struggling to catch the breath that her beauty was stealing. I remember thinking that her beauty had attracted me, but her soul was definitely the magnet that glued our futures together. I thought I couldn't possibly be there with the most perfect girl I'd ever met. Not only had I met her, but I was actually talking to her. I mean, I was shocked by the fact that she was really talking to me as if we'd known each other before.

Maybe we had, you know, known each other in another life? I don't believe in all of that crap to be honest, but there is something bigger between Mary Skeffington and me than the usual 'boy meets girl'.

Hey, but you know what, grand and all as that is, if I don't pay attention to her and work at what we've got, it doesn't mean that I couldn't lose it as quick as the next couple; particularly with the likes of John Harrison lurking somewhere out there in the shadows.

Although, you know what? While we were all up in Matlock for the celebration of Jean Simpson's life, we all promised to meet up in London. But it never came to pass – that day, the day of the celebration, would have been the last time Mary and I saw any of that crowd. It wasn't intentional or anything like that. Years had passed before we'd realised we just hadn't seen any of them in ages, and by that point they'd all probably moved on an address or two, so we didn't even bother to try. Maybe it was an easier way to forget Jean Simpson, I don't know. I don't think so, though; I think life just tends to be like that – you move on and people you once knew, you no longer know, and people you didn't know, you now know.

Chapter Forty-Two.

During that wee bit of an attempt to sum up there I started to grow self-conscious and I started to hear my own voice again. I mean, it came from absolutely nowhere, and it happened so gradually that I didn't even notice it coming. I suppose I started to consider that you might be thinking, 'God, how could he ever live with a killer?'

And let me tell you, over the years I've thought about that fact a lot, and sometimes it's bothered me more than at other times, but it's never bothered me enough that it disturbed the balance of our relationship. I have always felt that I loved Mary Skeffington and I loved her unconditionally. What's more, I really like her as a person. I hope you don't think that is too bizarre, but I had to admit it because it's absolutely, 100 per cent true and you know what's more? I would trust her with my life. I suppose that says more about me than it does about her.

Mary and I never discussed Jean's disappearance again, you know, apart from that one night on the Kopace Superstore building site. We'd talk sometimes about Jean Simpson and about Jean Kerr and about John Harrison for that matter, but we never, ever discussed again how Jean Simpson came to meet her Maker.

Mary Skeffington and I never had any children, though. I don't remember it ever being a big thing between us or anything like that; it just never happened. We never had any children. I often wondered deep down could that have been something to do with the fact that although I didn't mind living with and loving the person that could have murdered Jean Simpson, maybe subconsciously I didn't want her to be the mother of my children. It could have been the thing that prevented the magic from ever happening with us. I hope that I would never be so shallow, but you just never know, do you?

And that's nearly it, apart from one final incident I feel I should tell you about before we end this tale.

We're talking recent times here, Friday 23r July, 1998, to be exact. Mary had bought a couple of tickets for us to go to one of her Latin music concerts. The location was the once elegant Empire Theatre in downtown Shepherd's Bush. Mary and her mum are really into Latin music and I will admit it's so infectious that I don't mind being dragged along from time to time. I don't go to as many gigs as I used to go to nowadays; well, you just get other priorities in your life, don't you, and well, to tell you the truth, I started to feel that gigs have turned into big marketing exercises these days. The artists seem rarely ever to perform just for the love of the music – they're there to promote the latest album, or earn a wad of cash. But maybe that's just something to do with me growing older.

Anyway, we headed down to The Bush and you can imagine how excited I was when I saw the poster outside the venue proudly proclaiming: 'Latin Crossover featuring Steve Winwood, Tito Puente, Arturo Sandova and their All Star Band.'

As we waited for the concert to start I gazed around the venue, bewildered at how the presentation of live music had changed since I'd first started going to gigs at the Marquee Club and The Toby Jug in Tolworth thirty years previous. The venues are now actually audience-friendly, not just rooms in the backs of pubs converted for a bi-weekly gathering. And they're geared up to accommodate the marketing hype of the music business; you can now buy posters, t-shirts, caps, key rings, pens, jackets, iron-on tattoos, umbrellas, badges, shorts, CDs. CDs! Compact discs! CDs – now they didn't even exist in the Marquee days, but now the original magical 12-inch piece of plastic, enveloped in a piece of classic art, has been replaced with a high-tech, 6-inch disc of audio and visual information. The friends of the band who couldn't play an instrument but still wanted to hang out with the band (I'm talking about the roadies here) – the original, loyal roadies have now been replaced by numerous technicians all linked up with walkie-talkies. And whereas the artists used to play through a couple of small speaker cabinets on either side of the stage, now there is a wall of noise from either side of the stage, all controlled by more torch-carrying technicians back in the middle of the concert venue, blocking a large proportion of the audience's view. And the even funnier thing about all of that is at the Marquee I don't remember the sound ever being bad! I don't remember Rory Gallagher and the Taste boys sounding anything but brilliant. In recent times though, I do recall a few particularly iffy nights of audio, when the sound was in serious dire straits.

In the good old days you would pay half a crown for a ticket (that's twelve and a half new pence in unreal money), probably to a mate of the promoter who'd stand by a table at the entrance door and give you a tear-off stub as proof of admission (he'd also double up as a bouncer, nipping off when necessary to sort out any problems with unruly members of the audience). Now it's all computerised and automated and you usually have to book months in advance, and your £20 ticket will sit in a bank account gaining someone some kind of interest. I suppose the redundant box offices and computers have to be financed from somewhere. On top of the £20 you'll have to pay at least £2 to some ticket agency that has an exclusive on selling tickets for the particular venue you are attending. They'll give you a nice little ticket for all your efforts, though, with a McDonalds's or Burger King advert on the rear side. Which reminds me; the new, strange smell in our venues usually comes from the fast food being sold, all usually right beside the merchandising stands. In the new venues you'll be able to buy numerous designer beers whose sponsorship will be apparent from the many branding signs around the venue.

The security will be a well-fed team of large gentlemen and women, all dressed in black, also complete with walkie-talkies, and all still hungry enough that they will bite your head off if you even dare to ask them, where, when or how.

And what would you imagine that the other main difference between the nights at the Toby Jug and The Bush is? At the Bush there is not a single duffle coat in sight.

But all of that mattered not a lot because Stevie Winwood was going to be live on stage again! I couldn't believe it. I hadn't seen him live in years and years. It was an amazing night, with lots of dancing. Mary even managed to pull me down onto the dance floor for the infectious 'Higher Love'. We were about three rows from the front of the stage and Steve looked as young as ever in his bright orange shirt, opened all the way down, revealing a black t-shirt underneath. He was grinning from ear-to-ear and having a grand old night himself, and a few songs later he did a cracking version of 'Low Spark'.

We'd worked up quite a sweat by this point in the set and so Mary and I retired to the bar for a refill of liquid and energy. We found a comfortable corner and I think we'd both agreed to stay there for the remainder of the night but just as our joints were stiffening up from lack of activity, Steve and the band played the introduction to 'I'm A Man'. The bar simply emptied before the band had worked the classic Hammond organ-led intro into a rhythmic shuffle. Mary and I worked our way back to the edge of the stage again. Winwood proved he'd lost none of his prowess on the Hammond and the band seemed happy to be led by the crowd for the first time that evening. It's always an amazing atmosphere when the band and audience are as one. The song finished and the entire place went totally ape.

The applause eventually fizzled out not long after the musicians had left the stage. As the clapping eventually died out entirely, I heard this voice behind me say, 'Oh, that Stevie Winwood, he gets me every single time.'

I thought I recognised that voice immediately.

I turned around and came face to face with an ageing hippie. She was expensively dressed, but still a hippie for that.

I still couldn't put the voice together with the woman in front of me.

Then, when I focused back in on the voice again, the penny dropped.

She was still distinctive even in a crowd and even after all these years. Sure she'd changed in the intervening years, but her eyes and teeth looked exactly the same. Her hair was longer than before, but she hadn't put on an ounce of weight, nor did she wear a speck of make-up. Her once traditional miniskirt had made way for a long, flowing, light blue dress, which just about managed to hide her pink pumps. She'd a black jacket tied about her waist, freeing her up for dancing no doubt.

It was Jean Simpson, looking large as life and twice as pretty.

True, I kid you not.

I can't begin to tell you how happy I was to see her. I found myself hugging Mary so tightly I nearly took her breath away.

Jean Simpson didn't recognise me at first – I guess I'd changed a lot over the years, too. But she did recognise Mary (who obviously hadn't changed a lot) and by process of elimination and deduction, she realised who the crazy person beside Mary was.

We returned to the bar, Jean and her friend (she never told us his name) and Mary and I. We'd a few drinks before we were all chucked out, but we'd enough time to get up to date. John Harrison had been correct and I'd been wrong; Jean Simpson had gone off to a hippie commune in the West Country, Wells – near Glastonbury, in fact. She'd given up on them after a few weeks, in a way, I suppose, making me also right. She moved into a beautiful but extremely clean wee cottage, where she stayed for about six years, before returning to live in Derby.

She'd married (she didn't say to whom), and had a daughter, Joanna, who was now twenty-five years old and was just about to get married herself. Joanna's father and Jean had separated four years previously; she claimed that she had found out to her cost that she was too much of a free spirit to be tied down with anyone. Her friend looked decidedly uncomfortable at this point. Jean said that she had disappeared from London just because she was pissed off at all of us – at John for being a prat, at Jean Kerr for being so weak, at Mary for taking something she wanted, at me for deserting her and at her mother for not being a proper mother. She said that she felt that if she'd belonged to a stronger family unit she'd have been okay – her family would have seen her through her troubled times. She said that on one of the nights we'd been to the Marquee Club and I'd gone off to the toilet, a hippie had tried to chat her up. As ever, she'd blanked him. But she said he was well-mannered, gentle and polite, and he put a piece of paper with his telephone number into her hand just as I returned. She said the number came in handy when she needed someone else to take her to the Marquee Club. So that's where she'd been on that mystery night, when neither John nor I knew where she was – remember, when John came calling uninvited to my flat in the hope he'd catch her (and me) out? She said that she had originally only intended to go to Wells with this guy for a few weeks, and then come back and start afresh. But she found that after London, the pace of country life suited her much better. She said she'd waited nearly a year before getting in touch with her mother to let her know she was all right. She didn't realise until she'd called her mother how big a commotion she'd caused by disappearing, and on reflection, she said, she was not unhappy that she had.

During all of our time in the bar Mary never let go of my hand. She wasn't usually prone to such demonstrative acts while we were in public.

'So how have you been doing for all these years?' Mary asked.

'Great thanks,' Jean gushed. 'My husband was flippin' flush with money. He was a wee pet, really, we just grew apart. But he set me up in style back up in Derby. I enjoy my life up there. Our Jean is also living there now as well. So we're both back where we started.'

'How's she?' Mary asked, perhaps remembering her Amazon-like attack with her boots.

'She's great as well. She lived in Paris for several years, you know. She's now Mrs Debbs, would you believe? She's been married three times now, has our Jean. She's had two children, three homes and four cars, so,' Jean Simpson said through a laugh, 'she's ahead of her plan for the first time in her life! We're good friends again. But I haven't heard about or from John Harrison since the early days, though our Jean had heard that he'd gone off to America and apparently has an important job with Disney.'

I still had lost my tongue and so Mary, poor Mary, had been doing all of the talking for the both of us, but I felt it was time I needed to contribute something to the conversation. There was only one question I could think of asking; only one question I needed an answer to, and so when I couldn't think of a suitable alternative, I just blurted my big question out.

'So why did you leave your record player switched on and the record on the deck? And why did you file your Dylan sleeve in the Doors section before you left for Wells?'

'David!' Mary said, shaking her head in disbelief.

Jean Simpson smiled first at Mary with a quick nod to say it was okay and then at me.

'After all these flippin' years you still remember that I forgot to turn off my stereo and filed an album in the wrong section!' she said, before giving a fulsome laughing.

'He was convinced you'd been kidnapped,' Mary offered by way of explanation.

'Kidnapped? Not likely! It's quite simple really,' she said. 'When my new friend – you know, the hippie from the Marquee Club – invited me to go to Wells with him, but not with him, if you know what I mean,' she added quickly, still feeling a need to qualify it or justify herself even after all these years, 'it was a very loose arrangement. I mean, if it had all been planned out weeks in advance I'd most likely never have gone. In fact, I can tell you for a fact, I most definitely would not have gone. But he just rang me one night from Wimbledon Station, saying that he and a few of his friends would be around in two minutes, so be ready to say hi and wave goodbye at the same time. He said I'd need to run out the door in two minutes or we'd lose the chance of the lift. And I just laughed at him and was about to say no way, José! Then I thought, why not, why not just take the opportunity to just go, get out of London when I'd a chance to? You know, just flippin' get away from all of you and all of the bad vibes. When they arrived, I was still packing. I'd been listening to Dylan when my hippie friend rang from Wimbledon Station. As I finished packing I told him to turn off my stereo system and put my record away. At the same time, his friends were outside in the VW camper van, honking the horn for all their worth and so clearly the bottom line was I didn't pack properly and he didn't do his delegated chores properly either, but I did make it down to Wells that night. When I eventually went to rescue my record collection and stereo system, the girls upstairs told me you'd carefully removed the record, taking great care and attention to slip the sleeve into one of my spare plastic jackets without actually touching the sleeve at all. And then you'd turned off the stereo system. They were so intrigued by your little album-filing ritual.

'You've just solved the biggest mystery of our married life,' Mary Skeffington admitted, slowly shaking her head from side to side in disbelief.

I was still too much in shock to pay enough attention to what else was said.

Mary and Jean Simpson chatted away like age-old friends. I was occasionally called upon to remember the names of some of the weird and wonderful groups who'd played the Marquee Club back in the day.

'Oh, we'd don't go to many concerts these days,' Mary admitted.

'I very rarely get to go to any gigs these days, either,' Jean said, proving with her use of 'gigs' that she'd remembered at least some of the things I'd told her during our adventures away from the red carpet.

'But when I saw an advert for Stevie Winwood in Mojo I thought I just couldn't miss it. He's still great isn't he?' Jean said.

'Aye, but I'd like to have heard him do something on the guitar,' I offered up, but then realised I sounded too much like the duffle coat fans from the club days.

'And just look at you two – after all these years, still together,' she offered, thankfully ignoring the opportunity to share a duffle coat moment. 'I always knew he'd be dependable… for the right woman…'

Her last four words of that sentence disappeared in a mumble as she noticed the time, 'Oh flippin' heck, Pet,' she screamed, still not addressing her 'friend' by his proper name, 'look at the time! We need to get our skates on or we'll miss the last train.'

That was it, off she went into the night with her unnamed friend and off Mary and I went to our Wimbledon Village house in Marryat Road, very close to where George Carman QC lived until he died. Thanks to Mary's family money and what I'd made from investments during the Thatcher years, we'd been able to give up our work several years ago and were enjoying a very comfortable life.

And that is about it – really this time; I didn't tell Mary just how big a shock it had been for me to come face to face with Jean Simpson. You see, I'd never admitted to

Mary that I really had suspected that she had murdered Jean, and dumped her body in the foundation of the Kopace Superstore.

But you really wouldn't want to admit that to the woman you love, you know, that you think she's a murderer now, would you?

THE END

Acknowledgements

Thanks are due and offered to:

Mickey Connelly, Ann B, Miss Kerr, Miss Simmons, Taste, Rory Gallagher, Spencer Davis Group, Steve Winwood, Traffic, Musicland, City Week, Lucy Beevor, Chris McVeigh and all the Fahrenheit team.

Big, big thanks to Catherine (as ever) and my dad Andrew.

Other Books from Paul Charles

Detective Inspector Christy Kennedy Mysteries:

I Love The Sound of Breaking Glass
Last Boat To Camden Town
Fountain of Sorrow
The Ballad of Sean & Wilko
I've Heard The Banshee Sing
The Hissing of the Silent Lonely Room
The Justice Factory
Sweetwater
The Beautiful Sound of Silence
A Pleasure To Do Death With You

Inspector Starrett Mysteries:

The Dust of Death
Family Life
St Ernan's Blues

McCusker Mystery

Down On Cyprus Avenue

Other Fiction:

First of The True Believers.
The Last Dance
The Prince Of Heaven's Eyes (A Novella)
The Lonesome Heart is Angry
One of Our Jeans is Missing

Non-Fiction:
The Best Beatles Book Ever
Playing Live